PENGUIN BOOKS
# Secrets of the Heart

Elizabeth Buchan lives in London with her husband and two children and worked in publishing for several years. During this time, she wrote her first books, which included a biography for children: *Beatrix Potter: The Story of the Creator of Peter Rabbit* (Frederick Warne). Her first novel for adults, *Daughters of the Storm*, was set during the French Revolution. Her second, *Light of the Moon*, took as its subject a female undercover agent operating in occupied France during the Second World War. Her third novel, *Consider the Lily*, described by the *Sunday Times* as 'the literary equivalent of the English country garden', and by the *Independent* as 'a gorgeously well-written tale: funny, sad, sophisticated', won the 1994 Romantic Novel of the Year Award. An international bestseller, there are over 320,000 copies in print in the UK. Her subsequent novel, *Perfect Love*, was described as 'a powerful story: wise, observant, deeply-felt, with elements that all women will recognize with a smile – or a shudder'. Her last novel, *Against Her Nature*, published in 1998, was described as 'a modern-day *Vanity Fair* . . . brilliantly done'.

Elizabeth Buchan is currently on the committee for the Society of Authors, and was a judge for the 1997 Whitbread Awards and Chairman of the Judges for the 1997 Betty Trask Award. Her short stories have been published in various magazines and broadcast on BBC Radio 4.

# Secrets of the Heart

ELIZABETH BUCHAN

PENGUIN BOOKS

PENGUIN BOOKS

Published by the Penguin Group
Penguin Books Ltd, 27 Wrights Lane, London w8 5tz, England
Penguin Putnam Inc., 375 Hudson Street, New York, New York 10014, USA
Penguin Books Australia Ltd, Ringwood, Victoria, Australia
Penguin Books Canada Ltd, 10 Alcorn Avenue, Toronto, Ontario, Canada m4v 3b2
Penguin Books (NZ) Ltd, Private Bag 102902, NSMC, Auckland, New Zealand

Penguin Books Ltd, Registered Offices: Harmondsworth, Middlesex, England

First published 2000
1 3 5 7 9 10 8 6 4 2

Set in 12.5/16 pt Monotype Garamond
Typeset by Intype London Ltd
Printed in England by Clays Ltd, St Ives plc

*For my mother, Mary Oakleigh-Walker, and my sisters,*
*Alison Souter and Rosemary Hobhouse, with love*

'"Will you tell me how long you have loved him?"
"It has been coming on so gradually, that I hardly know
when it began. But, I believe I must date it from my
first seeing his beautiful grounds at Pemberley."'

Jane Austen, *Pride and Prejudice*

Several books have been invaluable during the course of writing this novel. Leo Marks's *Between Silk and Cyanide* (HarperCollins, 1998), *Elinor Fettiplace's Receipt Book* by Hilary Spurling (Viking, 1986), *The Farming Ladder* by George Henderson (Faber, 1944), Simon Schama's *Landscape and Memory* (HarperCollins, 1995), *Guide to Bees and Honey* by Ted Hooper (Marston House, 1997). I took factual information and drew on ideas from all of the above. Any mistakes are entirely mine.

Very many thanks are due to my editor, Louise Moore; the team at Penguin; my agent, Mark Lucas; as always, Hazel Orme; and Stephen Ryan. Especial thanks are owed to Richard Vines, producer of superb beef, who allowed me to pester him for details of how he runs his farm and business, Wild Beef. Also to Shervie and David Price and Elisabeth Murray for generously allowing me to make use of their material. I must also thank my family and friends for all their support and encouragement.

# I

When he was alive, Agnes told her uncle more than once that if he had been a different sort of man it would not have been the same story at all. 'Oh, no,' he said, 'the house was waiting for you.' Together they laughed about it, conspirators who understood each other perfectly.

Sometimes Agnes was taken aback by the depth of her feeling for Flagge House, the beautiful, big-windowed manor set in a water-meadow that had been in the Campion family for four hundred years. It was home and that was sufficient reason to love it. Yet it was also the material of fantasy and dream, an idyll of pastoral life and of a history that was vanishing. To all these Agnes clung – probably, she told herself, as a compensation for her sad circumstances. And as she grew from an awkward adolescent into a woman whose looks and success excited comment, she remained bewitched by her vision of the house and its past. As such, she was doubly bound in its coils of obligation and feverish romanticism, a maiden marooned on a rock but happy to be so. Her passion had been long-lived, for Agnes, now thirty, had first stepped into its flagstoned hallway, over which the sun had spilled a golden halo, at the age of twelve and had been instantly captivated and the intensity of her feelings had not diminished one iota.

Yet . . . and yet, as with all great enduring loves, occasionally in her busier, professional moments, when Agnes was away from home and operating as the documentary producer, she grew impatient with its demands, even perhaps a little embarrassed by its hold on her spirit.

But not for long.

Separated by a ten-year gap, her uncle John and his younger brother, her father, had not got on. 'Billy could never accept his bad luck at being the younger,' John explained. 'It made trouble between us and that's why your parents went to live in Cape Town.' However, when both her parents had been killed in the car crash on the dangerous Cape to Fishhoek road, John had immediately come to the rescue and brought Agnes back to Flagge House. 'Children,' he said staring at his niece through his glasses, 'are far more important than feuds. Never forget it.'

He and Maud, his wife, were childless and, for a time, they were at a loss as to what to do with Agnes. Maud's solution was to regard her with bewilderment, but John's was kinder and cleverer. 'Come with me,' he said. 'I've got such stories to tell you.'

*In 1589, the first Campion rode into Charlborough and surveyed the site.*

He led her from room to room and positioned her in front of the Campion portraits. Fighters, failures, wise administrators, spendthrifts and, a special category, religious martyrs. Here was a Rupert, who had died of his wounds at Naseby, there a bridge-builder in India. 'And this,' he said, placing his hands on her shoulders and steering her close up to the portrait in the hall, 'is the other Agnes Campion.' A large-eyed woman, fair hair drawn back into a tight knot with ringlets, she was wearing pearl earrings into which the painter had incorporated highlights with oil-slick colours. She had died at the age of thirty-one in 1650, from one childbirth too many. 'She can be your special companion,' advised her uncle shrewdly. 'And you have her look. We'll make it our project to find out about her.'

What had they found in their shared search through the family archives? That the dead Agnes had been a legendary cook, almost modern in her use of fresh vegetables and herbs. In January, she served her household with 'showlder of muttone and bagge pudding'. In December, 'salte pigge with boyled carrottes'. They found the letter written by her widower with instructions for her tombstone to be inscribed with 'From One Who Loved Her'. They found her will.

Agnes Campion. Her will. I give and bequeath to my husbande my inlayde cabnott, desiring him to accept it, should I dye being with childe . . .

They had never discovered if the ninth child, the one who killed her, had survived.

This is real history, her uncle taught Agnes, ushering

her through the rooms where thrift and utility had reigned: rooms where fruit and vegetables were stored, herbs dried, meat salted, where the women laundered and sewed and kept an inventory of every scrap of clothing. 'This history tells no lies. It is', he said, 'the small alleyways and courtyards, the mud paths beaten into iron by countless feet that make up the truth.'

A month or so before he died, her uncle went blind. 'No matter,' he said, in his gentle way. 'It is to be expected.'

Her heart breaking for the second time in a year, Agnes sat by the bed in the blue room where the spiders made free in the cornice and the cracks ran in dark tributaries across the walls. It was shrouded by the drawn curtains, and borrowed heaters exuded uneven pockets of warmth. She held his hand. 'Is there anything I can do to make it more bearable?'

His flesh felt lifeless. 'There is one thing,' he said. 'Do you think you could bring up my Jane Austens and put them on the bedside table? I miss them.'

Trying hard not to distress him with her weeping, Agnes went downstairs into his study, searched for the books amongst the papers and unpaid bills and carried them upstairs. She guided her uncle's fingers over the pile, which she had placed as close to him as possible. The encounter between his fragile fingers and the worn bindings was of old companions. 'All my life,' said John, 'these have been my friends, and I don't want to abandon them now.' Exhausted by the effort, he lay back and was quiet.

Neither Maud, John's wife of forty-five years, nor the nurse approved of this sentimentality. At regular intervals, they attempted to move the books out of the way of the medicines and necessary equipment. At one point Maud, threatened by what she saw as Agnes's indulgence, snatched up *Persuasion* and threatened to throw it away. Agnes won and was rewarded by her uncle's patient smile.

In the lucid moments that were left, John chose to say the things that Agnes already knew but wanted to hear again.

'I'm glad the house will be yours, Agnes. It is right. No one better.' The breath was measured between each word.

As the last surviving Campion, Agnes had known that she was to inherit Flagge House, since her uncle explained the position on her sixteenth birthday. It was a trick of fate and fertility that continually brought her up short.

There was another struggling pause. 'I'm glad we've always agreed on what needs to be done. But you will have to find ways. I've told you, there is no money.'

Agnes's mental image of the house grew hazy, and reassembled in sharper detail so that the defective roof and rotting windows were observable. For a second or two, she was shaken by doubt. Then she touched her uncle's cheek with a finger, willing him into peace as he laboured on. 'It won't be easy, Agnes.'

Inheriting an historic, if smallish, manor house was tricky at any time, and a rather vexed subject in the world in which Agnes had chosen to make her career. But she had thrashed that one out with herself. She had been lucky and others were not and, if the golden apple had been tossed into her lap, it was best to make the most of it – precisely because others suffered and had no luck. Anyway, there were her feelings for the house and she loved her uncle. *That* was important. Why waste energy on unnecessary scruples?

She bent over to kiss him. 'I promise to do my best.'

While John fought his last battle, she sat on through the bleak January afternoons and silently said goodbye to the security of their relationship. Resting on the sheets, John's hands were almost as white as the cotton and, occasionally, they clenched in pain. She stroked them, anticipating the time when he would not be there. No longer would his place be laid at the table; his key would remain on its hook in the hall; his voice, having joined the voices of the dead that crowded the husk of the house, would not be heard.

What a stealthy thief Death was, and what a dark and private business dying was. She had encountered it and its effects in her work more than once. They were lucky in the West: the span between the green light and the red was usually reasonable and, very often, by the time the latter flickered, you were aching and ready to go. She glanced at her uncle. That was true in his case but it did not make the passage easier.

Agnes squeezed out a cloth in warm water, to which had been added a drop of lavender oil, and bathed her uncle's face and wrists.

'Uncle John . . .' she whispered, but longed to say 'Father'. 'Thank you for everything. Thank you for looking after me all those years.'

He turned his head towards her. 'You were my daughter,' he said simply.

He shut his eyes and fell into one of his lightning dozes. Outside, in the dark winter world, the wind rattled frozen branches. It was grief-stricken weather: wild, moody and battering, which was only fitting. Slowly the sun abandoned the short day, leaving Flagge House and the water-meadow to the gloom. Complete and turned into itself, the house and the land settled for the night.

'Are you frightened?' she asked, when he woke with a start. She thought she saw that his features had sharpened.

He stirred and grimaced. 'I lost God a long time ago.'

Agnes did not bother him any more but sat, quiet and watchful. Slowly, infinitesimally slowly, John Campion raised his hand and traced the shape of the books he could no longer read.

*Are they there, Agnes?*

When she woke the next morning, still exhausted from her late-night watch, Maud appeared in her bedroom and told Agnes abruptly that her uncle was dead.

\*

The phone rang. 'Julian,' said the clever, faithful Angela, who was today dressed in purple Spandex, 'it's a Mrs Maud Campion. She says she lives near Lymouth and she met you at the Huntingdons' cocktail party.'

Julian was in his office at the Portcullis Property headquarters in London which, as chief executive, he had occupied for the past seven years, worrying over the figures which, for the first time in those seven years, were behaving unpredictably. 'Put her off.'

'She's been sitting on the phone for ages. And Kitty has also rung asking if you would call her back about arrangements for the weekend. She says . . .' Angela's pause was wicked '. . . she says that if you're not home in good time tonight there will be trouble. She did not specify what.'

There were many strands to knit into a day, strategic, financial, Kitty, the staff, the figures, but early on Julian, who had been born with an unquenchable curiosity and a capacity for risk-taking that had both pushed him to the top of his profession and, from time to time, got him into trouble, decided never to pass by on the wrong side of the road. Also, and this was an intellectual discipline, he refused to downgrade his experiences, especially the bad ones. Each one was useful and added a layer, another facet, polished up the idea of what he wished to be.

Sometimes this philosophy was tested to its limits. There was only so much that could be crowded into a day. He sighed but said therefore, 'Put her through and,

Angela, could you ring Kitty and tell her I promise to be home on time?'

He turned his attention to the phone. 'Mr Knox, we met briefly at Vita Huntingdon's at the Conservative do, and since your work is well known in the area I thought I would get in touch. My husband died last week . . .'

The voice was both confident and strangely muffled, as if the speaker did not wish to be overheard. Julian searched his memory for a Mrs Maud Campion. The call did not surprise him for he was used to approaches such as he assumed this one to be. Profit was a great dismantler of barriers and, because he lived there and knew it, Portcullis had quite a few projects under way in the Lymouth area. 'Is it to do with a property?'

'Well, yes.'

'I'd be delighted to discuss it and then I think it would be better if I put you through to the office that deals with the properties. I occupy a less important role. I merely run the company.' He spoke with his customary lightness, laced with irony, which made the less confident take fright. The word 'run' resonated in his head. Phone hunched on his shoulder, he tapped another key on his laptop.

'That's quite all right, Mr Knox. I prefer to deal directly with the top.'

The tone was old-fashioned. Julian raised an eyebrow at the hovering Angela, who had embarked on the grim task of getting him to a meeting on time. 'Perhaps you would like to tell me what you had in mind.'

*

Agnes felt in her dressing-gown pocket for her handker-chief which, not surprisingly, was damp, because she had done nothing but weep since John's death – secret tears that convulsed her between making the arrangements and seeing people, and which left her exhausted.

It's because I'm so tired, she told herself. Fatigue flays you open, and bullies you into thinking that you cannot survive such a loss. But I can. She thought of John's key hanging on the hook and his empty place at the table. She remembered looking up at him as he had taken her round the house, and the manner in which he had placed his arm around her shoulders and told her that her bad times were over. She had found her refuge and a place in which to grow up.

It was dawn, the day after the funeral, and Agnes, run ragged by the demands of her aunt and the organization of the details, had abandoned her efforts to sleep. In the frozen moment before dawn, she had pulled herself out of bed and crossed over to the window. Her feet left smudges on the floor and the darkness was as thick as velvet.

Out there in the meadow, the river clattered icily over the stones.

During the past four years, she had grown used to sleepless nights – *nuits blanches*, as Pierre called them – and to rising in the morning with a body racked with tiredness and stretched nerves. Nothing helped. They came with the job and with love affairs and, now, with bereavement. She had given up fighting them, for, in a curious way, Agnes felt her experience of them made her truly alive.

The cold knifed into her flesh and hurt her bare feet, and she tucked her arms across her chest, a defensive posture that she noticed she had adopted lately. Correction: that she had taken to since Pierre.

Happiness and unhappiness were so close that they were joined at the hip, except that unhappiness was longer lasting. But she had no intention of letting it become a life habit. Occasionally, Agnes dreamed of warm kitchens where she did feel happy – which surprised her as her interest in cooking was minimal – but put it down to some residual message to do with contentment lurking deep in her psyche. Perhaps there was a programme to be made that investigated the meaning of the kitchen?

Above all, Agnes wanted to live as completely as she could manage, for the ambitions that drove her were deep-seated. She had been battered and hurt, and now she was grieving bitterly for the end of a loving era and worried by the prospect of the new, but she wanted to understand what she was and how best to be that person.

Outside, the waxing light threw a transparent wash over the meadow. My land. With a tremor of delight and dread she said it aloud: '*My land.*'

With a grand sweep that made the rings rattle, she pulled the curtain fully back and stared at the shapes massing across her vision: the land, the trees, the perimeter wall snaking its way towards the village.

Silence. Except for the sound of the river running over those stones as it had since human memory began.

Agnes shivered and hugged herself for warmth. *Her land and house.* Flagge House had acquired its name because of the river and wild irises for which the area was famous. No longer did they grow in their masses but, if the year was propitious, the irises ran up a display of colour that aped the white and smoky-yellow carpet of previous glories.

It was good soil, whose mixture of clay and chalk produced a mix of vegetation, and where the river had thrown an ox-bow and slowed its pace, it was carpeted with moss and lush grass.

In the past, figures had moved over this landscape, purposeful, occupied figures, who understood and lived by the land. Her Agnes, the dead Agnes of the portrait, would have been among them. Silk skirts swishing, lace pouting at her breast, earrings jangling.

Sleepless and wrung out, Agnes felt the weight of those past lives. Something had ended. Something was beginning.

# 2

Maud had acquired the habit of inserting French words into her conversation on the annual holidays to Deauville with John. She did so whenever the mood took her, chiefly to indulge her desire to be noticed, but she maintained that it was to do with her inner ear, which was particularly sensitive to languages.

It was mid-morning, the day after the funeral. A post-mortem of the ceremony had been held and the conversation had turned to the next move. Not surprisingly, Maud was prickly.

'*Comment?*' she challenged Bea, her widowed sister, who had lived at Flagge House since the death of her husband seven years previously.

'I don't think you should have said what you did.' A pale, shrunken-looking Bea poured out cups of tea and handed them round.

Maud was sufficiently surprised by her sister's attack to snap back, in English, 'What did you say?' It was rare for Bea to criticize Maud: when she did, it was usually in the presence of a witness.

'I didn't like what you said to him that morning . . . just before . . . you know . . .'

Maud's still large, lustrous eyes – she had been an

exceptionally pretty woman – were sullen. 'I thought you were supposed to be comforting me.'

Maud was wearing one of her home-knitted jumpers, a professional-looking creation in mourning-black angora with a turtle neck, but she looked frozen. The diamond-paste ring that she habitually wore with her wedding band gave off a blackish sparkle that never fooled anyone who knew about diamonds. 'Aren't you?' she reiterated.

Agnes and her aunts were huddled at the kitchen table below a ceiling across which yellow stains sailed in cloud formations, surrounded by a litter of saucepans and the unopened cans of soup on which the aunts appeared to survive. The cold crept round their feet and an acrid underlying whiff of mould emanating from the leaking window seemed more than usually noticeable.

Agnes drank her tea out of the thick white cup that had once been of use in a station canteen before fetching up in a jumble sale. It tasted dead, if such a thing were possible, and her stomach protested. Grief was a funny thing, circling round like a tiger and pouncing just at the moment you thought you had it under control. Guilt, as she knew from experience, did not bother with the circling.

At any minute now, she must spring into action. With some amusement, she had read about how families assign roles to the separate members – the moneymaker, the fool, the dreamer – and now Agnes had been assigned hers. That was fine. That was what was expected of her, and what Agnes expected of herself. She knew, and they knew, that despite their sparring the sisters were united in their expectation that Agnes would take charge of both the argument and of the future. *Agnes will know what to do.*

'I had to tell John the truth. I was taught to tell the truth.' Maud raised her eyes to the ceiling and dropped them again when she encountered the colony of spiders in the cornice. She faced Agnes. 'You weren't the only one in his life,' she said, dripping bitterness. 'I was the one who was married to him, you know.'

Bea was apparently fixated by the dingy laurel tree that guarded the entrance to the kitchen yard. 'It wasn't kind, Maud.' She did not look at her sister. 'You must have peace when you're dying.'

Agnes braced herself. 'What did you say, Maud, that was so terrible?'

Maud's bulldog expression said: You can't shame me. 'That I was sick and tired of words like "heritage", and how ridiculous it had been that because he was the owner of a house like this we had been martyred all our lives to it. What's more, I told him I wanted to move out and live in a bungalow. A nice warm modern one. There, that's what I said.'

Agnes stared at Maud. In a normal marriage one hoped for a little peace in which to shelter. Pierre had agreed, adding that his marriage to Madeleine did not stop him worshipping Agnes's size seven English feet and long ash-blonde hair. As a result, a besotted Agnes in all innocence, no, foolishness, had spent four years imagining that Pierre would leave his wife in the flat on the rue Jacob in Paris with the three elfin daughters.

She knew those daughters as well as she might have known her own, for everywhere she went, in everything she did, they were there, like the tender, infant *putti* in the paintings: Katrine, the clever one, Claudine, the pretty one, and Mazarine, the plump little angel of the family. She had been jealous of them, the only considerations that gave Pierre pause. Their innocence, their physicality, their needs were balanced in the palms of Pierre's hands, and Agnes hated it, and hated herself for that.

That was before Madeleine had arrived at Agnes's hotel one evening and pointed out how terribly the family was suffering, and if Pierre said otherwise he was lying. After that, everything changed, and because Pierre was forbidden, Agnes wanted him even more. Yet the more she wanted him, the more she thought of Madeleine until, in some tortured fashion, Madeleine became more important, the one who occupied Agnes's thoughts.

After she had told Pierre it was over and that she was not coming back to Paris, Agnes had finally tumbled to the conclusion that the good and bad areas of a marriage were irrelevant. You grew round the other person, like fat and muscles over organs, and that was that.

Maud shrugged. 'You needn't look so disapproving, Agnes. I have a point, and John knew it. Anyway, he probably didn't hear what I said.'

'But he *did*.' Bea was as fierce as it was possible to be.

No fool, Maud realized that her trespass was too far and she adjusted her tone to a more reasonable one. 'You ought to sell this millstone, Agnes. It's done nothing but bring trouble and misery on all of us. Think. We could all have some money to buy somewhere sensible.'

Agnes's fingers folded across the cup and tightened but she said nothing. An empty bag is impossible to burst and it was best with Maud in this mood to be as empty as possible.

'For a start, there's a leak in the blue bedroom ceiling,' said Maud, 'and the roof is getting worse.'

'I know, I know,' said Agnes. Maud had a nose for the details. 'It's on the list.'

'Long ago,' Maud had once, in a rare soft moment, told the frightened little cuckoo who had dropped into her nest, 'John and I had to mend the roof. Nail fatigue, I think. The men found a plate in the rafters, one of the Delfts. A maid must have broken it and been too frightened to own up. She would have lost her place.'

That a plate could so alter a life had shocked Agnes. She had asked to see the pieces, and Maud obliged. Agnes cradled them in her hands: indigo blue and greyish white shapes, which had ridden over a dark sea from Holland to the sun-flecked drawing room in England. If she thought hard enough, she could still feel the sharp, gritty edges that had grazed her skin.

'But why ever not sell?' Maud saw the nice, clean, warm bungalow slipping away.

Agnes finished her tea. As clearly as if he was in the room, she heard her uncle's voice. 'Family, tradition, history, not letting go . . .' Those were the charges laid on her by him. To be fair to Maud, they probably did not make sense. But they made absolute sense to Agnes. 'By the way,' she said, 'the Jane Austens are missing from his bedroom. Someone has moved them. Do you know where they are?'

'You were *wrong*,' said Bea, for a second time. She whirled round, fierce and trembling.

Maud poured herself another cup of tea. 'Thank God I'm not a proper Campion,' she said. 'It's perfectly ridiculous.'

Both Agnes and Bea knew exactly what this outburst betokened. Maud had always felt excluded, an interloper of forty-five years who could never quite see her way into the charmed circle. The pretty bride who had married John had never truly found her niche.

'Actually, can we not argue?' Bea looked ill with distress.

Agnes reached for her bag and extracted her notebook. 'Let's sort a few things out, then we can have lunch.'

'I'll lay up.' Bea struggled to her feet.

Maud watched her sister bustling around with china and silver. 'Not *those* spoons for soup, Bea,' she said, after a moment or two. 'Will you never learn?'

A couple of hours later, Agnes tucked Bea into bed

for a nap and ordered her to stay put for at least an hour. Maud retired to the small sitting room, formerly the butler's pantry, in which the television and video-recorder were installed. Within minutes, music drifted through the house.

Tackling a pile of paperwork in her uncle's study, Agnes heard the familiar notes and knew exactly what Maud was watching. First, the unsoiled grey-green vista of an Alpine mountainside on which a dot appeared to fling wide its arm and loose a string of high notes. Then, in a director's sleight of hand, the camera panned down to transform the dot into Julie Andrews. Once again, Maud was worshipping at the shrine of *The Sound of Music*.

Agnes gritted her teeth and telephoned Bel, her co-director at Five Star, the production company they ran together. Bel operated from the London end and they kept in constant touch. Half-way through their discussion on the schedule for their project, *The Death of the English Apple*, she heard Maud cry out. Agnes shot down the passage to find her transfixed in front of the screen, which was now a mass of moving colour and song.

'It's so sad. I can't bear it.' Maud pressed a hand to her mouth.

Agnes sat down beside her. 'Maud, John was eighty. I know he didn't want to die but perhaps . . .' She could not bring herself to continue.

Maud stiffened. 'Oh, *that*,' she said. 'I meant,' she pointed to the screen, 'she looks so young and beautiful, so pure, and I can't bear it.'

Agnes looked. Julie Andrews was progressing up the aisle in her wedding dress, and the choir were singing like angels. She counted to five and leaned over to tuck the tartan rug around Maud's angular form. 'You know this is your home, don't you? Always. You mustn't worry.'

Maud dropped her hand and turned a countenance on Agnes on which incomprehension and anger were etched. (Agnes could almost predict the number of seconds required for Maud to slot into dramatic gear.) But Maud surprised her. She stretched out an arm to Agnes, the paste ring quivering on her finger like a roosting insect, and the aggression was replaced by a weary regret. She pulled at a fold of papery skin at her wrist. 'Look at me. Old. Drained. *Fatiguée*. If you take on this house, you will end up the same.'

'Hush, Maud.' Agnes tried to soothe her, but Maud grabbed her.

'*Believe* me.'

1939–45 was the era of yet another war, and of Morse code.

Before sending a message from the field to Home Station, an agent was required to key a message into a numbered phase. From there, he or she would hook it up to a second transposition, at which point the original message had been thoroughly scrambled.

The concept of double transposition appealed to Julian Knox, who, being fascinated by codes, had picked up a history of the Special Operations Executive during the Second World War in a bookshop and bought it. He had reached the section on coding. The mathematical constructions were fascinating. So was the neatness of a code and, in contrast, its risky fireworks and the dig-deep analysis to which he responded. He liked, too, the exhilaration of stalking an objective enfolded in cryptographic darkness and of dragging it into the light. He liked the puzzle and, when the key was exposed, its absolute rationality.

He was thinking about safety and danger, the closed message and the clear, as he drove down the motorway from London to Lymouth, where he lived and where Kitty, his mistress, was waiting. On the way, he planned to detour to Charlborough, which was only eight or so miles to the west of Lymouth, Mrs Campion had invited him to drop in at any time, and Friday afternoon seemed as good as any and fitted in with the weekend schedule.

In the period since Maud Campion had called, faithful Angela had been busy. She had extracted relevant material from the County Masterfile, which, because they did so much work in the area, was kept permanently up-to-date. It included a report on the river systems, its farming (the ratio of arable to dairy), its parishes, topography, recorded footpaths and hedgerows. She had also produced a large-scale map of Charlborough on which she had highlighted with coloured marker pens the railway lines, churches, glebelands, school playing-fields and conservation areas. Julian insisted that the team was meticulously briefed and, because he played fair, that included him.

Still reflecting on the subversions, the almost erotic moment of discovery posed by the code, he drove through the moorland that separated the snug, thriving coastal town of Lymouth from Charlborough, which was struggling to preserve its shop and bus route.

In the drive at Flagge House, it took only a few seconds to see that, if it was not quite in rigor mortis, it was certainly *in extremis*. The older, main section of the house was lovely but the Victorian addition was graceless, and the repairs that had been undertaken to shore up portions of walls and roof were inadequate.

Never trust an old house. It was a greedy thing, honeycombed as often as not with rotting roofs, collapsed windows and hidden problems which, naturally, were always the worst. Why did one old house fare better rather than another? The answers were various. Owners defaulted, families decayed, energy dwindled. As a loose Darwinist, Julian accepted the injustice of chance and survival, and built it into the underlying philosophy of his business.

He slowed the car to a crawl and assessed the terrain. The team could work their miracles here with a couple of well-designed but low-cost houses. Behind them, in the water-meadow, was easily space enough to build two expensive, sensitively sited houses, whose sale would subsidize the former and bulk up the margins. As a division of self-interest into altruism, the equation was sound and good.

He parked the car by what was obviously the old

kitchen garden. It was raining and he pulled his jacket out of the back before he stepped through the gate set into the brick and found himself in a walled garden.

His expert eye registered the subsidence in the bricks, and the shards of glass littering fractious unwilling soil. It was a place that no longer held energy and had given up the struggle. He bent down to pick up one of the pieces of the glass. It was thick and old-fashioned, tinged with green and lead deposit, smeared with snail slime. Probably from one of the wrecked Victorian cloches abandoned by the cold frames.

'Excuse me,' said a voice. 'What do you think you are doing?'

A girl with loosely plaited thick fair hair walked through the opposite entrance to the garden towards him, her hands dug into the pockets of her navy blue pea-jacket. Her skin glowed but there was a brushstroke of weariness under the eyes and anger expressed in the set of a large mouth. The effect was of long-limbed beauty, but beauty that was worn carelessly, disregarded even. The shock of discovery, which he knew of old, went through Julian.

Not now, he thought.

'You're trespassing,' she informed him.

Abandoning Maud to Julie Andrews, Agnes had seized her jacket and fled outside. The rain brushed her cheeks, light whispery drizzle that soaked everything it touched, and she made for the shelter of the kitchen garden.

A stranger was walking around it, a tall, confidently dressed man with reddish-blond hair. He was examining a shard of glass, in a manner suggesting energy and attack, and she observed that, under a battered jacket, he was city-suited, a type she tended to avoid.

She challenged him, and the stranger dropped the glass and turned round. Agnes looked into a face that was knowledgeable, sophisticated, clever and a little bit sad. It was a face that reminded her of the Greek masks, one laughing, the other tragic. The last always got to her. Her fingers closed around the fluff in her pocket. 'You shouldn't be here.'

He straightened up. 'A Mrs Maud Campion phoned me and asked me over. Apparently the house is for sale.' He peered at Agnes's flushed, set face. Rain had plastered tendrils on to her forehead. 'You don't look as old as your voice.'

'Possibly because it was not me. Maud Campion is my aunt. But you've been misinformed. Or perhaps,' she said coolly, 'you did not hear properly.'

The stranger's eyebrows twitched together, but he did not budge. 'I don't think so,' he replied.

The reporter and observer in Agnes took mental notes. *Does not like to be doubted.*

He shrugged, and the superbly cut suit obediently followed the movement. 'It's a wonderful place,' he said politely. 'It must have been beautiful once.'

True. On the wall behind him in the old days would have grown an espaliered peach: the nails were still *in situ* and traced their pattern over the pink brick. In the shade of its ripe, moist fruits would have flourished chard, spinach and sweet young peas. But, whoever he was, this man did not fit into the picture.

'It would be an ideal project,' he said, quick and calculating.

Agnes was on a short fuse. 'Were you hoping to find somewhere to buy in the village? There is a house by the church. It's in hideous brick, its architectural references are to suburbia and it's been built on part of the cricket pitch that had been left in perpetuity to the village but, no matter, the developer and the local planning officer did a deal and hey presto.' She looked again at the suit. 'But the price is good.'

'Sounds dreadful,' he said sympathetically, 'but perfect for me. Vulgar, intrusive and, no doubt, very expensive.' He brushed a runnel of rainwater from his cheek and added, 'I see you have me summed up.'

Despite herself, Agnes grinned. 'That settles that, and you need not stay any longer.'

He appeared to consider. 'Not quite. There is Mrs Campion to explain things to.'

Agnes did not respond and he continued, 'My firm develops sites. During my conversation with your aunt, she suggested strongly that this might be one of them.'

'Ah,' she said, after a moment or two. 'One of those.'

'I know what you're thinking.'

'Do you?'

He raised an eyebrow. 'Someone has to build houses. It *can* be done with taste and subtlety.'

This was an old chestnut and she had imagined that he would be cleverer than to produce it. '*Subtlety*,' she exclaimed passionately. 'Not always. Take at look at the houses on the edge of village when you leave. That was once a wood with medieval coppices and wild anemones. Now there are plastic swimming-pools and plate-glass windows.'

'I've upset you,' he said.

'My uncle loved those anemones. He died last week.'

'I'm sorry.'

Startled, she looked up at him and read his wish to convey a similar acquaintance with grief.

He said, 'I don't possess a handkerchief but I'm sure you're the sort of person who has one.'

'I don't.' She thought of the anemones lying under the bricks and mortar.

'How lucky then,' he said, 'that you are not wearing mascara.'

There was a moment or two of silence.

His feet crunched on glass as he moved away. The rain began to fall in earnest. 'There is a good case for pulling down a house in bad shape.' He turned to address her. 'A house like this can bleed you dry and there is always a need for new housing.'

Agnes pulled herself together. 'Fine,' she said, 'of course, but not here.'

'So be it.' He tipped a sliver of glass with the toe of

his shoe. He seemed to be considering the next move. 'In my experience, defenders of the heritage are never prepared to enter the debate and there are arguments on both sides.' Again he smiled, ironic and, this time, a little defensive. 'I don't blame them. It's easy to forget that if we want to develop our new industries we have to house people and give them the services they want. But I am holding you up.' He turned to go. 'Will you apologize to your aunt for me?' His gaze roved pointedly over the wounded glasshouses, the shattered cold frame in the corner, the barren soil. 'I should stick to sailing,' he remarked. 'It's less controversial and there are not so many people out for your blood.' He turned to Agnes. 'Do you sail?'

'No, I don't.'

She led the way out of the walled garden to his car. He opened the door and extracted his wallet. 'Here's my card.'

She looked down at the white rectangle. 'That's very kind, but I don't see the point.' It was balanced between his finger and thumb. There was no point either in being any more rude than she had been. Agnes stretched out her hand, took it and read the name printed on it. Comprehension dawned. 'I know who you are. You do a lot of work in this area. That's why Maud got in touch.'

Pepped up no end by this confrontation, she watched the car disappear down the drive.

# 3

*Saturday.*

'Why didn't you come last night?' Kitty Richardson asked Julian Knox as she slid out of bed and ran over to greet him. 'I was expecting you as usual. I waited.'

Yes, she had. She had stood by the window of her small, exquisitely arranged cottage for a long time that Friday evening, anticipating the crunch of his car turning into the drive, in much the same pose (had she but known it) that Agnes had assumed at the window of Flagge House. However, in Kitty's cottage, which she had bought outright herself, the curtains were lovely, expensive, clean, and if they bore a resemblance to those hung at the windows of Julian's house, which could be seen from Kitty's windows across the bay, that was because Julian had paid for the same interior designer to furnish both houses as a job lot.

'Sorry, Kitty,' said Julian, and Kitty tensed, for Julian did not sound *that* sorry. 'I had some business in the morning, then I went to view a possible project on the way down. By the time I reached Lymouth it was late and I wanted to go over the figures, so I went to Cliff House for the night. Forgive?'

Liar, liar, she thought, for Julian knew perfectly well

that, whatever the hour, Kitty always waited up. He had needed to go home to the house poised on the sea cliff, just to breathe, and she bitterly resented it. He knew Kitty could see the house from her cottage and would have been watching, would have seen the lights go on. He knew what Kitty would have felt, and her disappointment.

'Why didn't you ring?'

'It was late. I told you.' He paused. 'You would have seen the lights, Kitty, and known I was safe.'

He *knew* it was impossible for her to settle until she knew he was safe. 'It's *never* too late,' she said stubbornly. 'I keep telling you that.' Friday was their night, the culmination of a day of preparation and of mounting vigil. This Friday, she had kept that vigil at the window until it was very late and the food laid out in the kitchen had long congealed. Then, she had sat on the sofa with a glass of whisky and pictured Julian asleep at Cliff House, breathing lightly and softly. Remote and only half hers.

I will not let it hurt me, she told herself, the old hot, sick feeling threatening.

*I will not.*

Julian had made up for it, of course, by sneaking into the house in the early light, having been out for his morning walk. He smelt of sea and cold, and when he bent over to kiss her, her lips had fastened on his cheek with relief.

She laid her head on his chest, searching for the

heartbeat she liked to hear. 'Give me five minutes and I'll make you your breakfast.'

He plonked himself full length on the bed and closed his eyes. It was then that she asked him for a second time why he had not come as he had promised. He murmured, 'I wanted to get the research sorted. Think numbers. Work out logistics. All that sort of thing.'

*Without me.*

Kitty was brushing her hair, always an interesting exercise. If she brushed it back, then she was one sort of person, if she brushed it forward, or to the side, she was another. Transformations of this sort were her business, for she was a woman who made herself in the image of what others wanted. Well, what men wanted. The ones who kept Kitty in her so far successful career of being kept. She did not mind. Furthermore, it was easy: if Kitty did not possess conventional brains she understood more than most the value of metamorphosis.

Julian's prone figure on the bed was reflected behind her own image in the generous mirror. *I adore him.* Kitty transferred her attention to herself. Yes. That was her as he wished and, therefore, as she wished: a small, delicate, creamy-highlighted blonde with lovely bone structure.

Julian eased himself into a sitting position, picked up the phone and punched in numbers. He mouthed, 'Patrick Leache,' at Kitty.

'Oh.'

It was no use protesting. Julian relied on Leache, who was the area's district planning officer, for his information, which was often imparted in private conversations at weekends. Not, said Leache's enemies, that planning came into it but his friends in the building business were warm in their support of his work. I hate the Leaches of this world, thought Kitty, fiercely and illogically. Julian was explaining his possible interest in a house and could Patrick have a look at some point. He added the name 'Campion'. Like most people in the area, Kitty knew the name if not the house itself. 'Would there be a problem?' Julian was asking.

He put down the phone and lay back with an expression that Kitty knew of old. It meant that he was contemplating a challenge, one that pleased and stimulated him. It meant that he would often be too busy for her.

One step forward, two back. The anger never seen by others stirred in Kitty's soul. She fought it for she knew, from experience, that anger tightened the ligaments in her neck and hardened her features. Oh, Kitty, Kitty, what a sham you are.

If she was truthful, and Kitty tried hard to be so, her anger was really a form of grief and impotence, not the strong, cleansing emotion that psychotherapists advised it should be.

Come, tell the truth. She loved a man with a desperate passion that she knew was not returned, and would never be returned.

These days, being a mistress was a minority occupation. Rather old-fashioned, really. 'I am clever enough,' Kitty had once confided to her friend Amy, 'to know that I am a dinosaur, but not clever enough to do anything about it.' Amy rather disagreed. Over twenty years or so, she had witnessed Kitty moving with tact and grace from one lover to another (but not too many), providing, of course, they had sufficient funds. Kitty had done rather well out of it, she suggested, *very* much better than a nurse or a secretary. 'I mean,' added Amy, 'your career is being a Kept Woman and you've proved to be a high flyer. *It takes guts and nerve, Kitty, make no mistake.*'

Beautiful, discreet, charming and childless by choice – Kitty needed all her energy to concentrate on herself – it was too precarious a life to be otherwise.

True, she had worked at it.

She had not intended to be a professional mistress, but Kitty had made the mistake of becoming entangled with one married man after another, a practice that had become, she now realized, a kind of addiction but had not appeared like that to begin with. Stopping was impossible. In those early days, Kitty had *believed* that the Robins and Harrys and Charleses would leave their wives. Later on, she had grown to see the advantages of being single yet bound with delicate chains. In the style to which she had grown accustomed, Kitty had learned the secret. *There were always men who wanted a mistress.*

But things were changing.

'I'm longing for an orange juice, darling,' she pleaded. 'Then I'll do breakfast.' She had battered him into being good and contrite and, reluctantly, Julian pulled himself upright and went to do her bidding. Using a tissue, Kitty patted her face dry and applied expensive cream. Its glutinous, silken touch on her fingertips reassured her: her armoury and investment against . . . well, what? Against the vanishing beauty that had once been set and immutable and, at forty-eight, was now slipping.

Kitty got up and sat down at the foot of the bed, spreading out her manicured fingers on the counterpane, and was reminded of the things that went on in it, accomplished with shared greed and skill. Last night was not by any means the first Friday on which Julian had failed to turn up, but the shortfall mattered when you sensed that the slope was becoming steeper, or the precipice closer.

Was it significant? Freedom and space, and all the other abstracts Julian talked about with regard to their relationship, seemed at times to Kitty to come very expensive. In fact, because she loved Julian as she had not loved the others, she had grown to hate and distrust such terms. Anyway, most people didn't *want* freedom. It was, well, too free.

Theo, darling, mad, Australian Theo, who cleaned the cottage three days a week as part of his therapy, would understand. 'OK, darl,' he would say, bringing out all the clichés. 'He's a flaming bastard. A stupid, blind bastard.' And Kitty would bathe in the white heat of Theo's gratitude and affection, which was Kitty's repayment for having rescued him from the institution into which he had been binned. It would have the effect of thawing the ice-chip in her heart. Just a little.

Loving was so exhausting, so dependent-making, so hurtful. I have tried, *I have tried*, to conduct my career on the basis of good manners, affection and financial expediency, she thought, and I have succeeded. Yet I am continually surprised by how savagely love undercuts all of those things.

Before he left Lymouth on Sunday evening, Julian said goodbye to Kitty and returned briefly to Cliff House. London was the place where he worked and laid his head. Kitty's cottage was the place where he conducted yet another part of his life, but this generous, light-filled Victorian house was home. Poised on the cliff above its own tiny beach a little way out of the town, it was where the parts of him had been shaped – difficult, hard, puzzling, as the process had been. Here, where the smell of salt and spiky marsh plant intensified in the spring, the birds surfboarded the waves and, when the sea grew rough and tides pounded, he could hear the grinding of stones, slate and granite, one upon the other. When the water retreated, leaving rank memorabilia of weed and detritus dotted like a pox on the smooth sand, and the sticky bottom slice of the cliff crept into view, the old passion for the fossil chase flared. On quiet summer days, the sand shimmered, the stone grew hot and the sea turned transparent. Then it was possible to hear the shift of sand underfoot, the eddy of a current on the turn, the splash of a seabird, and he discovered, yet again, the power of insignificant objects – a shell, a stone, a piece of wood – to satisfy.

Sometimes on the beach a memory shifted, unfolded. Then he remembered how he had longed to grow up, not only because he imagined he would be given the answer to the questions that puzzled him but because he had imagined that being grown-up meant that you were never lonely.

Cliff House had belonged to his parents, who had astonished themselves, and their friends, by producing Julian when they were well into their forties. 'Never mind,' said the wives of Lymouth, agog at this evidence of geriatric sex, 'older people produce more intelligent children.'

Since the intelligence quotient mattered to his scholar father and quiet mother, they set about parenthood with the best of intentions which, unfortunately, were impossible to realize. They were too old and Julian too young.

'It is one thing to enjoy the idea of a clever child, quite another to experience it,' Julian's father was heard to say more than once.

Perplexed by it all, they had left their son quite alone.

His growing-up had been quick and solitary and, as quickly, he had gone away to seek his fortune in the heaving, seething money markets of the East, only returning on their deaths. Then, Julian had set about banishing the past and all its clutter.

Cliff House was ripped open. Bathrooms were installed, ancient radiators replaced, the bay window rearticulated. Wrapped in Cellophane, upholstered furniture arrived from London, and interlined curtains were hung at the windows. On the plain, empty walls, Julian hung paintings, landscapes and seascapes, shot through with the sun and isolation that he craved in his home.

By then, he and Kitty had met and agreed on their partnership and she had helped him with the transformation. But not too much. Cliff House was Julian's reclaimed domain. Kitty had hers, and the freedom and separate spaces provided the key to their ten years together. Separate territories gave space, light, flexibility: the elements he most admired.

It was very cold that Sunday evening in January but, after packing up his papers and books, including *Undercover During the Second World War*, Julian abandoned the house, walked down the garden to the path running along the edge of the cliff and slithered down to the beach.

The cold wrapped him with the curious sensation of being both icy dry and wet. The sea roared and the wind whipped any traces of warmth from his body and flayed the skin of his lips.

It was just as Julian liked it.

Nature was not often overly generous, but she had been to the girl in the walled garden. Whose genes had those been? The father's, the mother's? A plundering Scandinavian way back in the centuries? She had been tall, ash-blonde, her hair shading to white by the hairline, with a lustrous complexion and grey eyes. This was a beautiful, spirited creature, he thought, with the flight of fancy he always indulged at the beginning of a chase. Not yet tested, still stretching her muscles, pregnant with secrets and visions.

*Not now?*

She was not in the least like Kitty. The disloyalty made him pause, and it was entirely the wrong moment to become sidetracked. He knew the risks of taking his eye off the ball when the figures were on the slide.

A flash of light above made Julian look up. There, poised on the cliff path that ran between the cottage and Cliff House *was* Kitty, in her blue cashmere jacket, waving to him with a torch. Every line of her body and movement of her arm proclaimed her love. Waving goodbye. After a second or two, he raised his arm and waved back.

On the way back to London in the car, Julian worked out a campaign by which to get a better look at Flagge House and its owner.

# 4

Bel rang on the Monday after the funeral. 'Are you all right? I'm sorry I wasn't there but I thought of you.'

'Well, that's something.'

'Sticks and stones,' said Bel, 'will hurt me far more than your witticisms. You know me, death, babies, I'm hopeless at the messy things.'

Quite right, Agnes thought. It was as well to know one's limitations but, all the same, she could have done with the comforting sight of Bel's blue-streaked hair and matching fingernails.

She and Bel had agreed to found Five Star five years ago. Because they were both good, and lucky, the company had flourished. The previous year, they had won two prizes for their documentaries on micro-credit in the Third World, and the controversial look at whaling communities in Newfoundland. Five Star was run from Bel's Notting Hill Gate flat, where Agnes, who preferred to be based at Flagge House, stayed on her trips up to London and for which she paid Bel a healthy rent.

Bel was four years older, and the administrative genius behind the company. She was also hugely talented and experienced, but a snag in the psyche prevented her from achieving quite what she wanted. Reaching for the stars,

Bel shied away when they sailed into view – a binge or an illness – leaving Agnes to cope. Veering between brilliance and burnout, that was Bel, and Agnes would have walked on water for her.

Bel's papers were being rustled meaningfully at the other end of the line. 'What's up?'

Bel sounded dubious, which was uncharacteristic for she was not a creature that entertained doubt. It either was or it wasn't. 'A farmer called up from your neck of the woods,' she pronounced the words as if she was discussing a disease, 'and he thinks you would interested in a stash of letters he's discovered in his attic from the Second World War. They were written by a farmer to his girlfriend. They're all about his farm and their love affair. He says they're immensely passionate and compelling. There's about forty of them. He's sent in two.'

'Not our sort of thing,' said Agnes.

'He disagrees. Apparently he runs an organic farm, or something, and he's being evicted by the landlord who wants to sell to a property developer and he thinks the letters might help get some publicity.'

Agnes stroked her plait. 'Why doesn't he go to the BBC?'

'Apparently he read the article about your uncle's death in the local newspaper. He was especially taken with the idea that you had inherited the house and you ran Five Star. He thought you would understand.'

\*

Jack Dun, farmer, to his lover, Mary, who had gone away in December 1942:

After we said goodbye I walked on the moor. Everything, trees, grasses, even the stones, were white and brittle with cold. I followed the old drovers' path past the oak copse, and I heard the branches on the trees groaning and snapping with ice. Further up, at Tolly's Spring, I stood and surveyed my land. In winter, it is possible to piece together the clues of an ancient system. That strip there belonged to William, that one to Robin, and that one to the master. You can read the land, Mary, if you care to.

I was looking at the old laws of possession, a kind of love dug into the earth which made it bring forth. The land trusting the men who worked on it.

Yes, thought Agnes. *I understand.*

At dawn, Andrew Kelsey was up checking on his cattle in the pens, a twice-daily ritual in winter. He was a lean, weathered man, with a thatch of thick dark hair just beginning to go grey, dressed in a clean check shirt and corduroys. He moved slowly and methodically, running a hand over an animal here, casting a professional eye there. 'Quiet, my beauties, quiet.'

He talked to them in this hushed moment before the day took over. To the uninitiated, each one was very like the next. To the informed eye, each was different. Andrew knew each one as an individual, as instinctively as a parent identifies his child. Always, at his approach, they stirred in their pens, and he fancied that they pressed up against him with something more than indifference. Why not? He treated them with respect and affection, and he ensured they were bedded on straw in good-sized pens.

It was so cold that the manure and straw smells were cancelled out in favour of sharp frost. Andrew fastened the final pen, stacked a couple of sacks of feed ready for the afternoon and backed up the van in the yard because he was expecting Agnes Campion.

He could feel, but not see, the lowering presence of the moor to the north of the farm. *So old, so indifferent.* But he liked the idea of its antiquity, older than it was possible to tally, older by far than the man-made landscape.

His fingers were aching, as they always did. Two of them on the right hand had been broken, nothing unusual in his work, but the blood no longer ran freely over the knotty calciferous joints until he flexed them. He walked towards the farmhouse. The blood flowed through his fingers, and the words in his head clustered like his cherished birds in the north field.

Soon there would be no bees left to forage in the grass, and no meadows. That was the way things were going. No tiny friction of crickets in the crops. No insects. No fungi running spores through the earth. No sighting of hares perched on chalky outcrops. No skylarks to loose their black arrows into the sky. No cowslip, burnet, toadflax and green-winged orchid.

'Breakfast.' Penny, his wife, had opened the kitchen window a crack, shouted through and closed it quickly against the dollop of cold air that slapped her round, unmade-up face. She sounded . . . not cross exactly but unsettled, a tone that was becoming habitual.

The words slithered away.

Andrew let himself in by the back door, shucked off his boots, washed his hands and padded across the kitchen in his socks. Penny was frying at the stove. As usual, her kitchen was immaculate, dishes stacked, pans shining, noticeboards displaying the weekly schedule, addresses, the bill rota and social engagements. Over by the window that looked out on to the yard and to the clump of ancient oaks beyond, which marked the boundary of the farm, was the latest pile of the women's magazines that were Penny's reading matter. Each month, Penny bought her favoured ones – every year more numerous – and read them, word for word, digging up from their pages the explanation to everything. And if one contained information on infertility, it was always left open for Andrew's attention. Then his mind snapped shut and, invariably, he ignored it. Penny and Andrew were childless, and the empty space had burned into their marriage. At first they had talked about it and visited the doctors but, as their hopes dwindled, so did the occasions when he turned to her in the double bed, or she to him.

He had grown to hate the magazines, and their disinformation, especially as, in the early years when he teased

Penny about them – but never too hard for he was a gentle man – she sulked.

Penny placed a fried breakfast in front of Andrew and they ate listening to the radio. Eventually, she fixed her eyes on him and asked, 'When's this woman coming?'

In the early days, Andrew had loved Penny's habit of gazing at him. Loving and trusting, her eyes had seemed larger then. Nowadays, her scrutiny made him uncomfortable, as if she saw into his secrets, his conviction that the world was a greedy, unjust place.

'She asked if she could come as early as possible because she wants to do some research in Exbury. Ten? Ten thirty? Depends on the roads.'

Penny washed up with a lot of swilling of suds. 'I suppose this means you'll go all arty on me.' The implication was: and leave me out.

Andrew suppressed a sigh. Just because once he had confessed that, if he had not been a farmer, he would have liked to be some sort of writer, a poet maybe, Penny had held it against him. 'For someone who's so *bad* with words,' she said. 'Someone who can hardly string a sentence together. Who never talks to anyone.' She meant that she and Andrew did not hold the long marital conversations to which she had looked forward and which she seemed to think were open and healthy. From that moment, she had chosen to interpret Andrew's desires, as different as they could be from hers, as a criticism of her, his silences as a deep alienation from their marriage.

Lately, Andrew had begun to wonder if Penny was involved with someone else, specifically with Bob Howell, who ran a dairy farm the other side of the moor. He had no proof, only a gut feeling – a reference in a conversation, a phone call terminated when he entered the kitchen unexpectedly, Bob's refusal to meet his eye in the pub. Strangely enough, part of him did not care if she was. Or he thought it didn't but maybe that was something to do with the changes that threatened his life. And his marriage? If he was honest, Penny and he no longer functioned as a proper couple.

He searched in his pockets for a piece of paper on which he had jotted some notes, hauled them out and studied them.

'What *are* you up to?' asked Penny. 'What's going on with these letters?' She was breathing hard.

He raised his head. 'What are *you* up to?'

Her gaze dropped and she placed a saucepan on the stove with extra emphasis. 'That's not answering the question.'

'Isn't it?' he said, his secret settling like a dog in a basket.

'Just don't lose sight of the fact,' Penny was saying, 'that we've got to save this farm. You've got to fight, Andrew, so you can't get all distracted.'

Andrew heard the car drive into the yard, and went to greet Agnes at the back door. As she scrambled out of the car, his eyes widened in appreciation. 'The photo in the paper didn't do you justice,' he said awkwardly, and led her into the kitchen to introduce her to Penny.

The kitchen was basic, but blissfully warm and clean, with immaculate touches. A dresser with blue china, a pair of old carver chairs, and a huge, burnished mirror on one wall that did not belong in a kitchen but actually suited it. In contrast to her rangy husband, Penny was small and plump, with badly permed hair and sharp-looking eyes, which were fretworked with fine lines a lighter colour than the rest of her complexion. While Penny was making coffee, Agnes inquired as to the date of the house, which she had expected to be much older.

'This house? It was built in the sixties.' Obviously Penny took the speaking role in this marriage. She heaved the tray of coffee over to the table. 'The old house collapsed so Charlie Stone, our landlord's father, built this one and leased it to Andrew's father. When he died, Andrew took over. Now Jonas, his son, is trying to chuck us out.'

'So Andrew has lived here all his life?'

'Yes.' Penny seemed tired and unfriendly. Agnes gained the impression of a woman who, over the years, had been disappointed, not drastically, but cumulatively.

'And you say you're being chucked out?'

Husband and wife exchanged a look, and Andrew shrugged. 'As I told your colleague, the landlord has got into debt and wants to sell the land to a developer for a housing estate.'

'Aren't you protected by the law?'

45

'That's the problem,' said Andrew. 'The lease was reissued in the sixties and the landlord wrote in a water-tight clause that says he can chuck us out precisely when he wants to.' White-knuckled, he rubbed at his broken fingers. 'The solicitor has gone over it with a fine-tooth comb.'

She heard the underlying note of tension.

Andrew continued, 'We farm organic beef here. No pesticides, hormones or stress. The cattle graze on un-treated grass and live in family groups. We sell the meat all over the south. There's a growing market out there.'

This fidelity to the old ways and old knowledge fascin-ated Agnes and she was warming to this slow-speaking farmer, who had taken to heart the responsibility for his land.

'You say you've lent the letters to the local librarian,' she said. 'Is it possible I could look at them? If I felt there was something to work with, there is a television series which runs in the autumn called *Hidden Lives*. Do you know it? It occupies ten-minute slots and its brief is to explore the lives of ordinary people. As it happens, they're looking for a couple of historical ones. But I'll need your help on the research.'

'Oh,' said Penny, and stiffened. 'What sort of research?'

Agnes noticed the body language. 'Authentication. It's usually done with wills, electoral rolls, constituency maps, that sort of thing. Don't worry. Bel, my co-director, specializes in it. Usually it's not a problem.'

Andrew produced an unremarkable grey file with a clip to keep the papers in place. Written on the spine in faded ink were the words: 'Cattle Feed'.

'The letters were mixed up with old bills for cattle-cake and that sort of thing.' He slid the empty file across the table. 'They were all jumbled up date-wise,' he said. He reached for a leather tobacco pouch on the table, and his unfastened shirt cuffs fell back over wrists as warm and brown as walnut wood.

He made Agnes think of summer and the outdoors, of fields and sun, of blackberries and hips and autumn mist burned away by the sun. Her eyes slid past him to the mirror on the wall in which was reflected the trio at the kitchen table. Penny, cross and hostile; Andrew, intent, absorbed in the drama of the letters. Herself? Listening hard with the calm, professional expression she had perfected. The winter sun had shifted and light bounced off the mirror, directing a dazzling, exuberant beam at her.

'Are you sure the writer, this Jack, lived here at Tithings?'

Andrew tamped a bootlace of tobacco into a Rizla paper, working the calloused fingers around the shape. A match flared, and tobacco smoke drifted up to the ceiling. 'I'd recognize the landmarks he talks about in my sleep.'

'And you've nothing else on Jack?'

'No.'

Agnes made more notes. 'Sometimes memory is the only source. We'll have to ask around. I suppose he might have moved on after the war. Perhaps Mary didn't come back and he no longer wanted to be here – '

Andrew cut in. 'Oh, no,' he said, tapping the table to underscore the point. 'He would have stayed here. He wouldn't have abandoned the farm. Never.'

The chair screeched along the floor and Penny got to her feet. With a gesture that Agnes was not sure how to interpret, she dumped her coffee mug in the sink. An awkward silence followed, which Agnes endeavoured to fill. 'Could I see round the farm, if you're not too busy?'

She felt the other woman's eyes fixed on her back as Andrew led her across the yard to the cattle-pens. Penny had lent her a pair of boots, which were too small, and she couldn't help thinking that Penny would be taking pleasure in the thought of her cramped feet.

To ease the pressure on her toes, she leaned on the railing of the first pen and savoured a pleasing pungency of cattle and warm straw, pulsing hide, muddy hoof and a base note of disinfectant.

Andrew pushed open the gate. 'They're raised on strictly traditional methods. That means they can grow at their own pace and without stress. I try to be totally organic. Sometimes I'm forced to use antibiotics when they're ill, but absolutely no growth hormones.'

Agnes told the animals how lucky they were. Andrew tapped a warm flank. 'You are, aren't you, my beauties? I keep 'em in family groups. Aunts and cousins . . .'

'Have you always farmed?'

'Always. Originally my father had a big place up in Yorkshire, then we came here.' He caressed the ear of the beast nearest to him. Little feathery strokes. 'It's in the blood.' The phrase was heavy with private meaning. A little puzzled, Agnes nodded. 'Along with other things,' he added hastily, and changed the subject. 'Let me show you the rest of the farm. The weather's clearing and you have to seize the moment with the moor. I should explain that I never use chemicals. You know that on some of the bigger farms the soil is technically dead? Eco-death. It doesn't happen here.'

'I did a piece on it once.'

He sent her a shy half-smile of approbation.

Together, they walked up to the north field and Andrew pointed out a cluster of granite buildings on the moor. 'That's one of the oldest farms in the area. Much older than here. Bits of it date back to the thirteenth century.'

Good camera shot. Agnes peered at the solid grey shapes, and the green and duns of the moor into which they were set. A silent, ancient setting.

One eyebrow arched quizzically, he turned to her. 'I'd recognize it in my sleep.' He pushed aside a petrified waterfall of brambles to let Agnes pass. 'Over there . . .' Andrew pointed to the road snaking as perimeter around the farm, and Agnes knew that the whole point of the tour had been to lead her to this spot.

He was saying, 'There's where Arcadian Villages propose to build stage one of the estate. Stage two is planned for later and will reach up to the garden of the farmhouse. In all, a hundred and fifty houses.'

She felt his bitterness and anger, as sharp as the wind that was blowing away the rain. 'I know a little of how you feel. I had someone trying to buy up my house. I can't tell you how angry I felt.' She remembered the hot rush of words as she had told Julian Knox that her house was not on offer. 'So what is happening here exactly?'

He shrugged. 'The council has turned down the initial planning application but we had a letter yesterday to say that it's gone to a planning appeal, which will be heard in June. If we win, it will then go before the Environment Secretary and we can spin it out.

They were clever, these planners. They had a nose for the right setting. Agnes could see that. Situated where it was, close to the road, Andrew's farmland was the obvious place to site Exbury's overspill. 'I'm sorry,' she said, with real distress.

'They think I'm a pushover,' Andrew said, more to himself than Agnes. 'The capitalist pushing aside the small man. They can think again.'

The shyness and taciturnity were deceptive, for this was a man who was preparing to fight. And why not? She sneaked a look at his profile. Under the wind-scoured complexion, a fire obviously burned and people with a mission were, sometimes, magnetic: they had a way of drawing you in. Anyway, why should his carefully built-up farm be under threat? Agnes wanted to shout, 'I'm with you.' Then she felt rather stupid.

The wind had swung round and she buttoned up her jacket. The collar scratched damply at her neck. He let the bramble fall back into place, brushed against her and again she caught the faint scent of the farm.

'What are those?' she asked, indicating a series of white stands under the hedge.

He barely glanced at them. 'My bees.'

As she drove past the oaks on her way home, Agnes glanced in the driving mirror. Hands stuffed into his pockets and shirt cuffs flapping, Andrew Kelsey was rooted to the ground in the yard, gazing up to the north field, which rolled out under the moor. Tense and intent, his pose had a monolithic quality.

It was late afternoon when Andrew returned home for tea. Penny did not look up from her magazine, but said, 'She's pretty and all that, but I don't think she could cook for a moment.'

'Probably not,' said Andrew.

'She'd be no good as a farmer's wife.'

'That's lucky, then, as I don't think there's any question of it.' He drank the tea. 'Pen, if I nip down to the pub could you look in on the calves?'

'Sure,' she said.

It was not until he was ordering the beer in the company of his mate, Jim, that it struck Andrew that Penny had been quick to say yes. Usually, requests for pub slots required plea bargaining on a grand scale.

The weather had finally cleared, and the moon dominated the sky when Andrew drove back to Tithings, up the potholed road which, in turn, climbed past the oak clumps towards the moor. The axe he kept in the back of the van rattled against the tool box and he thought, Blast. There was always something that needed doing that he had not got round to, something he had not checked up on or put away.

It was old, old land, and demons raged over it. A fertile crucible, with blood-red soil, bisected by hidden lanes and drenched hedgerows. The wind that had blown all afternoon and evening stirred the oak branches as he passed. *Hearts of oak*. Andrew saluted them, symbols of liberty, stoutness, mercantile imperialism. Under their canopies had been consummated a marriage between the elements and all the best myths. The Green Knight, Robin Hood, the Forest of Arden . . .

Upstairs in the stuffy main bedroom of the farmhouse, the alarm clock ticked away in the dark. Andrew pulled back the bedcovers and encountered the patchwork quilt, made by Penny's mother. This was strange. Always, without fail, Penny removed it from the bed and folded it carefully. He put out a hand, felt across the quilt for the warm hump of Penny and found nothing.

He snapped on the light. The bed was empty and so was the room. There was a note on the pillow, which he snatched up. 'I've left you,' Penny had written, 'for Bob, who wants me. You don't and you never have. I'll fetch my things another time. Good luck with the fight.'

Andrew lurched into the bathroom and was violently sick.

When he finally managed to drop into a twitchy sleep, Andrew dreamed of Jack. He pictured him, tall and short-sighted, ranging the moor and thinking of Mary. He was a man who would have known how to calculate time and distance from the sun and moon, a man whose power and presence were growing as Andrew wrote him into the letters and prepared to deceive as many people as possible to save his farm.

> Who sows a field or trains a flower
> Or plants a tree, is more than all.

# 5

Early in February Agnes received a packet from Andrew Kelsey containing seventeen letters from Jack to Mary and dropped everything to read them.

She held them gingerly. These were fragile artefacts from which secrets must be coaxed. Written on various kinds of papers, they were mottled and foxed with age and, in places, worn almost into transparency. Some were in thick lead pencil, some in watery navy blue ink. The handwriting varied in its legibility, and showed signs of stress and cramped conditions. The sifting and making sense occupied Agnes for a whole afternoon.

Afterwards, shaken and moved, she sorted them into date order. It appeared that Mary had left the farm without an explanation and, vague as to where she was going, abandoned the lover who was too old? medically unfit? to fight. To reassure her, remind her, perhaps, Jack wrote in minute detail of life on the farm and, always, of his love for Mary. The list of her beauties was tenderly couched – the shape and colour of her eyes, her slender back and arched feet. A man of deep emotions and some poetry, he described over and over how he had fallen in love with her at first sight. 'I had no idea,' he wrote, 'how completely and utterly you know within the instant.

How mind, body and spirit fuse as the spear strikes into the soul.'

After she had finished, Agnes paced up and down her uncle's study, which was large enough to allow her to do so. *Her* study now. The letters had convinced her that this was a subject which would work. But how? She picked up the phone and put a call through to Dickie, a commissioning editor at the BBC with whom she had collaborated on several projects.

An hour later she was checking over her diary when Maud appeared in the study doorway. 'There's someone on the phone who wants to speak to you,' she said, in the ultra-polite manner that always gave Agnes pause.

'What are you up to, Maud?'

'*Rien*,' said Maud, and disappeared.

Agnes picked up the phone. 'Will you come out for a drink with me?' said Julian Knox. 'Please.'

'Why should I?'

'Why shouldn't you?' he replied. 'Six thirty at Buzacki's on Tuesday next week?'

Agnes sighed. 'I suppose you've been talking to Maud.'

'As a matter of fact, I have.'

'Then I must come and put the record straight.'

'Exactly,' he said.

At Buzacki's there was a discreet clink of glasses, the glitter of mirror and chrome, and bowls on tables heaped with expensive nuts and handmade crisps.

After a moment or two's study, she modified her first impressions. This was a different man from the successful opportunist prowling around the walled garden. He was still as sleek and groomed, but more fatigued, troubled, and she wanted very much to know why.

'Within the instant,' it had said in Jack's letter. Agnes helped herself to the nuts. 'I gather you laid siege to my aunt again. It wasn't very honest.' She gave him a direct look. 'Was it?'

'Honest? Yes and no. Your aunt was very keen that I had a go at changing your mind. I was interested in seeing you again. *Ergo*. Is that dishonest?'

She leaned forward. 'Preying on an old lady?'

'Is *that* what you call it?' He ran his fingers through his red-gold hair, which destroyed the sleek look and replaced it with a boyish one. 'I was practically kidnapped over the phone by your vigorous aunt and I had to swear on the blood of Julie Andrews that I would try to talk you round.'

Agnes almost felt sorry for him. 'So she mentioned *The Sound of Music*?'

He opened his hands in a gesture that said, I quite understand, enjoy even, the absurdities of human nature but this was a tough one. 'Put it this way, I hadn't appreciated its merits before. But by the time she had finished I did.'

Kindness to elderly ladies what not what she had expected, or the humour. Perhaps he was a Jekyll and Hyde character, a fiend in the boardroom, wise and tolerant at home. They did exist. Whatever, he was a little mysterious and that always appealed to her. Agnes rolled the wine-glass idly between her fingers. It never did to make assumptions and she should know that by now.

'Decent homes mean decent lives,' he said, laying out his case like gems in a jeweller's window. 'We need profit. Why not combine the two?'

'Flagge House is not a proposition.'

'Of course.' He poured out more wine. 'I quite understand. But situations have a way of changing, believe me. And you will be saddled with its upkeep.' He paused. 'Not to mention fending off everyone who wishes to give you advice.'

'Tell me, who should I trust?'

Again the quick, ironic smile. 'Obviously not me. But now that that's been said, and I have done what I promised your aunt, shall we change the subject?'

His capitulation was too easy and Agnes was immediately suspicious. She put down her glass and leaned on her elbows. 'Shouldn't you come clean?' she asked. 'About what you want from me?'

'Not a bad idea.' He captured the last nut from the bowl. 'You look like a schoolteacher,' he said. 'A divine one.'

She had forgotten the feint and counter-feint of pursuit, and lust, and the exhilaration of both. The tiny little pricks of anticipation, and the responses resurrected from their semi-death. Only a few weeks ago she would not have thought it possible but perhaps, perhaps, the spectre of an old and done-with love was, finally, banished.

'Will you come sailing with me some time?'

'Yes. If you don't mind a novice.'

He must have been watching her very carefully for he reached out with his hand and covered hers. Thin fingers that she liked. A texture of skin that she liked. 'I wanted to know if you're getting over your uncle,' he said. 'Does it hurt less?'

She looked down at their hands. 'I will be fine.'

'Good.' He removed his hand and desire washed through Agnes so powerfully that she was literally breathless.

After a moment, he asked if she was working on a project, and she told him about the letters and Andrew Kelsey. She also admitted that they had a problem in verifying who Jack and his lover Mary actually were. It was particularly difficult as there were no letters from Mary. 'She seems to have disappeared completely, leaving Jack in the dark. But it is odd because Jack is so besotted and what he writes suggests that she is too.'

'There could be hundreds of reasons,' said Julian. 'War was like that.'

'But to be so secretive.'

'Secret work, perhaps.' He refilled their glasses. 'For instance, the SOE made a point of using women during the war for undercover work. Jack sounds as though he was educated, and perhaps Mary spoke a language and was used in intelligence. I've been reading about it. If you make the assumption that Mary was sent into the field – for instance, France – she could not possibly have written any letters home.'

Not bad, thought Agnes, fascinated by the way he held the wine-glass.

'Can you imagine how lonely and isolated it must have been, knowing that you were living in a different box from everyone else? Being apart.' He spoke matter-of-factly but his body language suggested to Agnes that he had experienced this.

*Within the instant.*

Being apart and lonely was Agnes's main memory, right from the beginning. In fact, she had made a speciality of being miserable. 'Yes, I can,' she said. 'Very well.'

'It's only a supposition but I'll send you a book I'm reading on the subject, if you like.'

'Don't worry, I'll get my colleague, Bel, on to it.'

He did not seem to hear her. '*Think,*' he said. 'On the run, pushing your response to the limit. Diving into yourself. Digging into yourself.'

*Not bad, not bad at all.*

The air between them seemed charged, and the chemistry fizzed in the pit of her stomach. Agnes struggled to be sensible.

'I'm going away for a week or so,' he said eventually, 'but can we meet again?'

'For what?'

'What do you think?'

'Well, yes,' she said, and felt the pulses beat in her wrist and at her throat.

The following week, she and Bel waited in the reception of Television House. 'Tell you what,' said Bel, 'if this goes through and the figures are right, we'll go shopping.'

Bel was always trying to smarten up Agnes and it was true that she had not bothered much lately.

'I'm sick to death of you in those trousers and refusing to take an interest in what you look like. Pierre was a pig and you're over him, and it's time you got your hair cut.'

'You sound like him,' she murmured.

Pierre had berated Agnes for her lack of chic and her English indulgence in imperfection, and she had argued that what lay underneath was what mattered. He had said, 'You are so young, Agnes, so innocent. Do you want to succeed?' She had been so angry and so sure she was right ... Agnes was brought up short. For the first time she was thinking about Pierre without the accompanying hobgoblins of pain and humiliation. *Good*.

'OK,' she said, taking Bel by surprise. 'Let's go shopping.'

'Right,' said Dickie, opening the meeting. 'What have you beauties got for me today?'

They were in one of the conference rooms with huge plate-glass windows, no air – or, rather, only the conditioned kind swarming with menacing bacteria – and rows of bottled mineral water. Providing you nailed him in the mornings, Dickie's nose for a popular programme was infallible and Agnes trusted him. She outlined a couple of ideas: the Jack and Mary letters, a forty-minute exposé of the DDT breastmilk scandal in India.

'Breastmilk, great,' said Dickie. 'Just what we should be doing. Nice and PC. That will jack up the Brownie points. The other one . . .' He shook his head. 'I know we said we wanted history, but I'm not quite sure. Not sexy enough.'

Agnes said, 'Actually, there is a handle on this one. The farmer is about to be evicted by a landlord who wants the land back for development. There's a row brewing in the local community. The farm's been there since the sixteenth century.'

Dickie brightened. Bel, like lightning on the uptake, shoved the list of figures over the table. He glanced at them. 'Don't try and pull any wool over my eyes.'

'Why should I?' asked Agnes, softly.

'Because you're unscrupulous, sweetie, that's why. As I well know.' Dickie read on. 'Who's Mary?' he asked.

'His lover. We think she went off to fight somewhere. One theory is that she was an agent.'

'Oh, well, then,' Dickie said, 'that's great. I like it. Battlefronts, women in the front line, Mata Hari, injustice, war. Great.'

Despite working late into the night on budgets, Agnes woke fresh and clear-eyed at Flagge House. Today she had three meetings in London, a catch-up with Bel and a drink with Jed, her favourite cameraman. She stretched and her head fell back. It was too soon to jump to conclusions, and one crackling strike of attraction over a glass of wine did not a new life make.

She padded into the bathroom and endeavoured to concentrate on the meetings. The breastmilk project required more money. How could she arrange it by the autumn? More worrying, Jed had been booked for another project. But instead of solutions presenting themselves, the image of a blue, sunlit sea danced across her vision in an enchanted wash of colour and light. A wine-dark sea, over which she would speed with the freedom of the released.

Downstairs, she located a spare copy of the letters, which had been typed up and bound into a file, and packed them carefully into a padded envelope with her business card. On it, she wrote, 'I thought you might like a copy.'

This she sent to Julian Knox.

# 6

The card lay on top of Julian's papers in the kitchen of Cliff House. Kitty noticed it at once. She picked it up. 'Who's Agnes Campion?'

Julian was stowing a bottle of wine in the picnic cooler. 'Possible business.'

'Oh.'

Kitty scrutinized the card for further clues. Was his answer the usual ducking away from confrontation? She knew him so well, from back to front, from side to side, and she knew that he would work all night rather than face her questioning. And, oh, how he hated confrontation, particularly where feelings were concerned. But wasn't that like all men?

Julian fastened the cooler and placed it on the floor. Then he reached over and prised the card out of Kitty's hand. 'Business, Kitty. That's all.'

He was lying, she knew he was, but she had to carry on as if it did not matter a jot. Kitty put her head on one side in a manner that always made Julian uneasy. He had told her it made her seem arch, but she couldn't help it. 'Don't be a bully.'

'Then don't pry.'

'Of course not.' Kitty picked up her expensive pale

blue jacket and shrugged it on. 'Why *do* you insist on picnicking in mid-winter? Why do I let you bully me?' They were *en route* for Lincolnshire, where Julian was going to make one of his weekend site visits which, as chief executive of the company, was not strictly necessary but, as he explained to Kitty, only unwise emperors never visited the empire.

'It's nearly spring. It's good for you. For me.' Julian grinned and kissed her cheek lightly. 'Let's go.'

Everything was all right, really.

Nevertheless, the card cast a darkening shadow over Kitty as they drove north to Lincolnshire. It was always the way, she had discovered. Small things possessed a power to disturb out of proportion to their size.

*Agnes Campion.*

They drove across fenland, so flat that Kitty felt giddy, through which were threaded drainage ditches as straight as tram-lines. A ferocious wind buffeted the car and whipped over fields so large that Kitty wondered if she had strayed into the Russian steppes.

Mile after mile, the countryside was quite different from the pink-bricked, graceful landscape she was used to, but she had had the forethought to read up on it a little. Here had been traditional farming communities, governed by rote and season, by husbandry and tilth – she liked that word – but they had been invaded by new techniques. She peered out of the car window. If you looked carefully at the rich-soiled fields, said the guide, it was possible to see traces of the old ways.

Suddenly, miraculously, the fens folded up into the wolds and the road was tugged upwards by the swell of the land. Kitty was entranced and she reached for the guidebook. '"Once the wool market for England,"' she read out, '"the county is dotted with substantial grey stone churches and large houses built in a more prosperous age. The poet, Alfred, Lord Tennyson, lived and wrote in the area and called it the 'Haunt of Ancient Peace'."'

At Horncastle, Julian turned right towards Skegness and drove several miles. On the outskirts of Loutham, where the sea was just discernible in the distance, he stopped the car beside a field in which the skeletons of new houses were already in place. 'Welcome to the Tennyson housing estate.'

They got out of the car, Kitty already shivering inside her pale blue jacket. 'Why here? It's so windblown and . . . ugly.'

'Well, for one, Bristling's have built a large factory this side of Boston and it's a perfect dormitory site for its executives.'

'And where,' asked Kitty, surprising herself, 'will the badgers and foxes sleep?'

Julian hunted for his jacket on the back seat. 'I didn't know you were a naturalist, Kitty darling.'

'I'm not,' Kitty fought to tie a headscarf over her hair, 'but I could be.' She looked over to the sea. Dotted with only a few trees, the outlook was bleak, desolate, and she turned back thankfully to the car.

While Julian had his meetings with the group who had been assembled already by the Portakabin, Kitty drove herself to the nearest village and amused herself in a couple of junk shops. She bought a blue and white plate for her collection, a mirror for the staircase in the cottage, and a wooden coal scuttle banded in brass as a present for her mother. Signing a cheque always brought a satisfactory rush of blood to her head.

Eventually, she drove back to retrieve Julian, who was still occupied with the architect. Feeling more acclimatized, Kitty hauled on a pair of wellingtons and wandered around the estate, which was well over a mile in circumference. On the sea side, the foundations for a perimeter wall had already been dug, but Kitty felt instinctively that it would be no defence against the winds roaring in from polar regions, or rain lashing in from the sea.

She walked along the rudimentary roads and closes to the furthest end. It was part of her self-imposed mission to be curious for, lately, she had been feeling the lack of it in herself and had wondered fearfully if it was a sign of ageing.

At the end of the final close, one of the houses, much smaller than the others, was set at an angle to the rest. It faced in the direction of the coast, and the pale winter light illuminated its carapace of scaffolding and empty window arches.

Picking through the piles of bricks and mud, Kitty walked up to it and peered into the interior. Someone would settle here, put up pictures, agonize over the arrangement of the furniture, open the french windows into the tiny back garden, fry bacon in the kitchen, draw the curtains against the winter. As she gazed into it, she heard a soft voice in her head say, 'You must start somewhere.'

Kitty lingered so long that she began to shiver in earnest.

That night, in the hotel bedroom where they were staying, she asked Julian why that particular house was so much smaller. He looked up from a bound manuscript he was reading and told her that it was part of the thinking. '*Zeitgeist* housing, Kitty.' These days, marriages did not last, mothers were single and grandmothers did not live with their families. There was a demand for small accommodation for all those who did not live in large family units. 'The shape has changed,' he added, and Kitty saw the point, only too well.

'Why don't marriages last, do you think?'

But Julian cradled the pages of the manuscript. 'It's too much to ask,' he replied. 'I suppose we get sick of each other. That is our nature, and it can't be helped.'

Stupid, she thought. *Stupid, stupid.* Keep off these topics.

Julian returned to his reading and Kitty examined the wallpaper. She slid down on to the pillows. Reading was not one of her habits; she preferred the radio. Eventually, she tried again. 'What are you reading?'

Julian looked down at the face on the pillow. Then he leaned over and stroked it. 'A rather remarkable collection of love letters.'

Kitty's interest sharpened. 'Whose?'

'A farmer's. He was writing during the Second World War to his lover who had gone off to fight.'

'Male or female?'

'Female.' He seemed alight with an emotion she could not catalogue. 'Listen to this, Kitty. He writes that he feeds on her absence like the vampire. "I suck greedily on my unassuaged desire until my throat is blistered and burning . . ."' He put the manuscript on the bedside table, lay down with one of his quick, decisive movements and turned off the light.

The writer knows, thought Kitty. He knows how I feel. She wanted to reach out and to feast as greedily on the flesh that she loved so well but Julian was too silent, too still for her to dare.

I must start somewhere.

They were back in Lymouth early on Sunday evening. Julian drove Kitty to the cottage, unloaded her suitcase and announced that he would spend Sunday night at Cliff House because he had work to do. To her astonishment, Kitty heard herself saying, 'Julian, I've been thinking. Thinking that . . . it's time for a change.' She knew what he was likely to say, that there wasn't time, that he was busy and couldn't it wait, so she held out her hand, pulled him into the hall, shut the front door and leaned against it. 'No, you can't go yet. I won't let you until we've talked.'

'Kitty . . .'

Her courage was fragile so she got the words out in a

rush. 'I would like us to get married. We suit each other and it would be so much more practical.'

Fists clenched, she waited for his reply. She longed, how she longed, to live in Cliff House, so big and generous, sited so perfectly by the sea. How she would grace it, the trophy that, surely after ten years, she had earned. How well they would fit together, she and it. The serene, bay-windowed room framing the seascapes, the sunlight that poured through it, the garden she would make it her business to study. 'Say something,' she begged.

He did not look at her – a bad sign. 'I don't want to hurt you, Kitty.'

She felt his trappedness, or was it indifference?, like a thousand slashes, but pressed on. 'Why not, Julian?' He shoved his hands into his pockets, and she remembered the faint disturbance given off by Agnes Campion's card. 'Is there someone else?'

Now he did look at her, with a kind, too kind, expression, and for a few terrible seconds she thought she had hit on the truth.

'I'm not sure.' She winced and damned their agreement for absolute honesty. Julian continued, 'But I don't think we should make any changes. I don't know why exactly, Kitty, and I know I should explain it better. Except I've been happy with what we've got.'

'You *must* know why.'

He shook his head. 'Kitty, if . . .'

Ominous 'if'.

A picture of one future took shape in her head with appalling clarity. No Julian sitting in the chair by the window, an echoing space in the bed, which she took care to make up each Friday with Italian cotton sheets and which bore the impress of his body when he left.

'Stop,' she said, her courage and resolution vanished. 'It's all right. I didn't mean it.'

He moved towards her, took her in his arms and dropped a kiss on her blonde, highlighted hair. She shuddered with the humiliation of that light kiss. 'Is this making you unhappy, Kitty? I couldn't bear that. You must be honest.'

'No,' she lied. 'No. Not at all.'

Julian took her hand and pulled the fingers gently, one by one. 'I would prefer to stay as we are. I hope I look after you well enough, and you like it here in Lymouth.'

'Do I?' Kitty felt too weary to dissemble. 'What do you know about the weekdays?'

Now he traced the shape of Kitty's fingernails. 'Nothing at all, thank goodness.' His finger slid up her arm. 'So lovely to touch, Kitty,' he murmured, and she had an awful, awful feeling that the words were not really for her. 'That's what I've always loved about you. You're so well . . . tended.'

*Coward*, she wanted to fling at him. Coward.

'Soft, lovely Kitty.'

She hated his patronage, but also knew that he did not intend it in that way. He thought he was paying her a compliment, and it amused her that even the accomplished Julian stumbled. She also knew that she was not going to receive an answer to her question. She raised her beautifully made-up eyes to his.

'Don't rock the boat, Kitty.'

In his way, Julian was being loyal, for she knew now there *was* someone else. His warning was a kind of fidelity – the one they had agreed on.

There was silence, except the dim, muffled sound of a rough sea.

Oh, God, thought Kitty. Help me.

Patience. Instinct. Sexual perfection and expertise, a willingness to abandon. These were the elements that Kitty summoned to her aid. She reached up and kissed Julian on the corner of the mouth where she knew it roused him. 'Once upon a time,' she said, brushing the line of his jaw with her tongue, 'there was a fair princess . . .' Julian laughed and moved closer. Ah, thought Kitty. She could feel his response and stirred it further by nipping his lower lip gently between her teeth. 'Who lived in a tower. Untouched.'

Julian's arm circled Kitty. 'And she waited for a prince to come along. One day he did. Better still, he was tall, fair and rich.'

Safely encircled, Kitty sighed. 'But he had one fault.'

'Oh?'

'He was too bossy. And she wasn't quite sure that his lovemaking was up to it.'

'You devil,' said Julian, and pulled her even closer, 'for that.'

Kitty's spirits rose. She understood this particular exchange very well. In one way or another, she had played it with all her men. 'And what are you going to do about it?'

'I could take myself off. Or . . .'

'Or?'

'I could decide the last accusation was rubbish and deal with the situation in the way I think fit.'

Kitty backed towards the staircase. She raised a school-mistressy finger. 'Stay where you are, Julian. Right there.'

She turned and fled up the stairs to the bedroom.

In the middle of the night, Kitty woke. Julian's head rested against her shoulder and she smiled to herself. He had stayed, and such moments of sweetness made up for the doubt and confusion, and for her fear for the future.

It was only as she was drifting back to sleep that she realized that Julian was still awake.

# 7

Jim's reaction to Penny's departure stung Andrew. 'Grief! Penny's a stayer – you must have treated her rotten.'

Had he? Andrew reviewed his own behaviour. Rotten? He didn't think so. But the relief at being alone was enormous although he felt a queer, contrasting shudder of grief whenever he thought of his wife. A couple of days after leaving, and he still had not quite forgiven the bald note, Penny had returned to Tithings for a flying visit. 'To have it out with you,' she said.

He had done a bit of thinking by then, summoned his better nature and told her that of course she must go and find happiness and that she would be far better off without him. Even with the awful Bob, whom he disliked intensely.

She had listened impassively, then said, 'You're just easing your conscience, Andrew.'

She abandoned him to an empty kitchen, his beasts and the letters.

He was delighted, he wrote to Agnes, that the *Hidden Lives* programme seemed to be on the cards, but he had been notified that the planning appeal inquiry had been set for early June. Therefore, if Agnes wished him to be around while they were filming, it would be best if she and the team came during the last week of May.

He promised to send the remaining letters in the next few days. Meanwhile he enclosed a pamphlet from the conservation group to which he belonged. 'DID YOU KNOW?' it asked in very bold, badly assembled type. '200,000 MILES OF ENGLISH HEDGEROW HAVE BEEN RIPPED OUT, ENOUGH TO GIRDLE THE EARTH NINE TIMES.'

Underneath was printed a list of bird populations whose habitat had been destroyed. It included grey partridges, linnets, song thrushes and the cirl bunting. On it, Andrew had written, 'Can you do anything about this on the programme? NB. I layer and pleach my hedgerows in the old way. The birds on my farm are safe. I am looking forward to meeting the crew.'

It was a risk to attempt to write more letters, but Agnes had stirred him up – not that he needed stirring. She had imported the flavour from another world where what was said and done had an impact. Her programmes *affected* people.

He opened the desk drawer, took out a piece of the paper he had found in the attic, sharpened the old-fashioned lead pencil and placed its point on the grained sheet. He wanted to conjure her shape and colouring, and the impact they had made on him. At that one meeting she had sprung, golden and fresh, into his consciousness and elbowed Penny aside. Recapturing

Agnes on paper was an act of lust and fanaticism, which would make his letters live.

Agnes had become Mary. Defining Mary was the springboard that gave him power and a voice that had been silent for most of his life.

He began to write.


Agnes pushed the pamphlet Andrew had enclosed with his letter on to Bel's desk. 'I think this angle will work. We don't have to do anything except present it.'

'If you like.' Bel was preoccupied.

It was the weekly catch-up. Bel reported that her research on Jack Dun had yielded thin results. 'Ag, I don't think we should waste any more time on this one. It has "slog" written all over it. The Kelseys have no idea who this bloke was and nor does anyone else in the area. And, let me tell you, I've rung quite a few.' She contemplated her nails. 'Truth game now. No one cares much except a bunch of greens.'

Agnes had been riffling through her notes. Alerted, she looked up. She and Bel did not usually part company over the philosophical content of their work. 'That's not like you.'

Bel's answer was the flicker of a serpent's tongue. 'No, but we haven't had to deal with a joker like Andrew Kelsey before.' She peered at the schedules tacked up on the wall and wrote a couple of filming dates into the diary.

Bel's opinions were always worth taking seriously. Agnes frowned. 'How do you know he's a joker? You haven't met him.'

Bel kept her face averted. 'Instinct.'

'You're wrong. It's a good subject.'

'It's no way to do business. Fancying a farmer.'

Agnes said, with old hot insistence, 'I don't but if I did it wouldn't alter the fact that these letters have got it.'

'Why, Ag? Tell me.'

'Because they're about a life that is vanishing.'

Slipping. Dissolving. Dying.

She thought of this conversation as she prepared for a day of meetings at Flagge House. Things were always more complicated than they seemed. She had learned that. But trust in your own responses also had a part to play and Andrew had the convincing desperation of the wronged. Perhaps having no parents and siblings gave you an unnatural belief in yourself and she should listen more to observers like Bel. For, at the bottom of her heart, where the non-negotiable truths lived, Agnes was well aware that most people spend most of their lives pulling the wool over the eyes trained on them.

Think of the house. Surrounded by its water-meadow, its kitchen garden, its once formal parterre, Flagge House was a dreamscape of kind brick and generous windows. But, she knew, she *knew*, that under the eaves the birds scrabbled with sharp claws and rose abruptly into the winter grey, spiders spun intricate silk patterns and the mice constructed atria of pulped wood and stolen linen.

She picked up her rucksack, and let herself out of the bedroom. Strains of 'Edelweiss' led her to Maud's bedroom, where she knocked and heard a flurry of movement.

Both sisters were tucked into the matrimonial four-poster bed where they had obviously spent the night. Maud was knitting and Bea was propped up on pillows reading. Despite the blankets, both sisters looked cold and there was a distinct burnt smell.

'For goodness' sake!' exclaimed Maud. 'You're always coming and going, Agnes. We never know where you are.'

'Yes, you do. I told you twice I'd be coming in late.' Agnes crossed to the grate and poked at a lump. 'Maud, have you been burning things again?' Maud had a habit of gathering up unwanted papers or clothes and burning them in whichever fireplace was to hand. 'Fire is tidy,' she said. 'It clears the air.'

'We were so cold last night,' said Maud plaintively. On one hand, she sported a new bruise.

Agnes felt that hand slide around her and squeeze – the squeeze of the feeble on the strong. She straightened up, raised her eyes and looked into the mirror over the mantelpiece. Campion brides had always occupied this bedroom. Two of their portraits looked down from the wall: a Regency beauty in striped silk and a Victorian matron.

'I hope you didn't burn anything important,' was all she said.

'We're so bored,' snapped Maud. 'So bored. Aren't we, Bea?'

'Are we, dear? I don't think it's quite as drastic as that.'

'Darlings, have you had breakfast?'

'Not yet.' Bea dangled a pair of frail varicosed legs over the edge of the bed. 'You must be exhausted, Agnes. I'll go and get some.'

Agnes pushed her back gently on to the pillows. 'You stay where you are. I'll make it.' She looked at her watch. 'They'll be here at ten thirty.'

Maud drove the needles through the ball of wool with a samurai twist. 'Who? Do I know about this?'

Bea and Agnes exchanged looks. 'Dear,' said Bea, 'it's the lawyer and the others. You know. You promised.' She leaned over and prised the knitting, a lacy baby's shawl, from her sister's grasp. 'Let's get up, shall we?'

Maud grimaced and the dusting of pink-orange powder from yesterday's maquillage cracked. Bea patted it away. 'There, we'll make you all nice.'

Agnes said comfortingly, 'If I put them in the dining room they'll freeze and they won't stay long.'

Peter Bingham, the lawyer, arrived with Mr Dawkins, who was in charge of her uncle's investments and what remained of the Campion trust. They were standing in the hall as an unfamiliar Porsche shot into the drive and parked smack in front of the door. A short young man climbed out, walked into the hall and stood knotting his tie.

'Hi,' he said, 'I'm Paul and I'm here to do the valuations for probate. I rang.' His gaze ricocheted around the hall and fell. 'It shouldn't take more than a few secs.'

Maud, who was descending the stairs at that point, said, '*Tiens*, and the house has been standing for centuries.'

'How do you do?' said Agnes, and held out her hand.

Paul ignored it. He was busy pushing the ends of the tie into his waistband. 'As I say, shouldn't take too long.' He snapped open his briefcase, extracted a notebook and positioned himself in front of the portrait of the seventeenth-century Agnes. 'I don't care for this sort of thing myself. I can never see the point.' He moved on to examine the lamp on the side table made of spun glass in which a ship rode a crystal sea in full sail. When it was turned on, the ship flew through a sea of light.

Agnes reckoned he could not have been more than twenty-five.

Paul turned his attention to the elephant's foot, which was used for umbrellas. 'Now, that's more like it. There's a good market for this sort of thing out East.' There was a minute inflection of curiosity in his tone. 'How old is this place, then?'

She told him that it depended where you were in it. With a knowing smile, he responded, 'It's very flung together, then, isn't it?'

The dining room was in the Victorian wing, which

had been tacked on to the main house by an Archibald Campion, who had made money in jute. It was furnished with brocade curtains and had a series of dull portraits of later Campions on the wall. The room was north-facing, and within seconds everyone was freezing and could concentrate on nothing except the temperature.

They sat round the table and, their feet numbing, tried to agree on strategy. Peter Bingham was young, ambitious and computer literate. He and Agnes had quickly established an understanding. Coming up for retirement, Mr Dawkins belonged to a different era.

Bingham was at pains to tell the Campion women that although John Campion had done his best to protect his house he had been able to do little in the later years, just routine maintenance.

'Yes, I know,' said Agnes. 'I had talked to him about it from time to time, but the subject upset him.'

Agnes was used to meetings and to controlling them, but this one kept disintegrating as Maud demanded, first, the bungalow she craved and, second, more money to live on. Failing those, she wanted a new central-heating system installed. Then she burst into an uncharacteristic flood of tears. Bea hastened to comfort her.

'Mrs Campion,' Bingham was embarrassed, 'your husband's will stipulates that you have a home in the house as long as you wish. There is no need for you to move to a bungalow or anywhere else. Indeed, it would be impossible.' He turned to Mr Dawkins. 'Am I correct?'

Mr Dawkins shuffled his papers.

'Have you *anything* to say, Mr Dawkins?' Maud blew her nose defiantly, and Agnes deduced that these two were old adversaries.

'As you know well, Mrs Campion, there is money – just – put aside for the Inheritance Tax but nothing else.' Mr Dawkins refused to look at Maud.

''Scuse me.' Paul popped his head round the door. 'I wouldn't say no to a cup of coffee.'

Bea was on her feet before he finished speaking. 'I'll do it. Everything's ready.'

Mr Dawkins looked sick. 'I believe,' he addressed Agnes, 'you are going to have to negotiate a loan from the bank if you wish to do any repairs to the house.' He made a second raid on his papers. 'Of course, there are grants for this sort of house . . . Perhaps the heritage people would help.'

Agnes steepled her fingers and rested her chin on them. 'How much is there?'

Mr Dawkins named the sum, and Agnes winced.

'Oh, good, you're still there.' Paul's head reappeared. 'I've had a teeny accident with the coffee on the stairs. Do you have a J-cloth handy?'

By one o'clock, they had all gone, leaving a trio of strung-out women. Thinking of lunch, Agnes hunted for a saucepan to boil potatoes, and discovered one in the pantry with several pairs of dun-coloured stockings soaking in it.

The phone rang. 'Darling,' said Dickie, from the BBC,

'can't seem to get hold of you for love or mon. Just to say I've secured the budgets for the lovesick farmer and the breastmilk thingy. If you can find out where the girl went, terrif. Hurry is the word . . .'

She sighed, wiped her hands on her apron and got on with peeling the potatoes.

'Agnes,' Maud fiddled around with the food that Agnes had eventually served, 'John did say that you were to look after me, didn't he?'

'Yes.' Agnes was wary.

'Well,' Agnes had often wondered how eyes managed to look cunning, but her aunt's did, 'I would very much like to go on the tour devoted to *The Sound of Music*.' Maud did not wait for Agnes's reaction. 'We fly to Austria and are taken to the places where the film was made, and then to Salzburg for a special showing.'

Agnes sensed what was coming.

'Bea and I need a break. We *need* to go.'

Bea looked embarrassed. 'We don't have to, dear. Not if it's inconvenient.'

'*Please*,' wheedled Maud.

Agnes looked at her watch. 'I'll see what I can do.'

'While you *are* tackling the frightful Dawkins, Agnes, I need a bit extra for one or two things. And the headstone for John's grave. It *must* be organized.' Maud rubbed fretfully at a worm of lipstick wriggling at the corner of her mouth.

'I'll see what I can do.' There was no escape now from the next attack.

'I can't think why John didn't leave me all the money instead of putting it in trust for you.' The gear shifted into the role of the wronged widow – a role Maud had seized as one that held infinite possibilities. But, then again, Agnes thought wryly, she *was* a wronged widow. 'You would have got it in the end, Agnes. Do *you* know why your uncle cut me off at the knees?'

Bea assumed her frozen look, and Agnes knew that she was withdrawing into the still place that she had at her centre, a place where her sister failed to reach her. Agnes summoned her charity. She had to be fair, but dealing with Maud was like dealing with an ageing car. Some days it functioned smoothly, sometimes lack of oil caused the engine to blow up.

'It's so cruel of John to exclude me. So thoughtless of you to agree.' Maud looked round at Bea as if to say, There, I've cleared the air.

But Agnes flashed back, 'Perhaps you mentioned the word "bungalow" too often.'

On application for funds, Mr Dawkins simply replied that there was no spare money. That was that and, if Miss Campion would excuse the comment, he was surprised that Mrs Campion had considered such a thing.

'There's no slack at all?'

Mr Dawkins paused. 'No,' he said, with an unexpected

blaze of temper. 'I don't think I have convinced you, Miss Campion. There is *nothing* in the way of slack.'

Agnes decided to pay for the holiday out of her own savings, and Maud acknowledged the gesture with a flash of the complacent smile that had once, long ago, enraptured John Campion, but not with a thank-you.

'Dear Agnes,' Bea hastened to supply the gratitude unforthcoming from her sister, '*thank* you.'

To her astonishment, Agnes choked back a lump in her throat. Anger? Disappointment? Fatigue? She seized her jacket from the peg and let herself out into the kitchen garden.

*Nothing*. Ruined earth. Ruined plants. Ruined buildings. Echoes and sadness.

She closed her eyes, dug her hands into her pockets and encountered a small, rectangular business card. Her mood lifted, and she promised herself that she would ring him.

# 8

In late spring, the South Devons were due to be driven to their summer pasture – his dumb blondes, his gentle beauties, who required such pampering during the winter otherwise they drooped. Unlike the tough and hardy Welsh Blacks. Now *they* were cattle with an attitude.

Andrew checked with the calendar pinned up above his desk – 15 March – for in matters of the farm he was meticulous and knew exactly to the hour when any event was planned. For instance, the date of the planning inquiry, 10 June, was fixed in large letters above the calving rota on the calendar, and two weeks previous to that had been pencilled in for 'Agnes Campion and film crew'.

Time was flying on. It eluded his grasp, and the days dropped into the slot quicker than any coin.

The computer booted up and Andrew began the daily update of the records. Betsey, Bill, Caro, Carlo . . . Tammy, Violet . . .

In the past, Penny had helped. 'I do half of everything in this marriage,' she had declared at the beginning, and had kept her word for twenty years, she seated at the kitchen table, he in the study, where they shouted to each other through the open door while they attacked the wall of paper.

Looking back with his newly charged feelings, Andrew was prepared to give those peaceful, productive years more credit than he had done.

Granted, spring and calving had always been bad times for Penny. 'Everywhere is . . . ripe,' she had sobbed once. A mocking conspiracy of plant and animal to show up the Penny who was unable to conceive. 'It's the pesticides,' she accused, 'used on the other farms. They've killed my ovaries.'

A shape at the open window made Andrew look up and, to his amazement, Penny was leaning on the sill wearing one of her more battered anoraks. 'Hallo, Andrew.' She had a scarf crammed down over her head and was wearing unfamiliar pink lipstick. She was obviously nervous and triggered a bristling defensiveness in Andrew. He did not bother to get up. 'What are you doing here? Been let out of the love-nest?'

Penny's roughened cheeks turned white. 'I needed some things. Clothes. But don't let's discuss that now. I think Caro's in trouble and you'd better get the vet.'

Within seconds Andrew was in the pen and running a hand over the sweating heifer, trying to locate the position of the calf. She was in pain, and her hard, lumpy flanks heaved in and out with each breath. He almost groaned. It was almost certainly breech and vets cost money. The Devons were usually reliable breeders but you always got one in the bunch.

'How's the disaster fund?' Penny extracted a rope from the bin and tossed it in Andrew's direction. She was referring to the money they set aside each year under the heading 'Trouble'.

'Low. Very low.' The farm's finances were never good and each year there was a struggle to meet the contingencies. Andrew swore and caught the eye of the labouring cow. 'All right, girlie,' he said. 'Easy. It was nothing. Easy now.'

He knew what Penny would be thinking. *You treat the cow better than you treated me. You are gentle with her, but never with me.*

'You don't have to stay,' he said abruptly, because she was right and he didn't want to think about it. 'I'll manage until Peterson comes.'

Penny's features snapped into a familiar set. 'Don't get on your high horse. You need help. She's a valuable beast.'

'Fine.'

Together they arranged the pen, working as a team who knew exactly what to do, until a van drew up in the yard. The vet did not waste words.

'Breech,' he said. 'A Caesar, I'm afraid.'

Andrew did some mental arithmetic which, since there was no option, was a waste of time. Penny merely tied up Caro. Peterson administered a local anaesthetic and made the first sweeping cut with the scalpel. The flesh peeled away with a tearing sound and exposed the bulging uterus. Caro remained quite quiet and, seemingly, now not in pain. Gently, Peterson manipulated the calf, all legs and eyes, into the world and settled him beside his mother.

'I'll say goodbye, then.' Penny stuffed her hands into her anorak.

Busy with Caro, neither man responded. The smell of the birth blood was fresh and repellent, primitive, even. Before Peterson had finished sewing Caro up, she was nuzzling and petting her calf. The mother spoke to the calf, the calf spoke to its mother – and the alchemy between mother and offspring was safely conjured. As they watched, the calf looked at its mother and, with a cry, butted his head into her savaged flank.

Peterson gathered up his tools and Andrew hosed the floor. 'It's nice,' said the former. 'These days, it's like visiting factories on many farms. Still, you can't be sentimental.'

Andrew regarded the concrete floor, the corrugated iron, the empty feed bags, the bloodstrewn straw and the quiet nativity, and, with an uplift of spirits, thought, Yes.

To his surprise, when he returned inside Penny was still in the kitchen, sitting quietly at the table. She had taken off the headscarf and her dry, bleached hair sprang round her face. 'I thought you didn't live here any more.' Then, still buoyed by his flash of optimism, Andrew added more gently: 'I'm getting confused.'

She placed her hands on the table and levered herself to her feet. 'I had a quick cup of tea. The place is a mess. I knew it would be. I wanted to ask you something.'

He stepped out of his bloodied overalls and dropped them on the floor. Penny pointed at them. Andrew shrugged and picked them up. 'What do you want to ask me?'

She thrummed her fingers on the edge of the table, a curiously uncertain sound. 'These letters . . .' She seemed reluctant to frame her question. 'Why didn't you tell me about them when you first found them? Why did you leave it so long before you said anything? You told that girl before you bothered with me.'

Again he shrugged. 'It wasn't deliberate. I found them. You were staying with your mother. I sent them off and forgot all about them. Before I knew it the researcher was on the phone.'

The drumming increased. Then ceased. 'You didn't want me to share in them,' she stated flatly.

'Then why ask?'

She fumbled with the zip of the anorak. 'I suppose it confirmed that I, your wife, was the last person in the world in whom you would confide. That's all.' She placed the chair neatly under the table and stepped back from the piece of furniture at which she had spent so much of her married life. 'It doesn't matter.'

He knew from her clenched hands that she was willing him to contradict her and to apologize. In fact, Andrew knew *exactly* what Penny wanted, but he could not summon the charity to give it. He looked away, down at the table, which still wore a veneer of the polish Penny had applied with such energy when she ran the house, and felt his lack of charity more bitterly than he could describe.

'That's why I left.' Her voice was brittle with tension. 'I couldn't bear it any more.'

Her sadness encompassed the non-children, the silent husband, the threat to her home, the lack of a future and the battle they should be fighting together. As did his.

Cross, tired and a fish out of water, Bel came shakily down off the train on to the platform at Charlborough where Agnes was waiting, bearing schedules, budgets and the post. Her crossness intensified at the sight of Agnes in old trousers and hastily plaited hair. 'Oh, for God's sake,' she said. 'When will you learn?'

Bel had brought her own coffee from London and hunched over a full mug, which Agnes kindly made. 'This kitchen, Agnes, is a disgrace. Even you can see that.'

Agnes glanced up at the mesh freeways that belonged to the spiders. 'So it's no good me asking if you would like to run Five Star from here, then?'

'You are joking?'

'I am.'

The postbag was large and it was half an hour or so before Agnes slit open a packet from Julian Knox containing a photocopied chapter from *Undercover During the Second World War*, and an invitation to a reception for the coming Friday, plus a brief note asking if she would have dinner with him afterwards.

'Ah,' said Agnes, who had tried a couple of times to contact him at Portcullis but had been told by Angela that he was away.

'Intelligence-gathering as a metaphor, do you suppose?' Bel's shrewdness had returned with the intake of caffeine.

'For what?'

Bel was expert at interpreting Agnes's expressions. 'You've got this one bad,' she said wearily. 'It's the crusade.'

Agnes did not contradict her.

The idea had been for Bel to look over the house. But even with the coffee boost, Bel did not seem good material. Agnes toned down the planned tour of the house, omitting the attics and, having assessed Bel's fake snakeskin half-boots, the walk by the river. Yet if the shivers were a little overdone, Bel was reasonably complimentary about the rooms and the hall.

Agnes pointed out the depressions in the flagstones made by countless feet, the mark on the newel post where generations had put a hand to steady themselves, the burn in the wood on the bottom tread, made – family history had it – by the heated shoe of a horse fleeing with the news of defeat from a Civil War battle. She bent over and punched the tapestried seat of a stool by the hall window, and eddies of dust rose into the still, cold air. How do I keep this particular story intact? she asked herself, and thought of the dust-shrouded attics where once a maid had wept and hidden a plate.

Bel paused by the portrait of the other Agnes. 'She looks tough. Who was she?'

Agnes explained that she had died in childbirth at the age of thirty-one, leaving a husband, nine children and a household.

Bel's crossness returned. 'She wasn't a woman, she was an organ. No wonder she looks like death in life.'

Tenderly, Agnes touched the painted face. The other Agnes's lips were firm, composed. The silk dress was trimmed with lace and the mirror, held in a white, ringed hand, reflected the furniture and paintings in the room. 'She accepted it, or at least didn't question it. Those were the terms of her time and she exchanged them for status.'

'Gave her a prolapse more like.'

'Probably.' Agnes sank down on the bottom stair. 'I try to imagine what she felt, especially during that last pregnancy. Frightened, perhaps, knowing the luck had probably run out.'

Bel shrugged. 'I should think she was furious. Wouldn't you have been? *He* did not love her enough to stop giving her children.' She kicked one snakeskin boot against the other. 'Excuse me, kind husband, you have failed to impregnate me for the nth time. To your work, sir. I am ready to receive the death thrust.'

'But she had a family,' Agnes pointed out, 'which meant something. "Ladye. I shall no more delighte in any creature, but the Lord." Her husband wrote that on the cover of her housekeeping book after she died, and he had carved on her tomb, "From one who loved her".'

'Thank the Lord,' said Bel, reaching for her cigarettes, 'that childbirth is now an *option*.' She lit one and blew out a lazy, contemptuous curl of smoke.

'Yes,' said Agnes, after a moment. 'Thank goodness.'

# 9

*Friday.*

For Kitty, a day of preparation, dedicated to the readying of the body, as Catholics once reserved it for fish. It had been her habit since the beginning, since the Harrys, the Robins, the Charleses – and Julian – from when her flesh had still been sweet and pliant, and the preparations had been more of a celebration than a necessity.

Now, change was creeping in, and Kitty was forced to consider new tactics against the rigidity tightening her skeleton, and the slackness sliding into her slender body. This enemy – age – had to be fought, with exercise, unguents and discreet visits to the plastic surgeon. Kitty knew she was inviting mockery, contempt, perhaps, from those who did not need such props (yet) and from those who considered one should take whatever one was given, brittle bones, sagging chins and all, but to take charge of her disintegration helped Kitty a great deal.

I was brought up in a world, she told herself, where we were taught that to make our bodies pleasing to men was our prime function. I have obeyed my lessons. I am not about to change for the sake of new political theories.

Anyway, any fool knows that it works better.

She scrutinized other women for clues. Did that one betray a new wrinkle, the suggestion of fat pooled around the waist? Or did she exhibit a fullness in the upper arm, and the tell-tale collapse of flesh between the nose and chin? If she found the signs, Kitty was secretly, shamefully, pleased that she was not alone. Yet, even then, into that companionable sense of fellow decay crept competition. *She* would prove better at preserving herself than they. Her arms would be slenderer, her chin less full, her thighs more taut.

Sometimes she imagined climbing inside the mind of the younger woman and tasting her freedom, her shamelessness, her ambition. Then Kitty would be permitted to view the horizon as these clever, earning, self-sufficient younger sisters saw it. Then again, sometimes she imagined it was possible to knock a way out of the pretty shell in which Julian kept her. But not for long: anxiety and fear would reclaim her. It was ridiculous to think she could earn her living in the conventional manner. Anyway, she loved Julian too much.

To get on with Friday.

The morning. Around her breakfast tray lay copies of the day's newspapers, to be tidied out of sight. From them, Kitty extracted various opinions of the British economy and the latest play to hit London's West End, which she planned to recycle, with subtle amendments, during dinner with Julian. These days, having an opinion was always useful.

Next, the bath and the process of creaming, patting and disguising. After she had applied her makeup, Kitty shrugged off her dressing-gown and pulled open a drawer in the cupboard. It was stacked with silk shirts, all tenderly folded and stowed. So expensive, so beautiful, so desirable. A second drawer revealed cashmere jumpers: grey, écru and white. Kitty sorted through them, their texture emitting a luxurious message through her skin, and picked the one for the day.

She pushed her feet into a pair of new high-heeled crocodile shoes. Finally, she checked the financial pages of *The Times*.

Yes. The portfolio was in excellent shape. Each of her lovers had given her something, including the one who had left a large sum in his will. (Of course, the children had screamed blue murder.) To her surprise, Kitty discovered that she had an instinct for the stock market, a feel for the swell of loss and gain. Neither was she too greedy: Kitty knew when to cut her losses.

At the beginning, when Julian had been so besotted (but not, she reminded herself, enough to marry her), he had taken time to explain the market. It was a curve, he said, that went either up or down. But you had to be careful. If you magnified any portion of that curve, even smaller variations would be revealed. 'By all means take advantage of them,' he had said, 'but don't try to explain the whole picture from them.' Kitty always smiled at the recollection. It was so characteristic of her lover, interfering, cajoling, anxious to explain how to see things.

Oh, he had been at his best when expounding his theory: impassioned, alive, powerful.

But she had seen the point at once. One way or another, she had been operating on the same principle all her adult life.

'Of course,' whispered a cocktail-party acquaintance into Kitty's ear back in those early days, 'Julian's name is mud among certain elements in the City. They don't go much on his philosophy. Julian is thought to be someone who preaches the good of his operations and, at the same time, is completely ruthless. I *mean*,' murmured the putative friend, 'one does not like to be spitted and, at the same time, to be told it's good for you, does one?'

At the time, this view of Julian had disturbed Kitty, for it was not always possible to know what you were letting yourself in for when you made a sexual arrangement. That was before she fell in love with him. Now, Kitty felt her knowledge of Julian to be far superior. *She knew, she knew — because she loved him — that his cool, detached manner hid a sadness that she could not quite understand and never would.*

Kitty had taken her finances into her own hands, and Julian thoroughly approved. Now, she had such a sweet man to advise her, and they enjoyed very nice conversations on a weekly basis.

Kitty breakfasted on grapefruit and black coffee. Then she swallowed several vitamin pills, checked the fridge and put on her pale blue jacket. For years now, she had held a block booking at the beautician's for Friday mornings. Nine thirty sharp to eleven thirty. Today that resulted in the smoothest of legs and underarms, and in scented, massaged flesh. Now it was time to do the weekend shopping.

Lymouth was crowded. In the last two years, a couple of supermarkets had appeared in the high street and brought in extra custom. Kitty emerged from the second, more expensive one, and encountered Vita Huntingdon, who was bearing several monogrammed bags.

Kitty smiled. 'Special occasion?'

'Daisy Wright's fiftieth.' Vita's large, big-boned face was flushed. 'They're making quite a thing of it.' Having imparted this information so carelessly, Vita obviously immediately regretted it. Kitty knew why: she herself had not been invited.

Kitty felt the bars around her status in Lymouth lock into position. 'How lovely,' she said, in her lightest voice. 'Is it a big do?'

Vita attempted to steer into less choppy waters. 'It's on Wednesday,' she said, as if that explained the lack of an invitation on Kitty's mantelpiece. 'So, you see, Kitty dear, Julian wouldn't be around, would he? It's in the evening, with a marquee. I shall be wearing my thermal undies.' As she got deeper into it, Vita's jaw made a sawing motion. She swallowed. 'Must dash.'

Kitty stood aside. 'Lovely day.'

'*Isn't* it.'

It's not so much that I'm a kept woman, Kitty transferred the shopping from one hand to the other, but the *precariousness* of my position. They think that, at any minute, I might make a play for one of their husbands. They think I know the ropes of 'all that', the irony being that they have probably given up 'all that' some time ago. They don't like being reminded so blatantly of 'all that'.

Then she smiled to herself. It was perfectly true. She did know the ropes of 'all that'. Very well indeed.

Kitty put her shopping into the car and drove back along a sun-drenched sea-front. Today, as it was so often on this strip of the coast, the water was the light, joyous blue of spring, clear and controlled-looking.

How stupid of her to be affected by Vita.

On impulse, she parked the car and got out. The sun was almost blinding. She fumbled for her dark glasses and toyed briefly with the idea of a walk, but in her expensive high heels she would only sink into the sand and stumble over the stones.

If you were a married woman, you were invited to fiftieth-birthday parties, but if single or divorced you made do with flower rotas and coffee mornings.

So be it.

The gulls screamed and coasted on the updraughts above her head. Kitty felt disturbed suddenly by the sea's wideness, its infinite capacity, and turned away. A tiny cascade of sand slipped down a large black rock in front of the car, grain by grain, slipping down, like the days of her own life.

*Tell the truth, Kitty.* Do you care *that* much? The truth?

These days, you are not so anxious for company, but much more for companionship and intimacy. It no longer mattered that Kitty often spent days alone – except for Theo, of course. Sometimes, after one of these periods of solitude, she became jumpy and remembered that she ought to do something. Attend a lecture? Hold a lunch party? Take painting lessons? Yet none of these appealed very much, and an insistent voice continued to whisper, 'Look again, think again.'

She started up the car. The water was *so* blue today, reminding her of the blissful times with Julian when she had surrendered to passionate love in a way that had never been true of her time with Charles, Harry or Robin.

A salt smell, the slap of water running up the sand, the sudden eddies of a chill wind through the car window: it was time to go.

Back at the cottage, Kitty hung up her blue jacket on a padded coat hanger. It exuded a faint scent of wet wool and salt and, for a second or two, her mind went inexplicably, frighteningly blank, as it did sometimes. With a little cry, she buried her face in Julian's spare jacket, which hung on the next peg.

The phone rang in her small but fashionable kitchen, with its distressed paintwork and double cooker, while she was unpacking the shopping.

'Kitty,' said Julian, 'I won't make this evening. OK? But come over to me in the morning. Sorry.'

'What are you doing?' Kitty's body felt heavy with disappointment.

There was a slight pause. 'I'm taking Agnes Campion out to dinner after the Portcullis do.'

'Ah, the girl on the card.'

'Yes.'

No more needed to be said. From time to time Julian, well . . . did this. Nothing serious and, to be fair, Kitty was free to do the same. *But she did not want her freedom.* That they gave each other a little leeway was part of the bargain and Julian always insisted that Kitty trust him. She strove to do so, but each time it happened she felt she was hovering on the edge of an abyss which, as she forced herself to look into it, seemed ever darker and deeper.

It was on the tip of her tongue to ask why she had not been invited to the Portcullis reception – surely, it was her place to be at his side? – when he said, 'Listen, Kitty, I'll see you on Saturday.'

She put down the phone.

'Gidday, darl.'

Theo breezed his way into the kitchen carrying the bag with the Equipment. Dusters, bleached and ironed. Cloths for wet work. Cloths for dry work. A stiff nailbrush for obdurate corners. Dettol – the dead giveaway to fellow obsessives. Polish. Lavatory-cleaner. Sink-cleaner. Cream-cleaner. Drawer-cleaner. Bacteria-destroying-cleaner. Window-cleaner.

Sharp but a little madder-looking than of late, Theo grinned at the frozen Kitty. 'How's my beaut? Orright?'

She lifted her hand off the phone and her spirits lifted, just a little. 'Fine. And you?'

For a moment, Theo's face was a mask of terror and pain, a reflection of the anarchy occupying his head. Then because it was Kitty, whom he loved, asking the question, he pulled himself together. 'It's ruddy bad at the mo, if you must know, but a person has to trudge on.'

'Have they adjusted your medication, Theo?'

He shrugged. 'I don't ask.'

'Tea, then.' Kitty swung into action. In the grip of his bad times, Theo would launch himself at the house, bearing his industrial-size bottle of Dettol, and scrub until the house smelt like a field hospital and Kitty was forced to throw open every window.

They were both outsiders, and the echoes of destruction emanating from the battlefield of Theo's mind were a small price to pay for the comfort of having him.

'For the comfort of having each other, darl,' Theo would have corrected.

In the London flat on the Friday afternoon, Bel hooked a finger into Agnes's waistband and pulled. 'A tight black number, I think.'

Agnes allowed herself to be dragged into Bel's bedroom. 'Black's not my colour.'

'Believe me, darling,' Bel's thin hand lay heavy on Agnes, 'it's better to go forth armed. Ask any general.'

She opened the cupboard and peered in. 'It's a pity you're so big.'

In Bel's world a size eight was big. 'Sticks and stones,' murmured Agnes, submitting gracefully and thankfully, and pulled off her sweater.

So Agnes waited in a sleeveless black dress ('I'll freeze,' she protested. 'It doesn't matter,' replied Bel. 'Anyway lust will warm you') and glittering earrings for Julian Knox, who had insisted on picking her up.

When he arrived, punctually and decisively, but rather pale and preoccupied, he said immediately, 'You look stunning.'

'Thank you.' The dress rustled against Agnes's skin. 'I'm sorry I've made you go out of your way.'

'I wanted to pick you up.' As Julian helped her into the car, he added, 'There are no ulterior motives.'

'I expect that's rubbish,' she replied, happy and excited at the vista that was panning out nicely.

He fitted the key into the ignition but his eyes continued to rest on her loosened hair. 'You're right,' he said eventually, and both laughed.

At half past ten, Kitty went upstairs to her pretty bedroom, took off her clothes, folded them away and swallowed a homeopathic sleeping pill (less damaging to the skin). It did not work.

## 10

The reception was being held in a house in a renovated Queen Anne terrace close to the Houses of Parliament. It was, Julian informed Agnes, a contact party arranged by the lobbyists Portcullis employed to persuade key people that a project for a riverside development outside Peterborough was viable. A minister had promised to appear.

'But you're the host, then,' she exclaimed. 'And I've made you late.'

'Yes, I suppose you have.' He was unfazed by his dereliction of duty and she was impressed by his good humour. 'But not *too* late.'

'You should have told me.' Agnes got smartly out of the car.

He tucked his arm under hers. 'Yes, I suppose I should, but don't worry, not too many people will have turned up yet. They come late and leave early, and the trick is to drink and talk as much as possible.'

But by the time Agnes and Julian had ascended the stairs to the beautifully proportioned room, a couple of the minister's juniors were already tackling the champagne with an expression that suggested that no vintage could or would ever influence their judgement.

Agnes's spirits rose even higher. The party looked interesting and might yield some subjects for Bel and her, the surroundings were lovely and there was dinner to look forward to afterwards. She ran her hand over the material of her dress and felt the satisfactory concave curve of her waist. Sometimes, things did fall into place and it was possible to move on from mistakes. It was important, therefore, never to give up hope, or to lose grace and desire, and to try to build on what had gone before.

'Let me introduce Chantal.' Julian guided a chic-looking girl in a short skirt into Agnes's orbit. She was looking up adoringly at Julian. 'Chantal works for the lobbyists in the Brussels office and keeps us informed as to what is going on there. Chantal, you might have seen some of Agnes's television work.'

Chantal's expression adjusted into professional interest. 'I'm afraid not.' She smiled with wide, knowing eyes at Agnes. 'By the way, how's Kitty?' She floated the question past Agnes to Julian.

*Kitty?*

His answer was instantaneous. 'She's fine. She's coming up in a couple of weeks. She sends her regards. Agnes, there are people I must talk to.' He moved away and was immediately buttonholed by two well-known politicians.

Chantal's attention did not waver as she explained to Agnes that her company's role was to make sure that the right politicians received the briefing papers and to arrange site visits. Then they discussed the art of manipulating vested interests, which, they agreed politely, was one of the main functions of politics. Chantal's gaze slithered between Agnes and the figure of Julian, now surrounded by a circle of businessmen and politicians at the other end of the room.

*Who is Kitty?*

A chill made free with Agnes's bare arms and exposed spine. Gradually, the wonderful excited feeling drained away. No doubt Kitty was his wife, and she told herself wearily that she should have known, should have asked a few questions and, furthermore, she was a fool to be lured into an arena where it was plain that she was not the wife.

She looked around at the smart, hustling gathering and felt the beat of their indifference and the weight of greed. Chantal was talking smoothly about the possible release of tied agricultural buildings on to the housing market, and Agnes remembered Andrew Kelsey. She felt her anger stir for him too.

When Julian reappeared at her elbow after a *tête-à-tête* with the minister and the party was breaking up, she said, 'I'm sorry but I'm very tired. I'll think I'll go straight home.'

The excuse was transparent but he said at once, 'Of course.'

After a silent ride, the car drew up at the flat. 'You seem angry,' he said. 'Did someone offend you? If they did, I'm sorry. But I thought you might be interested in the set-up.'

It was as if all their conversations had never happened and a curious formality had taken over. 'I was,' she replied, 'and you've been very kind.'

He pressed his hand briefly against his eyes. 'Actually, I'm tired too, so I'll say goodnight.'

The gesture touched her and slipped past her defences. Anyway, she wanted to know who Kitty was. To be told, perhaps, that she was his sister. She wanted to smooth things over and go back to the beginning of the evening. 'Would you like to come in and have some scrambled eggs? I think Bel is out.'

He leaned back in the car seat. 'Do you mean it?'

'I mean it.'

He hesitated and she was terrified that he was listening to the voice of common sense. Then he said he would like that – if she wasn't too tired to crack an egg, and Agnes laughed and replied that her cooking was terrible, whatever her state, and the atmosphere suddenly changed.

He sat on the sofa with a glass of wine and watched her whisk in and out of the kitchen. 'There was another reason I asked you out.'

'Yes . . .' Agnes pushed some eating implements at him. 'Would you mind putting these on the table while I go and find a cardigan?'

'You sent me the letters and, like you, I became rather hooked and I got Angela to do a bit of digging. I know it's a coincidence that I've been reading up about the

SOE but there is some basis for thinking that my theory might hold water.'

He pulled a folded piece of paper out of his pocket and, while Agnes made the salad, he read out to her, '"The records show that in July 1942 the first women SOE agents went into France. They would have trained for at least six months previously." So Jack's first letter in January 1942 would fit.' He glanced down at his notes. '"They trained in various places including a manor near Guildford, Arisaig in Scotland and Beaulieu."'

Agnes put the food on the table and while they ate, pushing bits of information back and forth, a shared story began to take shape as to where Mary might have trained and been infiltrated. 'Don't you think she would have confided in him?' The eggs were heavy and leathery and Agnes's hunger was quickly satisfied. She put down her knife and fork.

'Not necessarily. It's possible that she wanted to leave Jack and used the war to escape.'

Julian and Agnes looked at each other across the table. Why not consider Julian's theory? thought Agnes. It was safe and containable. 'But even in war don't you have to trust?'

'It depends. I can think of lots of cases where you love someone very much but don't tell them everything for good reasons.'

She refilled the glasses, watching the red swirl of liquid until it settled. 'Are you being nice to me for me or my house?'

'Guess.' Julian cut into an apple from the fruit bowl. 'Why are you being nice to me when, clearly, somebody has told you something at the party?'

'Guess.'

They stared at each other. Then he leaned over and kissed her.

'Who is Kitty?' she murmured, through a welter of sensation, which ceased abruptly as he stopped kissing her, sat back, ran his fingers through his hair. I know that gesture already, she thought.

She pressed the point. 'I think I should know, don't you?'

All the ease and humour had fled from his expression. In their place was a frozen, at-bay look. Oh, God, she thought, not again. Not again.

'Would you mind if I told you about Kitty another time?'

A familiar angry, *hopeless* feeling took possession of Agnes. 'Yes, I do mind,' she said. 'I don't know what you're trying to do, but if you have something to tell me about Kitty, then you must do so now.'

There was a swish and hum of traffic on the wet streets outside, and the murmur of conversation, the click of car doors and clattering feet.

'Julian, who is Kitty?' He frowned but she persisted. 'Why can't you say who she is?'

He looked straight into Agnes's eyes and replied, 'Kitty and I have had an arrangement for a long time. We meet mostly at weekends.'

She was conscious of relief, as sharp and unmistakable as a mouthful of lemon juice. He was not married.

*Saturday.*

Very early in the morning, Kitty had slipped through the white mist shrouding the path to Cliff House. Now and again, her feet fought for anchorage on the drenched grass, and she blundered in the obscuring mist. The sea murmured quietly and the shrieks of the gulls tore out of the shrouded sky. As she slipped and slid along the narrow, stony path, she told herself that everything was quite normal. Absolutely normal.

Kitty let herself into Cliff House, via the conservatory, stopping to plump up the Wedgwood blue cushions on the white wicker chairs. She tiptoed silently into the house and halted by the open door of Julian's study. He kept his fossils in here – extinct sea animals with obscure names. Dull, implacable things.

She glided into the room to check them and stopped by the desk where a file lay open. On top of it was a list in Julian's handwriting. 'Virginia Marie, Claude, Katrine.' Kitty stared and a hand gripped her heart coldly. Virginia? Katrine?

She pushed aside Julian's list and bent over to read what was in the file. 'The enemy is now me . . .'

Oh, yes, it is, she thought. The enemy is me: my rotten, ageing body. She leafed further through the pages. '5 June 1942. My Darling. I am worried. I can't help feeling that you are exposed to danger, your white, slender body hungry or damaged . . . Remember you promised to return.'

Kitty sat down heavily in the desk chair. Tears began to flow down her cheeks and she let them drip down to her chin.

A hand descended on to her shoulder, causing her to rear up in fright. 'And what the hell do you think you are doing?' asked Julian.

She looked up at him, wet eyes meeting antagonistic ones, and faltered, 'Reading these letters. What does it look like?'

He sighed and ran his fingers through his hair. 'You're snooping, Kitty.'

She sobbed. 'I know, I know.'


Julian had woken suddenly, choked by a dream. He had been walking along the beach. His feet dug into sand so hot that it burnt his soles. Arms wide, he swung round to savour the heat and then, suddenly, he was in deep water, fighting for breath. Below his blurring vision lay rocks and sands and a world of undulating seaweed.

He lay and reflected on his dream. Its imagery and significance were embarrassingly obvious. He *was* in deep water.

*Not now.*

He turned and punched the pillow. On that Friday morning a journalist from the *Guardian* had rung to check whether the rumours that Portcullis's disappointing margin of return on the Hastings and Bournemouth project had been correct. Julian had been able to put him right – after a fashion. But it was a straw in the wind.

It was no good becoming involved with Agnes Campion at this precise moment. Why, therefore, had he asked before he left Agnes's flat that night if he might see her again? That she had refused meant nothing. He had asked a second time and she repeated that she could not see him again until they had sorted out the subject of Kitty. It had not occurred to Julian that Agnes might be a woman of scruple.

Kitty? Kitty was the thorn buried in Julian's flesh that, every so often, drove itself in deeper. It was a reminder, a penance . . . an anchor. How could he explain the position to a pair of puzzled grey eyes?

He said goodnight and left the flat.

The sound of feet padding softly in the kitchen broke his reverie. *Kitty.*

He heard the sound of stifled sobbing.

Agnes knew perfectly well that she had been obsessed by Madeleine. Madeleine the virtuous mother, Agnes the outcast sinner. Madeleine was dazzlingly soft and seductive, full-bodied, fragrant and powerful. Agnes placed her in a frame and arranged the objects of married life around the figure of the suffering wife.

The three elfin-faced daughters in smocked floral frocks and white socks. The *appartement* in the rue Jacob, painted a fashionable grey-white. The china, the glass-ware, the books.

But even all these considerations, and the domestic details, begged from the reluctant Pierre, had not stopped Agnes continuing the affair, and she had learned the lesson of the selfish power and persuasion of passion.

Yet Madeleine had triumphed. In their bed, she lay beside Pierre, and it was Agnes who grew bitterly jealous of the rightful wife. Equally, Agnes understood the other woman's grief and her desire to make Agnes pay for her trespass. In that Madeleine had succeeded superbly, for Agnes suffered as she had never before, her guilt ensuring that it was sharper, more intense and more damaging than perhaps was necessary.

Perhaps Madeleine had banked on that too.

The pattern must not be repeated; nor should she get back on the treadmill of hope and self-disgust. Yet the terrible thing was that the moment Julian had confessed about Kitty, Agnes's emotions slipped into a higher gear. She had fallen in love.

## 11

Everyone sat it out through March, which turned to April, a grudging, unspring-like April with squalls of rain and blustery winds, and into May, holding the equilibrium. At least, that was how Agnes saw it. She pictured Kitty – well, a notional picture of Kitty – willing the centre to hold and Julian, hair ruffled, eyes hollow with strain, dodging the issue. And herself?

She did her best to forget Julian. Heroically so. She and Bel had mapped the next six months' work, found the money, set the schedules. This left her free to concentrate on the house.

My house, she thought, so wounded by all that warm, careless flesh that has lived under its roof, by numberless feet treading through the centuries, by weather and by the slippage of energy and money.

First, a survey. ('If you want instant depression,' Julian Knox had told Agnes over that meal of scrambled eggs, 'talk to a surveyor.' He added, 'They are careful people.')

No doubt about it, Mr Harvey was indeed a careful man. He took one look at Flagge House and got down to work with his electronic tape-measure, which emitted a bee-like hum.

'Regular maintenance,' he informed Agnes, with the

satisfaction of a missionary faced with the most pagan of territories, 'can pre-empt all sorts of horrors, and I'm afraid the late Mr Campion did not invest in it, if you take my meaning.' Enraptured by the flight of his electronic bees, he adjusted the dial. 'An historic house can't look after itself.' His tone was one of reproof.

They made for the drawing room and Mr Harvey measured and paced with his tape-measure and dictated notes. Occasionally he became transfixed by a crack or a fissure, by the tilt of the stone fireplace and, in particular, the long windows overlooking the terrace.

Eventually he pronounced, 'Proper restoration is always expensive, but it depends what you want. A total overhaul or just bits and pieces.'

'Can you pick and choose what to preserve?' Agnes fingered a curtain, which had been bleached by the light. 'I would have thought not.'

Mr Harvey's machine hummed in agreement. 'I'd like to view the cellars and storage areas.'

The cellars ran the length of the house and were dark, cold, and bled damp. Agnes led the way. 'This one was known as the women's cellar,' she explained, embarrassed that anyone should have had to work in such conditions, 'where they did the pickling, spicing and meat curing. The men's cellar, where the wine and beer was kept, is through that door.'

The measuring and humming and dictating began all over again. If Mr Harvey was of a careful disposition, he was also a showman. He paused, milking his moment, and ran his hand over the brick on which a blotched mural had been painted in mould. 'It's a big story of rising damp, Miss Campion.' To emphasize the tragedy, he stamped his feet on the flint cobbles and showed her where the ooze created a lustrous setting around the cobbles.

Agnes went quiet. She knew death had been here, an uneasy death, or so it had been reported in the records. A-swagger with riches racked up from exploiting trade in cardamom, muslin and jute in the East India Company, Archibald Campion had been hot to build a grandiose Victorian wing. Driving their spades into the earth to set the foundations for the wing, the estate workers had hit a pile of human bones. 'There was no question that they were human,' noted Camilla Campion, Archibald's wife, 'and some were horribly charred. We were afraid that we would catch a putrid contagion.' The conclusion was, she reported, shocked, that these bones were the relicts of plague victims, denied proper burial in the graveyard.

Unquiet their death and, thus, unquiet their souls: they beat their anguish and disturbance against the brick and silence.

Mr Harvey was upset by what his inspection revealed. His machine snapped to a halt. 'I'm afraid that, over the years, the external soil level has risen. It requires to be stripped back and a damp course inserted.'

'I'd better get you some coffee, Mr Harvey, and we can discuss the options.'

While they sat and drank it in the kitchen, Mr Harvey

reeled off a verbatim report in which the word 'defective' featured heavily. The roof timbers were defective. The brickwork was defective and had the additional problem of soot disease – 'Sulphuric acid, Miss Campion, caused by a mingling of fumes and damp air, which penetrates the brickwork.' Further defects included damp in the roof and an almost certain infestation of lyctus and death-watch beetle, and the ivy growth on the Victorian wing.

'I know *that*,' said Agnes. She looked down at her untouched coffee. 'What are we talking?'

Mr Harvey shifted into a comfortable position on the chair and totted up sums under his breath. 'Thousands.' He peered at her face. 'Don't worry, Miss Campion. Once you've reached fifty or so anything else on top seems immaterial.'

At last Mr Harvey announced that he had done. With doom in her heart, Agnes accompanied him to his van, parked by the kitchen garden. He tapped the wall. 'These I like. Put me in front of a wall,' he said, 'and I can tell you such things about it. Like this one.' He pointed. 'English bond. Not to be mixed up with Flemish bond.'

'Certainly not,' said Agnes, with gallows humour.

'I noticed when I drove up that your boundary wall over by the river is knapped flint and brick. Used in Hampshire and here since Roman times. Needs repairing.' He took a final squint up at the house. 'Bucket repointing on the brickwork,' he said, 'and you'll probably have to stipple it for the weathered effect. Otherwise, you'll have the heritage people down on you.' He inserted himself into his van. 'Guttering? Well, needs completely replacing. Cast iron, I'm afraid, but we might get away with fibreglass for the hopper heads.'

Then, mercifully, Mr Harvey drove carefully away.

The house was bleeding to death and, for the moment, she was powerless to provide a transfusion.

Within an hour, Peter Bingham was on the phone to report that he had had a telephone call from a London estate agent, who wished to know if Flagge House was for sale. A housing association and a developer, who specialized in converting older properties into multiple-occupancy, had both expressed interest.

'Stop there,' said Agnes. 'Have you been speaking to Mr Harvey? Whether you have or you haven't, the answer is the same.'

While Agnes dealt with Mr Harvey, the sisters were upstairs practising packing for the *Sound of Music* holiday. Or, at least, Maud was. The bedroom was chilly, and when a depressed Agnes joined them, she scolded them for not turning on the electric radiator that she had bought in an effort to head off Maud's fires. Shoes clacking on the wooden floor, she crossed the room and turned it on.

Outside, the river ran strong and fierce, still swollen with spring rain.

'We wanted to save you money,' said Bea, edging closer to the heat.

Maud sailed about the bedroom, dropping pieces of clothing here and there and shuffling, to no point, through a discarded pile of blouses and stockings. Patient Bea waited on the sidelines and, every so often, stepped in to restore order.

'Only one suitcase, dear, don't you think?' Bea sorted the stockings into colour-coded heaps.

'You were always so bossy,' said her elder sister. 'Always.'

Bea's busy hands did not stop. 'Was I? Dick didn't think so. He liked the way I kept house.'

Maud's large eyes were veiled. 'Dick,' she said spitefully, 'was a saint.'

Bea dropped the stockings and plumped down on the edge of the bed. 'Yes, he was, wasn't he?' The characteristic serenity had cracked, and she showed her distress. 'And I miss him so.'

Agnes sat down beside Bea and slid her arm around her shoulders. 'What do you miss most?'

Bea picked at the folds in her skirt. 'I miss . . . I miss the journey. We moved forward . . . I can't explain quite what I mean. But, whatever it was, it ended when he died.' The concertina of material twitched between her fingers.

Not to be outdone, Maud was still rattling through her clothes. She held up a blouse against her chest, threw it down, picked up an alternative. 'The buttons are off this one.' She swung round and accosted the pair on the bed. 'Where did this . . . *journey* with Dick begin? Correct me if I am wrong, but I thought you lived all your married life in Shaftesbury. Or are you speaking in some kind of code?' Her voice crescendoed with echoes of a child's rage.

Agnes squeezed Bea tight. 'Darling Bea.'

Bea held out her hand for Maud's blouse. 'Give it to me. I'll mend it.'

Maud clutched it hard to her chest. 'Will it make you feel better?'

'Maud!' Agnes summoned her patience.

'Give me the blouse, dear.' Bea turned so pale that Agnes was alarmed.

'Have you taken your pills, Bea?' she asked.

Maud gave the blouse a final inspection and tossed it over to her sister. 'There.'

Agnes retrieved it from Bea's lap, folded it and laid it to one side. 'You can sort it out later. You are all right, aren't you, Bea?'

'Oh, yes, dear. Of course.' Bea was looking more her normal self. She seemed embarrassed by her revelations and twisted her wedding ring up to her knuckle. 'Don't mind what I say. I was confused. But the habit . . .' she considered '. . . of being with someone has to be unlearned.'

'*Alors.*' Maud hovered in front of her sister. 'Marriage is there to be endured, like bank managers and politicians, because there is nothing else.'

'Maud, that's foolish,' murmured Bea.

'I may be many things, but not a fool.' In a rare gesture,

Maud placed a hand on Bea's shoulder. 'I wish,' she said, 'that I missed John.'

There was a lull in the jealousies and hostilities.

Julian rang the day after. 'Agnes? I've been thinking. Would you like to come sailing at the weekend? I'll tell you about Kitty as I promised.'

Maybe the Kitty problem had been dealt with. Agnes anticipated being gracious and understanding, and pre-pared to dissipate any awkwardness, but was not offered the chance to do either. Julian greeted her at the station – Agnes's car was being serviced – and drove straight to the beach. There he busied himself with the boat, a J-24, issued requests and Agnes's high spirits did an about-face. The wind blew in smartly from a choppy sea and, despite the oilskins, her extremities were a mass of gooseflesh. Ignorance made her clumsy and Julian's com-mands became sharper. 'I said I was a novice,' she protested, when he ordered her to wind a sheet round the cleat.

He seemed amazed. 'What difference does that make?'

Eventually, sail flapping and sheets clacking, they nosed their way out of the protection of the point and headed for open sea.

Once beyond the spit, the wind screamed and the land bucketed across her vision. Out here, the sun was brighter, tougher, refracting off an expanse of white, wind-tossed water, and Agnes was the dazzled traveller gliding over its waves.

'I don't like to mention this,' Julian hailed Agnes from the tiller, 'but could you pay attention? The wind's backing up and it's going to get rough.'

Agnes hung on grimly to the side of the boat.

'We're going about,' shouted Julian, the wind whipping his hair into a frenzy. Agnes lost her balance and went sprawling against the railing.

'Novice's luck,' said Julian unfeelingly.

How she loathed being useless. She scrambled into a sitting position and rubbed potential bruises. 'Everyone loves a sailor,' she said bitterly.

An uncomfortable half-hour later, they beat shore-wards. Agnes shivered with anticipation of dry land, for any pleasure in the sailing had long vanished. She crouched lower on the bench and tried to cover her hands, now enticingly mottled, with the sleeves of her oilskins. In contrast Julian looked on top of the world and glowing.

'Aren't you cold?' she asked, and when he shook his head, said with some feeling, 'I hate you.'

Back on shore, they queued for fish and chips at the van parked at the harbour entrance then wandered to the nearest bench to eat them. Shuddering cold fits attacked Agnes, and she hiccuped and shivered.

Julian draped his oilskin over her shoulders. 'You didn't like that much, did you?'

She shook her head.

He prised the empty chip paper from her stiff hands. 'It's a bit early in your sailing career to be subjected to the rigours. I should have made sure that you went out on a sunny pancake.'

'I have a sailing career?'

'Oh, yes.'

'Since when?'

'Since meeting me.'

'I see. Forgive me asking. I just wanted to know, that's all.'

'A reasonable question.' He squinted, balled up the chip papers and launched them at the rubbish bin.

The chips and the strong tea were excellent restoratives. Agnes buried her bare feet in the sand, a thousand tiny abrasions pricking the skin, and slid her hands up inside the sleeves of her waterproof jacket, which almost persuaded her she was warm.

Julian leaned over and wiped a fleck of salt water from her nose. 'A walk, I think.'

He led her east along the beach in the direction of Cliff House. The tide was way out and they scrabbled for footholds among the stones and layers of beached seaweed. Agnes stopped to pick up a shell with a razor-sharp edge. 'How long have you lived here?'

She had the impression it was not something he talked about much, but he did now. Chilly parents, a small boy left to his own devices, silent meals, anniversaries unacknowledged. She watched a small figure in grubby shorts haring down the road on a bicycle, bird-watching on the dunes, solitary picnics accompanied by the music of sea birds on the cliff, the tired, cold return to a house where electricity was rationed by cost-conscious parents. Her imagination painted him as very small against the grandeur and sweep of sea and land, and she heard in the screaming wind the sobs of the boy whose tenth birthday had been forgotten.

We have no right to hurt the tender, curled child. Ever.

'Childhood is a lottery, I suppose,' she said. 'You can be born to the wrong parents, in the wrong skin, or the wrong place.' She let the shell drop to the sand.

They exchanged a look that surprised them both with its impact.

'The best thing about childhood is that it comes to an end,' said Julian eventually.

At twelve years old, she had scuttled and lolloped around the walled garden with no purpose, her companion the terror of being abandoned for a second time. 'That's why we go back. To make sure we are adults.'

'Nothing so complicated. In my case, Cliff House was available. I wanted a base.'

The wind slammed a handful of hair into her mouth and she grabbed it. 'Have it your own way.'

'I will.' He grinned and tucked her hand into his elbow.

They wandered on, their feet flicking up seaweed and pebbles, the wind attacking hair and clothes. In the spring light, stone, wood and sand appeared white and insubstantial. The gulls dived. Her hand was warm and safe in his pocket. Surely, once you had been through a love affair and were hovering on the brink of another the feelings and emotions would be the same. But, no, they weren't. Not at all.

Julian slowed down and pointed. 'Cliff House is over there. And over there . . .' he paused '. . . where the cliff path runs alongside, is where Kitty lives.'

'Kitty lives here? She lives separately?' She stopped in her tracks.

'I promised I would tell you about her.'

'I'm listening.'

She thought she heard his sigh above the wind. 'As I told you, I spend most weekends with Kitty.'

'Ah, I see.' Actually, she did not quite see. 'Not during the week?'

'Not usually. Sometimes she comes up to London.'

Agnes asked, 'Why have you invited me down here? To Kitty's territory.'

Julian did not answer directly. Instead he pointed to the smooth overhang of rock where compressed clay and shale formed a perfect fossil bed. 'As a boy, I spent hours hunting for fossils and I found my best ones there. Often in the least likely places. I learned never to give up the chase which, in the end, was a pity because word got around and the fossil hunters descended in droves.' There was a pause, and he added quietly, 'Kitty and I allow ourselves a degree of freedom. That was the arrangement. It's worked for a long time.'

A seagull screamed past and splashed heavily into the sea.

She stopped and pushed the obstinate strands of hair out of her mouth. 'Does it work for Kitty too?'

'I don't know any more,' he said.

'And you?'

He hesitated. 'Our agreement was that if we wished to go our separate ways for a little while then we were free to do so.'

'Was?' she reiterated.

He looked down at her. 'Things change.'

In the kitchen of Cliff House, Julian produced cakes and tea. 'I have a housekeeper who comes in when Kitty isn't here and organizes things.' He lifted the laden tray and conducted Agnes into the conservatory, which had an uninterrupted view over the garden to the sea. Through the glass, the sea appeared tamed and silent. Julian was still in his ragged, salty jeans, but he had combed his hair, and the wildness had been replaced by something smoother, less direct. The small, lonely boy had been put back in the cupboard.

Agnes drank her tea. 'Who does the gardening?' she asked, but she was thinking frantically about the business of Kitty. How did this woman, this weekend woman, fit in? Did he wish to get rid of one weekend woman only to substitute another? 'Things change,' he had said, and she flinched at the problems the two words encompassed. How could she have imagined that Julian would arrive unencumbered in her life?

'Theo. He's an outpatient at the local psychiatric

hospital. He works for Kitty too. In fact, he adores her. Gardening and cleaning are part of his therapy.'

'I need a Theo. Can every home have one?'

'Agnes, can I say something? Don't let your house drag you under for the sake of it. Preserving a house at all costs is . . . not clever. If you are going to do it, think hard.'

He looked so anxious and genuine, so upset for her, that she wanted to kiss him into tranquillity. Instead, she smiled sweetly at him. 'And you told me not to trust anyone.'

The phone rang and he got up to answer it. 'I won't be a minute.'

A minute stretched into two, then five and she could hear him talking fast in the next room. The daylight was fading and the sun was poised above the sea like a scarlet bauble, so bright that Agnes wanted to touch it. She let herself out of the conservatory and walked down to the gate that led on to the cliff path.

It was narrow and the cliff was steep, dangerous, no doubt, in the dark. Here and there it divided and forked down to the tiny beach, which was flanked by black rocks and pools, one leading into the other like a necklace of sparkling stones. The dying sun threw a red wash across the rocks and pools where the mermaid would – surely – rise to the surface to meet her calvary of human love, and Neptune ride in on the spume to impose his law.

Out to sea, a tanker steamed from east to west. The

incoming tide rushed in and flung a lacework, woven with orange peel, tin cans and plastic bottles, further up the sand.

'Things change,' she reiterated, feeling the first rays of real happiness steal through her. The prodigal returns.

'Hallo,' said a voice from below. 'Who are you?'

Agnes swivelled round. Ultra-slender, ultra-groomed, honey blonde, defensive . . . This must be Kitty.

# I 2

She *is* . . . young.

Twice before, during her 'career', Kitty had experienced an encounter such as she knew, instinctively, this one to be, and had observed the form. Take defeat gracefully. Negotiate the pay-off and move on.

This time it was different. Love for Julian made it different. Confronted by this fair, dreaming girl, she knew that her options had been violently narrowed down. Run? Run back to the cool white embrace of her bedroom, shut the door tight and lick her wounds? No. Whatever her fears, a grain of sense stuck in Kitty's brain.

'I'm Kitty.' She held out her hand.

'I thought you might be.' The girl took it.

Her touch felt assured and practised, and she seemed not at all fazed. Perhaps Kitty had got it wrong. 'Julian mentioned me?' There was the faintest relaxation of Kitty's features.

'Yes. He showed me where you lived. I'm Agnes Campion.'

'And I know about you. The girl with the house and the irises. The girl with the letters.'

She seemed surprised. 'You know about them?'

'Julian told me. He knows it's the sort of thing I'm interested in.' Tiny pause. 'He tells me most things.'

'Of course.' Agnes absorbed the message.

Kitty enunciated each word very clearly. 'I should have been visiting my mother but she cancelled. You know what mothers are.'

Agnes's unease deepened. 'Mine died when I was twelve but I can imagine.'

For a second, Kitty's veneer cracked. 'I'm sorry.'

A flash of sympathy darted between the two. *Loneliness, I understand.* Almost immediately, the hostile expression snapped back into place on the older woman's face. 'Shall we go in?'

Julian was stirring the contents of saucepans. 'I hope you like spaghetti with clam sauce.' He looked round at the door, and a frown came and went like lightning. 'Good God, Kitty! I thought you were with your mother.'

Interposing herself between Julian and Agnes, Kitty raised her face for a kiss. This is mine, she was saying. Thou shalt not steal. In the electric light, Kitty's beauty was impressive: this was the setting that suited her looks and she knew it. Creamy, serene, with reddened lips and highly tended porcelain skin. She had dressed casually in silk and cashmere, her hair was beautifully cut and her nails manicured. Not a woman of extreme style or of fashion, but one whose every item of clothing proclaimed self-conscious femininity.

'Mother did her usual nonsense and muddled up

arrangements.' Kitty checked her watch. 'Is Agnes staying the night?'

'No.' Agnes stepped in quickly. 'Julian drove me over and I was planning to catch the late train. In fact, I think I should be going. Isn't there one about now?'

'I'm afraid there isn't a late train on Saturdays,' said Kitty, 'only weekdays.'

Agnes was hot with embarrassment. It was not fair to pay Kitty back in this fashion. 'I think I should try to get home. It's not that far.'

But, for reasons of her own, Kitty cut off the retreat. 'Face and rout the enemy,' had been the instructions that her great-grandfather, the famous General Mabey, had given to his men up on the Khyber Pass. It wasn't bad advice. She assumed the smile of the hostess who has successfully backed a guest into a corner. 'Why don't you stay? There's plenty of room. We can put you on a train early in the morning, if you wish. Then you can enjoy dinner . . . and we can all have wine.'

There, she had taken charge. Kitty the orchestrator. *We are all very adult and mature and we can deal with this.* 'Come,' she said quickly. 'That's decided.' She marshalled Agnes upstairs. 'You can borrow anything you want. I keep quite a few things here.' She pushed open a bedroom door and said, in a low voice, 'I'll be staying too.'

The message conveyed, Kitty ushered Agnes into an immaculate room and extracted towels and a flannel from the cupboard. 'I'll get you a jumper. You must be chilly.' She ran her eye over Agnes's jeans and crumpled shirt. 'Would you like anything else?'

Agnes shook her head. 'You're very kind.'

Kitty knew that Agnes knew that kindness was not the point and, to her surprise, discovered there was some enjoyment to be had from this encounter. With the realization came enlightenment – *I can see her off* – and the tiniest flexing of her muscles. Quick, before her courage left her. With all the permutations of sexual arrangements, there remained an element of the primitive. *Do battle to the death.* Kitty trod confidently downstairs in her high-heeled shoes but on the last tread her heel slipped and she was forced to grab the newel post.

Glass of wine in hand, Julian was waiting in the kitchen for her. He was not in the least abashed. 'What's this about your mother?' He looked hard at Kitty. Reading her as easily as a book. 'What are you playing at, Kitty?'

'Shouldn't the question be addressed to you?' she riposted furiously.

He handed her a glass of wine. 'No, I don't think so. I've told you about Agnes, and I've told you that I have met her on several occasions. I told you I had invited her to sail.' He was unsmiling and very angry. 'At the very least you should have phoned.'

Kitty helped herself to more wine. 'Why on earth did you bring her here? To our house.'

He looked down at his glass. '*My* house.' But when Kitty gasped under her breath, he softened. 'Kitty. I'm sorry. That was unforgivable.'

The bravado had gone. She wanted to cry out that this arrangement of theirs might sound so cool and modern and sophisticated. And, yes, they had always agreed to tell each other the truth. But, now it came to the test, a river of hot and desperate feeling was drowning Kitty. She had read – where? – in one of the newspapers she combed for opinions, an article that inveighed against the impermanence of relationships and how people couldn't cope with no religion, no structures and too much freedom.

'Why can't you accept me properly? Why can't I live with you . . . acknowledged?'

He put down his glass on the table, and checked the clam sauce on the stove. In the spare room above the kitchen, they could hear Agnes moving about, turning on a tap, opening a window. Julian looked as sad and bewildered as Kitty felt. 'Kitty, we go round and round. Perhaps we should both reconsider?' He ran a hand through his hair. 'Perhaps I'm the one who's changed. But I hope I have never misled you.'

'Oh, stop it.'

Yes, he had been honest. She could never accuse him of not being so. Right from the beginning, when she had fallen for his predatory, energetic charm, he had been open, uncommitted, and the first to admit that he did not think fidelity was for him. But she had learned that honesty could not possibly cope with real, intense feelings. Honesty was only a fig-leaf.

'Come here.' Julian mastered his irritation. He put his arm around her shoulders. 'I'm sorry about this.'

All traces of her mini-rebellion seeped away, leaving her drained. With an effort, Kitty pulled herself together. 'You're right. Let's forget it. There are other things to worry about.'

'Good girl.' He slid his hands around her waist, reacquainting himself with her fragile frame. 'Dinner?'

She turned and ran her hand up the features she loved so well and which she was never quite clever or astute enough to read. 'Sure.'

Over the spaghetti they discussed the *Hidden Lives* programme, a safe enough subject, and speculated as to Mary's identity. Kitty suspected that she might have been a domestic or a Jewish refugee, someone at any rate who was undervalued in the social scale of the time, and when Agnes reported that Bel was working on several ideas, including the SOE theory, Kitty asked abruptly, 'Why does the explanation have to be so dramatic? What about real life? Plenty of ordinary people in the war fell in love with the wrong people and had to say goodbye because they had to go and pick cabbages or look after their parents.'

How on earth had Agnes got herself into this situation? Kitty's ambush had been masterly. Agnes was aware that Julian had been watching her, quietly, covertly, while she was being forced to watch Kitty smile, offer food, pat her hair. Kitty sat on her seat with possession, wielded her knife and fork as the owner. She turned to her lover with a smile that said, 'I know your secrets.' It was all designed for Agnes's benefit and Agnes understood.

With an effort, she refocused on what Kitty was saying.

'Hasn't it occurred to you,' continued Kitty, 'that she might – she might have been pregnant?'

Later, Kitty showed Agnes upstairs and stood pointedly in front of Julian's bedroom. 'Goodnight, Agnes.'

In the double bed, she drew Julian close and, despite her exhaustion, coaxed him into responding to her yielding, pampered body. Then as she straddled him, she gave a great cry of possession and pleasure and Agnes heard it, as was intended.

Early the next morning, Kitty awoke with a start beside the sleeping Julian. Someone was moving around the house. Agnes, of course. Kitty manoeuvred out of bed and glided downstairs.

She discovered Agnes in Julian's study where she had pulled back the curtains and was watching the sea. In the half-light, she seemed awkward, rumpled. *Ill at ease.* At Kitty's entrance, she swung round and her hair – so shiny, so touchable, so youthful – swung with the movement of her body. 'I've woken you, I'm sorry.'

How *dare* she be in here? thought Kitty. Julian hated people invading his study. She closed the door and advanced into the room. 'Are you feeling all right?'

'I couldn't sleep.' True, there were smudges of fatigue

under Agnes's eyes. 'I was going to make myself a cup of tea, I hope that was all right.'

Kitty knotted the dressing-gown around her tiny waist (achieved with such effort), her pearly pink nails catching the light. 'I'll make a pot.'

'Please don't. I'm sure you want to go back to bed.'

'No trouble.' Kitty spread out a hand in front of her and inspected those nails. It was a rude, off-hand gesture and she hoped Agnes took it as such. It was the action of an older woman who, conscious of the younger woman's power and beauty, was fighting back. Then she felt shame seeping through her. How trivial, how pointless. Kitty summoned her training. 'You've probably got a lot on your plate. Julian tells me you travel a lot.'

'Yes, I do.' Agnes pushed back her hair with a weary gesture, but she gave a polite smile. 'It was good of you to have me to stay . . . considering.'

'Considering . . . everything,' said Kitty. 'It was.'

'But I shouldn't have stayed.'

Kitty sensed that Agnes was curious about her. How *did* she live? she was wondering, with that knowing, professional attitude of hers. What did Kitty do? Surely, she would be thinking, this woman did not spend her days waiting for Julian? Agnes was not to know that Kitty also pondered these questions and concluded that the condition of waiting could be expressed as an art form, or a psychological state. Some people did things, others waited. Passivity. What was it exactly? Was it in fact, asked the articles, a form of aggression?

And this girl, Kitty crossed over to the window and looped back the curtain proprietorily, she is the kind who uses the freedoms I never could have imagined, which I was never permitted, with which to bully others into letting her have her own way. By being here, she is saying, I don't owe anybody any fealty. I demand personal space. Sexual autonomy. I don't care about anyone else. *Otherwise she would not allow herself to be interested in Julian.*

'I'm afraid I don't have anything for lunch, so we'll put you on an early train.'

There. The message had been conveyed. *Go away.*

'Yes, of course. I need to get back. If you can give me a lift. Or perhaps I could order a taxi.' Kitty crossed the room and placed a small, determined hand on the door-knob. 'Kitty,' Agnes added, 'I know that you and Julian have been together for a long time. I understand the need to preserve.'

In the moment between the first sentence of the exchange and the next, an old battle was fought. For possession, for supremacy. 'The reigning queen in the hive fights off the young nubile pretenders,' Jack had written, in one of the letters Kitty had read. 'She will kill, if necessary.'

How nice of Agnes to yield so publicly. Kitty smiled in triumph. 'I'll make the tea. Why don't you come into the kitchen? Julian doesn't like anyone in his study.'

In the kitchen, Kitty busied herself with pulling up

the blinds and setting out the tea things. These are mine by right, she thought, carefully placing teaspoons in the saucers and filling the milk jug. I should be mistress of this house.

She looked up and out of the window, exhaustion registering in every muscle. Sometimes the effort of existence was almost too great.

There had been an accident further down the line and Sunday morning trains were not running. Julian rang Kitty and told her that he was driving Agnes home and he would not be late for lunch.

He had set out to make Cliff House a house of the elements: light, sun and water. Pockets of darkness and awkwardness had been eradicated by his ruthless hand, and with applications of white paint. He had decreed that decoration be kept to a minimum. He had wished to harness space and natural colours so that, weightless and airy, the house appeared to float above the sea.

Flagge House was different.

'What do you think of *my* home?' In giving him the tour, Agnes was demonstrating to him where her heart lay. Intent and preoccupied, she dragged back the curtains and shutters of the big window in the drawing room to reveal the interior. Julian absorbed the exquisite proportions of the room and pale honey parquet floor and conceded that it was beautiful.

'Sometimes,' said Agnes, 'if I am quiet, I can hear the house sigh and breathe. It's living, you know.' She held up a finger and her eyes narrowed in concentration. 'Listen.'

She was trying to convince him of her crusade and because he was more – much more – than half in love with her, he listened. Agnes struggled with the shutters. One by one, oblongs of light tumbled into the room like dominoes to reveal the raddled face of age. Water had stained the parquet and pushed its blocks above the surface. Above the central window, the lintel sagged.

'It's perfect,' she said, 'isn't it?' Love was so blind, he thought, touched in a raw, unexpected way.

Agnes conducted him through the house, luxuriating in each room – the document room, which she explained had been her uncle's study and was now hers, the chilly arsenic-green dining room, the kitchen. She showed him the carved staircase, the window of thick lead-hazed glass through which the Campion women had watched their men ride off to battle, to Court or to discover more bits of the globe.

Almost, she succeeded in making him forget other contexts and other considerations. That was her witchery. Following in her wake, Julian was drawn deeper into the blindness.

She made him stand on the top step of the terrace and look over the meadow to the river. 'We don't have the right to destroy that.'

He pulled himself together sufficiently to say, 'We have to survive. And survive with others with competing claims.'

'Of course.'

They went back to his car, which was parked by the walled garden. 'This was the scene of your trespass.'

'Have you forgiven me?'

She touched her plait. 'No.'

'Quite right.' He dug his hands into his pockets. 'Agnes . . . I want to . . .' But he could sense her retreat.

'Did you know that walls can be read like documents?' she said, in a conversational manner. 'I'm planning a programme on it.'

Julian cut her off and grasped her by the shoulders. Puzzled and lusting, he searched her face for a clue as to why he was baffled by his responses to Agnes. His was normally such a clear-cut world. In his ears rang Kitty's cry of sexual possession and pleasure of the previous night.

'We are not talking about the one thing we should be,' he said angrily. 'Look at me, Agnes.'

Her eyes were clouded with distress. 'There is nothing to discuss, Julian. I've seen the situation. I *know* the situation. I've been involved with a married man.'

He felt her sadness. He felt Kitty's sadness. He felt his own confusion, and a sense of impending disaster.

'What you have with Kitty should not be broken,' she was saying. 'Some things have to go on. There is too much destruction everywhere.'

'So, no more meetings?'

She searched his face. 'No,' she said, desperately. 'Go away. Please go away and leave me in peace.'

He pulled her to him. She smelt as he remembered. Soft, clean, flowery, but this time with a just a hint of salt. As he pulled her closer, Julian felt that he was taking possession of centuries: of brick aged into rose, of wood fretted by time, of stone wearing a mantel of lichen.

Agnes pulled herself free as Maud rounded the corner in the drive, dressed in her church hat and full regalia of paste ring and a huge brooch brooding on her chest. She was on top form. 'Has Agnes offered you any coffee before you go? No biscuits, I'm afraid, but that's how we are. Frugality is very democratic, don't you think? Here we all are in this historic house practising self-denial as merrily as Mrs Cadogan in her council flat.'

# 13

Agnes drove the aunts to Heathrow airport, kissed them, and handed them over to the tour operator, who was dressed in a flowered dirndl and holding a placard with '16 May, Captains and Marias Assembly Point' written on it.

Bea's cheek smelt of fabric-conditioner. Maud's exuded a soft, powdery decadence and she jabbed a finger into the soft part of Agnes's arm. 'Good riddance. That's what you're thinking, aren't you? Tell the truth.'

Agnes tucked a magazine into their hand luggage. 'Don't forget to send me a postcard.'

'*Do* talk to that nice man about the house,' said Maud.

Agnes arrived back at Flagge House in the late evening. It seemed too much effort to cook supper so she opted instead for a glass of wine and settled down on Maud's sofa in the butler's pantry with a copy of the Jack and Mary letters.

She read till quite late. A harvest sun warmed her neck, the taste of cold, sweet cider was on her tongue, and the weight of a lover's arm was around her body. Jack to Mary. Wartime lovers, and a man and a woman who had chosen to pursue a life together.

At the end, she let the file slide on to the cushion beside her. Nothing really had happened between her and Julian, only a bat-squeak of promise. No hearts had been broken, not like last time.

What was an affair? A grand roar of passion and tempest, followed either by regret and sadness or by the clutter of saucepans, laundry and the peculiar smell of a fridge that was never cleaned by either party.

Anorexics argued that power came from starvation and that it was possible to thrive on an emotional monasticism. Certainly, it was safer and left her free to work. A man or a woman was mentally leaner, fitter and more active without with the fat of emotion.

Sometimes Agnes pictured herself as others might see her. There goes Agnes. Successful. Ambitious. Her arena, the world; her subjects ranging loftily through politics, social problems, ecology and the vastness of war, the lost spirituality of the century and the cry of the endangered dormouse. No ropes, thank goodness, bind her to a stove, a cradle, an occupied double bed. There was no need for her to be unselfish or to pull in the focus of her vision. Work ensured that you were whole: a thinking, acting, creative person.

'Agnes,' those observers would say, '*a modern woman*.'

She closed the letters file and the phone rang.

'It's me,' said Julian. 'I need to see you.'

'But I don't wish to see you.'

There was a pause. 'I'm ringing from the pub in the village.'

Julian must have heard the hammer of her racing heart down the phone.

He arrived within five minutes with a carrier-bag full of champagne, smoked salmon and home-made brown bread. He was tanned from sailing but pale and exhausted-looking under it. 'I hope you don't mind.' He watched her unpack the picnic and set it out on the kitchen table. 'I've tried very hard to stay away, but I've had a hell of week at work.'

'Does Kitty know?' she asked quietly, fetching a couple of glasses and cutting the bread into slices.

'No.'

'Will you tell her?'

'Probably.'

How clever he was. Sneaking past her defences, telling her she was needed. Agnes arranged the smoked salmon on the plate and said desperately, 'It won't do.'

'No, it won't, but I'm here. Look at me, Agnes.'

Eventually she raised her eyes and looked at him.

'Oh, Christ,' he said.

She accepted the glass of champagne, drank and looked up at the ceiling. The spiders were in residence and, in the dim light, the walls were deeply shadowed. She drank another mouthful. Fatal on an empty stomach. After a minute or so it did not seem such a terrible thing that Julian Knox was there in her kitchen. In fact, it felt right. 'What is happening at Portcullis?' she asked recklessly, feeling the champagne work its way up to the outer reaches of her brain synapses. 'Laying waste the fields of England?'

He frowned, and offered her a sandwich. 'Perhaps you should eat this,' he said. 'You looked starved. Since you ask so nicely, things are not brilliant. The share price is going down and I have probably over-extended the two northern projects. There is no lack of demand in the south for houses, but the north is lagging behind and what profits there are from the north are not sufficient to fund the extra-expensive south. But let's not talk about it. I've got something for you.' Julian picked up his jacket, extracted an envelope and held it out. 'Don't look so suspicious. Take it.'

She obeyed. Inside were a couple of closely hand-written photocopied pages.

'Go on, read it,' he urged.

'Number 20. Virginia Marie Lacey. Code name: Claude. Subject responding well. Physically slight, but very fit. Reflects hard on the tasks allotted her and succeeds in maintaining objectivity. N. B. Not good with drink. She must be cautioned to avoid it. She is very young and we question her maturity.' The report was initialled and dated 21 May 1942.

The second page was written in a different hand. 'Number 20. Code name: Claude. French excellent. Any slight irregularities in accent put down to childhood in Canada. Exceptional grasp of Morse code. Sometimes obstinate and does not get on with her immediate superior. Disobeyed orders on night operation. Not happy with explosives . . .'

'I thought it would interest you.'

Mary? A slight, too-young, determined figure launching herself into moonlit operations without the comfort of a whisky. Agnes stroked the pages and felt a glow of affection for these daring women. 'How did you get hold of these?'

'Imperial War Museum. They're very helpful. According to my source, most of the SOE records were destroyed after the war but a few remained. They didn't get much down on paper anyway, but these training reports are in the library.'

She drank yet more champagne. 'You mean, you spent an afternoon doing this for me?'

He took the glass from her hands and set it down on the table. 'It was a happy couple of hours as it turned out, researching. It took my mind off my problems, which I needed, and I'd rather think about you than Portcullis. Does it make a difference that it was me?'

Ashamed, Agnes looked down at her feet, which seemed bigger than she remembered. Julian had moved close to her and Agnes discovered she was breathless with the effects of champagne. She struggled to order her thoughts. 'Yes, it does make a difference.' She folded her arms to make a barrier between them.

He had decided she was drunk, and the idea made her hot with indignation, although she knew it was perfectly true. He put a hand under her chin and raised her face.

'I'm afraid I'm after both your body and your house.'

'You mean the land, don't you?' she countered. 'You want to plunder my land like William the Conqueror, or whoever it was.'

'Not entirely true. Oh, I admit that I'm happy to swing a hammer against centuries of reverence for the English house, not because I don't rate beauty, because I do.' He smiled and said gently to soften the impact, 'It is my opinion that Flagge House is at the end of its natural span.' He moved even closer and closed his fingers over a handful of plaited hair. 'How do you woo a woman? Like this?'

She nodded.

'And like this?'

She was helpless.

'And what do you wish?' His breath travelled in a pathway up along her shoulder towards her mouth.

'There is no point . . .'

'In what?'

But the champagne had stolen her subtleties of speech. Agnes found herself slipping down into the chair, where she laid her head on her hands. A longing for nurture, for assuagement of her hunger, for the safety-belt of some kind of certainty, pierced her.

She felt his hands moving over her shoulders and neck. 'What are you doing?' she murmured.

'Unplaiting your hair.' He sounded surprised that she should ask. 'I've wanted to do it for some time.'

She took his hand, and the tanned fingers clenched

within her own. 'Don't you see? There's Kitty.' She clutched the fingers harder.

He had the grace to look away. 'The honest answer is that I can't think about Kitty at this moment.' His fingers played music on her skin. 'But we do have an arrangement and always have. You can give yourself permission to do something, if you wish to do it. It *is* simple. You don't have to hedge it round with guilt and foreboding.'

True. Vexed by the seesaw of drunken emotion, she spread his fingers and slipped her own between them. 'Darling Agnes,' said Julian, 'don't look like that. I can't bear it.'

'Champagne . . .' She felt the tipsy waves wash through her. 'It's very lovely.'

'Enough.' He pulled her into the hall and up the stairs.

At the top of the stairs, he hesitated then pushed open her bedroom door, picked her up and laid her on the bed. Agnes gazed up at the spinning room, sighed and gave in.

Half-way through, Agnes thought, I've forgotten what it is like. Then she corrected herself, No, for it has never been like this before.

This incident was very *physical*. Hammering hearts, raised pulses, stomachs shifting. The world was on the move and she was racing to catch up with it.

The light from the corridor caught his face: absorbed, almost feral. Like the fox. No, that was wrong too. The fox sneaks across the water-meadow in search of a drink, his coat brushed with burrs and dulled from weather. I hear him bark, sometimes, at night.

Shaken, she turned to Julian and kissed him. He ran his fingers down the slope of her shoulder. 'You're lovely, Agnes, did you know?'

Her spirit lifted, and she caught her breath with the sweetness of the moment. Then she shifted her body towards him and twined her arms around his neck. He fitted his cheek to the curve of her shoulder – and fell asleep with a rapidity that startled her.

The noise of the river woke Agnes at first light. She turned her head on the pillow. Julian was still deeply asleep, a hand flung out, the fingers curled towards the ceiling. He looked exhausted and vulnerable, all assurance gone.

She had been here before. For a long while, she looked at him, the sweetness and elation replaced by a more familiar, dreaded emotion that she had got herself into another muddle.

Agnes slid out of bed, shivering as the air hit her nakedness, grabbed her dressing-gown, crept down the corridor to the bathroom and locked the door. It was important that she and Julian did not share any more intimacies.

While she ran the bath, the huge, stained, claw-footed Edwardian one that took ages to fill, she scrubbed her face with lotion. Then she faced herself squarely in the mirror and made some calculations. Since Pierre, she had not needed any form of birth-control and last night had been a risk. The calculations seemed to pan out in her favour, and Agnes's slight eruption of panic diminished.

She lay in the bath, head aching, face smarting, a small, voluptuous bruise blooming on her right thigh. In the corners of the bathroom were damp spots, orchidaceous green and brown, and the cheap straw matting that had been laid by Maud in the economy phase was torn in places.

She was wrestling with the gas stove when Julian wandered into the kitchen, stubbled and sleepy. 'There seems to be no hot water,' he said mildly, but it infuriated Agnes.

'I know, I've taken it,' she snapped. 'You'll have to wait. This is not Cliff House.'

'Did I say it was?' He sat down at the kitchen table and put his chin in his hands. 'Do you get cross often?'

'No. I rarely lose my temper,' she said, even more crossly. Then she checked herself. 'Actually, I'm known for my calm. Ask the team.'

He tapped a knife on the table, and she coloured at the memories of the night. 'I just want to know for future reference.'

Cheeks still flaming, she made the coffee. Its smell revived her. She pushed a cup across the table towards him. 'Julian . . .'

He held up a hand. 'No recriminations at breakfast. That's the rule. What's done is done.'

Did one ever learn? Could one manage to put someone else, a person one did not know, in front of one's own wishes? It was so little and, yet, such a tall order.

They ate breakfast largely in silence. At one point, he put down his cup and said, 'Agnes . . .'

She turned abruptly towards him. 'Yes. What?'

He looked at her face. 'Nothing.'

'I've decided you must go.' Agnes eventually addressed Julian across the remnants. 'I only know a little about you and Kitty but enough to know that I can't . . .' She filled the basin and plunged the china into the suds. 'I can't . . . I won't do it again. I can't make Kitty suffer.'

He studied the worn grain of the table. 'Isn't that having your cake and eating it?' He sounded weary and disappointed.

She sat down at the table and rested her aching head on her hands. 'Yes,' she admitted miserably. 'It is. Not very admirable, but it happens.' She looked up through her interlaced fingers. 'Julian, you never told me how long you have been with Kitty.'

His voice flattened. 'Ten years. And we've worked fine together. We have been a team.'

Ten years of a shared bed and intimacies of which Agnes could have no notion and to which she had no right. Of flesh touching flesh companionably, of shared cries, pleasures, irritation and silence. Of plans and expectations of each other. This was Kitty's territory, not hers. Kitty had yielded part of herself up to it. Kitty had staked it out, cultivated it and built her house on it.

'Do you often put it at risk?'

'Kitty has been faithful and true.'

'But not you?'

'No.'

Agnes fought to give the other woman her due. She knew why Kitty loved this man: for his energy, his gleaming house, his kindness, his knack of making money, his humour. His seriousness. For the lonely child in grubby shorts chipping away at the rock face. She understood precisely because she loved him for these things too.

Julian pressed on, 'Kitty and I agreed the rules between us.'

'But is she happy?'

'On and off.'

'Are you happy?'

Julian considered. 'I've been too busy to ask.' He stared at the face opposite him. 'Don't be angry.'

'I'm angry with myself.' The kitchen in Flagge House was a rotten, dingy place to end anything, let alone this. 'You must go back to Kitty. You've got ten years' worth of reward points . . . Anyway, I don't want to be part of a sort of harem, which is what, I gather, I would be. It isn't what I want. I feel more strongly about my love affairs than that.' She looked straight into the face that she had kissed many times only a few short hours previously. 'I'm sorry.'

He shrugged in a way that told her he was hurt but not showing it. 'Don't worry. This is not everything, Agnes. In the end, the flesh and the devil is only a little bit of life.' She flinched, and he pushed the pieces of paper with Virginia Marie's training reports over the table towards her. 'At least take these.'

She picked them up. 'Thank you.'

The chair scraped on the tiled floor. He stood behind her and she tensed. He lifted the heavy hair from the nape of her neck, pressed his lips to the tendon skimming under the skin and walked out of the room.

Agnes spent the morning searching the house for her uncle's set of Jane Austens. They had disappeared on the day of his death and she had never managed to locate them. She wanted them back. She checked the books in the document room and searched the drawing room, bedrooms and the boxes in the attic, then returned to the document room for a second look. But they were not there.

Eventually, unsuccessful, Agnes returned upstairs to the bedroom where she picked up her discarded clothes from the floor, stripped the bed, smoothed the bedspread over it and opened the window.

She thought of Julian's determined, experienced lust, and of her own response, of the drained, vulnerable, sleeping face on the pillow, the soft sigh of his unconscious breath, the tussle between them, and sat down abruptly on the edge of bed.

Some things you can have, some things you never, ever have. That was one of the laws that must be obeyed. Otherwise it was anarchy.

# 14

A week later, Agnes scooped up the aunts at the airport, plus a collection of plastic bags and suitcases, and drove them home.

As ever, Maud was on the case. 'Bea had to stay behind on some of the trips. Anyone with medical problems was not allowed up the mountains.'

'I didn't mind. I was quite happy resting in the hotel.' Bea gave an impression of being more than usually placid. 'The sun was out most of the time and you would have loved the colours, dear.'

'But the meat at dinner always had hairs on it.' Maud swivelled round to face Bea in the back of the car. '*You* ate yours.'

Agnes concentrated on turning off the motorway and, this culinary solecism out in the open, Maud returned to the subject of the coach trips. 'I'm afraid Bea missed a remarkable one,' she said, with satisfaction, and went on to describe how strong the sun had been, everyone commented on it, it had been almost *too* bright. Slowly, slowly, the coach had risen above the world up into the mountain, a place of solitude and green, cleansing light. 'And here,' the disembodied voice of the guide had declared reverently, 'is where the opening scenes of *The Sound of Music* were shot.'

Agnes could not resist it. 'Actually, Maud, Julie Andrews spent most of the time in a fur coat while they were filming because it was so cold.'

Maud pouted. 'I wish . . . I wish I could explain to someone as unimaginative as you are what it was like.' What exactly she wished to explain Maud was unable to convey, for she had had no practice in the consideration of abstracts. Perhaps it was a sense of rapturous abandon and of *purity* so lacking in the world? 'I was quite over-whelmed, if you must know. Particularly at the gazebo where Maria and the Captain kiss.' She shivered. 'I think we should light a fire when we get home, I'm feeling the cold.'

Agnes parked in front of the house. The aunts were back. 'Did you enjoy the holiday, Bea?'

Bea was fussing over her luggage. 'Oh, yes, dear, I loved it.'

Maud waited for Agnes to help her out of the car. 'Human relationships are so *vexed*,' she said, apropos of not much, leaning on Agnes and limping a little, 'but a person has to soldier on.'

'Yes, I suppose a person does,' said Agnes gravely. 'Have you hurt your leg, Maud?'

'My hip. It's getting worse.' She limped into the kitchen. Her gaze fixed at once on the draining-board and the two breakfast cups that had remained there since Julian's visit. 'Have you had people to stay, Agnes?'

'Yes, I did.'

'Overnight?'

'Yes, overnight, Maud.'

'I expect it was the nice farmer you've told us about.' Bea began to unpack the bags of duty-free. 'Talking over your film.'

'Actually,' said Agnes, 'it wasn't.'

The look Maud gave Agnes was not so much disapproval as envy.

The gazebo was not the only thing to have excited Maud. Over coffee, and the rapturous recollections, the name Freddie was dropped into the conversation more than once. Freddie, apparently, had been a good friend to them and very helpful, but a full explanation as to who he was had not been forthcoming until Maud cornered Agnes in the study.

'Agnes,' Maud was unusually polite, 'we've invited someone to dinner tomorrow. Will you be here? It's Freddie. You'll like him.' The ring flashed as she smoothed down the sleeve of her latest cardigan in moss green. 'You will.'

'Are you reassuring me or commanding me?'

Maud's eyelids dropped. 'You can be very irritating sometimes.'

Agnes regarded Maud thoughtfully. 'What you are really asking is, will I cook dinner?'

'Well, yes, since you're offering.'

Thus Agnes, who had planned to spend the whole of the next day working on the direction for the *Hidden*

*Lives* film, found herself in the kitchen. As she melted redcurrant jelly into the gravy, she cursed the ancient oven and prayed that it would yield cooked beef. Transparent, ectoplasmic, the jelly swirled in the liquid. She hoped it would taste better than the primordial soup it resembled.

Sounds in the hall alerted Agnes to Freddie's arrival. She put down the wooden spoon.

In full paste regalia, glittering, Maud led him proudly into the kitchen. 'Agnes, this is Freddie Loupe. Freddie, this is my husband's niece. She's the one who's making the programme about those letters.'

The blazer alerted Agnes. The material had a sheen acquired from over-zealous cleaning and age, and the buttons were too bright. A poseur, she concluded, possibly one who did not possess much imagination. He was tall, but his well-manicured nails had a blue tinge, suggesting that he had heart problems. But just in case the observer was inclined to write him off, Freddie had dyed his hair an improbable, almost hypnotic, glistening white.

He took Agnes's hand and peered short-sightedly into her face. She was taken aback, for he had a kind expression. He cleared his throat and said, 'Your aunt never stops extolling your gifts.'

She did not require the inflection on the word 'gifts' to know that he was lying. Maud would be dead before she extolled anyone's gifts.

During the dinner, he kept up a flow of anecdotes

culled from years of package tours. 'I'm the best of troupers,' and 'I know the form backwards.' Agnes imagined him moving from one honey-pot of a widow to another, prospecting for treasure. Realizing she must defend the aunts against the con-man and the gold-digger, she set herself to find out about Freddie Loupe. What she discovered was that Freddie liked life, and wished others to enjoy it too. Against her better judgement, Agnes succumbed to his charm.

The aunts' faces shone with wine and pleasure.

Agnes studied them with misgiving. They had *both* fallen in love with Freddie.

The evening wound up with Freddie promising to escort the sisters to the local theatre. Saying goodbye to Agnes, he remarked, 'You have a very beautiful house, dear lady, but I don't envy you. I've seen it too often. All history and tax. Thank you for an excellent evening.' He tapped the side of his nose with a finger. 'If you ever want to sell, just let me know.'

'What did you think of him?' Maud demanded, before the door was safely shut. Before Agnes could answer, Bea nipped in with 'Oh, he's so sweet. *Sweet*. He's a very, very nice man.'

Maud looked dangerous. 'He's *my* friend, Bea.'

'Of course, dear.'

Agnes put her arms around them both and propelled them towards the staircase. Two elderly women: Maud, the nutcracker-chinned crone of the fable; Bea, the selfless wraith consigned to the fireless corner of the room. One day, Agnes would be like one of them. Or both.

Having said the goodnights, Agnes went back to the study to catch up on her correspondence and the neglected schedules. At midnight, she went upstairs.

The washer on the basin tap in the bathroom was on its last legs, and she resorted to the pair of pliers she kept there for the purpose. She yanked at it angrily. Given the chance, someone like Julian Knox would rip out this bathroom. His sensibility was different from hers. He would ignore its period charm and superb Edwardian domestic engineering, its individuality, in favour of his boxed-in baths and shelves of white, crunchy chain-store towels.

She gave the tap a final twist. There was *nothing* wrong with this bathroom, except for a lick of paint and a sort-out of the plumbing. She stepped back and wrenched her toe on the split matting. The pain was intense enough to allow her to weep.

The last week in May was the date finally settled on for the shoot.

Agnes phoned Andrew from the flat to check that everything was OK and they talked over sleeping arrangements – Agnes and Bel had been offered a bed at Tithings, Jed and the others had been booked into bed-and-breakfasts – and the catering for the team.

Andrew took it in his stride. 'It will be interesting.' They discussed further details for a little longer and

Agnes was about to say goodbye when he cut in, 'I think I should tell you that Penny, my wife, has left me.'

'Oh.' He sounded so matter-of-fact that it was almost insulting to the departed Penny, she thought. 'I'm sorry. It must be a difficult time for you and I'm afraid we'll add to the confusion.'

There was a pause. 'It's double the work without her.'

Of course, he was the farmer who relied on his spouse and it had a certain logic. Farming was all about growing and harvesting and selling off the crop to plant the next. Perhaps Penny Kelsey had planted secret desires in herself and this was the moment at which they had pushed to the surface. Other people and their mistakes were a mystery. But how could they not be when she herself was a mystery?

She confided to Bel afterwards that she had found Andrew's reaction a little too detached.

'They probably couldn't wait to see the back of each other.' Bel fanned her fingers over her exposed thigh and inspected the dark plum of her nail varnish. 'Do you like this colour?'

'Bel?'

Bel wouldn't look at her. Agnes waited. Bel was brilliant at trawling low water in which she could detect scum and corpses quicker than anyone. And the atmosphere was not good. When she had an opinion, and the subject of Andrew Kelsey and the letters was as yet unthrashed-out between them, Bel did not hold back. 'Agnes, I think you've lost it a teeny-weeny bit over these letters. I'm asking myself why you want this programme to happen. I'm also telling myself there are plenty more ideas for me to toil over. Is it the brooding farmer who's got to you?'

A thought settled at the back of Agnes's mind: Andrew Kelsey no longer has a wife. 'The angle is important. This is an illustration of what is happening to the rural heritage. It's a good subject.'

But Bel was not easily won. 'There's better material to make the point with. Have you noticed how menopausal-male the letters are? I'm not convinced about this female Scarlet Pimpernel either. I think she is a fantasy.'

'Well, here's the script,' said Agnes wryly. 'Do, please, give me your opinion on that.'

Bel glanced at the typewritten pages, shrugged, extracted a bottle of nail varnish from her bag and repaired a chipped nail. Only then did she pick the first up. After a few paragraphs, she stopped. 'What is this?' she expostulated and flapped the hand with the wet nail through the air. 'No, don't answer. It's the crusade and I'm the dumb cluck who gets beaten up. It's the New-castle factor all over again.'

There are some things that stack up on the 'unforgiv-able, unforgiven' shelf. On it was the programme on the red-light district in Newcastle when Agnes had made Bel go undercover in a feather boa and a PVC skirt. Bel had only just escaped serious injury by an enraged pimp.

'"At first sight, Andrew Kelsey's farm is similar to many others of approximately a hundred and fifty acres.

A tumble of outhouses flanks a modern farmhouse, surrounded by fields in various stages of cultivation and fallow. Tithings is a working farm devoted to producing organic beef. Cattle of all generations, mothers, aunts and grandmothers, graze peacefully together, on a mix of herbs and grasses. When the time comes for the trip to the abattoir, they travel in pairs, and Andrew Kelsey will have checked with the slaughterman to ensure that there will be no waiting.

'"There is a world of difference between Andrew Kelsey's approach and the men who run agri-business.

'"Andrew Kelsey's farm enjoys an astonishing diversity of grass, wildflowers, insect and wild life. He has forbidden all pesticides. As a result, his soil is rich, friable and astonishingly fertile, unlike many other farms whose soil is biologically dead. His farm is notable for the wealth of birds: songbirds, swifts, martins and, even, the increasingly rare linnet. It is an example of man and nature co-existing in harmony and to the mutual benefit of both.

'"But this paradise is now under threat. Having fought off opposition to his way for farming, Andrew Kelsey is now battling developers who are planning to evict him and build executive homes to cater for the projected overspill of the local town of Exbury. Andrew Kelsey has a battle to save his farm, but he also possesses another small part of our heritage. A series of letters . . ."'

Bel sighed and put down the script. 'OK so far. But if we lose our edge, we're finished. The critics will crawl all over us. There'll be a fine old row and we'll have to fight our way up all over again. You are transfixed by the letters but there is not one shred of evidence to authenticate these scribblings, nice though they are. Beautiful, though they are. And there's a hard-luck story there, all right. But the two are not necessarily linked and the fact remains that we take the rap for what we produce now, as much as for what we've already done. Our names are on it, Ag. The dynamic partnership.' Bel cast around wildly. 'You were always the one to see through a pretty idea and insist on the facts. You *can't* make a programme on this flimsy basis.'

'It's good,' said Agnes. 'Believe me. This is what should be said.'

She and Bel traded a look. 'Agnes,' said Bel, 'can I tell you something?'

Agnes waited expectantly.

'You're a fool.'

## 15

Dead on schedule, the film convoy of a van and three cars eased its way down the track to the farmhouse, where Andrew was waiting by the back door. Agnes rolled down the car window and he leaned in.

'Do you always travel with an army?'

She laughed. 'Showbiz.'

'Lucky I have the space.' His eyes told her that he was pleased to see her. 'Can you ask them to park over there? Otherwise they'll get in the way of the animals.'

Agnes parked and got out. Groaning theatrically, Bel emerged from her car. 'It's a long way from civilization.'

'I heard that,' said Andrew, as the others decanted from various vehicles.

The group, who knew each other well, made straight for the back of Ted's catering van, which was already open and dispensing hot drinks. Clutching their clipboards, they stood around drinking and making bad banter. It was the ritual that eased them into the slog ahead.

'Eat, eat,' exhorted Ted, whose life's work was to stuff film crews with unnecessary food. 'Eat, my darlings.'

'OK,' said Agnes eventually, 'it's time to start.'

Jed hefted his camera equipment on to his shoulder

and he, Agnes, Bel and Andrew made for the north field, from which an uninterrupted view of the house could be had. They spent a lot of time discussing opening shots and assessing the light, with Andrew watching and listening. They were lucky and netted an opening sequence first time off, a pastoral composition of the cattle grazing in the field and the farmhouse behind. But filming is unpredictable, and Agnes knew this beginner's luck meant nothing.

After a while, she came and stood beside Andrew. 'Jed is just wrapping up some shots.' She glanced up to check the sky.

'I don't recognize you,' said Andrew. 'You look and sound different.'

It was a remark that frequently came her way. 'Aren't you different at work?' she asked.

He considered. 'No, I don't think so.'

Jed signalled to Agnes, who consulted her clipboard. 'Andrew, in this bit, the voiceover will describe your farm and its philosophy. And we'll do some shots with you tending the animals. Can you spare the time?'

'Oh, I have the time.' Andrew's mouth had set in a such a firm line that little white patches appeared in the corners. 'I'll make it. Look, Agnes.' He bent down and scooped some earth into the ball of his hand and thrust it under her nose. 'I'm not going to let anyone build on that.'

The earth was thick and dark with a fretwork of red tints. Andrew squeezed his hand shut. This was an angry man.

In the early evening, Bel and Agnes plodded back to the farmhouse while the bed-and-breakfast contingent headed off for baths and beer. Bel went inside to make some phone calls and write up notes but Agnes picked her way across the yard and discovered Andrew in the shed, occupied with stacking sacks of feed. She thought he was not aware of her presence until he said, without looking up, 'Finished for the day?'

She leaned against the concrete wall and scuffed the dust with her feet. 'We've made a promising start.'

'Good.' He hefted the last sack into place and leaned on the pile. She was riveted by an ugly slash over the fleshy part of one of his broken fingers. It was imperfectly healed, and the skin still weeping. 'Do you want to see something special?' The blue eyes were speculative.

She dragged her gaze from his damaged hand. 'Sure.'

He beckoned to her, led her round the shed and pointed to the sky. He placed his hands on her shoulders, propelled her round in a half-circle and said, 'Look at that.'

Agnes inhaled sharply. To the north, the moor rose like a giant phantom, but to the west, the sky was washed with rose pink and fire orange. Just at the edge of this palette of colour was the dark.

Surely this was the domain of the old gods who stalked through the rocks and trees. She explained the fancy to Andrew and his fingers gripped her shoulders. 'That's right. This land belongs to them, but I don't expect city dwellers to see it that way.'

She was startled and a little offended by his hostility. 'Why shouldn't they understand? After all, it's what the film is about.'

'Of course. I'm sorry.' He dropped his hands. 'I get carried away sometimes.'

As they headed back to the farmhouse, he said 'I'm sorry Penny isn't here. It makes catering a bit awkward.' He stooped to pick up his axe, which was propped up against the van. 'You've never been married, have you?'

'No.'

'I wish . . .' again Agnes caught the roil of anger under the surface '. . . that I had done things differently.' He put the axe in the back of the van and closed its doors.

Bel was waiting for them in the kitchen where Penny's rule was still in evidence but under attack from Andrew's careless habits. Lists were tacked up on a noticeboard, a small pair of rubber gloves hung from a peg by the basin, handcream stood by the soap tray and a row of knives had been arranged in descending size on a magnetic strip above the work surface.

But on the table there was a large, untidy stack of papers, which Andrew piled on a chair in the corner. 'That's all the planning-inquiry stuff. Masses of it. Then I have to send out copies to the organic farmers' defence group, who want me to keep them up-to-date.' He had a go at stabilizing the pile, gave up and dumped half on the floor. 'After a piece in the local papers, I got sent all sorts of strange things – pamphlets on self-defence, on making Molotov cocktails, instructions on passive resistance from the Gandhi Self-helpers. I had no idea there were so many interests boiling over.'

'There were a couple of phone calls.' Bel uncurled herself from her foetal slump. 'Whoever it was wanted to know the date of the planning inquiry. I've written the names down. I didn't know what to do about food.' She had not discarded her parka and shivered impolitely.

'Believe it or not, Penny came over the other day and left me food for you all.' Andrew padded over to the fridge and extracted a tin-foil container labelled 'Tuesday'.

'It's Wednesday,' Bel pointed out.

'Is it? I must have forgotten to eat.' Andrew looked around helplessly. Sighing, Bel removed the container from his hand.

'We'll do the supper,' said Agnes. 'Tell me how to drive the oven.'

Bel addressed Andrew: 'You don't know Agnes's cooking.'

Andrew said he would take the risk and went over to the cupboard, extracted glasses and opened a bottle of wine.

'Is a bath an impossibility?' asked Bel, in a manner that suggested she supposed it was.

Andrew took her upstairs, and Agnes hunted around in the drawers and cupboards for the correct utensils. Everything was in immaculate order; even the cake tins were wrapped up in oiled greaseproof paper and tied with string. Agnes stared at them. Penny's care was infinitely touching. It said: Even the smallest things are worth doing well.

Having got the stew under way, she searched in the fridge for some vegetables, failed to find any and called up the stairs to Andrew.

'Carrots are in the outhouse. To the right of the back door. In a paper sack.' Andrew materialized at the top of the stairs. He had stripped to the waist, and in the electric light his flesh seemed to gleam, sinewy with use and health. It was a surprisingly delicately fashioned body but lean and strong-looking.

Agnes swallowed. 'Thanks.'

On her return, a fully dressed Andrew was finishing laying the kitchen table.

Agnes washed the carrots. 'After her husband died an aunt of mine said it was like having her stomach removed. She still functioned but nothing nourished her.'

He put the final knife in place and reached for his tobacco pouch. 'Funnily enough, I haven't really found it to be so.' He glanced at the strip of knives. 'Actually, I castigate myself for finding it so easy.' Fascinated, Agnes watched out of the corner of her eye as he selected and rolled the shreds of tobacco into the correct shape.

He folded up the pouch. 'The strange thing is, the marriage might never have been. Twenty years have just vanished, short-circuited in the memory, and now I can't really remember what it was like having Penny here.' The match flared. 'I don't know what that says about marriage – or me, for that matter.'

Agnes inspected a stone crock by the stove, which proved to hold salt, and dusted a pinch into the stew. 'I don't know.' She kept her back turned. 'But a short memory can be life-saving, I suppose.'

'It's the watching over me, the fussing, from Bob's home where she's now living, that I can't cope with,' said Andrew.

There was an embarrassed pause. It was growing dark in the kitchen. Andrew got up to switch on a lamp in the corner of the room and nudged the pile of magazines lying beside it. 'Penny doesn't want to be here with me, yet she can't quite . . . Either she's left me or she hasn't.'

Agnes tested the stew. 'Delicious.'

Andrew regarded the magazines with a thoughtful expression. Then he picked up an armful and dropped them into the wastepaper basket. 'Penny was obsessed by these damn things. Agnes, can you still make the film if we haven't tied up who Jack and Mary were exactly?'

Agnes chopped up a carrot into nice, neat slices. 'We will find out who Jack and Mary are. It's a question of understanding where to look.'

'Good.' Andrew picked up the overflowing waste-paper basket and carted it outside. From out of the kitchen window, Agnes watched him lift the lid of the dustbin and, with one swift movement, tip in the magazines.

When Bel reappeared, with a face bare of makeup

– 'Behold, my country look' – the meal was ready. Afterwards they drank coffee and whisky, and the two women regaled Andrew with tales of filming on location.

'Do you get frightened?' he asked, after the story of the sinking boat on the whaling trip.

'Not really.' Without her painted-in eyebrows, Bel looked sweetly, and deceptively, childlike. 'There are worse things than a perishing cold sea. Like a BBC budget meeting.'

'Liar,' said Agnes fondly.

'I'm frightened that I'm going to lose the farm,' said Andrew, gazing into his glass. 'Very frightened.' The whisky had obviously clocked in. 'I hate builders, planners and landlords who think they can do what they like.'

He refilled his glass.

Bel had thought of something. 'You need Gordon the Gladiator. He organizes peaceful opposition to builders. I'll give you his address. We did a quickie fill-in on the eco-warriors not so long ago. He's probably up a tree, but don't worry, he runs a mobile off his social security.'

'Good,' said Andrew blearily. 'Up a tree, you said?' The idea of the tree-borne gladiator appeared to strike him as funny. His shoulders shook and he dropped his head into his hands. And, very slowly, Andrew collapsed on to the table.

Agnes and Bel looked at each other. Bel staggered to her feet. 'Come on, Ag. Upstairs with this one.'

They manhandled Andrew into his bedroom, laid him on the bed and closed the door. Bel backed theatrically into the minute third bedroom, which, Andrew had explained earlier, was once designated the nursery. Agnes had been put in the spare room.

Considering the amount of land surrounding it, the architect had been over-zealous in saving space in the house. This room was small, too, with a low ceiling and only just enough space to accommodate two single beds with a chest of drawers wedged between them. There was no room for a chair, the cupboard was too narrow for a coat-hanger, and every swish of water from the bathroom next door was audible.

Despite a dredging of dust on the chest of drawers, the room had been scrupulously maintained, and the absent Penny was evident in the clever curtains and bedspreads. Folded at the end of each bed were knitted rugs, of the kind often seen in charity shops. Agnes touched one. They reminded her of Bea, for it was the kind of thing she liked.

Someone had placed a vase of wild flowers and grasses on the chest of drawers with a lace mat to prevent the water staining the wood. It was a woman's gesture. Penny's, she imagined. The Penny who was performing the double act of both quitting and defending her territory. Andrew implied that you slough the skin of a marriage, just like that. Obviously Penny felt differently. Penny had made the dash for freedom and fresh air, but found her roots too strong and painful to pull up in one mighty heave.

After her parents had been killed, Agnes had not

known in which hemisphere she would end up. At night, she curled up in bed, hands tucked between her thighs for comfort. She knew she had strayed into a bad story but she was sure that the mistake would be sorted out — if she was patient enough.

Perhaps that was what Penny felt. That she had strayed into the wrong story and she was keeping open her options. Or perhaps it was guilt that made Penny cook a stew, ladle it into tin-foil containers and bring it over to her abandoned husband.

Agnes lay with an unfamiliar pillow denting her cheek, and Julian crept into the bed. Tender and importunate, weary and bothered. Go away, she said. I have not invited you. But she had. She had, because she longed for him.

'*Comment*?', Maud would say, and '*Tiens*', for Maud had the survivor's trick of trading through the bad times. Not a bad thing to possess.

Agnes thought about the grace she so desired, how it would feel and how she must set about attaining it. She twisted on to her other side and pressed her hand to her hot cheek. The nag of what might have been had never been so sharp.

She was woken by a crash in the passage. Sodden with sleep, she got out of bed and encountered Andrew sitting on the top stair. 'Sorry,' he whispered. 'I slipped.'

She regarded him blearily. 'What time is it?'

'I'm afraid it's only four o'clock.' Agnes emitted a little groan. 'I needed some water and thought I'd make less noise if I went down to the kitchen.'

'And an aspirin?'

'No.' He placed a hand on the stair rail. 'Go back to bed. We'll wake Bel.'

He looked terrible. Agnes grabbed him by the arm. 'You do need an aspirin. Come with me.'

He edged into the bedroom and she flipped open a pocket of her rucksack. 'Double strength.' She shelled two pills into his open hand and offered him her toothmug of water. He swallowed the pills and drank all the water.

Agnes slipped back into bed and Andrew slumped down at its foot. His fist struck a tattoo on his forehead. 'I'm sorry. Whisky always does me in. Was I obstreperous? Rude?'

He seemed eaten up by an intensely private emotion and Agnes's pity leaped into the breach. This was someone who needed care and comfort, which she could give at this precise moment. It was not easy to lose a spouse or, God knew – Agnes knew – to lose a lover.

He got up and opened the window to let in the air. Outside, it was quite still and he stepped aside to allow Agnes to see the first fingers of light trickling over the oak canopies.

The tousled hair and the curve of his back were unfamiliar but the thought, *This man is available*, swam into her mind, taking her by surprise. The night always performed tricks and did strange things. As a general rule, Agnes's history demonstrated that she did not get involved easily or lightly. *That* was her trouble.

Andrew turned and leaned back on the edge of the window-sill. 'I've been thinking a lot about you, Agnes. I've never met anyone who understands exactly what I am doing at Tithings. Do you mind me saying it?'

It was strange compliment. 'Thank you.'

She must have sounded a trifle wary for he said, 'Don't worry, I'm not going to pounce.' Andrew shoved his hands up the sleeves of his dressing-gown. 'Look, no hands. Apart from anything else, booze kills my performance.' He was beginning to shiver noticeably.

He turned to her and his whole body was shuddering. 'I'm at my wit's end. I don't know what to do.'

This was a cry for help. Agnes pulled back the sheets. 'Get in or you'll get pneumonia.'

'Are you sure? I have some sense of decency left.'

'Look, you get in under the blankets, I'm under the sheets. Will that do?' Andrew did not require further encouragement and his shaking, gelid body slid in beside hers, insulated by a couple of blankets. Feet. Thighs. Long, lean back. Unfamiliar bones.

'Sorry,' said Andrew, in the dark. 'You must forget this conversation and this drunken display. Whisky talk.'

She shifted her back against the wall. 'Don't worry.' She felt him relax a little. 'I was taken to a reception the other day. There was champagne and powerful people, intent on carving up land like yours. The talk was of the future. But it was a limited future for it was all their future.

So we have to make sure your sort of future is given a chance.'

'Didn't Jack say something like that?'

She smiled. 'Did he?'

They lay quietly, their breath steadying into a shared rhythm, Andrew growing heavy against Agnes, he seeking the comfort of being close to another human, she dispensing it. It was the solidarity of body against body, ranged against the terrors and anxieties of the night: a strange, unimaginable intimacy, which sometimes happens between people.

The alarm clock tore Agnes awake. Cramped and exhausted, she frowned, puzzling out the events of the night. Andrew had vanished. She pulled back the sheets and stumbled over to the open window.

It was a glorious early-summer day, so beautiful that her heart lifted. The sun was already warm and the air was clean, so clean.

Green and flower-strewn, Andrew's fields unfolded around the farmhouse towards a horizon that dipped and curved with female lushness. In the distance were the glimmering white squares of the beehives and beyond them the moor.

Poppies and cornflowers, whispering grass, herbs . . . Agnes cupped her chin in her hands and, voluptuous and life-enhancing, the sun warmed her. The canvas outside the window was a dialogue between man and nature. A clever con trick, for what was artificial had become natural. A master craftsman – no, an artist – had created such a wild and joyous sight. Andrew *was* the artist.

He came into sight round the corner of the house and, leaning out of the window, Agnes called to him and told him so.

# 16

*Friday.*

Kitty waited in her cottage until, one by one, the lights flooded through the rooms at Cliff House and slipped through the warm, late evening to join Julian. Her feet hurried along the cliff path, still treacherous from the spring rains, and the sea roared below. In her haste, she hesitated and stumbled as if the path were virgin territory instead of a route as familiar as the lines on her face.

He was already in bed, surrounded by papers, a sign that the week had been a bad one. 'Darling, is everything all right?' She cast her cashmere cardigan on to a chair and bent over to kiss him.

He looked up from his laptop. 'Hallo, Kitty. Nice to see you.'

'Bad week? The market seems quite buoyant. FTSE up at the close and the shares are holding.'

The corners of his mouth tightened: the bear-market expression. 'There are the glitches I mentioned. Actually, Kitty, a bit more than glitches. Quite serious, but I think, I hope, I can sort them out.'

She was conscious of a little glow of triumph that she had netted his response and sat down on the bed.

'Tell me.' On money, their talks were usually good, the exchanges easy and productive.

'I think we have over-extended ourselves on the projects in the north and I can't quite see how to limit the damage.' He leaned back on the pillows and smiled at her with sufficient steel to inform her that he was angry with himself. 'My mistake, Kitty. I was over-ambitious and bullied the others into agreeing. Classic stuff.'

Kitty turned over in her mind what she knew of Portcullis. 'Can't you transfer the profit centre? Or carry it over to the next year?' She ran a mental check through the summer schedule. 'Some serious entertaining of the big shareholders?'

He considered. 'No, I don't think so, but I'll look into it.' He leaned over and kissed her lips. 'Keep thinking, please.'

She picked up the file nearest to her and opened it. Her glow of triumph vanished. It was a copy of Jack Dun's letters. Inside was a sheet of Portcullis headed paper scrawled over in Julian's handwriting. 'Agents given a poem to help them memorize their wireless codes. Each radio operator's touch – the radio fingerprint – on the keys was unique and easily identifiable. The listeners at the home station were taught to watch out for the characteristic touch. Like handwriting?'

'What's this?' she asked.

'Some research I've been doing.'

'You mean, Angela has been running round.' She tapped the paper with a leaden finger. 'For . . . Agnes

Campion?' Kitty closed the file and held it tightly against her knees.

'Yes. But the funny thing is I've got quite interested in the subject. Radio codes, living undercover, all that sort of thing.' Julian snapped his laptop shut and shuffled his papers into order.

'I bet.' She hated herself for sounding bitter but she could not help it. 'Glamorous documentary-maker. Etc., etc. You might even get a credit if you're clever.'

She had spoilt things.

'For God's sake, Kitty.' Julian swung his legs out of the bed and made for the door.

She clasped the file so tight that her knuckles went white. 'Julian, is this woman going to be one of those . . . She is already – sometimes-we-go-our-own-way?'

He turned to face her. 'Yes.'

Kitty bent her head so the pain on her face could be private, known only to her. 'I thought so.'

She heard him go downstairs and into the kitchen. Kitty opened the file again and riffled through it, desperate for clues. She stopped at a letter dated 15 July 1943. 'You have been gone over a year and I confess that I am growing frightened. When you left, I was half mad with craving the physicalness of you. I bit on nothing and swallowed draughts of burning jealousy. I dreamed incessantly of your softness and silkiness . . .' Kitty's stomach lurched. That was what it would be like if Julian left her. She leafed further through the file. The letter of

November 1943. 'You have done a terrible thing, Mary. You have taught me how to hate wastefully . . .'

Kitty shut the file as Julian reappeared with a couple of glasses and a bottle of wine. He stood for a moment in the doorway. 'I'm sorry, Kitty.'

She sprang up, divested him of the wine and the glasses, pulled him awkwardly into her arms and ran her hand over his face. 'This is my radio imprint on you,' she whispered, pressing her fingers into his temples. 'No one else has this touch, have they?' Her hands slid down his body and came to rest. '*Have they?*'

'Oh, Kitty.'

'It's fine. Let's go to bed,' she said softly.

*Saturday.*

As usual, Julian was up early for a pre-breakfast walk, leaving Kitty in bed. She stretched luxuriously, sated and at peace. Perhaps they should get a dog. Then they could walk it together and it would keep her company during the week. Julian planned to sail, as he did at every available moment during the season. Kitty hated sailing but perhaps in future she should make an effort to go with him. Make that a statement of commitment.

Yesterday she had purchased the crushed raspberry linen suit that she had had her eye on for some time, and Julian had paid for it. They often exchanged presents – a feature of their arrangement. But as soon as she had carried the monogrammed carrier-bag into the cottage, Kitty had lost interest in it. She had chucked it on to the kitchen table where it remained. Theo had thrown her a knowing look. 'Retail therapy, Kits?'

Kitty closed her eyes. Am I unhappy because I am powerless?

But that was not true. She had the power to ask for expensive clothes from her lover. She had her own money and managed it. She had a certain routine and a relationship – of sorts. Looks excepted, from unpromising material she had made something of her life. It was not to everyone's taste but she had chosen it, worked for it (my God, she had worked for it) and it kept her in the manner she wished. But she had not expected the goalposts to shift quite so radically at this stage. When she had been young, she kept her emotions in a pretty little box into which she looked from time to time but which she kept securely locked. Now that she was older, she had become a neglectful concierge: she had dropped the box and spilled its contents for all to see.

She turned her head to check the time and encountered the wretched letters file on the bedside table where she had placed it the previous night.

Oh, Kitty, Kitty. By now she knew enough to understand that the body was not so very important in the long-term and to share it was not so very significant either. But she did not know enough not to let it hurt her.

Kitty embarked on her increasingly lengthy morning routine. Cleanse, tone, nourish. A little massage on the neck. Cold water splashed on the eyes. She sighed.

Years of this ritual lay ahead. Years of fighting, dodging, manoeuvring around age, of outwitting its incursion into her body, and of never giving up. Years and years – and the result would be defeat.

What did it add up to?

She looked up from the basin to the image in the mirror. Mouth slightly agape, hair lank in the steam, skin shinily nourished. A fish out of water? Automatically, she adjusted her expression into an acceptable one, reached for the towel and patted until the shine was dulled. Then she massaged cream into the base of her neck, where it was beginning to fold and thicken. A fragrant, feminine, highly constructed, accommodating Kitty took shape in the mirror.

That was better. The wild, panicking figure had been smoothed out of sight, and she recognized herself again.

Downstairs, she made breakfast and carried it into the conservatory. Later, she would make a picnic and wait on the shore for Julian to return from his sail. They would eat it tucked under the fossil cliff: good friends and companions with the memory of the fervent, burning, slow-motion sensation-seeking and -giving of the night still fresh.

After dinner, Kitty came into the study where Julian was wrestling with the Portcullis problems and shut the door.

He looked up. 'When you look all pink, soft and gold like that,' he said, 'it usually means business. The Kitty paradox.'

'It does.' In a waft of scent, she trod across the carpet towards him in her high heels and stood over him. He put down his pen but did not meet her eye. He's thinking I look older than last week, she thought, in sudden fear, and twisted the ruby and diamond ring he had given her round and round the finger on her right hand. *He's comparing me.* 'I know we've discussed this only quite recently but I want to talk about it again. I want to thrash it out.' In the silence that fell, she felt a prickle run over her flesh. 'Julian, please, I have some rights in this too. After all this time, I am entitled to make my demands.'

He pushed back his chair and got to his feet and she hoped, desperately, that it was to touch her. But he moved towards the window. 'Do we need to go into this again, Kitty?'

'I've had enough of being unsecured. I want an anchor. I can't explain it very well. Oh . . . I don't know. I would like to be invited to the social events in the area without being labelled the scarlet woman.'

He seemed genuinely taken aback. 'What on earth –'

She cut him off. 'You wouldn't understand because it isn't your world, and you don't think about anything except your own world, but it means a lot to me. Or it's beginning to. It's about belonging.'

He turned his face towards the sea. 'The weather's getting up,' he remarked – he was cruel, so cruel – and the wind's mutter could be heard through the window. It was a long time before he asked, 'Do you want the truth, Kitty?'

Too late to scuttle back into harbour: she had launched her boat. Kitty searched Julian's face for a clue, for a positive sign from which she could take heart, and found nothing worthy of interpretation. She summoned courage. 'Yes. I do.'

He seemed to be making up his mind to say something. 'Kitty . . . I think . . .' Terrified, she gave an involuntary little cry. At the sound, he stopped, appeared to change his mind, and began again. 'We've had ten years. Are you telling me you've had enough?'

She bit her lip. How like him to throw the question back. Always resisting confrontation. He was like a piece of galvanized iron, smooth and impervious, which over the years she had sought to pierce and never succeeded. 'I don't think you're being honest. Is it . . .' Kitty forced her mouth to stop trembling. 'Is it . . . my age? You'd better say if it is.'

He flinched. 'Kitty, do you think you should tear yourself apart like this?' He looked straight at her. 'If you want a change . . .'

And Kitty wished, *wished*, that she had never opened her mouth and, at the same time, she knew that it was impossible for her not to try to discover the truth. She longed to know how thin and insubstantial was the ground on which she stood but was terrified to look down. And yet she had come up against the limits of what she was prepared to suffer in silence. 'Go on, Julian, we'd better get the age question out into the open.'

'All right, your age might possibly have something to do with it.'

'Why . . . why?' She heard herself dart and jab like a stinging insect, a useless, irritating thing. 'Tell me.'

He looked troubled. 'Lately, I have considered the idea of children.'

'How strange. How very strange. I never imagined that lack of children would ever be an issue between us. We were both . . . so set. We agreed . . .' she gave a short laugh '. . . that we were always too self-absorbed.'

'You were always adamant that you never wanted them.'

'True.' Kitty twisted her ring and fumbled for the advantage, the light of battle still not quite extinguished. 'If – if you feel strongly, Julian, there are clinics and things that can sort things out.'

At last, he touched her. He slipped an arm around the doll-like waist and barely curving hips. Passionless and without curiosity, it was the gesture of a man who had been familiar with a body for a long time.

'I think I have my answer. But . . .' Kitty could not finish the sentence. She slipped from his grasp and left the room.

The door clicked shut.

*Sunday.*

He was finding it hard to look Kitty in the face, a trait he despised in others and particularly in himself. Kitty's haunted eyes, which shuttered briefly at the moment of passion, only to open to tell him she loved him. He had grown to dread the scrape of their flesh as they willed a response from each other.

Nor did he want her exquisiteness, which she presented to him like an expensive gift. Or the Kitty of the pale blue jacket who waited on the roaring, spitting shore with a perfectly planned and packed picnic. Waiting for him. Always waiting. And he hated himself for his unfairness and cruelty, but not sufficiently to do something about them.

Julian picked up the fossil and traced the rough undulations. Inside it, the separate chambers of the shell would have been divided by thin septa and connected by a tube, which was used for buoyancy control, like the air tanks in a submarine. Thus, each chamber was connected, each contributing to the life of the animal, and activated at different times and different situations.

The Kitty chamber? Did he regret falling in lust with her sexual poise and sophistication, with the delicate face and sensual body? No, he could not do that. In their way, he and Kitty had grown into each other. But tonight, for the first time, he had noticed a flush layered at the base of her neck and a crêpiness, which he was sure had not been there the previous week. The discovery hurt. Not so much that the signs were in place but, rather, that he had noticed them.

Time was folding, telescoping and vanishing.

Julian owed Kitty much. And more, he was responsible for her. But the variables of their life together were altering in a manner that startled him. His meeting with Agnes had changed him. Air was slipping from one chamber into another and, having made the mistake of forgetting that the condition of life – and business – was constant evolution, he felt helpless, and stupid, in the face of these forces. Temporarily, he hoped. The knowledge that the levels of his life were shifting flooded him with a mixture of exhilaration and despair.

# 17

Gordon 'The Gladiator' Rice lived in deepest Croydon where, for a fee, he masterminded guerrilla activities – 'nationwide' – to foil road- and house-building. As soon as the filming had finished, Andrew got up at dawn and drove up to see him, explained that the planning inquiry was in June and he needed a bit of advice on tactics.

The Gladiator was not good in the early mornings, but he pulled himself together sufficiently and said he was happy to oblige. He was sorry about the charge, he explained cheerfully to Andrew, but social security wasn't enough to fund his activities. If a top-up was on offer, he would nip down to Devon and teach the citizens of Exbury the art of civil unrest. After a lifetime of being a problem statistic, he could spot at once where the flanks were weak. His arsenal of ideas included sit-downs on major roads, living barriers stretched across the routes of heavy machinery, and digging tunnels through the foundations of the proposed houses.

'You must hit them.' He smacked a fist into his cupped hand, and Andrew was forced to take a step backwards: it was all too apparent that the Gladiator had philosophical objections to – or perhaps did not have time for –

laundry arrangements. He smelt of earth that had turned rank, of gas mains, sulphur and sweat. But above the filthy anorak and jeans his countenance seemed to show content with his role in the world. It was an expression that Andrew knew he had yet to find in his own face, search as he might.

The Gladiator gave full value for money, and issued a stream of advice and instructions. 'They scream if their budgets are affected, and if their name is branded in the press it's a bull's eye. You must make them scream. I *love* to make them scream. Are you on the Internet? No? Fix it up. That's how we pass information. That way, we can duck and weave past them. Meanwhile,' he shoved a heap of paper at Andrew, 'read these, but don't let the pigs in blue get their hands on them.'

The top sheet of roughly printed paper read: 'DON'T MUCK WITH OUR FUTURE.'

'One thing,' added the Gladiator.

'What?'

The truth dragged itself out of him. 'They win. They always do. But we have to keep on. Never, never give up.'

Anger hissed in Andrew. These days, he was surprised at the intensity of his feelings, sometimes rather frightened by them. After years of nothing, of no real change in how he perceived and reacted to his surroundings, his decision to fight his landlord and forge the letters, then the departure of his wife had wrought in him a sea-change. Very quickly, he had become this person with powerful feelings and the urge to act. He hoped that he would recognize himself.

The Gladiator shrugged. 'We outsiders,' he said, 'we know.'

Andrew thought then of Agnes, and of her hair tangled across the pillow. The intimacy of seeing her asleep had been erotic and dangerously satisfying, its secrecy thrilling.

It was a glimmer of hope for the farm. Agnes understood the situation. With her film she had taken on the role of keeper of Tithings. Its messenger, perhaps even its saviour.

The fact that he was deceiving her was something he felt she would understand when the time came to be transparent.

On the way home he stopped, on impulse, phoned Agnes at Flagge House and asked if he could look in.

The van bounced up the drive and the soft beaten colour and shape of the house was framed in his windscreen. At the sight of it, Andrew suddenly felt happy and in communion with Agnes. His meeting with her had been more than a professional one: it had ensured new connections. Unsure where to park, he drove round to the kitchen yard at the back. As luck would have it, Agnes emerged with a bowl of wet lettuce from the back door, looking strained and preoccupied. 'Good Lord, Andrew. I didn't expect you quite so soon.' But a smile lit her face and he felt better.

He unfolded himself from the driver's seat. 'I've come

to report that the Gladiator and I are now in contact.'

Shreds of lettuce drifted towards the stone flags. 'Good.'

The meeting did not seem as easy as his imagination had painted it, and he said awkwardly, 'I've got a present for you.'

He opened the freezer section in the back of the van and presented her with a large, bloody bag. 'This was Cromwell. Or, at least, his back end. I thought you would enjoy him.'

'Hallo, Cromwell,' said Agnes dubiously.

Andrew closed the van door. 'He rode in the tumbril with Nero, his best mate. They were happy.'

Agnes swallowed and checked over the dried lettuce. 'We'll put that in the freezer. You'd better stay to lunch. Come, I'll introduce you to the aunts, who think you're a very nice farmer indeed with lots of fluffy lambs and ducks.'

She shoved the meat and lettuce on to the kitchen table and led him down the gloomy Victorian wing and through the drawing-room window on to the terrace.

'Maud, Bea,' she said, 'Andrew has arrived.'

Maud had decked herself out in a large straw hat *à la* Bloomsbury and, a little unsteady on her feet, was leaning against the stone balustrade for support. Bea was sitting on one of the rusty chairs, sewing. Rust flakes had landed on her light green cardigan and one or two had migrated to a very pale cheek. She smiled at Andrew. 'We've been hearing about your farm.'

Maud commandeered the remaining chair. 'You look a bit undernourished,' she commented. 'Doesn't your wife feed you?'

Andrew was amused. 'I've always been thin, Mrs Campion.'

Agnes bent over Bea and brushed the particles of rust from her cheek. 'I think you'll like him,' she whispered. Bea snipped at a piece of thread and Agnes realized that she had been sewing a button on to Freddie's blazer. She watched the small fingers pat and dart, smoothing the material with enormous consideration. 'You're always doing something,' she commented, with a rush of affection.

Bea looked up in her unobtrusive way. 'Keeping busy makes me feel useful. It's the small things, I always think. They keep one in touch with what's important.' With the care of the trusted custodian, she laid Freddie's blazer to one side. 'You wait, Agnes, until you're older.'

'And what has persuaded you to leave your cows?' Maud was asking.

Andrew fixed his eyes on Agnes. 'I'm on my way back from a meeting with an eco-warrior.'

'A what?'

Andrew explained who the Gladiator was. 'He's an expert in burrowing and protesting against road- and house-building.'

'Burrowing? Is that really necessary?'

Andrew said gravely, 'I want to save my farm. Any tactic will do.'

'How refreshing.' Maud breathed in sharply, the powdered planes of her face working. 'There's far too much niceness about. *Non*? It will be the death of us.' She swivelled to face Andrew. '*I* plan not to be nice at all from now on. I've wasted my life being nice.'

'So have I,' said Andrew, at a stroke creating a skilful complicity between himself and Maud.

'We like each other. You can fetch the drinks now, Agnes.' Maud twitched at her skirt.

'I like the sound of your farm.' Bea spoke up. 'Do tell us about it.'

Maud fidgeted while Agnes handed out sherry. Andrew had begun a brief description when she cut him off. 'Agnes, you have remembered that Freddie's coming to lunch?'

Bea's sewing slipped to the ground. 'Oh dear, oh dear,' she said, as Andrew swooped to pick it up. 'I must go and do things in the kitchen at once.'

In the kitchen, the remains of Cromwell had dripped a pool of blood on to the floor which settled into the loosened grout between the tiles.

After lunch, Freddie took Maud off for a drive and Bea, who declared she felt a trifle under the weather, went upstairs for a rest. Agnes and Andrew set out for a walk.

Thermals of warm air rose from the steps. 'The house and grounds are about fifteen acres. It used to be bigger but various Campions have sold it off piecemeal.'

Andrew shaded his eyes and looked over to the houses

hugging the perimeter wall. 'Prime land, though. Who built that lot?' He gestured at the cluster of villas whose roofs peered above the wall.

'The farmer sold off his field and the developers went ahead, despite the protests, built them and sold them to people who had never even heard of the village. Half of them don't live here during the week.'

'Like you?'

She grinned. 'Hey, I *do* live here.'

They walked over the meadow to the river and she thought how much she liked his straightforward attitude. You knew where you were with someone like Andrew. He told you how it was. 'I like the idea of you going into battle as an eco-warrior armed with cyber weapons and old-fashioned spades.'

'You've probably filmed a lot of protest.'

'Yes.' She thought of the struggle she had had to get behind the lens and to get what she saw right. 'But as an observer rather than a doer.' She bent down, fingers tugging at the sappy grass. 'It's time to jump down off the fence. About the house, I mean.' She crunched a stalk between her teeth and he observed how white they were against the pink-red of her lips. 'But there isn't much money.' She threw the grass away.

He said, with a rush, 'The planning inquiry is coming up soon.'

'I know.' She paused. 'Andrew, what will you do if it goes against you?'

He said stubbornly, 'It won't. Or, put it this way, I'm

buckling on the armour. I won't make it easy for them.' He shoved his hands into his pockets with a force that threatened to drive them through the material. 'And there's the programme. I'm sure it will make a difference.'

It was not often that her work had such a direct bearing on a situation and she felt a small glow of selfish pleasure. Andrew wiped the sweat from his forehead and cleared his throat. 'Agnes, I don't often get drunk. I wouldn't like you to think that.'

She looked down at his tanned forearms. 'Andrew . . .'

'I apologize for that night.'

'We all do it,' she said.

'Penny isn't coming back.' He seemed anxious to let her know. 'Given the circumstances, I don't want her back.' There. He was saying: the way is cleared for you and me.

The level of the river had dropped, quite normal in summer, and the long weed streamed through it, like a drowning woman's hair. Andrew hunkered down and dabbled his finger in the chalk-filtered water. 'Trout?'

'Well, there are lots of fisherman's tales in the village.'

Andrew stood up and wiped his hand on his trousers. 'I imagine there's a bit of a frost pocket.' He indicated the hollow between two ancient oaks and the north wall. Then he bent down again and scraped away at the earth. 'Loamy soil. All you need is drainage, and you'd have very good grazing.'

'Goodbye, irises.'

'You ought to keep bees. They'd do well here. Lots of

nice rich clover. It's the swarming season. You could lure in a colony.'

Agnes threw away her grass stalk. 'Why do they swarm?'

'The hive becomes too crowded and unless they sort it out the bees becomes diseased and aggressive. Anyway, it's time to chuck out the old queen in favour of a younger one.'

'Poor queen.' Agnes took the path alongside the river and beckoned to Andrew. Her words floated back to him. 'Imagine, flying up into the sky, old in knowledge and bee sex, knowing that her airborne mating will result in another queen, who will usurp her.'

They walked as far as the boundary wall and leaned up against it. This was a good point from which to view the village.

'It's all very civilized and obedient,' he pronounced at last. 'Not like the moody moor.'

Agnes rallied in defence. 'Are you saying the supermarket and the motorway have won? No ancient gods?' She scraped at a curl of lichen on the wall, and its sage-green dust sprouted under her fingernail. 'They are still here. They just had to find new hiding places, that's all.'

His hand trapped hers against the stone. 'I can only see what's in my own backyard.'

Hand pinioned, she asked, 'How do you like my house?'

He kept his gaze fixed on Agnes. 'It's very fine.'

Agnes removed her hand, and Andrew was aware that he had disappointed her.

They walked back to the terrace. Thick clumps of Jamaican daisies bloomed in the cracks of the steps and the sun had picked out white and orange moss circles fanning across the stone. In the trees, wood pigeons cooed.

'You need to do some repairs.' Andrew tested the bottom step with a foot. 'This is pretty ropy.'

'You remind me of Mr Harvey.'

Andrew made the same criticism of the walls in the kitchen garden, and offered advice on double digging, compost and where to site the bees. A slight frown appeared on Agnes's face, so he did not mention that he suspected that all the sash windows would need replacing and the kitchen wing looked as though it was subsiding.

'Had you considered getting the kitchen sorted out first?' he suggested finally, noticing the frown deepen. 'You would feel better.'

They were loitering in the walled garden, enjoying the warmth. Agnes picked up shards of glass and stones and placed them in containers she had left there for the purpose. She straightened up. 'I dream of a warm, functioning kitchen with a honey-coloured flagstone floor.' She laughed. 'I don't know why, I'm a rotten cook.'

As he drove up the drive and parked by the front door, Flagge House levelled challenging and hostile eyes at Julian. Since that night, three weeks ago – three years –

he had gone over and over the situation and he could not work out if it was Agnes's rejection that so piqued him, or that he had lost control over the situation. He could see the problem, he could hear the explanation – a spoilt man wanting his way – but they did not add up. The mental picture of his life running on oiled wheels, work, mistress, odd love affair, was still clear in his mind but the edges had blurred, and he was conscious of serious shortfalls of feeling and tenderness, and of the wish to help himself to them.

Of Kitty he could not quite bring himself to think.

He hauled on the brake. At the same time, Agnes and Andrew emerged from the kitchen garden. They moved slowly, absorbed and at ease, deep in conversation.

Agnes looked up and gave a visible start. She sent him an angry, disappointed look which asked, *Why?*

At a disadvantage, and not a little sickened by himself, Julian waited for Agnes to approach him.

'I'm *en route* to a project in Dorchester and I thought I'd drop this off.' He produced a video from the back of the car. 'Angela tracked it down so I can't claim any credit, but it's about the SOE. I thought it might interest you.'

Agnes flushed. 'How nice of you.' Her voice rang strangely in her own ears. 'Can I introduce Andrew Kelsey, the farmer who discovered the letters?' She turned to Andrew. 'Julian had the theory that Mary was an SOE agent.'

It took only seconds for Julian to assess and conclude

that this man was also interested in Agnes. 'Agnes mentioned that your case has gone to planning appeal,' he said. 'I run a firm that develops properties.' He paused. 'From your point of view, that might be a good thing.' The video dangled from his hand.

A spat broke out between the wood pigeons. The sun slanted a beam of light into the driveway and shadow enshrouded the house. There was a moment of silence, a beat of impatience and rejection.

'Why would that be?' Andrew was polite, but only just.

'I don't think that district councils are always the best judges. They're too close to the problem and too easily persuaded. Some developers prefer to do things properly and work with the planning people.'

'Yes.' Andrew's eyes turned a cobalt colour with fury. 'I expect it's extremely satisfying concreting over an area the size of Bristol each year, particularly if you do it properly.'

Julian began to enjoy himself. This was straightforward. His wars (and this was war) tended to be fought politely but savagely enough with guile, statistics, words and paper plans. He knew the territory.

Agnes intervened: 'We've got most of the film under our belt, but we're giving a chunk of time to the appeal.'

'It will make good viewing,' said Andrew. 'Live executions do.'

'Have you been offered relocation?'

Andrew swung round. 'Can you relocate a life's work?'

'I think you can,' answered Julian quietly, for Andrew's anger had succeeded in touching him. It was on the tip of his tongue to present the usual arguments: fair compensation, government backing for new homes, the balance between the individual and the mass, working with the future, the vision that helps the ordinary person – people.

These were his beliefs, and that was the typically energetic language in which they were couched. But in the context of the distress registering on Andrew's face, he abandoned the emollients and kept silent.

Agnes stretched out a hand for the video. 'I'll watch it tonight.'

Julian released it. 'If Mary was an agent, she was a brave woman. You'll see what I mean.'

At this point, the conversation ran out, for the two men were not making any effort. 'Shall we have some tea?' Agnes heard herself saying, and watched herself make bossy, shooing motions with her hands. 'You two go through.'

She was waiting for the kettle to boil when Maud and Freddie returned from their drive, and she added more cups to the tray. She watched them walk across the sunlit yard, Maud's steps uneven, uncertain. Agnes turned back into the gloomy kitchen. Time had rushed on, and she had not marked it. Next birthday she would be thirty-one. One day her footsteps would be as hesitant and fumbling.

She hefted the laden tray through the drawing room to the terrace, where the two men had been joined by Freddie. All three were being polite. The latter had thrown himself gallantly into the fray and was regaling the other two with 'the business deals of my prime', a topic that united both men in a glassy expression.

Agnes smiled. Freddie was so sweet and understood far more than he ever let on. She was handing a cup of tea to him when a scream issued from the first floor, followed by another.

Agnes started and the tea slopped. 'My God, the aunts!' Followed by the men, she fled through the drawing room and up the stairs.

At the top they found a groaning Maud collapsed in an unnatural heap outside her bedroom.

'Don't touch me,' she managed, as Agnes knelt down beside her.

'Where does it hurt?'

'My hip.' Maud closed her eyes. 'I think it's broken. It's bound to be broken.'

Julian touched Agnes on the shoulder. 'Where's the phone?' In shock, she stared at his blue shirt with its pearl buttons. 'The phone?' he repeated, and gave her a little shake. She told him and he disappeared.

Agnes chafed Maud's hand. 'Do you hurt anywhere else? Did you hit your head?'

'I tripped on the floorboard . . .' Maud ground out, between grimaces. 'The one you said you'd get mended but never did.'

It was true. Maud had been going on about one of the oak planks, which had worked free of its mooring, adding double danger to an already uneven floor. 'Oh, Maud,' she stammered guiltily. 'How dreadful.' Panicked, she peered closer. Maud's breathing was both rapid and shallow, and shock had stretched her skin tightly across her jaw.

Julian took the stairs two at a time. 'The ambulance is on its way. They won't be long.' He knelt down beside Maud, and his expression gentled. 'Would you like me to find your sister, Mrs Campion?'

Tears spilling from her eyes, Maud whispered, 'Yes.'

Agnes said she was the best person to find Bea and Freddie offered as well, which left Julian and Andrew to deal with Maud.

'How can I help?' asked Andrew, pushing back the open cuffs of his sleeves.

Julian gestured towards the open bedroom door. 'She would be easier with a pillow.'

Andrew disappeared and emerged with a pillow and a rug, and the two endeavoured to make Maud more comfortable. 'Agnes's fault . . .' whispered Maud. 'She promised. She's . . .'

'Now,' said Julian, 'I'm going to hold your hand while your sister is being found.'

Looking sweet and fresh in an embroidered blouse and her favourite cardigan, Bea was in the laundry room folding the washing. As she had been taking it down from the line, the commotion had bypassed her. When

Agnes broke the news, she turned as white as a sheet. Just in time, Agnes swooped forward and caught her as her knees buckled.

'I'm so sorry, so sorry,' she murmured as, with difficulty, Agnes manhandled her to a chair. 'It's the shock.' For a while, she sat clutching Agnes. 'I don't think my new pills quite suit me.'

Agnes dashed into the hall and called to Freddie for help. Moving with the speed of a much younger man, Freddie reached the laundry room within seconds, at which point the ambulance arrived and Agnes left him to it.

The paramedics took one look at Maud and transferred her to the gurney, during which time Bea, who had struggled upstairs on Freddie's arm, fainted properly. It was suggested that she, too, went into hospital, which Agnes, alarmed by Bea's reference to her pills, urged. Eventually, the gurney was carried down the stairs with its burden. Maud clung to Freddie's hand. 'I knew Flagge House would kill me. I kept saying.'

'Well, it hasn't, dear one, has it? Just a knock.'

'Don't leave me, Freddie. Don't leave me.'

'Now, now,' said one of the paramedics, with practised patience, 'we're going to make you better, not eat you.'

The ambulance with Bea and Maud drove off. Andrew, Julian, Freddie and Agnes were left in the drive.

Agnes turned to them. 'I'm sorry,' she said, 'but I must pack a few things for Maud and lock up.'

'Of course.' Freddie extracted his car keys. 'If you

need help, just ask . . .' He tapped a finger to his nose. 'Just ask, dear lady.'

Andrew shot a thunderous look at Julian. 'If you're sure, Agnes, I must get back to relieve Jim.'

'Sure.' She nodded. 'Thank you for Cromwell.'

'Any time.' As he took her hand, she felt the uneven shape of his broken fingers, and the scar tissue on the cut one. Then he inserted his thin form into the van. He looked at Julian and said, in a voice which, technically, was intended for Agnes's ears but reached Julian, 'I'll see you very soon.'

## 18

Julian watched Andrew's van lumber down the drive until it was out of sight. 'Agnes, it wasn't your fault. Your aunt lashed out because she was in pain.'

She shook her head. 'I *should* have done something about that wretched floorboard.'

'One always should have done something,' he said lightly. 'King Alfred should have checked the oven and Bluebeard should have gone into therapy.' He made it sound so easy, so forgivable and explicable. 'I'll lock up while you pack,' he finished. 'Tell me what to do.'

She looked at him in a way that his mother had sometimes, with tolerance and a slight suggestion of impatience, and he wanted to shake her and tell her not to underestimate him. Then he took in the pallor, and an uncontrollable tenderness washed through him. 'Get moving,' he said.

Fifteen minutes later, the house was closed and shuttered, and they were back in the drive. Softly, evening was stealing in. Cloaking reason and principle and substituting yearning, the dying light tracing a different horizon to the day. The swifts were calling and the wood pigeons' fractiousness had stilled. A ring of darkness gathered and waited.

'Will you be all right?' He was now concerned by how pale she was and searched his memory for how to treat shock. 'Maud is in the best hands. It could have happened at any time.'

'Yes, of course.' She picked up her rucksack and Bea's bag. 'Thank you.'

He fingered his car keys. 'Agnes, I'm driving you to the hospital.'

'What about – wherever you were going?'

'I'll get up early.'

'I'm fine. I can cope. I can cope absolutely. I've coped with far worse.'

'Of course.' He put his hands on her shoulders. 'I have an awful feeling I'm always lecturing you, but self-reliance becomes ridiculous if it means you can't accept the offer of a lift when you need one. Furthermore, it doesn't mean you're making a claim on me. Or ruining Kitty's life.'

'No,' she said stubbornly. 'It's *fine*.'

'Agnes,' he said, and startled by the pressure on her shoulders, she looked up at him. He said quietly, 'Just get in the car.'

At the hospital the wait was long. Casualty smelt of blood and alcohol; it was noisy with cries of distress and impatience; it was overheated, airless, and overflowing. The doctors were weary. Maud's fracture turned out to be more serious than had been suspected, the consultant was unavailable and operating theatres were full. To complicate matters, it was decided that Bea should stay in overnight for observation.

It was after nine o'clock before a heavily sedated Maud was wheeled away and Bea finally settled in the twenty-four-hour ward. Agnes reeled out into the car park, fatigued to the bone.

Julian was waiting. He had made phone calls, dispensed cups of coffee, waylaid one set of nurses while Agnes dealt with the other, and even managed to procure toothbrush and toothpaste from the hospital shop. She got into the car and slumped into the seat.

'Don't talk.' He started up the engine.

'You're good at hospitals,' she said, and shut up.

Ten minutes later, they drew up outside the Hanbury Hotel, whose topiary and Georgian façade were lit by discreet, white lights. It looked expensive. Before Agnes could protest, Julian assumed command. 'You're staying here tonight and so am I. I've arranged it. I couldn't bear to think of you grappling with that bathroom by yourself. The hospital has the number so you are contactable.'

Speechless, she nodded. He reached over and kissed her on the cheek. 'Poor tired Agnes.'

A bottle of wine and a plate of sandwiches were waiting in the lounge, which overlooked a floodlit garden that had been laid out by a genius. The bread was home-made and the ham had been cooked by the chef. After Agnes had finished eating, Julian refilled her glass and talked to her of other things – painting, sailing, his fascination with codes, living in the East.

The wine bottle was empty. Agnes crumbled the remains of the bread on her plate. A progression of things flashed through her mind in a crazy, speeding way, while her body behaved like lead.

'Tell me about the codes. In the war, I mean.'

'I don't know much. There is someone at the museum who could help, if you'd like to talk to them.' Julian shrugged. 'There are the obvious things. The shorthand, for example. A Morse phrase like QTC meant: "We have a message for you." Or QRU: "No traffic for London."' He stood up and pulled her to her feet. 'If the enemy did net in a couple of similarly configured messages, same length, same repetition of words, it was known in the trade as "a depth of two". Cryptographers loved that. It was their meat and drink. From a depth of two all sorts of things could be worked out and all sorts of things depended on it, including, possibly, your life or death.' He paused. 'Bed.'

At the door of her room, he slotted in the plastic security card, unlocked it and stood aside. 'I'm down the passage. I won't see you in the morning as I'll have to get up at dawn, but I've arranged for a taxi to pick you up at ten o'clock.'

She leaned on the doorpost. 'Aristotle said you can only be happy when you are virtuous. On your showing tonight, you must be a happy man.'

'Agnes . . .'

'No,' she forestalled him. 'It's all been said before. Except one thing. I forbid you to be rude about my bathroom.'

He fingered the plastic card. 'Goodnight, Agnes.'

Agnes sat on the bed. Exhausted as she was, she was reluctant to undress. The moments before the sleep she craved were so black that she was afraid. What else was it that Aristotle had said? That there was no short-cut to happiness.

It was true. Wherever she turned, she had run up against obstacles. Was that so surprising? But she had been naïve in thinking that, after the squeeze and confinement of childhood, a little air would be let in. That she would spring out of her cage, a strong, capable human being who would deal with what life flung at her strongly and capably. Perhaps it was because she felt so low and dispirited. Perhaps it was true that broken childhoods resulted in broken adults who could never quite see straight, who never got to know themselves. Some people just drove through life, from A to Z, with no problems, and were able to accommodate the demands made on them and the demands of their own hearts. They did the right things, married, had children, gathered grandchildren around them and performed beautifully.

But, so far, whatever Agnes had set her heart on proved to have a canker at the centre. Pierre. The house. Julian.

She reached for the bottle of water on the table and drank a glass. She had never managed quite to eradicate her tendency to misery. As an adolescent anything could set it off. The feeling was so heavy and so particular that it ached physically. It took only the slightest thing: 'The

Lord is My Shepherd' sung to Brother James's Air, a flash of tawny African landscape on television and, especially, the conjured image of the other Agnes dying in childbirth – with the white faces of those bereaved children gazing at their dead mother. Those children were looking at a bleaker place where they would stumble, time and time again, against reminders of their abandonment. An empty chair. The scared feeling that there was no anchor. No one to take care of, or to mind about, the small intimate details that could not be shared. When she confessed how she felt to her uncle, he explained that it was a way of mourning her own parents, which was perfectly logical.

That was part of Julian's attraction. Agnes drank a second glass of water. She understood so well a small, lonely boy in grubby shorts, digging away at a fossil cliff. She imagined the rip of the wind, the smell of salt, the little clunking noises of the chisel on the rock, the slither and patter of falling scree. The fierce, intent, determined look.

As she had grown older, Agnes had learned to manage her misery and to keep it in check. In fact, she had been quite proud of herself. That was why documentaries appealed to her. Any misery, loneliness and injustice had to be dealt with in a disciplined, factual manner. Then it had been contained. Packaged. Made to be useful and creative. Until now.

As Pierre once said, *You are not smart.*

During the night she woke, nauseous and uncomfortable. She had been dreaming of the river and, in her dream, trying to puzzle out the paradox. Water ran through time and place and never changed, yet never ceased to do so.

When she returned the following morning, Flagge House was shrouded in a dead quiet, not the drowsy content of the living. But as Agnes stepped into the hall an orchestra struck up. Creaks, a scutter of mice in the roof, the movement of brick on stone, wood on stone.

She bent down to pick up the post on the mat and inhaled a sharp, musty damp. 'Drains and plumbing,' Maud had said bitterly. In the end that was what life amounted to.

No wonder Maud had fallen in love with a musical.

Agnes rang the hospital and was informed that Maud was post-operative and as comfortable as could be expected. Bea, having been examined by the doctors, would be coming home after lunch. Mrs Innes, added the staff nurse, had arranged her own lift home and had left instructions that Miss Campion was not to be bothered.

Agnes went into the kitchen. She washed up yesterday's tea things, swept the floor, cleaned out the fridge and wiped down the oven – work that women had done for centuries, to which she turned precisely because she did not want to think about being a woman and of the sweet, peculiar double helix of emotion, calculation and anxieties of being female.

She was in the study talking to Bel on the phone when Bea arrived.

Wearing Maud's paste brooch prominently on her lapel and the ring on her finger, Bea looked cheerful and rested. 'Hallo, dear, I'm sorry to have given you so much trouble but I'm better. Those nice nurses sorted me out. I had been taking my pills in the wrong order.'

Agnes felt the tug of familial *ficelles* settling around her. She led Bea into the kitchen and sat her down. 'Would it be a good idea if you gave me the pills? Then you wouldn't have to worry.'

'How very sweet you are.'

'Bea, who brought you home?'

The stay in hospital had done wonders for Bea – she looked as happy and excited as a child. 'Freddie,' she said. 'Who else?'

## 19

Penny agonized whether to go over to Tithings. In the end, she had wasted so much time debating the pros and cons that it seemed crazy not to. Bob was suspicious of her absences and, no doubt, would kick up a stink on her return but so what? The discovery that she did not mind what Bob thought was one of several surprises with which she had been presented during this strange episode in her life.

The roots of a marriage were stronger and tougher than she had calculated. Pulling them up hurt, and the little spurt she had made towards being more in control of her life had not amounted to much. It wasn't that one missed the good points about the person with whom one had lived, but the bad ones. Knowing their tempers and selfishnesses intimately made it so much more possible to live with your own. And she knew Andrew's so well.

Tithings' routine was fixed, and she chose a time early in the morning when Andrew would be out at the abattoir and she could be on her own in the house for a little. Just for a little. Penny's homesickness nagged at her and undermined the value that she placed on herself – for she was used to thinking of herself as practical and sensible. A make-do-and-mend woman.

The first thing she noticed was the absence of magazines. *That* hurt too, but after making a cup of tea and some reflection, she reckoned that it was fair enough. Andrew had always hated them and her reliance on their bright, glossy certainties. A virgin edition of her favourite was in the car and she was tempted to retrieve it but decided to resist. Instead, Penny flicked through the script of the letters programme, which happened to be lying on the table. Agnes's business card was attached to it. On it she had written, 'This is the third draft, and it's shaping up nicely.'

Agnes did not interest Penny – as far as Penny was concerned, she was a woman from another planet – but she was greedy to read everything to do with the letters. The letters that, in her view, had sent Andrew off-course.

Everywhere I smell scent – of pollens, flowers, grasses and early fruit. The world is awash with it, and with the clacking summer noises of animals, insects and birds. There is nowhere more beautiful than this moor . . .

This Jack person wanted his brains examining. He only wrote about the half. What about the endless mud? The precarious roads, dropped so tightly between hedges that it was impossible to see where you were going? What about the neighbours, the gossip, the endless work, the cold, the damp, the snip, snip of penny-pinching?

The gut-wrenching business of watching animals sicken and die, harvests turning black with disease, the stretching and pulling of muscle and sinew into premature old age? What about the disappointments?

Nature may be beautiful, Penny conceded, but it didn't alter the fact that all the red soil and cream teas did not make the countryside an *easy* place in which to earn a living.

Penny closed the file, resumed her vigil and tried not to notice the state of the kitchen, so sullied, so changed, so untidy. But second nature won and, after a short tussle, she bounced up and opened the tea-towel drawer. It was empty, and she slammed it shut with the fury of someone who had discovered exactly what they expected.

She forced herself to sit down and *do nothing.*

The van drove into the yard and Andrew emerged into the kitchen. 'Here again?'

He eyed her dispassionately – and that hurt too. Surely he could manage to look cross, jealous, sad, *something*?

'Has Bob got tired of you?

Andrew and Bob had first run up against each other years ago over EC farm quotas and, since then, they had enjoyed developing a fine vintage hatred. Sometimes Penny wondered if that was why she had chosen Bob. *To get a response.* She riposted angrily, 'I suppose I deserve that remark.'

'Well . . .' Andrew sounded marginally less hostile. 'What can I do for you?'

Penny folded her hands over her empty tea-cup. 'I came over because I knew today was the first day of the appeal. To give my support.' I have surprised him, she thought, with a catch at her throat.

Andrew sat down heavily at the table. 'That was nice, Pen. I didn't expect it. I thought I'd been abandoned lock, stock and barrel for the magnificent Bob.'

His softening made Penny's eyes fill and she looked down at the table. 'Will Stone be there?'

'No. He won't. That fat bastard has taken himself off on holiday.'

It was unlike Andrew to swear. Penny scrubbed surreptitiously at her eyes and asked, 'Are you all right? Will you cope by yourself?'

His reply surprised her. 'Are *you* all right, Penny?'

She flinched and told him the truth. 'I don't know.'

'I'm pretty nervous about this afternoon.'

'I'll make some coffee.' Penny hauled herself to her feet and searched for the jar in the kitchen which, once upon a time, she had known better than her own hands. Now, it was foreign territory – and the situation was of her own making.

Andrew inspected the mug she slid over to him. 'Tell me one thing, Pen, did you really prefer Bob to me? I find that . . . difficult. The one person I dislike and despise. Was it deliberate?'

Penny visualized her empty tea-towel drawer and the old wounds bled. How like a man to think of his pride. 'Dear Marge, the only reason my husband is sorry I left him is because it makes him look foolish . . .' She shrugged. 'Day after day, year after year, I did what was expected. I cooked, I cleaned and all the rest. But you never talked to me, Andrew. I bet you told more things to that girl from television.' She flicked him a look from under her short, colourless lashes. 'Bob wanted me, or he said he did, and I felt a bit – a bit desperate.'

'A fine time to choose, wasn't it?'

'It wasn't meant to be like that.'

Her distress must have got through to him and he had the grace to look shamefaced. 'Other people are always easier to talk to.'

'Even so. I was – am your wife. I thought we were meant to share everything.'

Andrew shoved the coffee aside, and said in a kind, measured manner, 'I'm sorry, Penny, if I failed you. You should have told me sooner what you were feeling. I was so sure that you were with me, and understood how I felt.'

'I did. If you remember.'

They had not talked so openly for years. Andrew looked out of the window. 'But it's a bit late now, isn't it, Pen? The horse has bolted.'

'Has it?' she asked pitifully.

Where do I go from here? She drew in a panicky breath. She had read her magazines and the advice they gave on retrieving crumbling marriages or setting up with a new lover, but now that she was actually between the frying-pan and the fire, the advice did not seem so pertinent, nor as authoritative as she had imagined. How do you build a bridge to a spouse who is so dispassionate?

Andrew slid his hand across the table towards Penny. Being pitched out of a marriage was new to them both, and both were stumbling. 'Don't cry, Pen,' he said.

Her hand crept out towards his. 'Have you got someone else?'

His determined smile told her everything. 'I may have found someone else, Penny, so there is no need to worry about me any more. I wish you well with Bob.'

In times of stress, Penny reverted to habit. Snatching back her hand, she fumbled for her notebook in her plastic shoulder-bag. 'Right. I'll make a list, then, of things we need to do.'

Andrew left Penny shovelling aside the clutter in her car to make space for another armload of her clothes. He watched as sweaters and jeans, faded and ravelled from too much washing, the men's desert boots and men's striped pyjamas that Penny favoured were stuffed angrily on to the back seat. Eventually Penny stood upright and slammed the car door. 'I dunno. It's those bloody letters,' she said. 'They've caused all the trouble. If you hadn't found them, we would be fine.'

'No,' he said. 'It was happening long before that.'

'Well,' she got into the car, 'I'm very happy with Bob. He suits me just *fine*.'

After Penny had driven off, Andrew went to inspect the cattle in the north field. The South Devons had clustered in one clump, the Welsh Blacks milled around over by the hedgerow. 'You racists,' he called affectionately. They butted and nuzzled him, and he bent down to examine a South Devon cow's udder, which looked a bit pink. Luckily, nothing too suspect. All the time, Penny's worn, angry face bothered him.

At two thirty that afternoon, dressed in a jacket and tie, he sat in Exbury's celebrated and elegant eighteenth-century town hall, ready to listen to the opening arguments as to why the proposed housing development, to be built on his farm, would or would not benefit the community. The officials were busy and the inspector, who wore tortoiseshell glasses that were too small for his face, conferred with his clerk. The audience was buzzing with interest – in some cases, self-interest.

The developers, Arcadian Villages ('Built by and for the people') had been clever. They had listened to the locals and their objections, noted them down, modified their plans, offered lures in return. During the opening proceedings, the ominous term 'planning gain' was mentioned more than once.

Andrew swallowed.

Increased traffic? Not a problem, said the smooth, expensive barrister representing Arcadian Villages. The main road would be rerouted around Exbury, with plenty of access points. The funding would be shared and Exbury's ancient centre would benefit. Public transport? This was not a matter for the developers directly, but representations had been made to the relevant council departments with suggested routes and timetables. Wild-life? The barrister effortlessly changed gear and went over in some detail the European directives on the environment to prove how careful they had been to obey the rules and to preserve what was possible.

Out of the corner of his eye, Andrew saw Penny edge her way into one of the few remaining seats. She had put on her best dress, which had red poppies on a black background and was far too long. Under it she wore a pair of battered sandals. As she sat down, she sent him a tiny smile.

Architecture? Yes, conceded the barrister, drawing out the word to suggest how significant had been the deliberations. His clients had been reflecting on the detail of the proposed housing, which they now saw did not quite match the local tradition and ambience, and were prepared to go back to the drawing board. Here the barrister paused to make the additional point that the government had a declared policy to provide new homes and, furthermore, the site to the east of the farm in question had already been removed from agricultural use and was used as a tip by the community.

Andrew hated the barrister's obvious intelligence, his fluency, his being so on top of his material.

Flanked by Jed, the cameraman, and Bel in a tight pair of shorts, Agnes eventually arrived – late – in a pair of new linen trousers and a linen shirt, which exuded the sort of chic otherness of which Bel thoroughly approved.

In her seat, Penny stiffened.

It was the turn of the opposition to put their case. Their barrister was less fluent, less expensive-looking, but he knew a thing or two about building a case. Earlier in the year, he had interviewed Andrew, pressing him hard to find the areas where Arcadian Villages' position was weak and where to whip up the widest possible support for the case against. He had advised writing to the correct councillors and alerting the press; he had shaped up Andrew's written statement and hammered out a timetable for action if necessary. Better still, he had accepted the fight out of conviction.

The room grew very hot and the inspector asked for the windows to be opened. Immediately, a roar of traffic drowned the proceedings and they had to be closed.

The atmosphere grew stifling. Sweat trickled from numerous armpits and left high-tide marks on shirts and blouses. The acoustics made it impossible for those at the back of the hall to hear. The chairs were hard and uncomfortable. One man grew desperate, got up and reopened one window. Again the room was invaded by the smell of car fumes and noise.

Half an hour later, Andrew was invited by the inspector at the top table to submit to cross-examination. He felt in his pocket for his handkerchief (oh, God, agonized Penny, in her seat, for it was obviously not a clean one) wiped his hands and noted with satisfaction the sheen of sweat on his opponents' faces.

'Mr Kelsey,' said the inspector, 'could you please identify for us what actual harm or disadvantage this development would have on the community? I should emphasize to the listeners that these are your opinions.'

Arcadian's barrister took over, his professional manner suggesting that he was quite used to filleting the opposition.

'Mr Kelsey,' he was deceptively mild, 'am I right in thinking that if the development is accepted you will lose your farm?'

Jed raised the camera to his shoulder and Agnes instructed him in an undertone. The big round eye of the lens followed obediently.

'Mr Stone has served me notice. Yes.'

'Do you like your work? Love it, even?'

'It is my life's work.'

The tone sharpened, carrying a hint of scepticism. 'Then it is fair to say that your opinion will not be unbiased? That you would hardly welcome having to surrender your business, and your arguments against would be motivated by a desire to preserve it?'

Agnes whispered to Jed, who padded down the side aisle. Andrew forced himself to remain calm. 'My business contributes to the community. Even if I wish, which I do, to save my farm from the bulldozers, it does not necessarily mean that my arguments are . . .' he tested the word '. . . invalid.'

'Quite right.' A woman at the back sprang to her feet.

Used to such interruptions, the barrister hardly paused. 'Mr Kelsey, would it be true to say that you could, if necessary, set up the same farm operation somewhere else?'

'Yes, I could, but it would take years to build it up again.'

He was cut short by the barrister. 'Ladies and gentlemen, the facts are here, that Exbury is overcrowded and in need of additional housing, which my clients plan to offer at some cost in order to make as sympathetic and viable a project as possible. It is not in dispute that Mr Kelsey would lose his undoubtedly useful and productive farm but he could move his operations else-where. The question must therefore be, which is of greater benefit to the community? The housing that is required? Or a beef farm run on traditional lines?'

This was it. Andrew found himself on his feet and addressing the audience. 'Remember, these people have no knowledge of the land. They are imports, hired at great cost, and they have to earn their wages. They don't care about our community. Only the profits from it.'

'Oh, really,' said the cool Arcadian barrister. 'May I remind listeners that Mr Kelsey is defending what he perceives as *his* livelihood.'

Andrew swung round, blue eyes blazing, and said, through gritted teeth, 'You sanctimonious bugger.'

At five thirty, the inspector closed the inquiry and requested that all parties opposed to the development should produce a list of conditions that, in their view, should be imposed on the development, if it was allowed to proceed. In addition, there would be a site visit at ten a.m. the following day.

By the time Andrew emerged from the hall Penny had vanished, but Agnes, with a pile of gear at her feet, was waiting.

'Hallo, Andrew.' She shifted a file from under one arm to the other.

Tense and angry, he grasped her by the shoulders and shook her. 'Agnes, I lost it.'

Agnes, Bel and Jed stayed in Exbury's best bed-and-breakfast. Agnes spent a restless night, and at nine thirty, feeling uncharacteristically out of sorts, she drove the other two over to the farm. It was a soft, beautiful day, and the cries of curlews and swallows and cattle noises batted to and fro in the warm air. The back door opened on to an empty kitchen. Agnes stuck her head through the study window. That, too, was empty.

She checked her watch and, taking turns to carry the equipment, set off for the north field. The route took them down the old drovers' road, between hedges so high that it was impossible to see anything except the oblong of sky above.

'Stop,' cried Agnes. There were raised voices, a whine of machinery being driven at high speed, followed by the short, sharp scream of a woman. Agnes broke into a run and, weighed down by the camera, Jed brought up the rear.

Emerging first from the drovers' track, Agnes came to a halt. 'Oh, God,' she said.

The north field had been earmarked by Arcadian Villages to fall first to the developer's bulldozer because it had the most convenient access to the main road. Now its lush, untreated grass, strewn with stars of red poppy and blue cornflower, was a mass of flame.

Smoke wreathed in layers over the field before, marshalled by a thermal, it streamed up towards the moor and into the sky. Under the pall it cast over the field writhed red and gold tongues of fire from seven . . . nine . . . ten bonfires, constructed of stooked straw bales.

Both the women clapped their hands to their mouths and Agnes gagged.

'Weird,' said Bel, a grin streaking across her face.

She beckoned to Jed and pointed out the inspector and a cluster of others by the gate. Andrew was perched on the bonnet of a tractor parked dead centre in the field. It was a mad but valorous sight: the warrior-farmer defending his land against an aggressor armed with plans, statistics and lust for profit.

The first shock over, Agnes snapped to attention. 'Get him up on the tractor, Jed. That's the shot to finish.'

Bel muttered, 'I thought it was Londoners who were supposed to be mad.'

On his tractor podium, Andrew cupped his hands over his mouth and shouted to the inspector and his team. 'This is to remind you that this land does not belong to you.'

Agnes, Bel and Jed joined the planning inquiry group by the gate.

'The man's a lunatic,' Agnes overheard one woman say. 'He nearly killed one of us driving that thing. He could be charged.'

The inspector now conferred with Arcadian Villages' architect, who looked mortified. Indeed, the only person present who appeared happy was the press photographer from the local paper who clicked away with a grin on his face that said front page.

Andrew had orchestrated his demonstration with some sophistication, and chosen his position with care. The tractor was parked so that the doomed oaks and the fields beyond were in the line of vision of the photographers. He cupped his hands and bellowed, 'Are you going to join me, Jim?'

'Sure,' answered Jim, who had driven up from Exbury. He pushed his way through the spectators into the field. 'I'm with you, boy.'

At this point, the press officer for Arcadian Villages took the inspector aside and talked furiously at him. Agnes tapped Jed on the arm. Jed's camera swung around – an eye that accosted the inspector when he looked up. He adjusted his ill-chosen glasses and moved away.

Another man joined Andrew and Jim and took up position, arms folded, by the tractor wheels. Agnes sketched a frame in the air. 'Go in tight, Jed.' Then, 'Jed, I'm going to be sick!' and she fled towards the oaks where she retched up her breakfast. The bout over, she leaned on a trunk for support. A dozen or so pairs of eyes observed her with interest, as she fumbled for a tissue and levered herself upright.

Jed hightailed over. 'Are you OK?'

'Sure. It's the smoke. Where's Bel?' Agnes pressed a hand to her stomach.

'She's talking to the photographer. Apparently most of Exbury is on its way over. I think your friend did some telephoning before he set about burning the county.'

'I expect he did.' Hoping she did not smell too awful, Agnes scraped her hair back from her forehead. 'We ought to be out there with him.'

The bonfire nearest to the inspector collapsed, sending up an additional plume of smoke. The solid rank of spectators sprouted gaps and the inspector ordered the architect to summon the fire brigade.

Penny, who had been rung by Jim and had got herself over to the farm fast, leaving a furious Bob, arrived as the crew from the local television station also pitched up with their van, together with a hard-core group of anti-Arcadian Villages protestors carrying placards.

'Agnes,' Jed grabbed her arm. 'Take a look at the old chap.'

'Oh . . .' Dressed in a tweed jacket and tie, with his trousers hauled up high, a major-general figure stood to attention and saluted the protestors.

The bonfires had been expertly constructed and burned for another good half-hour while television crews, the local press, protestors and the planning-inquiry team got in each other's way. Yet in the end even Andrew's skill could not prevent their metamorphosis into carbon and hot ash. He descended from the tractor and Jim and he set about extinguishing the remnants with the water he had ferried up during the night.

Bile. Ash. Anger.

Agnes abandoned Jed and picked her way over to Andrew. Obviously exhausted and somewhat wary, he watched her approach.

Sweat beaded Agnes's upper lip. 'They don't like it one bit.'

'Did you get it on film?'

She nodded. 'We did.'

The field emptied untidily. Protestors dismantled their banners. The television crew packed up their equipment. The inspector was decanted into his car and driven away. Arcadian's press officer sat in his parked car talking into his mobile phone.

Soon it was empty. A meadow gouged with round, black scars.

'I'm glad you showed up.' Andrew's obvious depression wrenched at Agnes's heart. 'I was hoping you would. I wasn't sure if my little demonstration would embarrass you.'

'Why should it?'

'Because it's not going to achieve anything, except a bit of publicity.'

'Driving your spade into the earth?'

'Something like that.'

She thought for a second or two. 'I hope the programme will do that.'

He said swiftly, 'You can't rely on it. You never know, do you?' She must have looked a little taken aback and he backtracked: 'Actually, my activities last night were the result of a rush of blood to the head.'

They had returned to the farmhouse where Andrew insisted on assembling a scratch meal. They sat at the table eating cheese with stale bread. Jed and Bel had left for London and the editing room. Agnes planned to join them later, via Flagge House, where she would check up on Bea.

'Were you up all night?' Craving something solid, she tackled the tough bread. 'Weren't you worried the fire might get out of control?'

Andrew sawed off a lump of cheese. The question amused him. 'I have a pretty good idea of the land and the weather. The ground's still wet and I may have looked demonic but I was keeping a close eye on everything. Anyway, the boys at the fire station would have been up in a trice if I had given them the word. It *is* still my field, you know.'

She wanted to seize a brush and paint out the circles under his eyes but she confined herself to leaning over and wiping a lick of grime from his cheek. 'Any chance of you getting some sleep?'

Under the light, dispassionate gesture, he stilled. 'Not

yet.' He slumped back in the chair, not exactly beaten but clearly at the edge. 'That barrister knew all the right words. He knew that if he chose the right ones, that would be that and the case is wrapped. If you pay enough for the best manipulator, you get your way. That's justice.'

She continued to chew the bread, praying that it stayed put in her stomach. Andrew stared out of the window. Eventually, she hazarded, 'Work is a good remedy when things go wrong. At least, I found it to be so.'

'You're not giving in?' he asked. 'Not backing off over the film?' His brows snapped together.

'No. For what it's worth, I was offering you the Campion patent for getting through.'

'I'll take your word for it.' He dug his fingers into his sticky, grimy hair. He watched Agnes chew the last of her bread. 'We used to have tea, you know. Every day. High tea. With scones and cream. Cake. Sometimes one of Penny's hams. She was good at all that. Penny had a picture of what life should be on the farm, which meant a lot to her. She made it work.'

He appeared to lose interest in the subject. 'Do you think it's too early for a whisky?' He fetched the bottle and two glasses. Agnes took a sip and realized it was a mistake, but Andrew sucked down several mouthfuls.

He stumbled through a confession and retraced the night's events. The loading of the trailer, the drive in the dark, the stacking of the bales. Sweating and cursing.

The wait. 'I had gone to war. With my own land.' He pushed his glass aside. 'I ought to check on the fires before I get down to everything else. Do you want to come?'

Leaving the door wide open, they exchanged the muddle and incipient loss threatening the farmhouse kitchen for the heat of a summer's day. The smell of burning was still almost sickening and the van was powdered with ash. Yet the day was quiet and clear, and the sun strong. Up on the moor, the heat and light had played tricks: bleaching out the colours and pushing them back into the far distance.

They retraced the path to the north field. Thickened by spiky growth, the hedgerow was wreathed in pale pink dog rose and honeysuckle. Andrew unsheathed his knife and cut off a length of the latter. 'Here.' He twined it into a rough crown. 'Come here, Agnes.'

Drawn by the heat, the wild, fresh smells, the sound of skylarks, she moved obediently towards him.

'Here.' He placed the crown on her head, pressing it down over her forehead until she felt the sticky sap spread over her skin.

He assessed his handiwork.

She smiled up into the blue eyes and it must have been an invitation for he bent over and kissed her on the mouth. And she thought, *Why not*? Not being hampered by love had the effect of making her more curious, less flattened by emotion. Andrew smelt of fire, straw, sweat and whisky, and by inhaling these scents of earth and land and in kissing him she was taking a step to shake herself free of the ghosts.

'You taste of summer.' He kissed the hollow of her neck.

The crown of honeysuckle seemed faintly ridiculous and she took it off. 'You're very unusual, Andrew.' She coloured. 'I mean, it's nice.'

'Kissing someone is not so odd, is it?' His strange intense expression was now replaced by the more normal flush of an aroused male.

'No.'

He defused the awkwardness that had sprung up. 'Come on, you can't leave Tithings without visiting the bees. This is my party piece.'

Agnes allowed herself to be drawn towards them through the scented air. 'Quiet,' he ordered.

She strained to hear, and rising from the hives was a murmur. 'What is it?'

'They're cooling the hives. It's hot and they've been making honey.'

Agnes was fascinated. 'They are extraordinary insects. They seem to have worked out how to live with each other.'

'At a price,' Andrew reminded her. 'They kill off the drones.'

'Even so.' Inside the hives, the bees stepped up the fanning. Higher and faster.

'If you come closer you can smell the particular forage for the day.'

She obeyed and caught the scent of wildness. Grasses, white clover, wild thyme. There *were* other possibilities, she thought. Unfolding wings that could liberate her.

He cleared his throat and she sensed what was coming. 'Stay here tonight, Agnes.'

She traced the knotty joint of his broken finger with her own and experienced the panic of making a decision for which she was not ready. 'Could you wait before I answer,' she said.

## 20

*Friday.*

'Do we want the electrolysis today?'

The beautician was new to the salon in Lymouth, obviously bored and more than a little distasteful of the tasks that she was paid to perform. Kitty requested the hand mirror and scanned her top lip for any traces of unwanted hair. You could never be sure when the markers of lost youth and dwindling hormones became obvious to everyone else. Because she did not want to see, Kitty knew she must ask to be told the truth.

Yes. There was one wispy hair and she directed the beautician to run the machine. The tiny prick hurt far more than its allocated franchise of pain. It hurt Kitty because it had been necessary.

'I think,' said the beautician, who was reduced to a huge eye looking at Kitty through the magnifying light, 'we should zap a few veins as well. Are you happy for me to do them?'

'I suppose so.'

That process was far more uncomfortable, especially in areas near the nose where Kitty was sensitive. The electric current aggravated the nerves and she ended up sneezing and weeping a stream of tears. Tomorrow, she knew from experience, would be bad and her skin would be blotchy and raised. Still, the situation was manageable for Julian had rung to say that there was an emergency board meeting, which was scheduled to continue through the weekend. 'Sorry, darling, it can't be helped. I'll explain when I see you.'

At first, Kitty had wanted to protest but then a great weariness with the condition of her life sapped her will. She made no comment, except to say that she was sorry and, of course, he must do as he wished.

*And she should do as she wished?*

Catching her at odd moments, these infant stirrings of protest were in danger of becoming the norm, and Kitty discovered that she relished them, welcomed them, even. They introduced a different note into the familiar lament in her head, of which she was growing tired. But for the irritants of the machine, the shuffle of the beautician's clogs and the smell of burnt capillary, she was entirely at liberty to think as she wished.

She flexed her finger, and felt the slick of moisture from the cream that had been applied. What was she doing engaged in pushing back time? Perhaps . . . here Kitty strained for the right words . . . perhaps, in itself, that was a waste of time. Perhaps she was wasting time in tackling it.

'Dear me,' said the beautician. 'These are toughies. Have you been sitting in the sun?'

The needle dug into the flesh of Kitty's cheek. After all, she *could* choose not to engage in such a difficult –

no, impossible – battle. Beauty, Kitty had learned in the hard school of survival, was in the eye of the beholder and mattered. Forget the nonsense about inner beauty, a thesis peddled only, she noticed, by those who had no pretensions to looks. Certainly, in the past, Kitty had ignored it in favour of the philosophy that worked. And yet, now that she was growing older, it was going to fail her.

Under the pink blanket, Kitty sighed and entertained the radical vision of life uncluttered by considerations of her beauty. No Friday preparations. No covert glances in the mirror. A mind washed clean and free of the tyranny of scrutiny.

Yes, she *was* free to be free, if she wished.

The beautician embarked on the final challenge of Kitty's left cheek. But it was not as simple as that. Kitty loved Julian and, to be free, it would be necessary not to love him.

'Leg wax?' intoned the beautician.

Kitty stretched out a slim leg in the manner of the sacrificial victim.

After the session was over, she went home to hide her blotched skin. At one o'clock she switched on the radio in her kitchen and listened to the news as she spooned up very clear, ultra-slimming consommé. But it was not filling and she was still ravenous. Normally she ignored growls in her stomach – the serpent that signalled her emptiness and her struggle for mastery – but today her hand crept towards the cupboard where she kept a tin of rice pudding as an emergency for Theo. At first it felt cold and smooth in her hand but, under her prolonged handling, this way and that – *shall I, shall I not?* – the metal warmed up.

Flinging open the kitchen drawer, Kitty scrabbled for the tin-opener.

The rice was delicious, a taste she had forgotten. Once eaten, it sat in a nourishing heap in her body, as heavy as if she were carrying a child. When she threw away the tin the serrations on the lid caught the flesh on one of her fingers. The taste of blood as she licked it mingled with the honeyed pleasure of the rice.

When Theo arrived, he peered at Kitty, who was wrapping her finger with Elastoplast. 'You look awful. Tell a fella.'

But she could see from the unfocused cast of Theo's expression that he was slipping into one of his phases and, if she required his comfort (as she so often did), she must catch him quickly.

It was too late. Theo had 'vanished'. Kitty was concerned that the warden in charge had not spotted what was happening before sending him out but at least she knew what to do. Talking softly, she prised the bag from his hands and sat him down at the table.

'Tablets, Theo. Where are they?' She searched in the bag and extracted a couple of bottles, read the labels, shook out the correct one and gave it to him with a glass of water. Then she stood, massaging his terrifyingly tense shoulders, muttering words of comfort, until the drug kicked in and his shoulders relaxed a fraction. On previous occasions, Theo would get up, rummage in his bag, extract the weapons – the cleaning materials – with which he managed his illness, and proceed to batter the house with dusters.

'*Battering the bastards,*' he explained. 'The ones that live uninvited in my head.'

Kitty was proud of the way she managed Theo and, in a curious way, grateful to him for his permission to do so. It implied trust and affection. It showed her that there were possibilities in strange places. 'Don't let them get you, Theo,' she cried now, her fingers kneading and soothing. She added feebly, 'I need you.'

'I'll try, darl . . .' Theo muttered, through the muddle in his head. For Kitty, as he had once confided, was the only person in the world he loved without reservation. By taking him on, she had rescued him at a time when he was plunging lower and lower. Kitty was the one person for whom he would make the effort to be normal.

Thank God, she had thought when, blinking hard with the effort, Theo told her how he felt. Thank God I won't go to my grave completely untouched by unselfish love.

Still rubbing away at the tortured back muscles, she bent over Theo and smiled at him, and Theo felt cool, soft rain fall on his parched interior.

Eventually, he pulled himself upright and looked up at Kitty with reddened eyes. 'Pass my bag, darl . . .'

He got up and began to attack the kitchen windows. Soon, they were glittering and shining like the most innocent of lives.

*Saturday.*

Kitty's skin throbbed and smarted, but Theo rang to say he felt better, and to thank her, and he would see her later at the Huntingdons. Today was a flower day and Kitty, whose skill at flower arrangement was legendary, had been invited – well, commanded – by Vita Huntingdon to arrange the flowers for the fashionable evening wedding of her daughter. And, of course, ever anxious to keep what social foothold she had gained, she had meekly agreed.

'You will understand,' Vita had explained, 'that we can't invite you to the actual do. Numbers, you know. But, please, feel free to take a peek at the buffet and presents while we're in church.'

'Shall we peek?' Kitty asked Theo.

'Will we hell,' said Theo.

Vita had requested pink and white flowers to match the striped marquee lining and the gilt chairs. Her daughter had demanded something more exciting and original. 'You know,' she suggested vaguely, 'some of those South African numbers.' Theo and Kitty had conferred and, disgracefully, she took a small and delightful revenge by creating an undisputedly stunning but, nevertheless, predominantly yellow and white display.

'Like the Aussie sun,' Theo pronounced, heaving the last vase into place. 'You can't miss it.'

'Have we peeked enough, Theo?'

'Are you ever afraid,' asked Theo, as Kitty drove him back to the hostel, 'that one of these days I might grow violent and do you in?'

The notion had crossed Kitty's mind more than once. 'Not really. Provided you did it quickly enough, I wouldn't have time to object.' She turned into the high street. 'Promise me, Theo, that if you do it, it will be quick.'

'I promise.' Shoulders hunched up to his ears, Theo stared straight ahead. 'Fish and chips, darl?'

That night when she was half asleep, Kitty experienced what she later referred to as a vision. In it, she was floating high in the sky and looking down at a very blue, very calm sea and herself on what she presumed was a life-raft. She expected to be out of control but, strangely, she was very much in charge and heading out towards the open sea and stagey setting sun, hair streaming out behind her in the wind. Hair that – perhaps in the most telling detail of all – had reverted to its natural colour of mouse brown.

*Sunday.*

Kitty got up and had breakfast of muesli and coffee then went upstairs to change into her raspberry linen suit. She brushed her hair at the dressing-table, this way and that – one Kitty, two Kitty, three Kitty, four – and anchored it with a pair of combs.

She glanced at the bed. Julian did not sleep here often because he found the house too constricting. Instead, he slept in his own bed at Cliff House whenever possible, arranged on his right side, the pillow bunched to support his cheek. Sometimes his neck was dark with sweat, sometimes his pyjamas fell open, like those of a little boy. Sometimes, he hunched his shoulders and muttered. She had grown used to studying the language of his sleep. He muttered when he was bothered. The deep sleep of renewal came after a hard week. Or there was the heavy unconsciousness after sex.

She did not look at the bed again but concentrated on producing the Kitty she knew and trusted. At last she was done, and pleased with the results. Before she left the room, she fastened the window tight and locked it.

Kitty sat in the car and stared ahead. She placed her hands on the wheel, then removed them. She rubbed them together. She opened her handbag and reapplied her lipstick. Again she rubbed her hands. Then stretching out the right, she turned the key in the ignition.

Half an hour later, she nosed her car up the drive of Flagge House and, at the first sight of the pink brick and elegant windows, perceived at once that it was an ageing prima donna of a house demanding love and attention. It was beautiful, old and sure in itself, but in need of maintenance and a face-lift.

She lifted her foot off the accelerator. The words that had seemed so urgent and rapier sharp when she had rehearsed them were vanishing. She had been so sure when she embarked on her 'raft', so energized, but now she suspected she had been guilty of a terrible misjudgement and if Julian *ever* discovered . . .

Impatient with herself, she stopped the car in the drive and rested her head on the steering-wheel. Out of the corner of her eye, she caught the deep blood-red of summer poppies blooming in the field up on the ridge. It was not a colour she liked – the blood-red of childbirth and of her own cycles, which were . . . coming to their end.

Kitty forced herself to look up at the house. Moss and lichen had built pathways across the flagstones and, above the front door, open windows glinted in the sunshine. There was one way out of the struggle, a way that would bring her peace. All she had to do was walk inside, up the stairs . . . and jump. So easy. And the grey-green of the moss would deceive her on the way down that she would land on a soft, springy bed and sleep.

The first wife offering her blood for the second – for she knew, oh, she knew, that Agnes was no ordinary threat. She wasn't We Will Go Our Own Way For A Time. She was the darkness that Kitty must face.

Wasn't that the way it went? First wives were supposed to go quietly, weren't they? But she wasn't a wife. She had been the mistress of Robin and Harry and Charles, those very married men who had kept her in the style she had demanded.

Would she look as good in death as in life? For the

stones out there were hard, unforgiving and, besides, it took years of practice to be a martyr.

A car manoeuvred alongside Kitty and stopped. The driver wound down his window and asked, 'Can I help you?'

It was Freddie who, at some cost to his Sunday beauty sleep, had come to keep his dear ladies company at lunch. He parked and introduced himself.

'I'm not expected,' Kitty said, as he helped her negotiate the gravel in her high heels.

'All the better.' Freddie rang the bell. 'That's what makes life interesting.'

'I'm not quite sure Agnes will see it that way,' said Kitty drily and looked up to the exquisite fan-light above the door.

## 21

Agnes stifled a yawn and glanced up from the Sunday papers at the mantelpiece on which she had arranged family photographs. There weren't many left in their thinning family. She yawned a second time and frowned. Feeling bushed in the aftermath of a big shoot was normal but this was different. An anchor had attached itself to her body, a great hobbling fatigue. This is what ill people must feel, she thought, with a quiver of unease. Since her return from Devon her body seemed to be changing, urging itself into a different way of behaving. Even her hair felt different.

Andrew had not been too disappointed when she answered, 'No,' to his request to stay, but she sensed that he flinched inwardly and was sorry. As best she could, she explained it was impossible to do anything but go slowly. She had learned that a little at a time had a better chance of succeeding. Andrew had been understanding and sensible, but when she got into the car, he grabbed her hand.

'You won't let me down over the film. *Promise?*'

The women were sitting in the big drawing room, which Agnes insisted they use. It was too beautiful to leave empty, she had argued. 'We live in this house.

We are not lodgers or squatters.' Maud and she had quarrelled about it, and Maud had eventually declared that Agnes must do as she liked, *as she held all the purse strings*, but she would not raise one finger to help. Agnes had had the curtains cleaned, the cornices brushed, and had polished the furniture with a mixture of turpentine and wax.

'Time for the *apéritif*?' Accompanied by the paraphernalia of the invalid, which included a walking-stick – of which she made cunning use – plus an electric alarm, Maud had progressed from the bedroom to the blue brocade sofa. There she sat, enthroned but still bad-tempered and weak, the velocity of her knitting increasing to a ferocious speed.

Agnes cupped her chin in her hand. Maud had been a bad patient and a worse convalescent, and Agnes and Bea had been run ragged by her demands. But Agnes had felt sorry for her aunt. Maud had been terrified by her experience, and the equation had been made that once you were dead you had gone. 'Before you are cold, you are forgotten,' she said, 'the waters close over,' and she wasn't ready for that by a long chalk.

Sunday lunch was cooking. The shutters in the drawing room at the big window were folded back and the sun streamed in. Well away from her sister, Bea sat by the window, hands folded in her lap. She seemed peaceful enough, and yet, as she squinted in Bea's direction, it struck Agnes that she was waiting for something.

On a previous visit, Freddie gently suggested that

Maud should try another musical, just for fun. What Freddie said usually resulted in magic and, for a time, the strains of *Les Misérables* replaced Julie Andrews in Flagge House. But the status quo soon reverted and once again raindrops and kittens filled the drawing room.

'I will never understand what you see in it,' said Agnes, driven to protest.

'I don't expect you to understand.' Maud threw down her knitting, consulted her watch and reached for her lipstick. 'Freddie will be here any minute.'

Bea pleated the material of her skirt, and the dust motes danced in the sun.

The doorbell rang. 'I'll go,' said Bea, and fled from the room.

A moment later Agnes, who was stacking the Sunday papers, looked up to see a poised, groomed Kitty in a pink linen suit preceding Freddie. To be with Kitty, even without Julian, in the same room did extraordinary things to her stomach and, for a moment, she thought she might faint. Fortunately, the cotton wool in her knees turned into proper muscle and she got to her feet.

'Hello, Agnes,' said Kitty, and flushed a violent red. 'I am sorry to drop in on you without warning. I would very much appreciate a few words.'

'Of course,' said Agnes.

'Is a chap going to be offered a drink?' asked Freddie.

Bea waylaid Kitty. 'Sherry? This is some from my special bottle. I have a kind man who sells it to me in the wine shop. Where have you come from?'

'I've intruded on a lunch party?' Kitty's poise appeared to desert her and she had gone from very red to very pale.

'The more the merrier.' Freddie presumed on his intimacy to good effect. 'Now, how are my ladies?'

Maud raised her head – the gesture of a younger woman which, in a younger woman, would have accentuated a swan neck. Her huge eyes were hungry and watchful. She tapped her watch. 'Hallo, Freddie. We've been waiting all morning for you.'

Agnes gathered her wits. 'Could you stay for lunch, Kitty?'

Kitty had already downed the sherry and Bea was refilling her glass. 'Actually, I only wanted a few words.'

'Lymouth,' Bea was saying. 'I had a friend there once. A champion jam-maker.' In Bea's book there was no greater compliment, a reminder that the world functioned on casseroles, jams and knitted rugs, a sub-stratum of thrift and skills that still held their own.

Jam-making was not a feature of Kitty's world or Agnes's. Their eyes met in mutual ratification of this fact. Antagonists but, briefly, allies.

'Could I use your bathroom?' asked Kitty.

Agnes led the other woman past the burnt-in hoofprint and the empty niche at the turn of the stairs, past the exquisite oriel window. Kitty put out a hand to the newel post. 'Someone loved this wood.' She ran her fingers over its curves. 'Very much.' She paused under the window.

There was silence.

Kitty continued, 'We only borrow houses for a while and then we hand them on.' Her high heels clattered on the stairs. 'You didn't see my cottage when you came down. It's tiny. Julian doesn't like it very much. He prefers Cliff House. If I'm truthful, so do I.'

Agnes showed Kitty the bathroom and suggested that they talk in her bedroom. When Kitty knocked and slipped into the room, Agnes was waiting by the window. She addressed Kitty calmly: 'The best view of the river is from my aunt's room, but this one is pretty good. On still nights I can hear the running water and, sometimes, foxes.'

'Really?' Kitty straightened her shoulders.

Agnes continued, 'This is the bedroom in which the maiden aunts always slept. One of them, Great-great-aunt Lucy, slept here for the whole of her life. I found her riding boots at the back of the wardrobe. So slim, they were like pencils.' Reluctantly, Agnes faced Kitty. 'I think they were happy in here, the maiden aunts. I feel they were.'

Kitty now patted her hair, her wrist weighed down with a gold charm bracelet. Oval-nailed and fine-skinned, they were the kind of hands the Victorians would have delighted in casting in plaster and displaying in glass cabinets. Then she fussed with her bracelets. 'It's obvious why I'm here, isn't it?'

'Yes.'

'So.' Now Kitty smoothed the strap of her handbag. 'Let's get on with it. I want – I want you to leave Julian alone. I thought I had made that clear at our previous meeting, but not clear enough. Anyway, it's worse than I thought, for I can see . . . I know that he is very taken with you. It doesn't often happen, although there have been . . . others. He's quite – quite reserved.' She paused, and said simply, 'But he's mine. We've been together for a long time and that counts for something, don't you think? You've seen enough in your work to know what goes wrong when people take things that don't belong to them.'

Agnes swallowed.

'You are there in my home all the time,' cried Kitty. 'All the time. I know you are. He's obsessed with you.' She brought herself up short. 'But other things matter too . . .'

Yes, yes, I am wrong. Without meaning to be so. Truly, truly, without intent, I have blundered into being put in the wrong and heaven knows where that leaves Julian. Didn't he think that ten years of reward points earns a tranquil old age? Kitty does. That is why she is here. And me? Never mind that the blossom on the tree is so scented, so beautiful, so tempting.

'. . . All I need,' the soft, inexorable voice of Kitty drove on, 'is a little peace. Then I can manage. Then I can pull it together.'

Agnes was shaking. Not even when faced with

Madeleine had her reaction been so marked. Of course Kitty was in the right and the complications stretched out in great web of misunderstanding and crossed connections. Yet . . . there was nothing in this world that belonged exclusively to someone else and she was tempted, almost, to conclude that it was a question of who was the stronger. She heard herself saying, 'Isn't that up to Julian?'

Kitty shook her head. 'It's taken me a long time to discover this. Ten years, in fact, but no. *I* have a say in it too.'

'I understand.' This was the real battle, the big one. Compared to this, the others had been skirmishes, and she felt quite breathless with pain.

She turned to face Kitty, the pink and fragile Kitty, who had chosen to confront Agnes at Flagge House because . . . of the shared bed, because the moments of despair were shared equally with moments of pleasure and content. Because what Kitty had built she was not going to allow Agnes to knock down. Because Kitty had made an act of will to fight and now chose to exercise it.

'You might not believe this, Kitty, but I did consider you,' she said at last. 'Ask Julian.'

Kitty's handbag was a crocodile one with gold fastenings. It slipped with a clunk to the floor. 'I don't want your name mentioned by him ever again.' She bent over to pick it up. *'Ever.'*

'Will you go now?'

Kitty joined Agnes at the window. 'How I dislike your type. Nothing personal, of course.'

'My type?'

'Women who have no investment in anything. You younger women imagine you have it sewn up. You have recast your role and have made it your business to pity women like me. Oh, I don't mind the careers and the money-making. I had my chance, I suppose. But I do mind your greed and the way you trespass on us because your bodies are younger and firmer and you have no rules.'

Agnes made to turn away but the other woman grabbed her. 'You will listen to me. You are younger but you have no idea. Yet.' She released Agnes, and fiddled with the ring on her right hand. 'I even thought about killing myself because I find the situation so exhausting and unfair, and it would pay you back.' The confidence was dropped clumsily. 'But I won't. I won't.'

Appalled, Agnes placed her hand on Kitty's shoulder and pressed it. Thin and sharp and brittle beneath her *younger* – and therefore, more powerful – fingers. Those fingers now bore down into Kitty. 'Just go, Kitty. Now. Before anything else is said or done.'

Kitty struggled for control. After a few seconds, she asked in a normal voice, 'Do you mind if I do my hair?' She sat down at Agnes's dressing table and pulled off her earrings. 'These ones always hurt. I don't know why I wear them. Well, I do, actually. Julian gave them to me.' She picked up Agnes's hairbrush. Agnes flinched. How dare Kitty touch her things? Kitty examined it thoughtfully, opened her handbag and extracted her own.

The mirror was old and spotted with age and the reflection in it was unclear. Deft and skilled, Kitty worked away at her hair and traced the line of her lips with a lip pencil, remaking the pretty object. She assessed her handiwork. 'Julian is difficult.' She trailed the sentence, releasing her insider knowledge in a tantalizing fashion. 'Pernickety. Demanding. He has his moods . . . and his tastes. I always make an effort.'

Agnes pictured Julian sitting on the sofa in Bel's flat, balancing a glass on the arm. He was talking about the Lincolnshire project, pulsing with attack and energy, one leg crossed over the other. She closed her eyes. It had been then that she had noticed he was wearing socks whose wool had worn thin with age under the impeccable suit.

'No, Julian is not easy. He works to his own timetable.' Kitty closed her handbag with a snap. 'Thank you so much for letting me freshen up. I'll find my own way out.'

What did Kitty think she was doing with her poisoned drip, drip of intimacies? Perhaps, she imagined that she had wrestled Agnes into a boneless heap on the floor where she could administer a kick with her crocodile shoes. Agnes's emotions did an abrupt change-about. There was a rush of waves in her head, the screech of a million small stones pulled into the riptide and she felt the cold, salt shock of her anger. 'There is one thing . . .' Ever after, she was never to be quite sure of anything, least of all herself. 'One thing . . .' Clearly expecting to hear Agnes's final capitulation, Kitty was arrested with her hand on the door handle.

'I think I'm pregnant!' Agnes cried out, in protest and despair.

Kitty fled down the stairs and into the still summer afternoon.

'Why did she tell me?' she sobbed in the safety of her car. 'Why did she *tell* me?'

Above her, the wood pigeons cooed and fluttered in the trees.

## 22

The following morning Agnes made her way down Charlborough's main street to the surgery, a modern building perched on the outskirts of the Bee Orchid housing estate.

Duggie Sutherland had been taking care of Agnes since she was twelve and knew her every nook and cranny well enough to ask any question he pleased. Duggie hated the new surgery and longed to be back in the cramped, damp rooms he had once occupied before they metamorphosed into a Group Practice. 'How's the air-conditioning?' she teased, knowing that it sent him into a frenzy.

'Do not ask.' He did a quick test and it did not take him long to confirm what Agnes suspected. 'About seven weeks.'

In the clinical surgery, the confirmation seemed so matter-of-fact with none of the panic and disbelief of the past few weeks. Agnes slid back into her T-shirt. 'Sod's law of averages,' she remarked. 'It happened only once after months of abstinence.'

'Hold out your arm.' He attached the blood-pressure equipment. 'This is not a scientific answer, Agnes, but it could be because you were ready.'

'*That's* pop psychology, Duggie.'

'Why didn't you come to see me at once? Or anyone?'

She looked down at her lap. 'You know what they say about people in burning houses hiding under beds and in cupboards?'

'No. Tell me about it. You might like to know that your blood pressure is down in your boots, which will be making you feel a bit odd. It will readjust in a couple of weeks.' He chucked her under the chin. 'Optimism, my girl. New life.'

She sat down on the chair by his desk while he wrote up the notes. 'Duggie, I find the prospect of having a baby terrifying. I wasn't planning it. I'm not ready . . .' She pulled desperately on a strand of hair. 'I wasn't envisaging this bit of biology being thrust on me quite yet.'

He put his head to one side.

She knew what he was going to say. 'No,' she said sadly. 'Don't even think it, Duggie. I can't have an abortion or send it away. I couldn't. I haven't managed much in the way of coherent thought but I just know I couldn't do it.' She shrugged. 'More fool me.' She tugged at her hair and winced. 'How typical of Nature to make a muddle.'

'Or you,' suggested Duggie.

She pushed her plait back over her shoulder, dug her hands into her linen skirt pockets and sent him a tiny, tremulous smile. 'Point taken.'

She pictured herself bowed down with a buggy,

nappies in a bag, a baby on a hip, encumbered and struggling with the tired, I-can't-take-much-more expression she had so often seen on mothers. They looked so battered, so shell-shocked and resentful. 'I don't want this baby, Duggie. I don't know how I'm going to manage and I can't feel anything for it except terminal crossness with myself.'

He tucked her notes into the folder. 'Is the father involved?'

'No, he isn't.'

Later, Agnes knelt by her bed – a old, childish pose, long discarded. She rested her head on its hard edge and the position soothed the nausea that tormented her.

*Why did I tell Kitty?*

The clear motives and clear vision had vanished. So had the Agnes who knew what was what, who believed in the rules. In their place was confusion. How could she have done what she had done?


On Thursday, Kitty left a message for Julian at the office with Angela to say that she would be coming up to London for the evening and that he was not to worry about supper. He returned to the flat in the Barbican to find the table laid with candles and flowers and Kitty busy in the kitchen.

It had been an awful day and he craved peace and quiet, but he forced himself to look pleased. 'Have I missed a birthday or something?'

She put a couple of steaks under the grill. 'Hallo,

darling. I hope you don't mind. I'll be gone in the morning and I won't see you at the weekend.'

Kitty never went away without elaborate checking and cross-checking. Presumably he was being sent a signal about which he had no inkling and, at this precise moment, no curiosity either. Kitty fiddled with the cutlery. Expectant.

'Where are you going?'

Kitty's expression was the one she assumed when she was giving him a present. 'I'm going to be checked out at a clinic.' She bent down to look at the meat. 'To see if everything is working.'

'Oh, Kitty.'

She turned away to attend to the salad in the sink. 'I just want to be sure, Julian. Before it's too late.'

All he could see was her averted back. 'Kitty, please stop doing that and look at me.' Obediently, she turned round. 'Now, listen. You don't really want children, do you?'

She fiddled with the gold chain at her throat. 'But I think you do, Julian. You admitted it that time when we talked before.'

'That was just an aside. I didn't expect you to take me so literally.'

'Asides are often very telling.'

Kitty was on form. *Full marks, Kitty.* He studied the expression on the flawless features and saw a new stubbornness. 'But you can't construct an entire case around a remark.'

'Don't be pompous, Julian.'

'Am I? Sorry.'

Kitty picked up the salad dressing. 'Think about the theory of evolution you're so interested in. I've thought about it, Julian, carefully. It must have occurred to you – and you were sweet to understand my wishes in the past – to understand what sort of woman I am, but one of the fundamentals must be to reproduce. It's taken me a bit of time to work it out. But that makes it sound so clinical. It isn't meant to be like that.' Under the grill the meat was spitting and she dived towards it. 'I would like to give you what you want.'

'Kitty, this is madness.'

She straightened up, flushed and, clearly, already pregnant with this new development in their strange life together. 'No, it isn't. It's just another stage.'

In the office the next morning, Angela appeared in skin-tight shiny trousers and a little jacket and informed Julian that Harold wished to see him urgently.

Harold approached his boss with the wariness of the messenger who understands there is a more than even chance he will have turned into the kill by the end of the interview. If he had not known what was coming, Julian might have been amused.

'Julian, I can't make those figures work as you asked. In particular, the Lincolnshire figures. They don't look good.'

He slid papers on to the desk and Julian gave them

a quick once-over. 'You're wrong, Harold. It's not a question of them not looking good. They're disastrous.'

'I think I meant that.'

'Well? Can I have a breakdown?'

Harold looked even worse. 'For example, the Lincolnshire project. The take-up on the houses is less than a third. That means . . .' He cleared his throat. 'It means only thirty houses have been sold, and none of the ones in the higher bracket price range. We needed to sell sixty-five to achieve the margin. I've run a check on the local employment figures. Not good. The young are moving south to look for jobs and agricultural wages have hit rock bottom. The upturn we calculated on has not happened.'

Julian informed Harold that he could add to the list of woes. A letter had come in from Bristling's factory, who had decided to pull the plug on the Lincolnshire project for precisely the same reasons.

Harold was trying hard to keep some sort of control. 'Protest is also building over the Sussex site. The antis have discovered that the houses would be built on part of an old smugglers' route. The heritage people are jumping up and down.' Harold dug his hands into the pockets of his fashionable linen suit.

'I believe it,' said Julian.

The two men were silent.

'Maybe,' offered Harold, 'we could palm off the Lincolnshire project on the council.'

'I think not.'

Julian took another look at the figures. If a profit warning on the next quarter's results was going to be necessary, then the share price would be affected. He ordered Harold to arrange a couple of emergency meetings and to get himself a cup of coffee. Harold disappeared.

Although he had known for some months that this might happen, Julian needed a few minutes' grace. Daily, he had watched the figures, adjusting projections here, strategy there, but his fire-fighting tactics had not been sufficient.

At some point, he had made a mistake and, like the gene pool heading for extinction, taken the wrong turning. Nothing overtly dramatic, but decisive nevertheless. Kitty had talked about evolution, and wrong turnings littered evolutionary history. He was desperate for this not to happen to Portcullis. Nor should it have done so. In theory the genes for survival were in place – his team, their experience, the backers and shareholders. Surely it was a question of reshaping projections and vision to fit into an altered context. Yes. He must act. He *would* act. He spread his fingers along the edge of the desk and pressed down hard to release the pressure in his shoulders, then rang for Angela.

Thus, Julian went into battle to hammer a rescue package into shape.

By the end of the day, he was exhausted, all attack played out. Gradually, the building emptied, leaving a series of lit rooms. Julian got up, extracted a bottle of whisky from the cabinet and poured himself a slug.

Much later still, he picked up his papers, stowed them in his briefcase and left the office. He needed to go home, to his real home, and the need was so powerful that he could think of nothing else.

When he arrived he found he was almost gasping with relief.

Inside Cliff House, the heat had gathered and the rooms were stifling. Julian flung open the windows one by one and let fresher salt air stream in. He leaned on the window-sill and listened for a long time to the sea. He may have lost his way temporarily in the City's wild and dangerous waters but he had returned to this anchorage. As he always did.

Then he went to bed.

Agnes spent a good part of Saturday morning recovering from the morning nausea. This was of a different variety from the one that floored her late in the afternoon and different again from the late evening bout that Mother Nature slipped in for good measure before bed. So far, she had tried everything: eating cream crackers, no breakfast (that had been bad), a brisk walk, copious amounts of food. Nothing helped and, struggling to achieve all that she had to do, Agnes was astonished that reproduction ever took place, because it was so awful.

She was in the study preparing for a day of financial

planning. Probate was through, and she had to face the problems that riddled Flagge House.

Money? Yesterday she had endured a session with Mr Dawkins and the bank manager, and walked over the house with Mr Harvey to work out the priorities. In the Action file on the desk lay various forms for grant applications, all complicated.

She slid her fingers inside the waistband of her trousers and pulled at it gently to give her growing stomach a breathing space. An unseen agency had packed her head with wet wool wadding and reduced her concentration to the level of the average rabbit.

Should she tell Julian about the baby? Surely the tiny package of cells growing inside her had rights. 'Picture your baby,' she would say. 'A smart, hungry, demanding squaller who needs you. When you look back over your life, you will want him or her in the family photos. In place, and part of you. You will have wanted to stand on the rugby touchline cheering him on, or to have ferried a daughter to a late, late party in an unsuitable new dress. Little things that make the throat prick with tears and pride and which make the photograph more alive and better than the one without them.'

The shabbiness of telling and distressing Kitty shamed her; her weakness in having done so shamed her – and she feared the future to which she saw no solution. But she longed to see Julian, with a miserable, aching longing.

She looked round the study, still cluttered with her

uncle's things. A massacre in Africa, dying children, whale slaughter – these and other outrages she had tackled in her work, grown angry over and recorded so that others might feel the same. Yet the terrible truth was that when it came to this point, her own predicament and desires won out.

Agnes picked up the phone and dialled.


An hour later, she drove up to Cliff House, where Julian was waiting.

On the phone, she had said simply, 'It's me.'

There was a pause. 'Agnes, I'm so glad you rang. Can you come down here. Just for the afternoon. Please.'

She hesitated. 'Actually, I did want to discuss something with you.'

*'Please.'*

So there she was at Cliff House and he was opening the door of the car. He bent over and touched her hair. 'You don't look well. Are you all right?'

'And you? You look awful too.' He shrugged. 'Kitty?'

'She's away.'

Julian took Agnes's hand and led her through the house.

Lunch was waiting on a table under an umbrella on the terrace. They sat down and Julian passed her a spinach salad. 'All my own work. Tell me what you've been doing. Is your aunt better?'

The conversation was heavy with the unsaid. They

exchanged news but it was not until he had drunk half a bottle of wine that Julian told her about Portcullis. He was concerned but resolute. 'I've had to do some thinking. I confess that I had been led to believe in my own myth. I wanted to believe in it. But financial pratfalls happen in a business life, and more people struggle back from the brink than is supposed.' He looked over to Agnes. 'Unfortunately there's a good chance that I will fail the people I employ.'

Agnes reached over and held his hand. It seemed to comfort him. 'I'm sorry.' The telephone rang but Julian ignored it. It rang and rang, then went silent.

Agnes stirred in her seat. 'Where is Kitty exactly?'

Julian frowned. 'She's gone to a clinic – the subject of children seems to have come up. Look, I don't want to discuss Kitty's business.'

She looked down at the table littered with the remains of their lunch. Her baby needed a champion too, she thought passionately, and she was all it had. 'But we must talk about it. What is Kitty doing?'

He turned his head abruptly away from her and she tumbled to the fact that he hated to be confronted.

'She thinks we ought to try for a baby.'

She felt the sun beat down on her skin. 'Do you want children?'

He stirred restlessly. 'Actually, I think I do.'

'So Kitty is going to try to give you one.' Cold in the sun, Agnes put down her fork. She remembered a famous novelist once saying: 'Relations with people never finish, only stories have an ending.' Clever Kitty. She understood the precept so well. Faced with Agnes, the enemy, the pregnant enemy, she had gone underground. Kitty was a natural *résistante*. Oh, clever Kitty, for she had ensured that if she became pregnant Agnes could not possibly take Julian away. Kitty held the prior claim.

Between them they could bat babies back and forth like balls. Not my baby, she thought tiredly. It is not going to be treated like that.

Later, Julian fetched a rug and spread it in the shade by the long grass. The sun was blazing, the sea had calmed to a murmur and, far out, white-sailed boats tacked to and fro. Sleepy and full, they stretched out on the rug and Julian's arm cradled her head. 'You must sleep and get rid of those shadows under your eyes.' He kissed her eyelids. 'Then you'll feel better.'

She obeyed, and drowsiness crept through her limbs, anchoring them with a delicious lassitude.

When she woke, the sun had moved and her arms were flushed pink. Dazzled by the light and by sleep, she turned her head to encounter Julian's next to hers. 'Magic.' Her gaze alighted on the long grass. Each blade seemed extra sharp. Some were rolled as tight as a pupa's case, others were upright razors, yet another hung with downy seed-heads. As she watched, an insect crawled through this green underworld. A small, lumbering creature, intent on survival.

Silently, Julian turned Agnes's face to his and kissed her. 'It's very odd, or perhaps it isn't,' he informed her, 'how the longing for proper love infects you at the wrong moment. Or when you least expect it.'

At sea, the tide turned and began to run in.

They were at the end of the garden, leaning on the gate that led on to the cliff path and talking, when they spotted a figure in a pink linen suit walking towards them.

'Hallo, Julian,' said Kitty, her red mouth set in a bitter grimace. 'Didn't you hear the phone? I rang at lunchtime to tell you I was coming back earlier than planned.'

Kitty's groomed exterior was immaculate, but underneath there was a terrified animal (the same animal that had taken up residence in Agnes), who was frantically weighing up the options on how to get rid of that enemy.

'Hallo, Kitty,' Agnes said, knowing that Kitty was in mortal terror that she had told Julian about the baby.

The two women sized each other up. 'This time *I'm* telling you to get out,' said Kitty, her voice shaking.

'Kitty . . .' Julian took a step towards her.

Kitty squared up to him. 'I don't think there's any point in beating around the bush. Tell Agnes to go,' she demanded. 'Now. At once.' She tugged at Julian's arm.

'Kitty . . .' Julian removed her hand from his arm. 'Agnes is here at my invitation. This is *not* your business.'

Kitty rounded on him. 'On the contrary, it is my business. We may not have a piece of paper, Julian,' she was trembling, 'but we have everything else. We have a marriage.' She snatched her hands behind her back to hide them. 'I know it started out as something else, but that's what it's ended up as. I must defend it.'

Oh, God, thought Agnes, noting Julian's at-bay expression, I should not be here, and she looked round blindly for her bag. The baby deserves better than this mess. 'I'll go.'

She allowed Julian to see her into the car, placed the key in the ignition and said, 'I shouldn't have come. I should have stuck to what I said.'

He looked so miserable and defensive that she almost laughed, the kind of laugh that is the only response to profound misery.

'Agnes, what did you want to talk to me about?'

'It was nothing. Go back to Kitty.'

'Listen,' he said urgently, 'you're right. This can't go on. Once I've sorted out Portcullis, I will sort this out. I promise.'

'When will Portcullis be sorted out?'

'I don't know.' He placed a hand on the car door.

She avoided looking at him but gazed down at the hand with brown fingers, brushed with fine gold hairs. At least she knew now where she stood.

On the drive back to Flagge House, Agnes's face and arms glowed with sunburn, and black depression gathered in her heart.

Fact. She had desired and taken, and got herself pregnant. The so very clever, practical Agnes.

Fact. She had an unborn child to consider — and

other considerations clustered as thickly. House. Aunts. Herself.

Each time, with both men, she had left a little bit of herself behind. And who could say that if she had told Julian about the baby that, in the end, they would have tired of each other too?

The situation she was in was not new, and there was nothing startling to be deduced from it. She gripped the wheel and drove on far too fast. The struggle between will, inclination and stricture was as old as time.

After the sound of Agnes's car had died away, Julian said, 'I want to talk to you, Kitty.'

'No.' Kitty had collected herself. She smiled her society smile but avoided looking at him and proceeded to lay out her agenda. 'There's no point in raking it over. We shall have to forget this incident. I shall. Let's be normal. Let's just be very, very normal.'

Kitty, the skilled, emotional debt collector. In little 'normal' ways, Julian would be asked to pay – as he had in the past. He considered producing the old arguments about their arrangement and their separate freedoms, but they no longer applied. 'I'm sorry we've reached this point.'

'What did you expect?' she flashed.

'But you agreed.'

'Sometimes, Julian, you have the emotional age of an newborn.'

'OK. OK.' He paced up and down. She was right to

question him. 'Kitty, if my behaviour is making you so unhappy that you feel forced to go off to clinics, then we must do something. Make a decision.'

The look she gave him made him flush. It was of pity and superior understanding. '*Nonsense*, darling. We're fine. It will all settle down.'

Kitty fetched her luggage from the drive, dumped it in the hall and followed him into the kitchen. 'Shall I make some coffee?'

*Let's be normal, please, let us be normal*

Julian was searching in the cupboard for the mineral water. 'No, thanks.'

Kitty surveyed the washing-up and ran water into the bowl. She spoke with the same light, relentless note. 'Having visitors has obviously turned you into a pig. How long has this lot been here? By the way, did I tell you that Vita Huntingdon's daughter is already pregnant?'

'Kitty, I know this is difficult, but please concentrate.'

Kitty scraped the plates clean and tipped them into the hot water. 'Julian, over the years I have learned many things from you. One of them is, don't give up easily. You have given me excellent tuition.'

'Clearly.'

His sarcasm lashed Kitty into retaliation. She dug her hands into the water and said furiously, '*Don't* talk to me as if I was some business rival, or someone to play boardroom games with. I'm not one of your projects and I'm not a profit margin. I am the woman you live with. Or, rather, your version of it . . . Like it or not, you're committed to me.' She seized the dishcloth. 'How often have I been in this kitchen, organizing operations to keep your life running smoothly? Countless times. How many times have I sorted the house out, rearranging cushions, hanging clothes, putting everything back into the order that you like? You *demand*, Julian. How many times have I bitten back requests to accompany you to London and stayed here as you wished? I have been here, in your life as well as your bed, and I will make you acknowledge that, if it kills me.'

It was enough. Without another word, he walked out of the kitchen and the study door banged shut.

He emerged just as Kitty's hand was creeping towards the half-empty wine bottle on the kitchen table. 'Fatal on an empty stomach,' she murmured, with an irritating laugh. Julian refilled his glass with water.

Kitty gave in. 'I'll have some wine.' She drank, her lipsticked mouth sipping fast and neatly. 'I needed that.' She put the glass down and fiddled with a charm on her bracelet. 'Julian, I'm sorry for my outburst.'

The depths of his indifference to her apology terrified her. 'I understand.'

'I was defending my territory,' she added hastily. 'It was a hitch, nothing to worry about. All marriages have hitches. People survive. It's a matter of will, an act of will. Anyway, I came to tell you that the clinic was very positive and – '

'Kitty, we are not married. The contract was different.'

She gave an impatient tsk. 'Words, Julian. You may be

good on numbers but you need a few lessons in what matters.'

He stared at her. Kitty was correct. What expertise he possessed lay not in emotions but in theory and, at this precise moment, he was too embattled to change anything.

Kitty straightened in her chair and ran her hand over her hair to check that it was in place. She spoke with the fluency of someone well rehearsed in their lines. 'We are married. You may think that this performance of weekends only and separate houses keeps you nicely insulated. But it doesn't.'

'You accepted it.'

'Well, now I don't. I've changed.' She leaned over the table towards him, her face so soft with love that he could not bear it. 'I know what you're thinking, Julian. You're feeling sad and trapped and besotted with someone else. But you know it will fade. If love isn't fed, it dies of starvation . . .' Kitty faltered, for the irony was cruel. 'The other night you were honest and said that ten years is about the limit for any one relationship. Maybe that's true. But it seems stupid to be condemned to repeating it with different people. Why don't we just accept that we're at a different stage?'

He looked down into his glass. 'Why do you put up with all this, Kitty?'

'You know those letters you were reading?' asked the desperate Kitty.

'Those damn letters,' he muttered.

'Well, the farmer wrote something along the lines that his life was empty without Mary, for she was the other half of his soul and without her he possessed only half a soul.' Kitty reached up and took off her large, gold clip earrings and laid one down on the table. 'That is me, Julian . . .' she placed the second beside it '. . . and how I feel about you.'

'Kitty. I can't say the same. I'm sorry.'

She sprang to her feet and her chair went winging back along the floor. 'I beg you, Julian. Don't leave me.' She flung herself at Julian's feet and slid her arm around his knees.

Guilty, despairing, repelled, Julian looked down at Kitty, a woman he had partly made who was wholly his responsibility. Sick with love that was not for Kitty, he put out a hand and stroked the highlighted head bent in front of him.

That night in the bedroom, they undressed. Kitty opened drawers, creamed her face, blew a drift of powder off the surface of the dressing-table and brushed her hair. Julian soaked in a bath, listened to the radio, ran more hot water, dropped a large towel on the floor and left it where it fell.

They lay in bed, exchanged a few words about the alarm clock, the whereabouts of the water glass, what time they would get up. The light snapped off and, with profound thankfulness, they waited for the dark to hide them from each other.

Eyes burning and chest occasionally shuddering from

the aftermath of her crying, Kitty lay awake for a long time. Then, very daring, she put out a hand, touched the form beside her and . . . Julian flinched.

At that, Kitty walked to the edge of the precipice and was forced to look down.

On Monday morning, Angela greeted Julian in his office in a tight Lurex dress with a fake peony in her hair, which did nothing to hide her intelligence. On the desk were a list of calls, his appointment book, a tray of coffee and biscuits and his correspondence.

Before the afternoon was out, Julian together called his young, trendy, socially aware team and gave them a rundown on the situation. Then he dispatched some of them by helicopter to reconnoitre twenty acres of farmland near Bath being sold by its broke owner – land so expensive that the margins might prove impossible. He also called in Harold, who was wearing yet another variant of the crumpled linen suit but whose trendiness was cancelled out by his ashen face. Again they went over the figures.

By mid-morning on Tuesday, the crisis was full-blown. None of the banks had shown any interest in putting together a rescue package and the share price was on the slide. Worse, Legatt's, the rival firm, had sniffed what was in the wind and was hovering, ready to launch a hostile takeover bid.

Harold was white to the gills and shaking. Julian took pity on him. 'This won't be your last crisis, or your worst.'

Harold closed his eyes for a second. 'If you say so.'

They were standing together by the office window, overlooking the clogged street below. Julian punched the younger man's shoulder gently. 'Use your wits to think up something, but don't worry too much. The Somerset deal might come through.'

He knew, and Harold knew, that it was touch and go.

Much depended on the Somerset deal, and on Wednesday morning Julian helicoptered down to the area. It was land owned by a farmer who, as soon as the subsidies came in from Europe, had abandoned mixed farming in favour of turning specialist cereal grower. But his profits had been eaten into by the variety of diseases that tend to attack monocultures and, despite huge applications of pesticide, the farm had failed to thrive. Now, the soil was dead and the farmer wanted out, to retire to France.

Julian walked the bare fields, the dry chalky soil crumbling under his feet. It offered the sort of opportunity on which Portcullis thrived, and Julian returned to London feeling marginally more positive, especially as the share price had steadied.

He returned to the Barbican in the late summer twilight, in the cusp before the razzle of lights took over from the dusk, through a city rattling with discarded polystyrene, and clotted with commuters.

The following morning a phone call from Harold

woke him at seven thirty. 'Legatt's have launched their bid,' he reported.

Julian swiped a finger across his throat. 'That's that, then.'

## 23

Some people reckoned their fifteen minutes of fame was their due and, if he ever thought about it, Andrew imagined he could be one of them. Yet when faced with notoriety, he discovered it was a dangerous thing. Too close to the bone of exposure. He did not like the questions it made him ask himself, and he hated the reminder that he was fraudulent and might be exposed as such.

After pictures and a report of his fiery protest appeared in the local press, he was besieged by the media and by phone calls. From being a case that had been virtually ignored, it now excited local interest, with supporters and detractors hurling insults at each other on the letters page of the *Exbury Herald*. A regional television company arrived to film the field of charred circles with Andrew and the Gladiator, who had hastened down from Croydon declaring that he would waive his fee for the sake of some action.

It was the lovely, somnolent moment of high summer. In the daytime, the calves slept, hidden by the grass in the meadows, their secret couches betrayed only by their flapping ears. In the evenings, the cows, weighed down by milk, soaked up the evening sun while their offspring, tails at full mast, capered in gangs.

The idyllic pastoral scene whipped up the film crew into excitement, and they responded with the delight, reverence even, usually aroused by great artefacts. They could not believe how perfect it was, they told Andrew, how marvellous, how picturesque. And they regarded him with the quizzical gaze of travellers in a foreign land.

'I am proud of my farm.' Andrew permitted himself a rare moment of satisfaction.

He looked out of the window. With their summer foliage, the oaks made a stately clump. If Stone got his way, they would be the first to go under the bulldozer. His mouth tightened.

Enough. The tasks for the day needing checking. Flora and Gudrun were due at the abattoir. Afterwards there was hay and sugar beet to pick up from Exbury, then the orders for the meat delivery to be worked out.

Before he could get going, Penny rang. 'Listen, love, there's a story being put about that you're burning carcasses illegally.'

'You know me better than that.'

'*I* do. But they don't.'

He glanced at his opened post. 'I've had a letter from the Meat Marketing boys. They want to inspect the farm.'

'Andrew, that's no coincidence.' Penny sounded troubled. 'There's something going on. Stone wants the money, and us off the land, and he's using tactics. You

279

wouldn't listen because you're too stubborn. But it's true.'

Penny was probably right. She had an ear to the ground and a practicality that enabled her to put two and two together and reach the correct conclusion.

'I wish I was there to defend you.'

He cocked his inner ear. If he was not mistaken, Penny was angling for an opening. To come back? The thought made him recoil. The shock waves from her departure had ebbed, and he had moved on in all sorts of surprising ways. Penny had chosen how it was to be and they had all better get on with it.

'Good Lord,' he said. The sound of his own laughter was increasingly foreign to Andrew but Penny's stout defence struck him as funny. 'I'd better warn Bob.'

He wished he had kept his mouth shut. With a little gasping sigh, Penny said, 'I suppose I deserved that.'

Bea waited up for Agnes, who returned to Flagge House in the late evening from a London trip. Maud was having an early night, she explained, adding, 'So should you be, but I'm afraid you're due a visitor.'

'Who?' Agnes dumped her rucksack on the table in the hall. In the evening sun, the glass ship lamp on the table glittered and rode through the crystal water.

'Andrew Kelsey. He was most insistent. He said that he wanted to ask you a question.' Bea looked puzzled. 'Does that make sense, dear?'

'Oh, yes, it makes sense,' said Agnes. To her horror, she felt tears spring into her eyes.

'Agnes, dear,' Bea looked concerned, 'you must stop this at once. It won't do in your condition.' Agnes gave a visible start. 'I am told, but I agree I don't have first-hand experience, that it is not a good thing to get upset while having a baby.'

Agnes was forced to lean on the table. 'How long have you known? Does Maud know?'

'No, dear, she doesn't. But you've had a funny white look about your lips. Very tell-tale. Could I say . . .' Bea was hugging the news as a personal affirmation of joy '. . . I'm so excited, and I'm so glad you haven't got rid of it. I was rather frightened – well, I said a little prayer. But it is bad timing. Babies always happen when one least wants them. Or when one thinks that's the case.'

'Good God,' said Agnes. 'I should have talked to you earlier.'

'You could get rid of it,' Bea was handling this delicate topic with the fluency of the worldly woman she was not, 'but you might end up living with a ghost.'

'Goodness,' was all Agnes could think of to say. 'I had no idea you had views on this subject. Aren't you shocked or upset?'

'Don't be silly, Agnes. We're not living in the Stone Age. Everyone welcomes the future generation.' She placed a small, dry hand on Agnes's shoulder, indicating that she forgave the younger woman's patronizing tone. 'Goodness is such a funny thing, isn't it? In my day, goodness meant you gave your baby away if you were unmarried. Now you can be unmarried, have a dozen babies, keep them and be considered a woman of principle.'

That made Agnes laugh.

Bea looked very earnest. 'Things have changed. Your generation is freer than we were. I expect that makes it harder.'

Agnes reached out her hand and touched the ship's crystal sail. 'If I need my head put in order I must remember to come and consult you.'

She went out on to the terrace and settled in one of the rusting iron chairs to prepare for Andrew's arrival. It was hot, with just a hint of thunder to the north. Then, as the static settled, the sky cleared and darkened and the stars began to make their appearance. A large August moon bellied up into the sky. The shadows over the water-meadow deepened, dimmed and vanished.

Once upon a time, a posse of men – for it would have been men – among them a Campion, rode into the village. They saw the potential of this site, struck the first spade into the earth and built the house. They had taken wives, had children, added wings, demolished others and, for a time, thrived. Unlike Agnes, they had not imagined that time and money were finite.

When Andrew stepped through the window, Agnes was sitting quietly, with a glass of water in her hand, staring over the water-meadow. 'Hallo, Andrew,' she said.

He walked across and raised her hand to his cheek, awkwardly but with a fervour that touched her. 'Here,' he said, and shoved a bag on to Agnes's lap. 'Honey this time.'

She exclaimed in delight. 'From your bees, I take it?' She kissed him back. He smelt of sunburn, straw and feed. 'I put a bottle of white in the fridge. I'll get it.'

When Agnes returned, Andrew had settled himself on the top step of the terrace and she dropped down beside him. The stone was warm and flaky dry. Andrew was hot from his drive and the sun had tanned his face and a deep V beneath his neck.

'Any news?' she asked.

'Good and bad. The anti-Arcadian lobby is growing in Exbury, and they've been forced into having a public meeting to try to show how much they're going to contribute to the town. It's delayed the results of the inquiry. The bad is that Arcadian are thinking of funding a sports centre as a trade-off.'

Silently she filled his glass.

He rolled it between his fingers and put it down on the step. 'I can't stay very long, but I think you know why I'm here.' There was no point in pretending and Agnes nodded. 'I'm not very good at this sort of thing or with words but I wanted to stake my claim . . . if you'll have me.'

She shifted on the hard stone and her sandal dislodged a shard of it, which bounced down the steps.

'I like you very much.' He gazed down to the grass that lapped the bottom of the flight. 'I imagine it's significant that you haven't been in touch since my rather bald request when you came down, so I came to put it right.'

Knowing what was coming, she stirred herself. If she had decided to have this baby, then she had to do things properly. Square the circle. Face up to the confrontation. 'Andrew . . . there is something . . .'

Andrew was in too much of a hurry to listen. 'I've no idea what the future holds but Penny has gone.' The blue eyes narrowed – stormy, chilly waters. 'I may lose the farm. But I may not. I may have to start again. Even if I keep Tithings, money is going to be a problem. Always. Farming does not buy luxuries. At least, my version.'

'If you lose Tithings, you'll be due a reasonable compensation?'

'I suppose.' He shrugged. 'And I suppose I would accept it. But I can't accept that because I'm small I have no rights.'

'Andrew. I've got something I must tell you but I'll find it easier if we're moving.'

He followed her down the steps, their feet swishing through the grass. The downy whisper of seed-heads shivered over Agnes's bare legs. She halted by the river-bank and drank in the familiar beauty. The façade of Flagge House was pitted in a dreamscape of light and shadow – a moment of lush, dreamy, sensual exchange between deep evening and night, accompanied by the sound of running water.

'Andrew,' she said, 'I'm pregnant.'

Andrew exclaimed, a sound full of anger and frustration, and swung on his heel away from her. A second passed. Two, then ten, twenty. 'I needn't ask whose it is?'

'As a matter of fact, no.'

'Does he know?'

'No.'

'Will you tell him?'

'No.'

'Why not?'

'Because . . .'

'You are sure you want it?'

'Yes . . .' She took a deep breath. '*Yes*.'

'It's spoilt, then,' Andrew said bitterly, and abandoned Agnes on the riverbank. Conscious of the weary drag of her body, she lowered herself to the grass, listened to the water and watched him go.

The dusk intensified.

If she remained quiet and concentrated, her reward might be a fox's bark, the rustle of a tiny rodent in the grass, even the slither of a grass snake cooling after the heat of the day. She undid her sandals and wriggled her feet in the cool, sappy grass – the action reminding her of the early years at Flagge House when her body had been wild and uncontrollable in its growths and surprises.

She had been solitary then, so why should she be surprised at her solitude now? No one held a blueprint for anyone else's well-being, and at least – at the very least – the tiny beating heart tucked under her pelvis gave her an entrée into another kind of love.

She was a professional, used to coping, and she would cope. Register at the hospital, move her bedroom upstairs to the nursery floor, find someone in Charlborough to look after it when she was away . . . Agnes ticked off a list in a dreamy fashion. She felt her mind shift into another gear, a certain pride that she was going to take control, a curiosity as to what was going to happen to her body.

The heat was sucking up the air and lowered over the water-meadow. Agnes dipped her feet into the water and her toes knotted up with cramp.

Then there were footsteps behind her. Heavy, circling. Andrew loomed out of the dark and dropped down beside her. 'Agnes?'

'Yes.'

'I came here to sleep with you. To *make* you give in. I wanted an affair.' He put his face close to hers. 'I still do.'

For a second, she heard an elusive echo . . . tap, tap . . . and the flight of anguished footsteps, the sound that an agent on the run, like the Mary of Julian's imagination, might have made. 'Do you?' she replied, and touched his cheek. 'Even now?'

He kept his lips close to her ear. 'Listen to me. It changes things, but not entirely. Perhaps it's a good thing.'

'Why?'

'We have no secrets. The worst has been done. I had Penny. You have a baby. You will need support. I can offer it. Come and live with me. I'll divorce Penny and we could get married. Think about it. We can pretend the baby is mine. It's happened before. Often, in fact. In lots of families. I can adopt it. Actually, no one need know.'

'I had decided that I could cope on my own.'

'No. *Listen.*' Andrew placed his hands at either side of her face. The pressure made circles dance in front of her eyes. 'It came to me in a flash. You'll need help when you have your baby.'

His hands moved down to the neckline of her linen blouse, sought entry and found it. 'Could you love me? Now, in the future, sometime? I could love you. Very much.' Gently, he caressed the skin at the base of her throat. 'I don't mind about him.'

His touch neither stirred nor alarmed her. It was a pleasant physical sensation, reliable and male, and she could live with it. Then, without warning, her pulses quickened and she was pierced by a longing for Julian so acute and anguished that she almost gasped. *Why?* she cried, in silent despair. *Why?*

The feeling vanished. Andrew drew her closer and she closed her eyes.

Moonlight and heat rising from the ground. The sensation of skin slicked with sweat, an ever-present hint of nausea, the harvest dusk . . . These increased Agnes's sense of unreality. Andrew both unsettled and reassured

287

her, and she yearned to yield to the drifting, drowsy persuasions of pregnancy. Her hands slid down her body and touched the tiny swell of her belly. Perhaps it would be better. A calm, considered partnership where there were no secrets, where the partners had looked at each other, dispassionately and without heat, before they had made the choice.

'You must take time to think about this, Andrew,' she said. 'And I shall too.'

He leaned back on his hands and watched the water. 'I don't have to. I like the idea of a family. But you must promise one thing.'

'What?'

'That he never knows.'

She turned her head away.

'You *will* think about it?' He leaned forward in a swift movement and cupped her chin so that her face was turned towards him.

'Of course . . . And, Andrew, thank you.'

Cloud had smeared itself over the sky and it had grown insufferably hot. Agnes could smell thunder rolling in from the west. 'Let's go inside,' she said, and with Andrew's arm now lying as heavy as wood across her shoulders, they left the shadowy water-meadow.

Before he left, Andrew asked Agnes, 'Could you come and live at Tithings?'

She thought of the lanes banked high with dog-rose and honeysuckle, of ancient oaks and the sweep of the moor, of Andrew's pastures threaded by wild herbs and dashes of shimmering colour. Beside this was the picture of her own house, so steeped in history, its foundations eroded, its structures brittle with age and disrepair, its significance dimming and the prospect of an extended, tortured struggle to preserve it.

Agnes promised him she would think it over.

After he had driven away, she pushed heavy iron bolts into place and turned the huge old-fashioned key in the lock. Then she switched off the lights, and the spun-glass ship was instantly extinguished.

## 24

Clutching her knitting-bag. Maud collared Agnes in the kitchen after breakfast. 'Was someone here last night?'

Agnes explained that it had been Andrew.

'*Tiens*. What the neighbours must think with all these men popping in and out . . .' Maud peered at her. 'You don't look as though you enjoyed the visit.'

With an effort, Agnes continued to clear the dishes. She would have given a lot to be quiet, and to be alone. 'To be honest, Maud, I didn't.'

'Oh, well, that's that.' Maud searched in the knitting-bag. 'Did I tell you I wrote to Julie Andrews over a month ago? She hasn't replied.'

Agnes deposited a crust into the bin. 'What on earth did you write about?'

'I wanted to know exactly what she felt when she fell in love with the Captain.'

'Maud, Julie Andrews is not Maria von Trapp.'

Maud extracted her knitting. 'You mustn't be so literal, Agnes.'

Agnes placed a plate in the rack. 'Maud, I thought you should know that Andrew asked me to marry him and I'm thinking about it.'

'He did *what*?' Maud almost screeched and Agnes

steeled herself. 'If that means he wants you to leave here it's out of the question.' She added the sly rider, 'Your uncle would turn in his grave.'

Agnes was arrested in the act of running hot water into the sink. 'Don't worry. You know what I feel about the house and I suspect . . . I have an awful feeling that Andrew might lose the farm. If he did, living and working here might help him get over it.'

'That's the first sensible thing I've heard you say.' Maud brightened. 'That gives you a clear choice. Have him if he comes here. If he won't live here say no.'

Agnes wiped her hands and sat down opposite Maud. 'Actually, there is another reason why I have to consider Andrew's offer.' Reluctantly, she confessed her pregnancy. Maud was thunderstruck and there was no trace of French in her retort. 'Good God, that's not what John would have meant by an heir.'

Agnes could have sworn there was a glint of satisfaction in Maud's eyes at this latest proof of her stupidity.

'You'll be calling it one of those silly names – Jack, Sam, Millie – that everyone calls their children these days.' Maud looked scared, out of her depth, triumphant and fascinated, all at the same time. Agnes traced the grain of the wood on the surface of the table and waited. A couple more seconds of further reflection had Maud modifying her position. 'Oh, well, quite a few Campions have been born the wrong side of the blanket. Perfectly respectable ones. These days, it *is* perfectly respectable. Your generation don't know how lucky they are. You indulge yourselves and keep the baby to boot.' A thought struck her. 'I don't suppose this means you'll think again about selling the house?'

Agnes put her head into her hands, retched and tried not to think about her body. 'No, Maud.'

Maud observed the all too obvious signs and embarked: 'I suppose you're going to be endlessly sick and no help to anyone?'

'Looks a bit like it. Duggie says it'll wear off soon. I'm just taking my time, that's all.'

Maud's gaze drifted to the window. 'Maria would never have allowed herself to get pregnant before marrying.'

Having recently been shown a photograph of the real Maria and the Captain, Agnes rather thought this might have been the case.

Maud picked up the abandoned knitting. 'It will give us something to *do*,' she observed.

'Maud, did you enjoy being married?' Agnes looked up from the shelter of her hands.

Maud sighed heavily. 'My generation did not have any other choice.'

'How you must have disliked having me foisted on you.' Agnes had seen the photos of Maud standing in the front door to welcome the new arrival. Her hair was arranged in little sausage waves and she wore a shirtwaister floral frock and pearls that had long since been sold. She looked faded and middle-aged, and her expression suggested that she just wanted to get life over.

'I did . . . and I didn't. You were a lot of trouble.'

There was a lot of buried history contained in the remark and neither woman wished to dig it up. 'About the baby –' Agnes hazarded but Maud cut in.

'Bea's telephoning and I don't know who. She's very secretive these days.'

It struck Agnes that Maud was rattled. She went and sat down beside her. 'Is anything wrong?'

'Of *course* not.'

'How is Freddie?'

Maud yanked at her ring. 'I haven't seen much of him lately. Busy, busy. Bridge and things. He has a full and interesting life but he's very nice to me.' There was a tiny pause. 'Freddie's a fine man, the best, actually.'

Agnes went in search of Bea. She walked down the kitchen passage, past the rooms whose original uses she had researched so minutely under the tuition of her uncle: one for vases, another for shoe-cleaning, another for baskets. Imagine, such luxuries of space, such opportunities to build a domain around your polishes, brushes and dusters. A maid might have felt a sovereign of the trug and the pannier. She might have enjoyed her sole discretion in arranging the silent vases and jars. She might have chosen this one for the blue delphiniums, another for the buttery rose, and that one for the lily. In its absolute autocracy, the house was fashioned around little kingdoms in which its slaves could rule.

Bea was washing clothes in the laundry room. 'Feeling better, dear?'

'Much.'

Bea nodded. 'Being miserable is so flattening, isn't it?'

Agnes let down her guard. 'I seem to have spent a lot of time being miserable, Bea. Do you suppose Misery spots someone and says, "Aha, someone to live off for life"?'

Bea sent her one of her looks. 'Nothing that middle age won't put right. I've discovered you must keep busy. It works.'

'Yes, I agree.' Agnes watched Bea's small pink hands chafe the clothes in the suds and suddenly realized that she was washing her new bits of underwear. 'Bea. You *mustn't* wash my clothes.'

'They'll be nice and soft by the time I've finished, and you don't have the time.'

'But, Bea . . .'

Bea wrung out a white cotton bra. 'You mustn't take away my role. There, it looks lovely.' The reproof was mild but effective.

'Maria would have approved, would she?' Agnes could not resist saying.

Bea put her head on one side. 'Now, Agnes, you know perfectly well that Maria is far too busy singing and running up mountains to have an opinion.'

Agnes dropped a kiss on Bea's cheek, and inhaled scrupulously clean, powdered elderly lady. 'Please don't think I'm trying to take away . . . anything.'

Bea seemed mollified. 'I've told you, you're still young, Agnes.'

'Here, let me.' Agnes helped her to drape the washing over the pulley. 'Are you trying to tell me something?'

'No, dear.'

Agnes hoisted the pulley up to the ceiling and hitched the rope around the cleat. 'Sure?'

'Freddie's a *great* traveller,' Bea turned the subject. 'Intrepid, even. He's been to Karnak and he might be going back there at Christmas. I'd love to go with him.' She picked up a pile of laundry she had ironed earlier and pushed Agnes towards the door. 'Enough of all that. I want to give you some hot milk. Then we must think about lunch.'

How had she managed, Agnes asked herself, to avoid so many daily acts of keeping clean, fed, of soothing relatives and disentangling their sticky demands? Occupied with work, she had missed the flow of unobtrusive existence in the background.

Dickie from the BBC phoned to say that the transmission date for the *Hidden Lives* programme had slipped to October. Apparently the chief honchos were not so hot on historicals 'just at the mo'. Plus, a couple of hot alternatives had come in on the Princess's manicurist and the leader of the opposition's milkman.

'Just take it on the chin, sweetie. OK?' said Dickie.

He did not suggest a spot of lunch, which was the normal procedure, and she took it to mean that her ratings were slipping.

After lunch Agnes went to bed, and staggered down an hour later to make herself a cup of weak tea. There was no sign of life in the kitchen but someone – Bea – had washed up a single cup and saucer and placed it on the sideboard. The afternoon sunlight shone harshly on the stained wooden draining-board and made it obvious that it was rotting at the edges.

'You've been there a long time,' she informed it. 'Hang on a bit longer.'

As she went upstairs, she heard a heated exchange coming from Maud's bedroom. Alarmed, she knocked and went in.

Maud was sitting bolt upright on the bed, her huge eyes fixed in an expression of such fury that Agnes recoiled. 'Get her out of here,' Maud ground out.

Agnes wheeled around. Bea was standing by the window in her heavy winter coat, which was far too hot, her handbag crooked over her arm. 'Are you going out, Bea?'

'I'm waiting,' Bea announced, nervous but confident. She was making a point of occupying the space she stood in, and Agnes suddenly perceived how Bea normally appeared shrunken in the presence of her sister.

'I can see that. But what for?'

'I'm waiting for Freddie.'

'You're going on one of your expeditions?'

'I'm waiting for Freddie,' said Bea, 'because we're eloping. I've just told Maud who is, as you can see, a little upset. I've told her there's no need.'

Agnes was so stupefied that she said the first thing

that came into her head. 'The whole point of eloping is its secrecy.'

'It doesn't alter the fact. I can say a tree is a pond, but it does not change its essential condition,' continued this new, astonishing Bea. She checked the drive outside and transferred her handbag from one arm to the other. 'Your underwear is all ironed, Agnes. I think you'll find it's nice and comfy.'

Maud cried, 'Freddie's *mine*. He belongs to me. He was going to marry me.'

'I've put a shepherd's pie in the fridge and you must promise me that you will eat it.'

'Agnes, tell her she can't.'

Bea ignored her sister and peered through the window. 'I can see his car,' she said, 'so there isn't much time.' She approached the bed, but not close enough to be within reach. 'I've been keeping this quiet, Maud, because I didn't want to upset you so soon after John and everything else. Or put dear Agnes in a difficult position. But Freddie . . .' a clear, happy note crept into her voice '. . . he loves me and I love him in return. He's been very lonely since Alice died and I want to look after him. That's what I'm good at.'

Maud pushed ineffectually at her skirt. '*Help* me. Don't just stand there.' Agnes did as she was bidden, and as Maud was hauled unsteadily to her feet, she said, 'Freddie can't *possibly* prefer you.'

Bea's smile was one of quiet, earned triumph. 'But he

does. I do see your point of view, Maud, and I'm sorry for your disappointment. Ah, there he is.'

'He'll spend the little money you've got.'

'I certainly hope he does. We want to enjoy ourselves.' Bea leaned forwards, tapped at the window-pane and mouthed, 'Just coming.' She turned back to the two women. 'We've made *such* plans, you know.'

'Freddie . . .' Maud launched herself towards the door but Agnes caught her arm.

'Maud, don't make it worse. It's obviously quite decided between them.'

'She's stolen my –'

'No I didn't.' Bea kissed Agnes. 'Do take care and . . .' she gestured at her collapsed sister '. . . I hope she isn't too difficult.' She patted Maud's arm. 'I'd better say I'm sorry because I am in a way, but not enough. It's funny how things turn out. I thought Flagge House would be home for ever, but it's only a stop-over after all.'

Agnes followed Bea into the passage and helped her negotiate the stairs. 'Bea, you're walking a bit oddly. Have you got a bad hip too?'

'Oh, that,' said Bea, and hauled up her skirt to reveal a wad of banknotes tucked into the top of her lisle stockings. 'A little precaution I always take.'

In comforting Maud, who would not be comforted, Agnes witnessed a rage that was terrifying, she told Andrew when she phoned him to tell him what had happened and that it would be impossible to make any decisions at the moment.

Maud knew that she had no options left. 'What will I do?' she sobbed, lonely, humiliated. 'What can I *do*?'

When Agnes went upstairs to investigate Bea's room, she discovered Bea's possessions, neatly bagged up and piled by the window. Every shelf was wiped, every corner brushed. The room was immaculate – but for the large crack that appeared to have spread across the ceiling since Agnes had last been in there.

## 25

*Friday*
    Kitty was reading.

Bees are excellent home-makers but they are also committed to the good of the colony. When it becomes too crowded and insufficient, they take action. A skilled bee-keeper can always tell when they are about to swarm by the sounds issuing from the hive.

There is a shriek as the useless drones are exterminated [Kitty put down her new half-moon glasses], the starving, ageing queen cries and begs her workers to feed her. But they ignore her and continue to groom her, ready for flight and for her final mating.

When had she faced the truth and known her reign was over? When she had seen Julian's face as he looked at Agnes? Or the lonely days and nights that had followed without Julian, who had stayed in London to deal with the crisis, and she had realized that summer was slipping away into the flux and change of autumn, and that she must quit the hive for the young, fertile queen? But she wasn't going to be pushed out, oh, no. Kitty was going to quit on her own terms, when she was good and ready.

For weeks she had been busy and was now putting the final touches to her plans. In the drawing room she talked on the phone, first to the sweet man who managed her finances. Second, she had cancelled her Friday appointment at the beauty salon for the foreseeable future. Instead she drove into Lymouth to shop and to see her bank manager and her lawyer.

The bank manager knew Kitty well and together they talked over the options, pushing them this way and that until they reached a compromise. Eventually, Kitty rose to her feet and thanked him, but instead of bidding her goodbye he asked if she wanted to take a little more time to think over her decision.

She said, 'No.' Definitely no.

After a snack lunch, she abandoned her normal routine of planning the menu and sorting the linen, the weekly chores that were required in the maintenance of two houses. Instead she took herself off for a long walk along the seashore. Pink and white and yellow, the little town drowsed under an autumn sun: so pretty and prosperous. By the time she had returned to the car with ruined hair and wet feet it was past five o'clock.

Julian phoned at seven and said he would be late.

'Fine,' said Kitty, and sat down with a cheese sandwich to watch a television programme. At ten, she tidied up the kitchen and went upstairs to have a bath in which she lay for a long time.

I am practising to be good at this. I am practising to release my soul.

'Kitty?' Julian arrived at the cottage a few minutes past eleven. He let himself into a silent, empty kitchen, expecting to see his supper laid on the table. No supper was evident, and he extracted a can of beer from the fridge and trod, reluctantly, upstairs.

Kitty was in bed, reading. At his entrance, she put down her book. 'Hallo, Julian.'

He sensed at once that her manner towards him was changed. 'Is everything all right?'

'Yes.' Unlike all those other times – those many times when, scented and sensual, she had pushed herself out of bed and run to kiss him – she made no move. 'Busy week?'

He sank down on the side of the bed and emptied his pockets on to the bedside table. 'The worst possible. But I'll tell you about that later.'

She did not say, 'Oh, please, tell me. Let me help.' In the old days, her heart would have beaten extra fast with the desire to comfort him. But tonight there was not the answering thud in her chest. Only the still remnants of an upheaval that had arrived, ripped her to pieces, and moved on.

He was curious. 'Is that a new nightie?'

She glanced down at the plain Viyella affair she had bought that morning. 'Yes.'

He assessed it with the care he gave everything to which he turned his attention. 'Not your usual style, is it?'

She plucked at the soft sleeve. 'It's warm and comfortable, and the weather is getting colder.'

'Still, I miss your beautiful silk one.'

'Oh, for God's sake,' she burst out, 'please don't patronize me. As if it matters what I wear in bed.'

Julian was puzzled. 'It's always mattered before.'

She turned away and put up a hand to shade her face. 'That was before.'

'Kitty . . .'

'Yes.' The word was dragged out.

He sounded very, very weary. 'What is going on?'

Kitty drew up her feet. Their years together had vanished entirely in a fog of mutual distrust and forgetfulness and she wanted to create a space between the two of them. *She had gazed into the precipice, and perceived that there was no bottom, and said, 'All right. You win. I give up.'* He checked the pretty, elegant bedroom and noticed that it appeared emptier. Stripped. He indicated a dressing-table which, except for her hairbrush, was almost shockingly nude. 'Kitty, where are all your things?'

Kitty clasped her knees tightly. 'I've been getting rid of them. I decided that I don't need them any more.'

He managed a smile. 'That sounds rather serious.'

'Does it?' Discarding the frilled skirt of her youth and dressing in the colourless, concealing robe of the *sadhu* to wander the earth before death. Yes, I suppose that was serious. 'I don't need them any more.'

Silence. Kitty felt a heavy ache mass at the back of her throat.

He frowned. 'And you don't need me any more either? Is that what you're saying?'

The lump subsided, and Kitty shook her head. 'Isn't it the other way round? You don't need me. You have other . . . well, I don't know.'

Julian cracked open the beer and took a mouthful. Kitty threw back the bedclothes and reached for her dressing-gown. Out of habit, she tied the belt extra tight around the waist to emphasize its slenderness. The gesture was not lost on Julian and, out of habit, he reached over to touch her but she stepped out of the way.

'What is happening, Kitty?' he asked quietly. 'I thought we two had to make a go of it. That was why we had that ridiculous scene with Agnes.' He wiped his mouth with the back of his hand. 'As with a lot of things, you were right. If that is the case, it is important that we keep on trying.'

She knew that expression. It was Julian being kind, which he was being a lot these days. 'It's not just Agnes,' she said. 'She was the symptom.'

'Perhaps we should leave her out of this.'

But she had seen the sudden quickening in his expression, which he strove to hide, and the worst of Kitty erupted. 'It may suit you to do so, Julian, but I don't think we should exclude the famous Agnes from this conversation. The minute you saw her, she took up residence in our lives. Agnes made you realize that you did not feel enough for me and our companionship was not . . .' she struggled to continue '. . . was not strong enough to build it up again. But, don't worry, I'm over that now. I tried. You know I tried hard, but even I can tell when I'm beaten.'

She waited for anything he might have to say, and when he remained silent, she extracted an envelope from the dressing-table drawer. 'This is a statement of our financial arrangements, up to date. As from today, please will you stop anything else coming in from you. Everything is in order.' She held it out. 'Take it.'

He ignored it and said haltingly, as he digested the implications, 'I wish you hadn't done that. It wasn't necessary.'

'Why not? It was part and parcel of our relationship.'

She dropped the envelope on to the bed and sat down at a distance from him. 'I was educated wrongly, Julian. Women aren't like me any more. They've changed, and they do things differently. I've been left behind.' She swallowed. 'But I suppose, in the end, they will face what I'm facing.' And in the act of liberating the words into the ether, Kitty's heart grew lighter.

See? The prison bars *are* dissolving.

There was enough truth in what Kitty said to make Julian wince. 'I'm sorry, Kitty.' He felt he ought to say more: she was owed explanations but he did not seem capable of making them. 'Shall I leave now?'

Sudden panic and the terror of what lay ahead almost choked Kitty. She remembered how well they had dealt with each other – in the early days – and what passion and love he had drawn from her. Perhaps she was wrong. Perhaps half a loaf was better than no loaf.

'It's so hard growing old,' she burst out.

On that first meeting, ten years ago, she had been so aware of her looks. She posed no complications, was realistic yet properly appreciative of the erotic – and judged shrewdly that Julian was used to helping himself to the good things. She had seen to it that it had all been made to seem so natural.

Julian looked at the beer can. 'Kitty, I should never have got you into this.'

She reared up from the bed. 'Oh, no,' she wept. 'I don't want you to say that or to suggest that it's all been for nothing. But look!' She tore at the belt of her dressing-gown, and wrenched off her nightdress. 'Look at me. Look at me properly.' White, curved and shadowed, she squared up to him like a fighter. 'Now do you understand? Age. And it is time the prince rode off to find a younger trophy.'

Suppressing a shudder, he picked up the discarded dressing-gown and draped it around the small, delicate body. 'You exaggerate. There's nothing wrong with you.'

'At least let's be honest.'

But she knew that he knew better than to be honest. That much he could do for her. He moved over to the window and pulled back the curtain. It was impossible to see the sea from Kitty's cottage and it was one of the reasons he had never liked it.

'You love Agnes,' she accused him from the bed, dressing-gown trailing awkwardly from her shoulders. 'You can be truthful.'

There was no point in subterfuge any longer. Kitty had received, deciphered and read the message. 'It is nothing to do with you, or how old you are, Kitty. It just is. That's all.'

Kitty gave a gasp. 'You never once told me that you loved *me*.'

'No, but I should have done.'

While rehearsing this scene, Kitty anticipated the quality of the pain she might experience. She had considered its thrust and sharpness, and trusted she would come through on the other side. But she had misjudged. The pain was, literally, making her breathless.

'Will you let me explain, Kitty?'

She could see that he wanted her to allow him to justify himself but her curiosity had died. Or, rather, her curiosity had shifted away from Julian and was directed at herself. A different Kitty was pushing her way through an unlit, constricted passage towards the circle of uncertain light at the other end, and she was consumed by impatience to get there.

As a birth, it was quite different from anything she had ever imagined.

Julian finished the beer. 'You've got foam on your lip,' she informed him, and he wiped it away. Kitty continued, 'I think it's time to stop talking. Some things can't be explained. I will never, never understand why you couldn't have married me but I have to accept it.' The old Kitty drove her to add, 'Once I worshipped you, body and soul, and a punishing God you proved, Julian.' The new one added, 'But it was not your fault.'

Julian abandoned the window and picked up his keys. 'What can I say?'

Kitty sat down at the dressing-table. 'Theo and I agree that most of the time we travel on the main road but, occasionally, you stop and take breath in a lay-by. Maybe that's what you need to do.' For all her determination, she was terrified that she was going to cry but fell back on habit. She picked up her brush and swept the hair from her forehead. Obediently her reflection followed suit – *not bad, not so very bad.* 'Please go now.'

He slid his arms down her shoulders, tracing the old pathways of desire with his fingertips.

She permitted him this last latitude. The bad Kitty rose, fought and conquered her better intentions. 'You may love Agnes,' she said, 'but you might not get her.' In reply, Julian bent and kissed her neck – in the way that she had loved. Under his touch, her flesh stirred and her pulse quickened. He looked up and caught Kitty's gaze in the mirror.

She let herself say, 'I wish I had not been so stupid, and we had had a child. A child would have made a difference.'

'Perhaps.' He looked over to the bed they had shared. 'Who knows?'

'One more thing.' She did not turn to face him. 'I know you are in trouble, and I thought it would be nice to help, so I've put in to buy one of the houses on the Tennyson estate. I thought every penny would come in useful.'

*Saturday.*

The fen was as flat as her waking memory of it, and the earth was dark, sodden and tinged with a green varnish of permanent damp. Only a few houses were visible, huddled inside their palisades of *Leylandii* cypresses. Otherwise, there were crops as far as Kitty could see, mile on mile of unlovely potatoes and cabbages, threaded through by drainage ditches. They have to grow somewhere, she thought.

Note . . . Kitty copied into her notebook from the gazetteer before she went to sleep. 'It was against this backdrop of fen towns and their surprisingly rich and sumptuous churches that the King Edward potato had been developed.'

It was cold and raw in her dream, and Kitty woke up shivering. After a while, she got up and dressed, slipping her feet into her elegant shoes, and went downstairs to eat breakfast. Theo had already arrived and was at work in the downstairs cloakroom.

'Don't come in, darl.'

Kitty knew better than to try. She knew exactly where and how to step in between the war zones drawn up by Theo and his cleaning panzer division. 'Kaboom,' said Theo. 'Every mad stinking bacteria of you.'

She poked her head around the door. 'Tea?' The Marigolded hands halted – Monday was yellow, Wednesday pink, Friday blue (after each session Theo dried them and dusted them with talcum powder).

'Yup.' He stripped off the gloves and placed them carefully on a clean cloth spread out for that purpose.

Over tea – drunk out of good bone china with a strawberry pattern – Kitty asked, 'Would you consider moving, Theo? I mean to live somewhere else.'

He whistled, out of tune and discordant. 'That's a bit of a whammy.'

Kitty took a deep breath. 'I wondered, if I moved . . .' she looked round at the small, fashionable kitchen '. . . if you came with me, I would look after you. See that you were all right. Care for you as well as I could.'

'What *is* this, Kits?'

'Me. Thinking again. Taking a grip of my life.'

Theo's brow puckered in an effort to make sense of her question. 'I've travelled far enough, Kits.' He meant not so much the passage from the red dust of his birthplace to this neat English seaside town, but more the journey in his mind.

'I understand.' Kitty got up, balancing neatly on her spindly heels, and tucked her chair under the table. 'It was just a thought. You can always change your mind.'

The tea-cups were empty. Theo gave them to Kitty, who took them over to the sink and washed them up. After a few seconds, she was aware from the faint chlorine bleach smell that Theo was standing silently behind her. She swivelled to face him and wrinkled her nose affectionately at him, a gesture she would never have dared make to Julian. Theo edged closer, a habit that in the early days had frightened her but now she knew to hold her ground. He circled her neck with his big hands and squeezed very gently.

'Spit it out, Kits.'

His hands were like a big, warm, reassuring collar and she nudged her cheek in a gesture of affection against one of them. 'I have to move, Theo, before I go under. For a long time, I imagined I was not capable of doing anything, but I am, Theo, I am. Aren't I?'

He nodded. If Kitty required reassurance he was going to supply it.

'So, I've decided on a new start, and the strange thing is, I . . .' *I want to discard, peel away, empty myself* '. . . have this urge to be somewhere harsher and colder. I'm not sure why.' She paused. 'I know it's unfair to ask you to come with me but I thought I would anyway.' She paused again. 'If it's money, Theo . . .'

The collar around her neck loosened and fell away. 'I don't think I could cope with a move, Kits.'

She was disappointed but not surprised. 'As I said, you can change your mind.' She arranged the cups on the rack to dry. A trickle of water escaped towards the sink and she dammed it with her finger, but it oozed its way round it.

'You know that the drugs make me impotent?' Theo dried up a strawberry cup.

'Yes, I do. I guessed that a long time ago.' Kitty drained the washing-up bowl and wiped it out.

'I like it. It's easier. I don't want to see women in that way.'

'It was you I invited, Theo, to look after you. I would miss you. Nothing else.' Kitty bent down to shut the door to the cupboard under the sink.

Theo gave a little chuckle. 'That's a girl.'

'Girl?' said Kitty, straightening up with the rudiments of a smile. 'I wish.'

Theo returned to his duties in the cloakroom. 'Where do you think you'll go?' he called.

Kitty's mind was filled with pictures and one was of the raven hanging in the wind above a wild, grey sea in which seals traced foamy detours around the rocks. Behind unfolded the flat, featureless land across which she was going to walk. 'Lincolnshire, I think. I don't quite know why. Except ... except I have a feeling I should divest myself.'

'Masochist?' Holding his gloves out and playing surgeon in the theatre, Theo returned to the kitchen.

Kitty's mouth tightened in anguish. 'I shall grow old, Theo, and I will no longer be desirable.' She paused and then whispered, 'I shall have to face it. I *must* face it.'

*Sunday.*

But when she woke on Sunday morning, a dull rainy day from which summer had fled, it was to peace.

# 26

'I shall have my revenge.' Maud opened her knitting-bag. '*Je reviens.*'

Agnes looked up. 'But you are here, Maud.'

It had been three weeks, three difficult weeks, since Bea's exit – and a lifetime since she had last seen Julian. Maud's behaviour had disintegrated. Grim-faced, she refused food, veered between tears and rage and drank industrial quantities of bad sherry. This catalogue of misery had culminated in a binge the previous night. Drunk and despairing, she flung at Agnes, 'What is my life? *Nothing.* Except debt and decay.'

The words, so it seemed to the listening, mopping-up Agnes, had been wrung from Maud's failure to connect on a deep and real level with her husband, her house and her sister. An important component had not clicked. A warning sounded in Agnes. *It was so easy for it to happen.*

Today the removal van came to take away Bea's furniture. The two women watched in silence the departure of the dressing-table, the glass-fronted Georgian bookshelf and some handsome chairs. Only Bea's clothes remained, and these were packed into suitcases and stacked in her room, to be picked up later by Freddie.

Bea had gone. *Debt and decay.* Tentatively, Agnes slipped

her hand through Maud's elbow and held on to her as Bea was erased from the house.

They retired to the drawing room and Agnes lit a fire. High summer had gone and autumn had arrived. 'There,' she said, the Scout leader banking on bossiness. 'That's brighter.' For once, the fire took and burned cheerfully, and Agnes and Maud huddled close to the warmth. Outside, wet leaves lay like mislaid gloves over the water-meadow and the rain fell.

Maud was crying again, and Agnes wondered if she should call in professional help. 'Maud,' she said gently, 'I think you should see someone.'

The mere suggestion was enough to provoke a hostile reaction. Maud was arrested mid-sob, hauled out her handkerchief and blew her nose. 'Are you mad?'

'Sorry,' said Agnes.

Maud's bony fingers paddled inside the knitting-bag. 'I shall knit Bea one of my jerseys. Black angora, *très chic*, and I shall knit a curse into it.' She extracted a pair of needles and cast on the preliminary stitches.

'*Maud* . . .'

Clack. The needles emitted hidden sparks. Clack.

'Only joking,' said Maud, her large, swimming eyes shuttered by her eyelids. 'Bea deceived us. There she was, all mealy-mouthed and full of good deeds, and all the time she was laughing at us.' Maud raised her head, and Agnes was treated to the full blaze of despair and jealousy.

'I don't believe that of Bea.' But Agnes suspected that

Maud might be correct, for Bea had surprised them all.

'If I was a young woman, I'd be interviewed in *The Times* on the pain of being deceived. But that's about as likely as coming back from the dead. Don't look so pained. I know that the old should be quiet and house-trained.' Maud tapped a foot on the parquet floor.

Agnes gave a snort of laughter. 'Oh, Maud.' But at least she had stopped crying, even if the grieving, weeping version was easier to handle than the runaway train. 'Of course, you must say what you feel to me, Maud. But . . .'

As therapy, the idea of revenge worked beneficially and Maud was looking marginally better. Agnes trod carefully. 'Did Freddie ever say anything to make you think . . . that you were special?' Silence. The rain sent a drum-beat down the long window. 'Did he?'

Maud shrugged. 'It was an understanding.' She sent Agnes one of her looks, picked up the knitting and embarked on a third row.

Agnes levered herself upright, prised the knitting from Maud, unravelled the stitches and rewound the wool on to the ball. 'I know enough to know that what you're doing is wrong. I've seen revenge, Maud, and the results, and for what it's worth, once it's done it never seems to come to an end.'

The older woman stared up her, and Agnes felt rather sick for she had hit the soft, exposed part of her aunt. 'I wanted to escape too,' Maud whispered.

Agnes tucked the wool and the needles back into the

bag and placed it gently on Maud's knee. 'I'm so sorry.'

The defiance was replaced by a soggier variant. 'You're so busy, Agnes. Always travelling. I never know how to take you. Never did. I was supposed to have enjoyed being busy with the house and the village. It never occurred to John that it bored me. And you did, too, Agnes. You were a very boring, ugly little girl.' Maud looked longingly at the knitting-bag. 'But . . . oh well.' She buried it behind a cushion. 'I have always wanted to know why I was supposed to fall in with everyone's wishes. Nobody consulted me. Merely because I wore a skirt.'

'Did you never love the house?' Agnes did not inquire about her uncle, for she knew the answer.

'How can you love a millstone?' Maud fingered her ring. 'There were no excitements for John and me. Only Charlborough, drains and rats in the roof.' She added crossly, 'I had no option but to live here.'

She was beginning to sound exhausted and, recollecting that Maud was still convalescent, Agnes took action. 'Bed. Now.' She helped Maud upstairs, undressed her and settled her down.

'Thank you, Agnes.' Maud leaned back into the pillows. In this setting, she grew smaller, beaten, her difficult qualities smoothed away. On an impulse, Agnes bent and kissed the cheek that smelt of cheap face powder. Sighing, Maud touched with her forefinger the place where Agnes's lips had rested. 'I'd forgotten what it's like to be kissed.'

She closed her eyes and appeared to be drifting into sleep. 'I imagine I'll get a letter from Maria tomorrow, don't you?' she murmured.

Agnes woke up. It was dark and she was drowsy. These days, she slept, dreamed, shuttled between her own and Maud's bedroom. A swelling, sleepy receptacle. Pregnancy was nausea and a craving for sleep, thick, lengthy dollops, and the drifting in and out of dreamscapes.

She closed her eyes and thought of the house. The irises were dying in the water-meadow. They could not speak out against time and change, or defend the stoicism of the many women who had lived at Flagge House.

She imagined its glory days: the kitchen basking in the stove's heat, and rooms overflowing with vases, baskets, shoes and balls of string; footsteps sounding on the stairs; the occupants' grievings and longings in each room. And from an attic room, the maid's stifled weeping echoed. Heavy, awkward earrings swinging, the other Agnes moved through them, ordering her garden, her stillroom, her children, until she lay down in the room allotted to the Campion brides to give birth.

Today – the now that she had inherited – the sun rose on ghostly greenhouses, birds swooped up from the eaves and vases did double duty as sarcophagi for mice. Must cradled a basket and a frozen torrent of books . . .

Something smelt terrible. Startled, Agnes turned her head on the pillow towards the window and gained an impression of unexpected colour. The smell intensified.

She shot out of bed and into her clothes, was down the stairs and haring in the direction of the kitchen.

The window to the courtyard was open. Agnes leaned out and recoiled. Underneath it, flames were crawling up the wall towards the roof and, as she watched, the first tongue licked the lintel. The kitchen was black with smoke and Agnes grabbed at the metal latch of the window, felt her flesh sear and vanish, and fell back with a cry of pain. The metal was red hot. Whimpering with shock, she cradled her fingers.

Behind her, there was a movement and she swung around. Resplendent in her nightdress and paste jewellery, Maud was sitting at the kitchen table. Close by her was a box of matches.

'What have you *done?*' Agnes flew towards the telephone in the hall and dialled for help. Doubling back, she careered into the pantry, snatched up a couple of large saucepans, and ran the tap.

'Oh, they'll be here in a minute,' said Maud. 'And, personally, I don't care if we fry.'

Agnes did not waste time in arguing but concentrated on heaving saucepans of water out through the window and on to the fire.

Maud was correct. Within minutes the fire engine had arrived and dealt with the problem. A sea of foam, water, blackened ash and mud rained down from the roof and settled in the yard.

A fireman poked at the pyre under the kitchen window with his boot and a shape sliced away, shedding a slough of incinerated plastic. It fell apart, revealing a white rectangle seared round the edges. It was from one of the missing set of Jane Austens.

The fireman drew Agnes aside. If she had been trying to burn the house down to get at the insurance, he said, it was ill advised. The insurance company would take a dim view of the situation. He was sorry, he had no option but to outline his findings in his report.

No insurance, then. 'What were you doing?' Agnes rounded on Maud the minute they were alone.

Maud looked terrible. Grey and sweaty. 'I couldn't sleep and I came down here and had a nip of . . . something. Then I decided I had to punish Bea, whatever you said. So I burnt her things. Cleansing the hearth.'

Because she was having trouble believing what she heard, Agnes made Maud repeat the story. 'But how on earth did you manage it? *Don't* say anything in French.'

'There was petrol in the outhouse. Just a little.' Maud held out her arm with a huge burn seared across the wrist. 'It burnt me too.'

'Let me have a look.' Agnes inspected it and said wearily, 'We can't take any chances, you'll have to go back to hospital. Do you realize you could have killed yourself and burnt the house down? As it is, it's going to be almost impossible to repair all this.'

Ash may have powdered Maud's hair and smeared her face but she was not in the least penitent. 'It's an ill wind, Agnes. We need a new kitchen and you'll get it somehow, I have no doubt. And, despite your holier-than-thou attitude, Bea deserved to be punished.' Maud winced. 'You know how I like a nice fire. Anyway, you gave me the idea.'

'I did?'

'The fires on the farm. You know.'

Agnes dropped her head into her hands and pressed hard. 'There was no need to act as if you were the first Mrs Rochester,' she said, through gritted teeth.

Maud's tears, which now flowed, were copious enough to have made the fire service superfluous. 'I thought if I burned her away I would feel better, but I don't.' She held out her arm, which was blistering. '*I don't.*'

Maud cried and cried. She cried at the doctor's, in the accident ward of the hospital, and she cried in her hospital bed when it was arranged that she should be admitted for a little while.

It took most of the day to grapple with the insurance company and electricians, and to clear up the worst of the mess. The smell made Agnes gag as, alternately wincing and cursing her painful fingers, she extracted tins from cupboards and tried to wash the worst of the mess from the walls. Then she tackled the china on the open shelves and bore it away to the laundry room.

Various experts arrived to assess the damage. The window needed replacing and the kitchen was unusable and out of bounds. Agnes abandoned it to the spiders, miraculously still occupying the cornice, and the sickening ash.

That evening, Bea rang. Agnes was wrestling to cook

pasta on a portable Calor gas stove that she had bought in the village. She felt sick, barely able to lift another finger and at the end of her tether. For once, she had little time for the gentle voice. 'Was it necessary to be quite so secretive?' she demanded.

Bea tackled the *froideur* head on. 'You're quite right to be cross. But, remember, I know my sister very well. In the end, she drives you underground. I wanted to spare Freddie any scenes.'

'If Freddie was spared, I wasn't.' Agnes described the events of the morning, and had the Pyrrhic satisfaction of hearing Bea's shocked response. 'I'm so sorry. I never imagined . . . Most of my clothes, did you say, dear?'

After a few minutes' more conversation, Agnes was aware that Bea, kind but secret Bea, no longer cared, although she was making a valiant effort to hide it. She had travelled far away into the shiny, insulating bell jar of a new life.

'It's only a kitchen, dear,' she said, as her parting comment. 'It can be repaired.'

'Your aunt has done me a favour,' said Andrew, when Agnes told him about the fire. 'If you don't have a kitchen, you must come here. I'll fetch you. Please send the respects of one arsonist to another.'

# 27

When Julian let himself out of Kitty's house, he savoured the curious, unfamiliar taste of being truly at liberty. The night air was cool as it would be for early October. A touch of salt, the thick, felty chill of the turn of the season.

In the end, it had been Kitty who had sent him packing and destroyed the pact. Yet her action appealed to Julian's sense of justice – the symmetry of justice in the rough. In doing what she had, and throwing down the gauntlet of the purchased house, Kitty had gained control and that was only right. The balance had evened, easing his conscience, and it struck him that Kitty had been more generous than she had meant to be.

Always he welcomed the moment of change: the point when the needle quivered on the marker before falling into a different quadrant. But it was usually concerned with his business life. Then the search was on for the undiscovered continent somewhere out there, unknown and challenging. But this was different.

He looked up to the illuminated bedroom in the cottage and the contrary impulses that accompanied a big transition made him pause and cast his mind over what might have been, feel the pang of regret. He would miss Kitty or, rather, the glimpse of the Kitty she had manifested tonight. With that flash of spirit, that cleverly judged segue of patronage and revenge, she had blotted out the irritations and trapped feelings of the past few years.

How would she manage in the harshness of marshland and wold, his soft Kitty? For a second or two, he was tempted to return to the house to instruct her to wrap up warmly, to buy stout boots and to make sure that her car was serviced. Always, she had required warmth, cherishing, protection against her fragility, a gentle easing in to new surroundings.

The light in the window went off.

Julian got into his car and drove home.

Cliff House was quiet and, of course, empty. Its rooms smelt of air from which the oxygen had been sucked. Cold as it was, Julian flung open the window in his study and sea sounds flowed into the room. Shivering a little, he sat down to work.

At three thirty, he finished for the night and, stiff and chilled, got up to close the window.

The figures on which he had been working closed a story whose finale was not good – no happy ending for him – and in which his role was not illustrious. At least he had known in advance and had had the grace of a couple of days, which was time enough to practise being the figurehead of a firm that had been taken over.

Looking back, his successes had been spectacularly

easy. Cushioned by thriving markets and solid finance, he had made choices and they had worked. But perhaps luck had played more of a part in his success than he had calculated. Perhaps the successful genes – for which he could claim no credit – of strength, intelligence and ruthlessness on which he depended had, this time, failed to outmanoeuvre luck's skittishness

The precise ingredients of the situation would be difficult to analyse – or perhaps they wouldn't, but of one factor he was sure: he was tired of thinking, arguing, bolstering, and of the depression that had weighed him down for the last frantic weeks through which he had struggled. Dying by degrees, he almost begged for the *coup de grâce*.

He ticked off the pointers: the proposed deals and alliances that melted on examination; the unreturned telephone calls; the meetings that were changed; the not-quite-engaged gaze of the financiers; the wooing of shareholders by others.

'What am I going to do with my hats?' a Conservative MP's wife once asked Julian at one of the dos where he had automatically worked the floor. The question, and her aggrieved manner, had stopped him in his tracks. 'I am redundant and elderly,' she continued. He had smiled politely, but without comprehension. 'A hat-wearing wife is no longer required,' the redundant political wife explained. 'What *is* required is a younger, efficient, hatless wife.' Now he was more open to that type of remark. Julian pictured a stack of silk and felt circles arranged one over the other, dust-powdered coffins of unrealized ambitions.

Now he understood.

Consider. If it was not rectified, the implications of a wrong turning multiplied and grew into a mass. Ask any mathematician. That was precisely what had happened at Portcullis. He had made an error in investing in projects that could not produce the profit margin, and a prime misjudgement had been to invest in a farmer's field in Lincolnshire.

How astute Kitty had been to buy one of the houses. In doing so she had weighed perfectly her judgement on the lover who had failed her.

He picked up the fossil anchoring his papers. The inefficient were eaten, or taken over, by the more efficient, and he hated the idea that his trendy, clever, visionary team would suffer as a result of him.

He thought of Agnes. He was sure that she had sussed his bad and weak sides, the bits of him that hated to face up to feelings and scenes. Did she think of him as emotionally retarded? Could she pull those bits into shape? Did he wish her to?

Last time he had seen her, sitting at the wheel of the car with a spitting Kitty lurking in the doorway, she had looked so young and tragic that he had almost swept her off there and then. But he hadn't because of Kitty.

It was growing lighter.

Julian picked his way in the semi-darkness down the cliff path to the beach below. With each step, the susurration of the water murmured louder against his eardrums. Over to the east, where the sun was rising, water and sand were tipped with a cold brilliance.

Long ago, the centre of the earth had growled and shaken, shifting and folding a mix of shale and limestone, and this coast had been made. Layer had been thrown down on layer, trapping animals and micro-organisms, flattening and crushing, until all that was left was the scratch of rock on rock, the hiss of decomposing bodies as they were turned to stone, and the echoes of sand falling into the water.

Imprinted on the beach was a record of the past and of what had taken place there, events indifferent to anything but the energy of themselves.

Julian was humiliated by the idea that his time was over and that layers of new rock would close over him. Once his role at Portcullis was finished, as it would be, he would have no more relevance than the fossil on his desk. Nothing more, nothing less than an interesting example of a wrong turning taken by the evolutionary river.

He kicked off his espadrilles. Sand oozed between his toes and the pebbles pressed uncomfortably into his feet. The rest of his clothes followed. Cold air ran up his body: the hair on his chest and groin responded, genitals tightened. He made his way down to the water's edge. There, the sea swirled over his feet, pummelling his toes, and receded, weaving its improvised, spumy lacework. Julian had swum here countless times. He knew the precise slope of the shore into the water, the formation of the rocks at its edge, and had explored their private rooms, daydreaming, inserting fingers into the anemones in the rockpools, and preying on transparent filigree shrimps. He knew where the rocks poked up out of the sea and where the tide exposed their hidden places.

It was here that he had gone over and over the puzzle of childhood. 'Of course we love you very, very much,' said his repressed mother when he asked her. He could not remember her kissing him.

Feet edging gingerly over the stones, he waded into the water until it reached his waist. The dense, cold mass sucked at him, willing him to strike out for the new continent. Gasping at the shock, Julian launched himself into the water.

Hair sleeked into a black cap, he swam for a long way. The sand in the water flayed at his skin, rubbing away the layers of habit. It flayed the image of Kitty, leaving a memory, as sticky but abrasive as the salt that licked over his body.

Agnes began to bleed.

At first reluctant, for he was of the opinion that nature should take its course, Duggie Sutherland finally arranged for Agnes to be admitted to hospital where she lay, pale and sweating, and gazed in panic at the ceiling.

They told her it sometimes happens at sixteen weeks, fitted a drip, rebandaged her burnt fingers, took endless notes and left her alone. Terrified that she might lose the baby, she struggled to find the rational, calm Agnes on whom she relied.

But that Agnes had fled, over the dew-wet meadow, leaving only her footprints – for she had never really existed.

Now she imagined herself on the operating table, knees raised while her baby slid away.

Desperately she focused on the small shape that was trying to leave its shelter. The curve of thin eggshell skull, the webbed feet, the tiny articulated shoulder. No, she cried out to it, you must not. You must hang on. You are not ready.

Forgive me for my doubt and for my busy, unattached life.

Perhaps you thought it was best to get out while the going was good. Perhaps you chose death in preference to what is on offer.

I promise to take care of you. I will wrap you in the softest of coverings, and lull you carefully and tenderly into being.

It was time to put down the anchor. When she got out of hospital, she would ring Andrew and tell him that she would marry him. Then she would settle to tidying and shaping the ends of her life in order to be ready for her baby. That was the least she could do. It was what she *should* do.

Agnes's head hurt, and she moved restlessly in the white hospital bed. Somewhere, in the distance, she heard a woman screaming. Was it the other Agnes, struggling to give birth, held down on her bed by other women's hands? Above her in the attic, mice scrabbling from beam to beam and the spiders spinning their webs?

For the tenth time in two days, Andrew picked up the phone and dialled Flagge House. For the tenth time, there was no answer.

In the end, he rang Bel. As he waited in his study at Tithings for her to answer, the sun came out behind the oaks. They seemed bigger, sturdier, more intrusive than he remembered from the morning. Stag-headed in shape. Oak was the hardest and stoutest of woods. It had built a navy and carried a nation. It resisted. It repelled fungal dry rot and teredines, boring molluscs – the invaders. The oak would face the bulldozer – and repel it.

When she eventually answered, Bel was crisp, never having troubled to conceal that she could not take Andrew seriously. Andrew didn't care. Early on he had dismissed Bel as a woman of no substance and a sharp tongue. The theatre of her cropped, moussed hair and rainbow fingernails had never entertained him.

He asked Bel if she knew where Agnes was, and Bel replied that she was taking a few days off but was not sure where.

Andrew suspected she was lying.

'Oh, by the way,' said Bel, 'did Agnes tell you? The *Hidden Lives* programme has slipped in the schedule. It looks like late October.' She was maddeningly smug. She added, 'Agnes is doing her best to get it out earlier, but she has other things to do, you know.'

'I hope she is,' he said. 'The results of the planning inquiry have been delayed. I'm not sure quite when they're due, but possibly early October and the timing could be critical.'

'Goodness, the tension must be unbearable for all you farming folk.'

'No need to be like that.'

'Who do you think Mary was?' Bel flashed the question, which, as it was meant to do, took Andrew by surprise.

'Mary? Oh . . . Mary. To be honest, I can't make up my mind about Mary.'

'Mary,' said Bel flatly, 'is a probability, not a definite, wouldn't you say? You can chase her down the byways of parish registers, electoral rolls, through the dusty corridors of Somerset House, but she eludes us, doesn't she? And, believe me, I have chased her. Mary, the eternal woman who inspires such passion, the epitome of courage, suffering and mystery. How do we decode Mary? I've tried and failed, and I have to tell you that I'm pretty sharp at spotting weak links. She almost seduced me too.'

'Ah,' said Andrew. 'You, too.'

'Come on, Andrew.'

For a moment, he was tempted to lay down the burden of his secret. Only the notion that it would be Bel's multi-studded ear receiving the confession prevented him. He did not want to waste his passion and effort on a woman like her. 'Will you tell me where Agnes is?'

'No, I won't. She needs absolute peace and quiet. OK?'

# 28

The waiting was terrible. Having put back the date twice already, for no good reason as far as Penny could see, the worse-than-useless inspector was taking delight in spinning out the torture. Stuff about further evidence and extra figures. Gossip in the pub had it that Stone, the caring landlord, was hopping mad at the delay because he needed the money, pronto.

At night sometimes, lying beside Bob, Penny prayed that Stone would go bankrupt, and when he did she planned to send him a postal order for five pounds with orders to buy himself a good meal.

Wouldn't they laugh, if people knew her terrors? The brisk, unflappable Penny reduced to a sleepless bag of nerves. Bob hated her tossing and turning but she didn't care, one way or the other, what Bob thought.

If Andrew lost the farm, it would kill him.

Some things you know, and you have no idea why you know, but if you feel something so strongly, it is unwise not to pay it attention. Penny *knew* she must keep an eye on her husband.

Unable to bear it any longer, Penny drove over to the farm at the next opportunity. It was lunch-time,

Wednesday, the slot between checking the meat orders and the journey to the abattoir.

'As I thought.' Penny edged into the kitchen to find Andrew eating a crispbread and cheese. The sight that greeted her was expected: unwashed dishes, a tangle of clothes in the corner and a muddle of cups and tins on the table. She directed her gaze to her husband. 'When did you last wash those jeans? Get 'em off, they're filthy. And everything else.'

Habits were strong. Andrew stepped out of the offending clothes, revealing his lean, worked body. A little softer, perhaps, around the contours, but the same man Penny had married twenty years earlier. She flashed a glance past the flat naked stomach and legs to the countenance above, which seemed so frighteningly indifferent as to whether she was there or not, and knelt down to retrieve the clothes, sick with longing to turn the clock back nine months.

He watched her sort out the clothes into their respective colours and stuff the first load into the machine.

'Go and get dressed, Andrew.'

Out of the same habit, he obeyed, and Penny cursed herself for being so practical and bossy. Perhaps she should try to say something. Now. *Tell him of her mistake, her terrible mistake*. Despite the magazines, her habit of reticence, and of hiding behind briskness, was ingrained. She was not good on the emotional stuff, and talk of the counsellors with whom some of her friends had ended up made her cringe. She decanted soap powder into the tray. These were naked areas, best kept private.

Andrew reappeared in clothes that were in no better shape. Penny scented her opportunity. Clearly the house needed to be taken in hand, actually a thorough overhaul was required, and if necessary she could spin it out for the whole day.

While he was changing she had whipped up one of her nourishing, quickie soups, with the already diced veg she had brought over in Tupperware boxes, and gave it to Andrew, who spooned it up hungrily. As hungrily, she watched. It was one of the better things of her life, dispensing food and comfort. 'I don't think you're looking after yourself.'

He brushed aside her concern. 'I'm fine. You needn't bother about me.'

She flinched. 'I *am* bothered about you.'

He did not even look up. 'Not any more, Pen. You concentrate on Bob.'

'Andrew . . .' Penny searched down the inarticulate years of marriage to find the right words. 'I could be bothered again. I mean . . . Bob is, well, not so very important to me.'

He shook his head and put down the spoon. 'Thanks, Pen, but I don't think so.'

It was at this moment that Penny made a discovery: if driven into a corner, it was possible to be other than yourself. She came out fighting. 'Don't be a fool, Andrew. You can't run the farm on your own. God knows, it needs more than two. And if we – I mean, you – are to fight the planners all the way we – you – have to show that we have a thriving enterprise.'

Her vehemence struck home. 'True. I must think about it.'

'How are sales of the meat?'

'Take a look at the accounts, if you like. They're half yours.'

'So they are.' Penny had quite forgotten her material interest in the farm, which was indicative of her confusion and her doubts.

'But not Bob's, mind. Remember that. He can't have a penny.'

'Of course.'

Let her husband be as angry, vicious and unfair as he could be over Bob. *Throw down the gauntlet*. It would prove that he *felt* something. That was what she wanted.

He needed feeding up so badly. Penny got up to butter a slice of bread and put it in front of him. 'Look, I'll bring some more food over.'

He shrugged, but she could tell that he did not dismiss the idea out of hand, which was good. 'If you like.'

As a come-on it wasn't that hot, but it was better than a definite rejection. Penny was not sure but she had an impression that Andrew was registering her properly for the first time in a long while and she burst out, 'I can't bear this business with Stone any longer. It's gone on long enough. It's not fair.'

'Who said life is?'

Penny drew in a deep breath and put down her marker. 'I'll come over with the food this afternoon.' Perhaps I can slide back into my place easily and quietly, and then we'll continue as we were. It's possible. It has been known. Lots of people do it. They break up, have a fling, come back, because habits are strong and it's better the devil you know.

Penny did not quite understand why she was doing what she was doing, or why she had done what she had – only that her marriage was an anchor and she had hauled it up without thinking properly.

If she was truthful, she blamed the magazines.

Andrew looked at a point above her head. 'Penny, you made your decision and I accept it. I can't say it didn't hurt at the time. It did.'

I must cling on to that, she thought. *He did mind.*

Then Andrew spoiled it by saying, 'You must get on with your life with Bob, I'll deal with the farm. I'll make sure you get your cut.' He paused. 'Whatever happens.'

The disappointment was so overwhelming that Penny almost choked, and it was doubly bitter for being self-inflicted. She thought back over the years when she had lived and worked alongside her husband, knowing that they had lost the point of contact, neither understanding the other. How she had toiled and made do, and lost her looks in the process.

*But it had been better than nothing.*

'Maybe. There's going to be some changes, anyway,' he said.

'Oh?' She flinched at his expression, which had switched suddenly to one of joy and hope, quite different from the Andrew she knew. 'What changes?'

'Someone is coming to live here.'

'Who? Who?'

'Agnes.'

Penny clutched the bread-knife. 'The television person? She won't come here. Not in a million years.'

'We haven't sorted out the details, but we will.'

Shaken by awful, debilitating doubt, Penny sat down. *I must not scream.* 'Andrew, please think. Is this just another bee in your bonnet? You know what happens when you get one of those. Hedgerows, pesticides, you name it.' She sighed. 'We've been there.'

'I've been thinking about a divorce, Pen.'

She forced herself to remain rigid but the word 'divorce' sprouted fins and a sharp point that buried itself in her chest. 'And what did she say when you asked her to live here?'

He got up to fetch his boots from the passage and wrestled with a knot in the laces.

'I see,' said Penny. 'Can't take the hard work?'

'I know what you're thinking about her but you're wrong. Agnes understands.'

She wanted to lash out: *I understand too.* But her flare of combativeness had been doused by misery. 'Andrew, I know how you work. You see yourself as some kind of white knight battling with baddies out for profit. You reckon you're going to save the world.'

'Someone has to.' The blue eyes masked deep waters. 'But it's more modest than that. At the moment, I just want to save my farm.' He fiddled with the lace then handed over the boot to Penny. 'You're much better at knots, Pen, could you do that one for me?'

Penny's fingers rattled at the knot. It was all very well, but martyrs and warriors were so extreme and unreliable. So inappropriate in an age that had parted the heavens and explained space. At this point, Penny checked herself. If any progress was to be made between them, she must make an effort to understand and to get round the problem. 'Here,' she said, and handed him back his boot with the knot untied. I know what he thinks of me. He thinks my dreams are the earthy, non-visionary type, and I'm not capable of anything, but I *do* possess a soul like this Agnes woman, and I can, if I want, lay claim to those feelings.

Andrew glanced at the clock on the wall. 'I've got to get on. I'm a bit worried about Molly and I must check her out. She hasn't picked up since her calf.'

'Is she eating?'

'Sort of. But she doesn't look right.'

'Bring her in, then.'

He considered. 'Yes, I think I will for a day or two, that's a good idea. She won't like it, though, will she? I'll see you,' said Andrew, tying the final lace. 'Sometime.'

Left alone, Penny went into Andrew's study and flicked up Molly's record on the computer screen. It was as immaculate and up-to-date as she expected. Nothing deflected Andrew from the business of the farm. Not sickness, or worry, nothing. Thinking hard, she sat down in the swivel chair and turned it so that she had the best view of the oaks.

*If she was going to reclaim her husband, Penny would have to move back into her own home before another woman dug her spade into her patch . . .*

It was as simple as that.

She tucked her handbag into the drawer in which it had always lived – just in case a passing tradesman took a fancy to it. Forget the food. If she got cracking this minute, she could boil, dry and iron the tea-towels and the rest of the laundry stuffed into the basket. By evening she could have a drawer full of white, ironed rectangles and – perhaps – her feet under her own table.

In the late afternoon, Andrew took a break from chopping up a branch that had come down in the north field, and rested on the shaft of the axe. To his surprise, Penny's car was nosing its way around the potholes in the track leading up to the field. 'Shoo!' he shouted to the Devons, who had come up to investigate his activities and were clustering as thick as the field thistles they stepped around so daintily. In response, they pressed their hard, hot flanks up against him, almost, he reckoned, with affection. The younger ones were playing games. Mothers and offspring swapped places, butted, challenged, circling their aunts and cousins in the way of cattle who are at ease.

'Go on, shoo,' he repeated, and flicked at a pair who were jostling for the front row of his attention. *They have to know who's in charge.*

It was October weather. A wind was funnelling down from the bronze moor, its chill fingers ripping apart the last traces of warmth. Above it, rainclouds were waiting to release their load.

At Penny's approach, the cattle fell back and away, leaving Andrew isolated. He watched her struggle out of the car and trudge towards him. Penny had always trudged, and always would.

It wasn't fair that the light was so harsh and truthful with her sturdy figure, her acid green nylon jumper and inexpertly tinted hair. Familiar, good-hearted Penny. Of course he loved her, in a friendly, uncomplicated way and, now that he had Agnes, he could afford to be kinder and more honest.

But, as she drew closer, something about her manner gave him pause. 'Thought you would have gone,' he said, warily.

'The postman came. I've brought this.' She held out an envelope. 'It's from the inspector.'

'It's not due yet,' he said, after all his preparation for this moment, feeling both foolish and unprepared.

Dear Mr Kelsey,

I am writing to inform you of my decision, made after due consultation and consideration and weighing all the factors involved. After assessing the needs of Exbury, and in recognition of the fact that part of the land under dispute is already used for an industrial purpose, to wit the tip that abuts the main road, it is my opinion that the housing estate, proposed by Arcadian Villages, should be permitted with the following modifications . . .

Andrew sat at the kitchen table with his head in his hands. Shock made him thick-brained, slow, stupid.

It was a blow to the head. The whirl of the axe blade descending. The terrible thud as it came down on bone. That was it. The end.

Once upon a time, the land had been green and fertile, crammed with species, layered one upon the other, flowers, fruit, grasses, bisected by the routes of animals and insects intent on pursuing their small, interlocking existences. Once upon a time, men had moved through the crops with their oiled, sanded scythes, their women in sun-bonnets clustering at the edges.

Once upon a time . . . the corncockle had thrived, the marsh marigold blazed and the wind was scented with wild marjoram.

All good stories must end.

He had already made the obvious telephones calls. Jim, Gordon the Gladiator, the posse of indignant protestors and friends. They were massing in response, making banners, writing letters, urging him to keep fighting.

The Death of a Farm. It made good copy in the newspapers. It would make excellent television. He knew

Agnes would see to that. Thousands would quiver with indignation – and put the kettle on.

But it was *his* farm that would go under the bulldozer. His soil, patiently tended and brought to life. His careful tilling, rotation, doctoring, mending, caring . . .

What happens when a mind splits? When strain and despair crack it into a thousand pieces? Is there a glue to piece it together, patiently and with knowledge? Andrew's fingers tightened on his scalp and he pressed as hard as he could until circles swarmed behind his closed lids.

Penny was talking to him. He looked up. She was pushing a cup of tea in his direction, but he could not take in what she was saying.

What did it matter? What did anything matter now?

Her face, wide-eyed, anxious, swam across his vision. Andrew pushed back his chair and left the kitchen, snatching up his axe from the yard. Penny stood in the doorway and yelled after him, 'Come back!' He ignored her.

*If it's destruction they want, they shall get it.*

The wind was rising, and the cattle had clumped at one end of the field, nervy now, with the weather, and restless as the wind plucked at their tails and ears. One or two watched Andrew as he ran past, the others paid no attention.

They would think him mad, as they had declared him mad for firing his field. He had heard the tattle in the pubs. Let them. Sometimes madness is sanity. He was panting, and his heart was thumping in strophes of grief and rage.

And as Andrew ran towards the innocent white hives, he raised his axe and brought it whirling down on the first in the line. It splintered and cracked. A moment of hush before the high-pitched response of the bewildered, angry bees.

The fascist guards sprang into action.

For a second time, Andrew raised his axe. High and poised. Then, it cut through the air towards the second hive. *Nothing shall be left. Nothing will be as sweet and pure as the honey. As untouched, and as ancient, as you, the bees. You must die for there is no place left for you.*

And as the gods on the moor roared their anger, and let loose the wind and rain, the wounded, violated bees massed, re-formed and struck at the one who had nurtured them for so long.

This is what I want, he thought, as their poison was driven in a thousand places through his skin and he felt it sear through his veins. To go.

'Andrew! Andrew! Where are you?' Up in the north field, Penny cupped her hands and shrieked into the wind, and the rain mixed the ash remnants from the bonfires into paste. *'Where are you?'*

She had already rung Jim who, good friend as he was, had come right over. 'Jim, I'm frightened Andrew might do something crazy. He looked so awful. We must find him.'

'No,' said Jim, reassuringly. 'Andrew would never do anything silly.'

'Yes, he would. Over this,' insisted Penny. 'I know him, Jim.' They fanned out, Jim to the south and Penny towards the bee-hives.

When, eventually, Penny stumbled across the figure in the grass, she was terrified that it was too late. Andrew lay spreadeagled and motionless in front of the splintered hives, covered in a moving shroud of bees. Every visible inch of flesh was swollen beyond recognition. Even his eyes.

'Oh, God, Andrew. Dear God.' Penny took in the destruction and sank to her knees. 'What have you done? Your bees. Your precious bees. Oh, Andrew.'

He managed an infinitesimal movement of his hand, and muttered, through the monstrous, puffed lips, 'Go away.'

'Jim!' Penny screamed, in her terror. 'Over here. Quick. How do we get them off?'

Jim came running. He knew what to do with the bees and managed to coax them up into the tree. Together he and Penny managed to manhandle Andrew to the edge of the field, and Jim hared up the path to fetch the van. Before they left, Penny ran into the kitchen, snatched up a pile of the fresh, ironed tea-towels and threw them into a bowl of water. All the way to hospital, Andrew whimpering with pain, she applied them tenderly to his destroyed flesh, wrapping him as tightly as a mummy.

## 29

As it turned out, Maud and Agnes were both in hospital for a week and sent messages to each other, via one of the support staff in a pretty pink apron, who reported back to Agnes that Mrs Campion was surrounded by flowers and eating well.

The doctors ran numerous tests on Agnes, including a scan. The technician had been kind and pointed out where the obscure grey shadows made sense. Agnes had puzzled and frowned but, under the technician's tuition, pieced together a fluttering, pulsing shape.

'Look,' invited the technician. Agnes obeyed, and peered through a gateway presented by science into a mystery enacted and re-enacted since the first cell assembled itself in the primordial fluid. The observer could watch through the camera lens. 'Ah,' she breathed, and her own heart leaped in greeting. What she was seeing flowed in from the river of time. The indistinct beating shape strung on to a necklace of bones was being built out of genetic information passed on hundreds and thousands of years ago.

She gave a little cry.

'Please keep still,' admonished the technician. 'Look.'

And Agnes finally stepped out from behind the lens

and looked deep into another human being. Into its heart, and through its heart to beyond. Beyond the image, beyond the genetic assembly, into another dimension for which she had no explanation.

'We can see the foetal heart,' said the technician. 'And everything looks fine. Do you want to know the sex?'

'No. No, thank you.'

The experience left Agnes weak and shaky, but with a burning determination that this baby would be born.

During her week's stay in hospital, she swam back up to the surface. The sickness lessened and she grew stronger and felt better. Of course she would manage the clutter and muddle that had been thrown into her path. A full, rich life absorbed the unpredictable, and did not throw it away. The house, baby, unsuccessful love affairs must not be wasted on mean, niggardly regret. Now that she had struggled to this point, her power would grow. She would cope, drawing on strengths lying dormant.

She pictured growing fonder and fonder of Andrew, with the real, solid affection she had witnessed between couples who relied on the steady beat of trust and liking, not the great, gusting emotions of passionate love. Between them they would work out a division of labour and locations. They had many things in common, a shared purpose. She felt Andrew to be a man she could trust with the baby and with herself.

For long hours, she lay and looked at the ceiling. What a challenge and labour it was to be the woman that she wished, requiring an interweaving of maternity, creativity, practicality, which were all constantly altering and progressing. And she wanted, she very much wanted, to achieve this state of mind and hold it with grace. No anger. No looking back.

Yes. With the sickness gone, her body more biddable, it was time to plan and schedule commitments. Agnes's certainties had returned.

As she lay quiet and dreaming, her thoughts returned to the other Agnes. Petticoats wadded around her feet against the draughts – often complained about in contemporary letters – the other Agnes had sewn samplers, one for each of her children with their names and birthdates. Rupert, Charles after the King, Henrietta, Margaret, Henry ... But not the one who killed its mother. That child had remained nameless. In hushed moments, she must have told her children stories. Of battles and kings, of witches and demons. And, leaning over and speaking directly to little Henry, of younger sons winning fortune.

In a few months' time, Agnes would assume her place in the circle of story-tellers. She, too, would be easing a child into its context, settling it into it with tenderness, and with colours and banners of imagination and history.

She rang up Bel and discussed fixing up a couple of schedules, to book in Jed, and to set up a meeting with Dickie.

First she needed to talk over things with Andrew. It was at this point that Penny phoned.

*

When Andrew finally opened his eyes after the sedation had worn off, his body was on fire with pain and hot, swollen tissue. Anxious and rumpled, Penny was sitting by the bed, a handkerchief between her fingers, her eyes trained on him.

'Am I dead?' he muttered.

'No, but you had a bad reaction.'

He digested this information. 'I was stung once too often.' He managed the half-joke, and watched her expression clear miraculously. If it was possible to feel pleasure at such a moment, it gave him pleasure.

Poor Penny.

'Why?' she asked. 'Why hurt the bees? They did no harm.' She moistened his lips with a sponge and he sucked at it gratefully.

'Penny. Could you do one thing?'

In the act of dipping the sponge into the water for a second time, she paused. 'If I can.'

'I know this is a difficult. But could you get hold of Agnes for me?'

The sponge dropped on to the floor with a dull sound.

Penny's phone call to Agnes left the latter in no doubt how much effort it had cost the other woman to make. 'The reason I'm ringing is because Andrew's had this accident,' Penny explained, in a voice wrung out with tension and nerves.

Agnes had only that morning arrived back from hospital. She sat down on the tenants' chair in the hall. 'Is he hurt? Badly?'

'A little.' Penny doled out the information with reluctance. 'But he's asking for you. The doctor thinks it might help if you came. After we got the news about the farm, he had a bit of a breakdown.'

'You've lost the farm?'

'Yes, we have.' Agnes noted the 'we'. There was a hint of triumphalism that the worst had come to the worst, a brand of *I knew it*, as Penny outlined a version of the events that had taken place at Tithings. 'He wants to talk to you about something. He won't say what. Actually, he can't talk much just at the moment. We're in the cottage hospital.'

Agnes agreed she would come.

Penny continued, 'There's one thing you should know. I moved back into Tithings yesterday, for the time being. Andrew will be staying in hospital.' She added, 'I wanted the situation to be quite clear.'

'Oh,' said Agnes, the careful future that she had plotted and planned dimming dramatically in her mind's eye. 'Perhaps we can talk about that.'

She drove sedately past a misty moor, whose uplands had once been home to the Bronze and Iron Age settlers. In the watery sun, the stones appeared less monolithic and important. The wildness of the plain had been tamed by the road, and the mysterious connection between land and human, earth and sun was obscured by the mist, as the Iron Age settlements had been subsumed under a shroud of chalky soil.

Agnes gripped the wheel and drove on.

At the sight of Agnes hovering at the entrance to the ward, Penny's mouth tightened, but she got up at once to greet her.

Agnes said warily, 'It was very nice of you to contact me, Penny. Under the circumstances . . . which I am not quite clear about.'

'Who is?' said Penny, brusque to the point of rudeness. 'But that's Andrew. I never know with him.' She folded her arms. 'At least, he's stable.'

'Good.'

'I can't believe – I mean. His bees . . .'

Greatly daring, Agnes touched Penny's arm. A gesture intended to be reassuring, friendly. Unthreatening.

'It was . . . so odd . . . mad,' continued Penny, and described haltingly, but intelligibly, the dark, unpredictable force that had been unleashed in Andrew, which had rocked Penny to her foundations. 'Lighting bonfires I can understand – to make a gesture – but . . .' The revelation of this side of her husband had been a terrible shock for Penny, and her anguish and revulsion overrode her natural distrust of Agnes.

Penny had not known her husband's secret landscape.

'I had no idea that Andrew was capable of that sort of thing,' she said, more than once, her boots leaving imprints on the green linoleum floor. 'He went mad. He attacked them with an axe, sort of goading them to sting him. He wanted it.' Eventually, Penny ran out of steam. 'Oh, well,' she said miserably, 'that's life. I'll have to do my best with him. Although I will never understand . . .' She looked straight at Agnes and sent a silent message: *I am his wife and you are not.*

Agnes thought of her plans and the solution Andrew had offered. She thought, too, of his hidden passions and despair, which she had imagined would become a second nature to her.

But Penny's anxious, worn face was implacable. *Leave us in peace.*

Agnes raised her hands to push back her hair and her changing shape was revealed. Penny's hands flew to her mouth and she emitted a little sound, such as a beaten animal might.

'No,' Agnes cried at once. 'It's not what you think. It's not Andrew's.'

'My God,' whispered Penny. 'Oh, my God.'

Agnes had no griefs to bear against Andrew, no years of whittling down, no bleaching out of optimism. Nothing to forgive. But Penny had, and he of her.

'Can I see him?'

Penny collected herself and led Agnes down the ward to Andrew, who was propped up on pillows, with a drip in his arm.

'Andrew . . .' Agnes had been anticipating a horrible sight, but even so she flinched at the violence that had been done to him. Andrew's skin was blistered and weeping. His face and limbs looked swollen and pulpy, like rotten fruit. Even the blue eyes had vanished, reduced to watchful slits.

Penny announced that she would leave them to talk and would be in the canteen. Agnes promised not to tire the patient. Penny flicked a look that said, 'Don't try me too far.'

She watched Penny retreat down the ward. 'Penny tells me that she's moved back into Tithings.'

The split, swollen lips worked with difficulty. 'I don't know what's going on.' He spread his hands out on the sheet – a bag of sausages with nails attached.

'That must change things between us.'

'I want to talk to you.'

He turned his head awkwardly on the pillow and the strain of the movement registered in the flare of mottled skin on his puffy neck. She stifled her regret and the questions, for he looked too ill. Very, very gently she covered one of the swollen hands with her own. 'The farm?'

'I have until December to slaughter my cattle, dismantle my fences, pack my bags . . . scatter my hay to the winds.' He struggled hard with his speech.

'And to fight?'

'I fought it. I fought as hard as I could.' He winced. 'In all ways.'

She cradled his hand as gently as she could, and it seemed to comfort him.

'Agnes. I have something to tell you.'

'Do you?'

Sometimes the truth is buried. You can ignore it, walk round it, refuse to look at it. But it is there all the same. Buried. The fossil in the cliff. She heard a faint, echoing tap through the salt water and the million million shifting grains of sand.

The confession was halting, guilty and agony – for both of them.

She recoiled. He lay quiet, gazing at her, waiting for her anger to be unleashed.

*You wrote Jack's letters.* 'Why? But, of course, I know why you did it.' Agnes sat stony-faced, her hands folded in her lap.

Andrew had been driven to the brink by the threat of being evicted from Tithings. 'I thought and thought about what I could do. Then I saw the write-up about you in the paper and the solution arrived in a flash. I wrote them at night when Penny was asleep. I read up about old paper, went to see some period letters in a museum. Knew there was a bundle of my father's pencils in a drawer and an old pot of ink. Then I began. It was as easy as breathing. Jack was in me. Mary was in there. I knew them as well as I knew myself.' Again, Andrew shifted his poisoned body and winced. 'It was strange. Everyone wished to construct a story around them. All I had to do was sit it out and hope the timing fell into place before the balloon went up. But I miscalculated. I had hoped the programme would go out before the verdict from the inquiry.'

He gazed out of the insulated hospital window, as if he hoped to see reflected in it his land rolling out its soft, brilliant colours, hazy in sunlight, washed by rain, diamond bright in frost.

'What I loved about you, Agnes, was your belief in the letters. And from there it was easy for me to persuade myself that you believed in me.'

Agnes struggled to make sense of what he was saying and to reconcile it with her goal of the rich, full life. She sought the truth and it hit her cruelly in the face. What did it tell her? It was this, bald and unedited: in wanting to believe in the letters, in allowing them to supply some of her own needs, she had ignored warnings and made a fiction of her judgement and experience. It was impossible to be much more stupid.

He flinched at her expression. 'That was deception on a grand order,' she said, 'and I was taken in.'

He shrugged painfully. 'Sometimes the end justifies the means.'

Agnes smoothed a lock of hair back from his forehead, her fingers brushing the skin as lightly as foam. Under her touch, he lay quiet. All her tidy structures and plans lay in an untidy heap. 'When were you going to confess this?'

'I would have told you eventually. Some time in the future.' He turned his face to hers. Swollen, desecrated flesh. 'I calculated we were even. You are carrying another man's baby and I was going to act as its father. You would have had to forgive me.'

'Yes, I suppose I would have done. But at a price. It was a risk, Andrew.'

'Possibly.'

She looked at the floor and he edged his hand over the sheet towards her. 'I hoped I would get away with it and keep Tithings.'

A long, long pause.

'Say something, Agnes. Please.'

She shuddered with anger and humiliation, then pulled herself together. How could she judge? Every day human beings used each other, not always carefully or wisely or kindly, and it would be a good thing to find words that would give him comfort. 'You are an artist, Andrew. The letters and the farm are part of that. The letters are very fine.'

That was all she could manage.

Moisture oozed between the puffy flesh around his eyes. 'They *are* true,' he got out with difficulty. 'I have lived every sentence.'

The activity in the ward continued. Trolleys. Tea-cups. The muffled sound of a radio. Voices.

Agnes bent down to pick up her bag and her plait fell over her shoulder. He watched her through watering eyes.

'You were Mary,' he insisted. 'You stepped into her place. I could not believe my luck.'

She shrugged.

'I liked you in the honeysuckle crown,' Andrew was saying.

Agnes looked away.

A nurse appeared, swished at the curtains around the bed and the side-show of the ward was blotted out. He seemed to be in increasing discomfort. The nurse flicked an eye over him and fed him some water through a beaker with a spout. Then she was summoned elsewhere and Agnes took over.

'What are you going to do?' he asked, between painful swallows.

Her sigh was dredged from the depths. 'Maybe, maybe, I can present your story as the hidden life. We can get at it that way.' She shrugged and her flicker of enthusiasm was doused. 'But I don't really know, Andrew. I'll have to think about it.'

Slowly and painfully, he circled his fingers around her wrist. 'Forgive me,' he whispered.

She disengaged her wrist and went to look out of the window. In the car park below, traffic was edging in and out of the exit and entrance. A couple of dead flies lay between the vases of flowers on the window-sill. The recycled air felt hot and heavy.

Her throat ached in a familiar way. Had it all been a waste, that fumbling towards a different understanding?

The ache spread to her back and, as she moved, there was a sharp twinge of stretched tendon down her side. She brushed her hand across her waist, which was no longer a curve but something lumpier and more mysterious. A nurse called out sharply. There was the clatter of a trolley moving down the ward. Agnes pressed the ache in her back and shifted her stance. Her body had been invaded and, at thirty – nearly thirty-one – it was time.

There was no point in not forgiving. Life flowed in one direction and it was impossible to go back.

She turned and leaned over the bed to kiss the hot, swollen forehead, forcing her lips to touch the flesh in farewell and regret. 'Of course.'

When Penny poked her head around the curtain, she was bearing a tray loaded with polystyrene cups and a plate. 'I don't know if you've managed to eat, but just in case you haven't I've got a sandwich. Egg without mayonnaise.' She balanced the tray on the locker. 'I wasn't going to spend good money on beef.'

How very like Penny. Flowers in a spare bedroom. Sandwiches on the tray. Her courage could not be questioned.

Agnes accepted the tea and the sandwich. 'You are kind,' she said, and meant it. 'How much do I owe you?'

Penny looked from Agnes to Andrew and drew her conclusions. 'Nothing,' she said.

# 30

The phone call to Dickie at the BBC was one of the more difficult ones that Agnes had ever made. She outlined the situation as matter-of-factly as possible, and suggested the new scenario.

Dickie sympathized. 'Such a prang, sweetie, but better to 'fess up on the bended. Anyway, as you know, the honchos weren't quite so keen on this one. Not very here-and-now, if you know what I mean. But hurry to get some more of your usually scintillating ideas in, otherwise it's slippery-slope time. Be there, sweetie. Do something.'

Agnes laughed. 'What would I do without you, Dickie?'

'Think future,' advised Dickie. 'Think bright lights. Think Oscar level. I mean, darling, how do you *see* yourself?' There was a pause as he gathered breath. 'Dear, oh dear, Agnes. I'm afraid the costs of this little fiasco will be roosting in your little nest.'

After a week in hospital, Andrew begged Penny to take him home. He wanted to see the animals, he said.

In the tidy, clean-smelling kitchen, he leaned gingerly against the Rayburn, so frail-looking now that the swelling had gone that Penny was shocked. *Burnt up. Burning.*

She hoped, oh, she hoped, that it was not for Agnes. The thought terrified her but she would make herself carry on. So she rattled around in the drawers, made coffee, put things away, boiled milk.

'Coffee?' She shovelled Andrew's hospital-smelling pyjamas into the machine.

He was watching her. 'Why are you doing this, Penny?'

'Because . . .' she straightened up '. . . we're in this together.' She held her breath against what he might say next.

The machine whirled and clicked. 'You mean for better and for laundry.'

It was an appalling joke, but she was so thankful that he had made it that she could not speak. It was so much better than nothing. Much, much better. Screwing up her courage, Penny pushed her husband's hair away from the features that were settling back into their proper focus. 'I know I'm not what you want . . .'

He arrested her hand. 'You don't know what I want, Pen, so you mustn't worry.'

In the past, she might have said something brisk or cutting, or resolutely practical, but Penny had learned the value of silence. And she had also learned that it was impossible to be the companion to the inner life of your spouse. That was hard. Even so, she could not prevent herself saying, 'After all these years I have some idea.'

The washing circled and recircled on its cycle. Unexpectedly, Andrew slid his arm around Penny. 'Yes, of course you do, Pen. I was wrong.'

Penny followed Andrew into the sitting room. He looked at the chair. Sitting down was risky, for his skin was still broken and weeping. What the hell? He lowered himself into the seat. Penny bustled around, drawing curtains and serving the coffee.

She brought his mug over to him and knelt down. 'One of the things I found so difficult was that you never told me what you were feeling.'

It was an uncharacteristic pose for Penny, and it would have cost her to make it. Andrew's deflated sausage fingers lifted and dropped back on to the arm of the chair. 'I don't like to think I drove you to his . . . bed. But I obviously did.'

He was sorry for a lot of things. The poetry he had once meant to write. His failure to rout Stone at the first hurdle. His failure to make his marriage a success. To have snapped up Agnes and taken her away. To accept that he had to move on.

Penny got up, went to sit in the chair opposite and crossed her legs in the manner that reminded him of when, young and slim, they had begun their married life and each had seemed complete.

'Would you like to look at the telly?' Her tone was light and brisk.

He shook his head.

'Radio?'

'Nope.'

'Andrew, don't go all dreamy on me. Smile.'

He turned his head away: his longing for what had never been, and would never be, was a physical hurt.

'Andrew. Please smile.'

How is it possible to gather in a harvest from barren land?

'Andrew . . .' Penny's eyes had filled with tears.

Summoning his resolution, Andrew did as he was asked for it was the only thing possible, the only route left. He turned back to face his wife, and the image of a girl with flowing blonde hair, dressed in green and white, shimmered through his vision with the shock and pain of the dead.

Obediently, he smiled at the anxious but loving woman who shared his real life.

Julian drove over to Kitty's cottage and parked. It looked odd, unfamiliar, for the windows were bare of curtains and large for-sale notices decorated the drive.

It was even odder to walk up to the front door, to knock and to wait. But wait he did. Kitty called to him to come in, and he discovered her kneeling on the floor of the sitting room by a large packing case, surrounded by objects. Julian recognized the Staffordshire figurines and the glasses he had given her. Every object was being wrapped with the exquisite care and attention to detail that Kitty took with all her things. Tissue paper, bubble-wrap, a label, neat blue lettering: 'Jacobite Spiral Stem, circa 1740'.

This was Kitty's fingerprint. The radio operator's 'fist' transmitting codes from the field. And, if luck held and your agent was a brave and resourceful spirit, its stream of Morse could be heard welling up through the betrayals and deaths. Reliable and strong.

Kitty did not look up. 'What do you want, Julian?' To keep up her courage, she wrapped a second glass and bedded it down in the packing case. Packing was easy. Laying up difficult memories was less so. But she was getting better. Every day was a little easier.

'I've brought over some of the things you left behind.' Julian held up a couple of bags.

Kitty did not stop what she was doing. 'Could you put them over there? I'm afraid I'm a bit pushed so I can't offer you anything.'

He did as she told him. Covertly, she cast him a quick look. Just to see. Just to remember. He seemed . . . troubled.

'Kitty, are you sure you're doing the right thing? I'm very grateful you've bought one of the houses. But to live there?'

She hunkered back on her heels. 'Did I hear that right? From the great proselytizer for Homes for People?' She resumed her wrapping. 'That house will be perfect.' Another object was placed in the packing case. 'For what I have in mind.'

'What do you have in mind?'

She did not answer directly. 'Did you know that there are beaches up in Lincolnshire that are famous for their samphire? But only those who belong know which ones they are. Not many outsiders are told. I shall be very pleased if, one day, I am invited to go and collect samphire.'

She could tell that Julian was at sea. He gestured at the object-strewn room. 'It's all happened very quickly, Kitty.'

'On the contrary. It's taken far too long.' A china plate was next on the pile and she picked it up. 'As you well know, the house is empty and waiting in Tennyson Court and I've had two offers already on this one. One of them a cash buyer.'

She saw the flare of admiration light up his eyes. 'But are you really, really sure?'

The tissue paper rustled softly. 'If you don't mind me saying so, Julian, it's none of your business.'

There was just room for the plate and another vase in the case and she stowed them skilfully even though her hands were trembling. She was holding on. Just. 'I think you'd better go,' she said.

'Of course.'

With a swift movement, he bent down and took her in his arms. 'I'm sorry, Kitty,' he breathed into her hair. 'Is there anything else I can do?'

Safe in his embrace, she closed her eyes and, to her surprise, thought, Truly, I don't want this back. *I have been released.*

Julian let her go and stood back. 'Kitty, I know that I took ten years of your life.'

She snatched her trembling hands behind her back to hide them and lifted her chin. 'I chose my life,' she said. 'That's something.'

When he had gone, Kitty sank down on the floor and pressed her head against the buckled surface of the packing case. The air vibrated with her loss.

Think of the flat sheet of fen. The light. The raven, and seals in the grey sea. Think of the smells of dark earth and of harvest.

She would learn, she must learn, to be tough, spare, not made-over, the reverse of the image she had constructed so ardently over the years.

Eventually, Kitty climbed to her feet and went upstairs to the bedroom. For a long time, she looked at the bed she had shared with Julian. One by one, she recalled the sensations: sweet, slippery desire. And the ache of a throat gripped by passion, the deep, deep happiness of love that was going well.

But time went on. Change. Decay. The flesh that had so tormented and pricked must drop away. She would let it go, stepping into a land where she would no longer hear its moist, insistent murmur. There she would live, her bones whitening and ageing until, dry as summer dust, she would be laid in the flat earth.

The extinction of desire.

One by one, Kitty opened her drawers, shook out

their tenderly folded contents and strewed her burden of cashmere, linen and sea-island cotton around the room, until it flowed with grey, white and écru. Then, she stepped out of her high-heeled shoes, bent over, picked them up, held them over the wastepaper basket and dropped them in.

A new pair of shoes lay in the cupboard. Flat and inexpensive. Kitty put them on and, treading experimentally, went downstairs, leaving behind her shipwrecked room.

Goodbye, to this part of her life. She neither wanted nor desired anything more.

Theo was cleaning the hall and tut-tutting – the pictures had left dark rims on the paintwork. Kitty held out a foot, which already ached a little. 'Do you like my shoes, Theo? Say you do.'

Late that afternoon, Julian pulled into the drive of Flagge House and rang the doorbell. Maud answered it, seized on Julian and demanded that he take a glass of sherry with her.

'Agnes has gone to Exbury,' she said. 'Something to do with that farmer. Was she expecting you?'

Unused to jealousy, he tensed but made himself step into the hall. Then he sniffed. 'Have you had a fire?'

Maud's eyes widened. 'My fault, I'm afraid. I had a go at burning down the kitchen.' She led him into the drawing room. 'I was trying to exorcize Bea. She's run off, you know, with that Freddie person, and I wanted to tidy up after her. But it got a bit out of control.' Maud fiddled about with glasses and the bottle. 'Agnes dealt with it. Insurance and all that sort of thing. She was very cross.' Maud fiddled further. 'Why did you want to see her?'

Julian ignored the question. 'How are you managing without a kitchen?'

'This and that. We boil a lot, Mr Knox. You can probably smell the fish from last night.'

'A little,' he admitted.

Maud wiped the bottom of the glass and handed it to him. 'Agnes has been in hospital. Badly burnt fingers. Rather apt, don't you think?'

'No,' he said flatly. 'I don't.'

Agnes was everywhere in the room. A new cushion on the sofa, a re-covered stool, a row of invitations on the mantelpiece, mostly to media parties, a copy – of course – of the *Hidden Lives* script on the peeling veneered table. She had tried, she was trying, pasting over the cracks and brushing out the spiders.

'Do you have any views on what Agnes should do with the house?'

'Yes, I do, but I don't think they would interest Agnes.'

'How very safe you are, Mr Knox.' Maud sounded disappointed. 'I hate it,' she said, apropos of the house.

'Yes, I know you do.'

'We've had a bit of trouble with flooding as well as fire,' said Maud. 'It's a nuisance, this river.'

Julian glanced out of the window to the water-meadow,

where little flashes of light were trapped on the river's surface – a code flashing information to the aqueous life under its surface.

'Yes. It must be.'

'Do have any messages for Agnes?'

He smiled his professional smile 'No, I haven't, and I think I'd better be going. I just thought I might catch her, that's all.' He picked up the script. There was a typed list attached to the first page: 'Uprooted Apple Orchards and the Death of the English Apple', 'Death in Life: The Orphans of Eastern Europe', 'A Whaler's Defence'. Underneath, Agnes had written, 'Confirm Andrew, parish records?'

He frowned.

Agnes's work. Agnes's world. In this room, he could hear her inveighing against the developers' skilfully thrown lure and against the concrete rolling over water-meadows and apple orchards.

Maud had tackled the sherry yet again. 'In the stories, Jack always gets his Jill, but it isn't true, is it?'

He put down the script. 'I'm afraid it isn't,' he said bleakly. 'I don't think this Jack did. I think it all went wrong.'

'So why did you come here, Mr Knox?'

In the flat autumn light, every wrinkle on Maud's face was emphasized – indeed each shadow and plane in a face that regarded the world with parsimonious optimism. It was a selfish face, and it was possible that his own was set in a similar cast. He hoped not.

Love should be unselfish. Yet it was far more complicated. Love was unselfish – but it was also unutterably selfish. He needed Agnes and a future, and it was a desire that was both fierce and passionately egotistical. He needed to find the new continent.

He heard himself saying, from a long way away, 'I came because I wanted some comfort.'

'Oh dear,' said Maud, giving him one of her madder looks. 'We don't have any of that. Dear, no. None at all. If there was any lying around, I'd want it for myself.'

## 31

'Maud,' Agnes trod warily, 'Bea has sent us a letter.'

The two women were in the drawing room and both were swathed in sweaters. The atmosphere was both stuffy and cold and, in the cornice above them, the spiders moved through the webs with complete freedom.

'I suppose you had better read it to me.'

'"Dear Ones,"' began Agnes experimentally, '"Freddie and I are positively frisking around Egypt. The *Isabella* is very luxurious and the food gorgeous. Dancing most nights. The Nile is warm and mysterious and we surge up it like a great white swan . . ."'

Sailing across deep, transparent water, lit by the reflection of glowing lamps. New land. Enchantment. Magic. Mystery. Love.

Agnes winced.

'" . . . We've been to see the tombs with their beautiful wall paintings. Freddie is very dashing in his whites. In fact, I call him my Captain von Trapp . . ."'

To her surprise, Agnes felt indignant on Maud's behalf, for that last remark was cruel.

'I hope she breaks her hip.' Maud knitted away furiously at a fluffy blue garment, destined for the children's hospital.

'She's enclosed a photo.' Agnes examined it. It was of the group, assembled by the ship's rail. They were all in evening dress, and most of them held a glass of champagne.

Maud dropped her knitting and peered at it uncertainly. 'Where's Bea? Can't see her.'

Bea was standing at the back of the group, and it took a moment or two to pick her out. There she was, smiling gently, in a long green dress. In the picture, her waist appeared as slender as a young girl's.

Agnes got up and propped up the photograph on the mantelpiece. She tapped Bea with her fingertip but of course the figure did not respond. Funny old Bea, she thought. Running off with Freddie, pinching the Jane Austens. Lifelines, perhaps, in a bumpy sea.

After a moment, she slid the photograph behind an invitation.

'By the way,' Maud was uncharacteristically subdued, 'did you send that property developer packing?'

One hand on her aching back, Agnes bent down to throw another log on the fire. Dislodged, yet another spider crept out from the basket and Maud put out her good foot and crushed it.

'In a manner of speaking. He lives with someone else.' Agnes hesitated for Kitty was owed her name. 'She's called Kitty.'

'What a useless name.'

Agnes sifted through the rest of the post and listened to Maud, who had launched an offensive against unmarried mothers and the selfishness of Agnes. While she was ranting, the knitting was shaping up into a matinée jacket of the kind that had gone out of fashion. Angrily, Maud delivered her valedictory shot. 'I've held back from asking, but are you ever going to grace us with the name of the father? Or perhaps you don't know.'

Agnes was taking a long time to read the single sentence on a postcard. In fact, she read it over and over again, just to be sure. She said quietly, 'I will ignore that remark, Maud.'

'Maria would never have got herself into such a hole. No husband. No money. No prospects.'

Agnes turned over the card and examined a photograph of Lincoln cathedral. 'No doubt, but it's different these days.' She put the card to one side then picked it up again and held it, as if it was of utmost preciousness. 'Maud, I've arranged a small loan from the bank for the kitchen and I've worked out a timetable for the most pressing repairs, which can begin next year in the spring. In the end, the bank was helpful but not generous. If we go carefully they might stump up more.'

'Oh, don't be silly,' Maud interjected. 'Even I know there's no collateral and we need hundreds of thousands.'

Agnes could not bring herself to reply.

Again Maud opened her mouth, and out issued the jangled, dissatisfied spirit that dwelt in her. 'How are you going to manage? What are you going to put on the birth certificate?' The voice cracked. 'Don't expect me to help. *I don't know what to do with babies.*'

The words flowed on but Agnes was not paying attention. She was thinking of how inadequate some words were. Some like 'snazzy' and 'perfumed' did a good job. But 'joy' and 'surprise' and 'indebtedness' only performed half their function. In no way could they match the feelings behind them.

'I never told you he turned up here the other day when you were in Exbury.'

Agnes looked blank. 'Do you mean Mr Harvey?'

'Don't be witless, Agnes. The property developer.'

Agnes dropped the postcard and retrieved it. 'Julian? Here?'

In the study, which was stacked with videos of her work, including the orphanage programme, and an emergency spare of *The Sound of Music*, Agnes was going through her papers.

This much she knew. When Thomas Campion had returned from the Armada in 1588 and, with his companions, looked down from the ridge to the water-meadow and made his plans to build his 'bigge howse', he had not been thinking of the past, but of a future.

In the records, it was set down that he spent £550 on wood and, since oak was becoming scarce, he had ordered it from the wrecked ships on the shoreline. He had paid £37 12s. for the marble fireplace, £50 for the tapestries, stripped from a Catholic house in the next village. Finally, £100 had been paid over to the sovereign for the rights of 'assart', the holding of private property within the boundaries of a royal forest.

The records told the story of Thomas's fine burial stone, of his son's extravagances, of his son's marriage to Agnes and her goodly portion. She knew of Agnes's great-great-granddaughter's unwise decision to build a folly on the marshy land by the river, and she knew, too, of Gervase Campion's passion for flowers and his death in the Himalayas on a bulb-hunting expedition. She could read of the remodelling and adapting of the house to accommodate new ambitions. A second staircase. The Victorian kitchen. How one member of the family had decided on change because the old ways had run out. How they shifted, adapted, expanded . . . and, finally, the story reached Maud and Agnes.

The past was a rich and fertile place, where Agnes had wandered to make up the shortfalls in her own existence. With her camera, she had projected her portrait of Flagge House on to an inner canvas – its richness of brick and wood, its beauty, its virtuoso stonework and glittering fenestration, its intimacies and poise. It had been a time of enchantment and profound disappointment. Of course it had been, for the past could never be trapped and preserved.

Agnes gathered up the family papers – incomplete, untidy, some indecipherable – and fitted them into the old-fashioned box file that had belonged to her uncle and put them away in the cupboard.

It was finished.

*

Julian arrived within two hours of her phone call. Agnes was sitting in the drawing room, looking over a sodden, flatly lit water-meadow. When she heard the car she got to her feet and went outside to meet him.

She saw instantly that he looked terrible, pale and bruised around the eyes, and felt the awesome depth of her love and tenderness, which burst to the surface, so intensely that she knew she could never have substituted anything else.

They stared at each other without moving. They needed that moment of harsh, pure feeling before the needle dropped into another quadrant. Then she asked, 'Bad?'

He thought. Damn the figures and the dig-deep analysis. I can't begin to explain this. He returned the smile, drinking in the iridescence of her radiantly happy grey eyes. 'As bad as it could be. Portcullis is finished, and finished with me. Legatt's have taken over, the shareholders have been offered their pound of flesh, snatched at it, and the new masters want me out fast. It's just a question of negotiating the pay-off, which they will do because they want my silence.'

'I'm very sorry.'

She knew the words were inadequate – *what would Kitty have said?* – but she would practise and become expert.

Julian made a visible effort and came up with, 'What news of the letters programme?'

'Dropped from the schedules. But I'll tell you about that later.'

She seemed reluctant to elaborate and he probed further: 'Wasn't the Exbury trip successful?'

'Andrew lost the farm. He's in quite a state.' Agnes was shivering in the chill, and she led Julian into the house.

'And?' He waited, breath stilled, for her answer.

'His wife has gone back to him, if that's what you are asking.'

'Ah.' Julian walked over to the window, a man whose energy had been diminished and drained. 'I thought I might be too late.'

Agnes picked up the postcard of Lincoln cathedral. 'I received this from Kitty. She writes, "I'm living here now."'

He looked down at it. 'Kitty decided that enough was enough.' His fingers drummed on the shutter, the tap of impatience that Kitty engendered in him but, following as quickly, was a scorpion's sting of regret and nostalgia. 'It was my fault because I met you . . . Ten years is a long time.'

'I'm sorry,' she said, for a second time.

'I wonder if ten years is all we can ever ask of each other?'

'I don't know, but that's what I want to talk to you about.' Agnes sat down on the sofa. 'I want to tell you something, Julian. I'm pregnant.'

'A baby?' It took a couple of pulse beats, then: 'Whose?'

Agnes smiled and shook her head. 'Didn't you notice? I'm huge.'

He ignored her. 'Whose it is? Please tell me.'

Struggling through the flat tone was fear, wonder, excitement. Agnes took pity. 'It's yours, Julian. Of course.'

'Are you sure?'

She scrutinized the exhausted face. 'You and Maud have more in common than you realize. You both imagine that I have a particularly lurid love life.'

He smiled bleakly. 'Then I must help you. You must let me.'

'Sail away to the land where the bong trees grow?'

'Nothing wrong with that.'

She reached up and placed a hand on his chest. The new, powerful Agnes. 'I want to give you something.'

He caught her hand and pressed it on to her stomach. 'Aren't you giving me this?' he demanded. 'You must say that you are. Otherwise I will imprison you on the island, where you will go mad with boredom.'

The response pleased Agnes more than she could say. 'Go and sit down and listen to me, because this isn't easy.' He hovered. 'Go on.' Julian did as he was told.

Agnes looked out over her water-meadow. Its music and the play of light on the water were about to change. 'Julian, I'm giving you the grounds of the house. I come with them. That is, if you want me . . . us. I've reached the conclusion that things cannot go on as they are. If Flagge House is to survive, then I must contrive.

377

Survivors are survivors, *because* they are survivors. That's something you've tried to tell me. Survivors are there at the right time. It is a present to Darwin, I suppose.'

'Remind me sometime to explain the theory to you properly.' Julian was digesting the implications. 'Agnes, do you mean it?'

Already the energy of the old Julian was flowing back, investing his features, pulling the weary body into shape. He was shaking himself back into a skin that was comfortable and familiar. 'Let me think. Finance. I'll be hobbled by investors because of my history, but that's OK. Once I've got a team organized and I'm out of Portcullis, we'll design you houses that will look as though they belong here.' He checked the water-meadow from the window. 'Four.'

'Two, Julian. No more,' she cried in panic.

He grabbed her hand. 'Three.'

'Two.'

His fingers squeezed hers hard. 'I promise it will work, Agnes. I will make it work. I'll leave the river, make it the focus of the planning.'

She was beginning to shiver violently with cold and with the reaction that follows great change. She also felt a little sick.

She looked out through the window. The figures that had moved across the meadow and plundered her imagination had vanished.

He stood beside her, hair ruffled, narrow-eyed and calculating, and she looked at the profile and wondered at the contrariness and yet the vastness of her love for him and for the unknown person she carried. 'Ten years you said . . . for a relationship.'

He frowned. 'Did I?'

'Ten years is not enough for a child. It must be longer.'

He touched her stomach. 'Will you come and live with me?'

She thought of the children surrounding the dying other Agnes. 'Yes. For the time being.'

His grip tightened on her.


'Maud.' Agnes led Julian into the kitchen. 'You wanted to know who the father is so I'm introducing him. Furthermore, we're going to get married.'

Maud poked at the pork chops that Agnes had put out for lunch. 'Very nice.'

'Are you hungry?' Agnes removed the plate. 'Listen, Maud, I have agreed with Julian to develop the water-meadow and then Flagge House.'

Maud sat down with a thump. 'Pull down the house?'

Agnes slid her arm around Maud's shoulders. 'No, of course not. But the money made on the field develop-ment will be used for renovating Flagge House into a proper home, including a flat for you. A nice, warm, centrally heated one.'

'But you won't change the house? Make it different?'

'*Maud!*' cried Agnes in exasperation.

'You mustn't do it.' Maud was shrunken and wild-eyed at the prospect of the changes she had begged for all her life. 'I didn't mean it, Agnes!'

'How long have you been bullying me to sell the house?'

Maud assessed her captive audience. 'You can be so stupid about things.' She hunched a shoulder. 'I had to make my stand somehow. Anyway, I feel differently now.'

'This will be better, you'll see.'

'But it won't be the same. The house won't be the same.'

Agnes stroked the angora-clad bony outcrop of Maud. 'No,' she agreed, filled with a weary, desolate feeling. 'It won't.'

But Julian was watching. 'Agnes,' he said. 'Trust me.'

She looked up at him and smiled.

Every line of Bel's body conveyed messages of outrage and betrayal. 'You're going to do what?'

'I'm going to marry the father of my baby and strive to give it some kind of security, and I'm going to live in Lymouth while everything is sorted out.' She added, 'I'm on hold, Bel, for the time being.'

Camaraderie. Exhaustion. The noise and smell of planes, bad food, the murmur of the team at work in the dawns, late at night, the bad habit of one last nightcap in the hotel bar. The absolute desire to get a vision on to film, absolutely as it should be. That would all go.

Bel's frosted blue nails vanished as she searched in her handbag for a cigarette, which she lit defiantly. 'What happened to you, Ag? You've gone off message. You've gone bush, native . . . whatever.'

'Sticks and stones, Bel. I'm having a baby. It changes you.'

'Doesn't take your wits or your ambition, does it?'

Agnes perched on the edge of the table, a manoeuvre that, these days, required thought. 'Did you ever believe in the letters?'

Bel's expression hardened, glazed. 'No,' she answered. 'I reckoned you were being led up the garden path.'

Agnes's eyebrows lifted. 'You always were sharper. I'm sorry, Bel.' She picked up her rucksack. 'Look, I've had a word with some of our contacts, and there's a couple who'd be very interested in you joining the team. Here they are.'

Bel picked up the list, scanned it and her eyes widened. 'Good grief. Thank you.'

'Just remember when you're the big successful shot, and I want to come back, which I will, that you owe me one. OK?' Agnes made for the door. 'I'll see you soon and we'll wrap up the ends. And, Bel, thank you for everything.'

'Agnes . . .' Bel's expression had not softened one jot. Nevertheless, she said, 'I wasn't being quite truthful. There were moments . . . Once I even thought I heard her, transmitting her messages from the field.'

*Oh, Bel.*

Bel hunched over the keyboard. 'Goodbye.'

## 32

Punctually, the bulldozers arrived at Tithings, followed by a procession of lorries, cars and Portakabins.

Andrew, Penny and a substantial crowd of protestors had taken up their first line of defence by the oaks. High in the branches above, the Gladiator was putting the finishing touches to a series of airborne ramparts, spinning a spider's web from branch to branch. Delicate gossamer structures, shaking in the wind. From here, he and his willing recruits from Exbury's teenage population planned to launch missiles.

The lead bulldozer forced its way into the north field. An oiled, hungry metal beast. It was the signal for the protestors to link arms and begin their chant. The local press photographer clicked away and the television cameras whirred as the bulldozer described an arc across the tender grass. Lowering its digger, it cut into the earth as cleanly and sweetly as the plough might have done, and moved on.

At the sight, Andrew broke ranks and walked with clenched fists directly into the path of the machine. He and the driver eyeballed each other, Andrew willing the other man to make the first mistake, to mow him down. But the driver merely touched his steering-wheel and drove around Andrew without any obstacle to his progress at all.

Almost a year to the day since John Campion died, a heavily pregnant Agnes stepped out of the drawing-room window on to the terrace to watch the first lorry negotiate its way over the meadow to the sites of the houses. It came to a halt by the river. Three men began to pace out measurements and to drive pegs into the earth.

While she watched, a new pattern was formed on the meadow, and the wind, a savage breath of winter, blew her short hair back over her shoulders.

With each swing of the hammer into the earth, Agnes felt the blow. Behind her, the windows of the house glittered in a cold sun, and the icy water in the river clattered over the stones.

She touched her stomach. It was a hard death and it would be a hard birth, and each would be a trade-off for the other.

For a long time, she stood quite silent and alone, until Julian appeared and led her to the waiting car, where Maud was sitting, and they drove away to live in the house by the sea.